Solar Minimum 4

Blood Memory

Greg T Meyers

Paperback edition 2015

ISBN: 1533226571
ISBN-13: 978-1533226570

For Shelley,

my Veronica. Thank you for saving me.

CONTENTS

ACKNOWLEDGEMENTS

Special thanks to all those who have gone before and left such great anecdotes of living both in the positive and the negative. The rich history of all of our ancestors who toiled through centuries of hardship, disease, war and evil. Their examples of piety and honor are perhaps never more needed for us to remember than today. May we be as courageous and selfless as they in the next hundred years.

Jacob Abbott for his volumes on English and European history that have greatly added to the historical accuracy and color of my work. I am especially grateful for his moral judgment and commentary on the histories he wrote, an asset that is painfully missing from many historical works.

Special thanks to Kim Mercer and her hours of pouring over this manuscript and who provided valuable direction when my storytelling was not completely converted from my imagination to paper.

Stanley and Diane Blackett for their support and excitement, love of my story and the characters I created.

My wife Shelley, the love of my life who was my inspiration for Veronica—sweet, kind, colorfully audacious and dangerously beautiful. I am a lucky man.

For England and letting me live with her for a time and her rich history of survival and moral right—peppered with terribleness.

CHAPTER 1

BROKEN GLASS

Conwy Castle rose majestically toward the sky in the distance just as it had done for over eight-hundred years, since the time of King Edward I. In the last light of the day, its imposing grey stone towers were soothed by the evening, soft amber light as it welcomed the King of England and his soon to be Queen. Two years ago, the King commissioned the complete rebuilding and restoration of Conwy Castle and the surrounding city walls. It was to be the region stronghold and official residence of Queen Veronica of Wales, but now that the Tower of London had been sacked by an unknown enemy, the King saw it as good a place as any to base his command until more intelligence could be had concerning Mercia and Kent, both areas whose allegiance was still unknown.

Just before the battle in Wales commenced, a rider sent from the Tower announced that London was lost to a very large and violent army. The Tower Captain had ordered the messenger to ride, just when all appeared lost and instructed him to tell the King that the army in all likelihood belonged to Wales. However, now that the King learned Veronica had nothing to do with the taking of the Tower and that they had been reconciled to one another, as well as engaged, this was certainly a falsehood. Veronica only commanded one ragtag army and that was the army she commanded herself in the Sevren River Valley against the King.

Even though the immediate and most dangerous threat of civil war had been resolved in Wales, it was still unclear where Mercia, Kent and East Angles stood. At last report, there was a sizable army marching from East Angles across Mercia supposedly to assist the Queen so the King dispatched General Clancy with two-thousand men into Mercia to intercept them. Gus rode north with just over three-thousand to Northumbria where the real battle was supposed to occur with the Celts. It was reported that the Celts were growing more numerous by the week as more men and supplies were shuttled from the former country of Ireland and the King greatly feared that they may have already advanced beyond the M6. Once the unrest in Mercia had been put down, General Clancy was to then march northward to assist Gus. This just left the heptarchy of Kent unaccounted for. Who or what had taken the Tower certainly invaded from the south of England or entered the through the Thames. After the Sevren River Battle, the King sent a small battalion of spies to investigate and learn all they could about the invasion while he prepared to unite the Kingdom by marrying the Queen of Wales and then immediately march for war in Northumbria.

Not since the Civil Wars of 1646 had an English monarch been so preoccupied with defending his Kingdom and during the long journey to Conwy, Veronica and the King discussed the topic in detail. They concluded it was no coincidence that the date of England's last civil wars also coincided with the last solar minimum period. More than just the reduced temperatures and the reappearance of mythical creatures, the very mindset of the world had changed and they along with it. The grim reality of the world and their place in it settled deeper into their minds, that place where the intricacies of the self are defined. The more they discussed their roles and the plans of the Kingdom—their Kingdom—they understood more who they were becoming and who they were destined to be. They were not actors in a medieval-like world, they *were* the very King and future Queen of England, scheming together how they would quiet the rebellion of their people and defend them against a very real and very violent alien invasion. Their final transition from being survivors of the Minimum world to the rulers of it was now complete and it descended upon them almost unnoticed. The ruins of their lost modern world were everywhere but viewed in much the same way that ancient ruins were before the Minimum, that of being a sign of the past, but slipping further and further into folklore and obscurity.

At some unknown hour during the night, Veronica derailed their conversation, her heart at last rising above her head, and said, "I loved Matthew and I still love his memory," she blurted out as the King stared back at her blankly, unsure of how to respond.

After a few awkward moments, he softly replied, "I know."

Veronica mentally paused as she considered her next words and how they went against every courting rule she had ever been taught but once she convinced herself such rules were all stupid anyway, she continued. "More than being your Queen, I want to be your wife, without secrets or guile. Under the right circumstances, I may fall to pieces from Matthew's memory, but I pray you might not be wounded by an image in my heart." She reached out and took the King's hand and gazed into his eyes tenderly, trying to connect with his soul but despite her longing, he inwardly seemed closed off to her. It was easy for her to find a reason, they had nearly killed each other less than a day ago and due to their quarrel, over four-hundred men were being buried in a mass grave in Aberbechan. Even still, she wanted to be completely in love with the King but she had to remind herself that this was not a fairytale, nor was this the modern world before the Minimum where life was a fairytale. The grim reality of their union was to first save English lives and she concluded that love would have to wait. When Veronica didn't speak after taking the King's hand he finally turned to her and asked, "What is it?"

"Oh—Nothing," she replied, shaking her head slightly and deciding that someday they would have an intimate conversation but that time was not now.

The King patted Veronica's hand nervously, which wasn't lost on her and she couldn't help but wonder if the King's emotional distance was more than he wanting to kill her only hours ago. The truth was, he had a terrible secret that was gnawing through his gut on its way to his heart and he wondered how he could ever live with such anguish. His bride was desperately trying to clear the air between them by confessing her greatest crime against their future union—a beloved memory, when all he could think was how he had created that painful memory her by killing Matthew.

"Perhaps you should get some rest. We can talk more when were both back to one-hundred percent," he said, escaping from the broken conversation.

Jess had preceded the King and Veronica to Conwy Castle by nearly a full day so that he could announce their arrival and prepare a place for the royal wedding. Since the state of Canterbury was unknown, there was no sense in returning home, besides the King wanted his marriage to Veronica solemnized as soon as possible. The village of Conwy was built at the mouth of the River Conwy, where it flowed into the Irish Sea and was anciently an impregnable stronghold. In addition to the castle itself, there was a completely intact, eleventh century wall that surrounded the nearby village. After the invasion of Holy Island two years ago, the entire region gathered within the safety of the Conwy walls, only venturing out to conduct their farming and trading. With the military supplies the King had brought, the fortress would complete its full return to its former glory and unmistakable military stronghold in Wales.

As the King, Veronica and their five-thousand man escort made their final approach to the south gate of the Conwy walls, they could see that torches had been lit upon all eight towers of the castle, as was customary for all royal residences in England by order of the King, but before tonight, Conwy Castle was not an official residence, therefore when they were lit, cheers were heard throughout the village as the King's arrival was announced. Even still, it was customary for only a single torch to be lit on each tower and as the King and Veronica watched, they saw over a dozen torches on every tower, making their arrival honored and very celebrated. Approaching the Llanrwst gates however, they saw that they were closed and they noticed that the former road into the village was sunk and full of water. The Minimum had destroyed all modern structures which included the three bridges that spanned the Conwy River near the castle, creating a low-lying dam where the river now beautifully cascaded over the concrete debris and they had been appropriately named the Conwy Falls. Consequently, on the ocean side of the dam, saltwater fish could be caught and on the river side, freshwater and both were in great abundance.

Due to the new dam, the power of the Conwy River forced its way up the Afon Gyffin, which was a small and rather insignificant river that flowed into the Conwy River just below the southern wall of the castle. Not to be denied its course to the ocean, the Conwy River cut through Llanrwst Road around the front of the castle and into the Irish Sea, creating a natural moat. Not being able to now enter through the Llanrwst Gate, they made their way to the west gate where they were greeted by the residents of the village. The press of peasants along the streets was nearly unbroken all the way to the draw bridge where they were then greeted by torch bearers that lined the pathway into the barbican.

The outer ward of the castle looked just as it must have done in the eleventh century with fires burning in iron baskets and servants rushing about. But as the King entered through the gates, everyone stood still and bowed as a new reverence for the King settled on the fortress. His subjects had always revered him but their fear of the Celtic invasion caused many to rally behind Veronica since she had defeated the last invasion of the kingdom nearly single-handedly. Now that the King and Veronica were to be married, confidence in the monarchy was again very high as were the spirits and fortitude of everyone in England from the armies to the peasants.

The renovation of Conwy Castle was magnificent and was certainly the crowning achievement of any building project in the Post-minimum period. Every wall had been washed, the centuries of decay removed and replaced with new cement and newly quarried stone where needed. The roofs had all been replaced and reinforced with steel, which was in great abundance in the debris of larger cities. The outer ward of the Castle was the business end of the fortress where the stables and kitchen were located as well as the chapel and the great hall where the monarch could hold court.

Once within the outer ward, the King quickly dismounted

so that he could assist Veronica—not that she needed any assistance dismounting from her mare but he saw it as an opportunity to smooth over the awkward and broken conversation they had just had. Placing his hands around her waist, he gently lifted her from her mount and cradled her in his arms as her long red velvet dress cascaded over his shoulder in the gentle evening breeze. Just before he sat her down, she tenderly kissed his cheek amidst cheers from the soldiers and staff while the stable hands escorted their horses out of the keep. Similar to when Veronica arrived at Powis Castle, they were introduced to the attending staff and escorted toward the inner ward where their personal quarters were housed. As they approached the inner gates, the King seemed a little anxious but then smiled and chuckled slightly.

"Did I miss something amusing?" asked Veronica turning to the King, wondering what was amiss.

"Not yet," he replied as the inner gates were raised and the six-inch solid oak doors were pulled wide.

The entire inner ward now had a roof covering wall to wall and the interior was dark, very dark and Veronica stopped, waiting for a torch or a candle to be lit. When no light was forthcoming, she turned to the King and asked if they were supposed to feel their way to their chambers. Just then King commanded, "Go ahead, turn it on."

Just as Veronica was trying to make sense of what he had just said, the room suddenly exploded with light as a very grand chandelier came to life, pushing away the heavy medieval darkness. It was the first electric light Veronica had seen since the Minimum four years ago and its brilliance was astounding. For several seconds, she could say nothing at all and only looked at the room in disbelief. Being so used to fire and candle light, the electric light seemed over-powering and after looking around the expansive room in awe, she finally replied slowly. "What the hell?!"

The King laughed hardily, enjoying her surprise and compete exasperation. "Consider it my wedding gift," he said.

"But, how did you accomplish such a thing? Wow, I had forgotten how powerful a simple electric light was!"

"We were able to salvage a generator from Liverpool and place it in the new river that flows around the west of the castle. The channel is very narrow and the flow of the Conwy is very extreme at that point, more than enough to power this building. If we had more generators, we could power the entire village."

"Then why not power the entire castle? Is the outer ward is without power?" asked Veronica.

The King nodded. "Yes, that is by design actually. I'm not sure how the country would react to such luxury to say nothing of our enemies. I thought it best if electricity at Conwy Castle was kept a secret—at least for now. When the engineer informed me of the possibility, I immediately sent men into Liverpool to find a generator." The King sighed as he remembered his secret, romantic frustration with Veronica and said, "I so wanted to bathe you with lavish gifts and demonstrate my love for you without saying the words but…"

Veronica leaned over, kissed him and held him tightly, thanking him for both the electric gift and his love. "It is beyond all imagination Your Majesty."

"There's more, my Queen," replied the King as they

continued their tour of the castle and all its many chambers. Instead of damp and dark corridors, there was adequate ventilation and electric heat that enlivened every corner of the castle, making it warm and comfortable. Amidst the rustic architecture were thick fenrir skin rugs and wall hangings, tastefully dyed to match the rest of the décor and lavish furnishings. After the tour, the servants left Veronica and the King alone in the private drawing room near the east barbican that featured an elegant row of French doors that opened up to views of the new Conwy Falls. Veronica sat down on a plush brown leather sofa, swung her legs up and laid down with a long sigh. The Castle wasn't the Ritz or even close to the comforts of most middle-class homes before the Minimum, but it was the most elegant dwelling in the Kingdom and possibly the entire world.

The King walked over and sat on an ottoman near Veronica and smiled. "I trust you are comfortable my Lady?"

With her eyes closed and without moving she replied, "Mmm, very much so. I think I could fall asleep right here."

"Well, we have bed chambers designed for that—if you can imagine."

Veronica smiled and looked over at her King and replied, "Imagine that—bed chambers too?"

"About that," replied the King. "I must insist that I be the perfect gentleman before our marriage and shall take a chamber near the Chapel Tower. Old-fashioned perhaps but—we are living old fashioned."

Veronica nodded, agreeing with him and also

understanding what he meant. Not only had the world changed but their minds and hearts had also. Honor was everything in the Post-minimum world as was virtue and being chaste—which was why Veronica's man shot down the King's soldier who had so grossly offended his Queen.

"Of course," replied Veronica smiling.

"Then with that, I suggest we retire. May I escort you to your bed chamber my Lady?"

"Indeed My King," replied Veronica as she took the King's hand and walked with him arm in arm to the chamber near the old King's Tower in the southeastern corner of the fortress. It was the grandest chamber in the castle and when the King opened the door and turned on the lights, Veronica was again astounded.

Unlike the rest of the castle, the floor of her chamber was black and white Masonic marble, covered with bleached white fenrir skins stitched into a grand rug that nearly covered the entire floor. There were thick glass windows that over looked the Falls with a winding oak staircase that led to the top of the King's Tower. She recognized the grand bed as the same one from Powis Castle, complete with vanilla-scented bedding.

"Oh Corinna!," she exclaimed even though Corinna was not in the room. She knew the attention to detail was all because of her and she walked over and opened the bottom drawer of the chest. Just as she expected, there were her warn, but very beloved Oxford sweats she had purchased her second day in England.

"And for the highlight of your tour my Lady," said the King, standing at the door of her washroom and turning on the light.

Veronica walked into the washroom and gasped. Not only was there everything that should be in a bathroom including marble counters and large mirrors, but a toilet and—a tub. She turned to look at the King for confirmation.

"Yes, they both work. We installed a pump that draws fresh water from the ancient well beneath the castle and of course an electric water heater—for your bathing pleasure. We were also able to salvage a septic tank from the Liverpool ruins."

A small tear escaped her eye as she embraced the King. "I truly am the luckiest woman on the planet. It is a wedding gift I could never equal. What shall I ever give you in return?"

"You have already promised to give me two—your hand and your heart," he replied as he held her right hand in his, inspecting the deep laceration from his sword. "Oh my Lady, you are a remarkable woman," he said as he then brushed back her long brown hair and inspected the wound on her neck. "Are you holding up well enough—any pain?"

"Oh, the pain is manageable but, yes—it hurts very much, thanks for asking," she replied.

The King rolled over her hand and kissed the back of it, then bent down and turned on the water for her tub and after testing it for a perfect temperature, he turned and strongly embraced her which made her feel not only very protected but also cherished, more than any man she had ever known. She sighed within herself and raised up on the tips of her toes and kissed his neck, under his beard.

"You have already given me your gift, and I have also given you yours—only one however. You have all of my heart, for all of my life, but my hand must wait until Sunday," she said with a tender whisper.

The King kissed her soft lips and bid her good night then walked out of her chamber. As he shut the door behind him, he sighed deeply, his heart pounding. He was hopelessly in love with Veronica, more than he ever thought possible. Perhaps it was because of the sheer brutality of life that made love so much sweeter but no matter the cause, his heart was in complete surrender. However, in the back of his mind he could not stop thinking about killing Matthew at point-blank range. *I am worse than King David*, he thought, disgusted with himself.

Leaning against the door he wondered if Veronica would love him as deeply if she knew the truth about Matthew. As he walked to the opposite side of the castle to his personal quarters, he wrestled with the thought of telling her and taking the chance that she might repulse him. Reaching his chamber he had almost concluded that he must tell her, but then he retracted and reasoned that, he had a responsibility to protect his kingdom and his people. The situation was a complete lose-lose and he reasoned that regardless of the moral implications, telling Veronica the truth right now would completely unravel the delicate tapestry of his country. As he rounded the corner, he saw Jess waiting for him on the stairs.

"Good evening Your Majesty, I was hoping I could have a word," asked Jess, bowing.

"Of course Your Grace, let us step inside and obtain a little privacy," replied the King, opening the door and allowing Jess to enter first.

Before the door was scarcely shut, Jess turned around and announced his business while the King locked the door. "I understand you killed Matthew two nights ago?"

The King turned the key in the lock and sighed. Like King David, his secret would never go away and after slowly turning around, he walked to an empty chair and sat with a heavy heart. He rubbed his forehead for a few seconds as he collected his thoughts and shifted his radiating thoughts of Veronica to matters of murder.

"Yes, that is correct," he finally replied.

Jess didn't say anything but just stared at the King as he took a seat opposite his across from a fireplace that was not lit. After a few minutes he replied and started to shake his head. "Your Queen can never know Your Majesty. I cannot imagine a scenario where she would accept such news—on any level. When I visited her on the anniversary of Matthew's disappearance, she was completely overcome with grief, more heartbroken than I have ever seen in another human being. She was in love with him Your Majesty, deeply in love."

The King sighed with despair. "Yes, she told me that very thing during our ride here. I pray that I might have the strength to keep it hidden from her. I almost told her this evening and it has troubled me ever since. I'm not sure I can keep such a secret for very long."

It was far from Jess to encourage someone to lie, but he was counseling the King on matters of kingdom security with thousands of lives in the balance, greatly obscuring the lines of right and wrong. "Your Majesty, if you feel this is something you cannot withhold, I plead with you to leave so that you might not be so tempted. I know you love her, but for the love of your Kingdom, you simply cannot do it!" Jess leaned forward on his knees and continued. "Think of it Your Majesty, not just for Veronica's sake. No matter how the secret is told, your subjects will see it only as a vile, cunning plan conceived only to stop Veronica from becoming the sole monarch. I have to say, it would be difficult to find any army that would support you in that hour."

The King sat back and folded his arms as he considered Jess's council. "You are right of course, but reason and strategy are not a part of the arsenal of love. And let's face it, Matthew was more animal than human that night and he most certainly would have killed the General. Surely that accounts for something—surely."

"Between two friends, yes. But your Kingdom will not see you as the hero I assure you. You won the day yesterday because you and Veronica became united. I shudder to think if you gave them a reason to doubt your integrity—indeed, there are many who are still looking for that reason." Jess then bit his lip, stopping himself from saying what was on the tip of his tongue. He then finally realized it had to be said and with a deep sigh he continued, "If Veronica—and I mean a very big and bold *IF*. If Veronica ever needed a reason to convict and remove you, she would have the ultimate weapon against you that you could not defend."

"Well—I wouldn't be the first powerful man to place his fate in the hands of the woman he loves. Legend says that is how Merlin become disempowered. He told his lover a spell that would render him like other men and it was his eventual undoing. Why are we men created thus?" he sighed as he stood up and walked over to the bed and began slipping off his boots as he continued. "A man can lead an army into hell and return victorious, but when he lays with the woman he loves, he willingly places his dagger under his own chin, if not through his own heart."

Jess had never considered love on such morbid terms but the King was absolutely right. When man falls into true love with a woman, she powerfully holds his life in her hands, though she will not even know it—or even believe it. Jess sat back and thought through the implications and after several long minutes he finally sighed and asked, "So you will tell her then?"

"My head will never do such a thing, but I fear my heart already has. Tonight I felt she knew there was a tourniquet around my heart. I have no plans to tell her but I will tell. I know I will."

Jess sighed deeply. "Then we should do it sooner rather than later, while we can control the outcome. There is no Transnet or bloody social media so we can be sure that there will not be a leak, especially if we keep the secret close. Which reminds me, who else knows about your deed?"

The King had to think. Certainly Clancy knew as did Gus but there were two other soldiers present that night and he wasn't sure he could remember who they were. This was potentially disastrous and the King slowly responded saying, "I—I don't know. There were two unknown soldiers present that I believe belonged to the General's army but I can't even be sure of that let alone pick them out in a line up."

"Well, I hope he can identify them," replied Jess in alarm. "There is not a moment to lose Your Majesty. I will send a dispatch to the General and order him to identify the men and…"

"And then?!" interrupted the King.

Jess got to his feet very unsettled and tormented while he nervously placed his arm on the fireplace mantle and said, "Damned unfortunate this all is, but so much is at stake we have no choice Your Majesty. The men must be found and—executed."

Putting his head in his hands the King groaned, "Jess! Life was so much easier when right and wrong were a simple choice. This has now become so complicated that I can no longer see the line of morality. I suppose the line draws between the number of lives at stake—two verses thousands. Perhaps we could only imprison them. There is a very strong prison here in the castle and we could release them once we can be sure their secret holds no power."

"What do they say, dead men tell no tales? So long as they are alive your Majesty, they are a liability to your crown." Jess then laughed incredulously, "Look at me! I am standing here trying to convince you to kill someone."

He then walked over to the bed and sat down next to the King as he remembered the night before the battle in Veronica's tent. "I can't tell you what it was like to sit next to your soon to be bride the morning before yesterday's battle, trying to find the words that would console her. She and I both believed that she would be killed in the morning and that reality shook my priestly foundation. Right and wrong for the first time in my life was more than a blur, it was a tempest that stormed in my soul up until the moment you proposed to her. I concluded eventually that the only right there was in the world was the preservation of good over evil. I concluded that both yours and Veronica's army were good and the evil was the situation that had caused you to want to kill each other." Jess looked the King in the eye before continuing. "I saw that evil yesterday. It only has one agenda and that is to destroy man. This secret of yours is not evil, it is merely a weapon that evil can and will use. We must take it from evil's hands, but the longer I wrestle with this moral morass, I realize I cannot condone the murder of the innocent. We must find a way to defuse this grenade and render its power useless and the only way I know to defuse a grenade is to detonate it under safe conditions."

Jess's words were very convincing and the King began to think he was right. The secret was so potentially deadly that it had to be removed from the world. After a long pause the King finally nodded and said, "As you will, Your Grace. Your council is both timely and wise and I thank you. Join us tomorrow on the east Barbican for breakfast and we shall have our defusing confession."

Jess got up with heavy dread and walked to the door. He then stopped as he thought deeper about the secret and asked, "Two you say—besides Clancy and Gus?"

"Yes, I'm very certain of it. Why?"

"What of the men who attended the General to Veronica's camp the night of the Hellhounds. I have it on very good authority that he did not come alone."

"All dead," replied the King. "Clancy was the only one to make it back alive—and only barely at that."

Nodding, Jess opened the door and then bowed respectfully to the King and said, "Good night Your Majesty."

Veronica rolled over to see the brilliant Welsh sunrise streaming through her window as her dreaming mind united with the day. She smiled almost to tears as she remembered the morning before the battle, fearing that it was her last day on earth. Now to be where she was, her feelings for the King made known, being in love again and having had a hot bath and a good night's rest in vanilla-scented sheets was overwhelmingly wonderful. There were few things she enjoyed more than taking a stroll on the balcony of the Powis Castle and remembering the spiral staircase that lead to the tower above her chamber, she quickly got out of bed, grabbed her robe and ascended to the top.

The sun was already a hand's breadth from the eastern horizon across the Conwy River and as she looked to the west, her ship was anchored in the estuary and she smiled, almost having forgotten about it. It then occurred to her that the ship was still without a name and she thought. In a few days' time, she would be married—to the King of England and she smiled briefly and then considered the circumstances of how it came about. While the engagement was certainly forced, quite literally at the point of a sword, she also remembered their long and frequent nights at Kensington and how she caught his admiring gaze many times, the first of which was when she, Gus and Matthew were invited to the Palace before the Minimum.

Just then, she heard a voice calling her from the bottom of the staircase. "Your Majesty, are you up there?"

"Corinna! Yes, I am. I am coming down," she replied as she descended the steep stairs into her chamber.

Veronica embraced Corinna as this was their first meeting since arriving at the castle as she informed her that His Majesty would be here in only minutes for breakfast and that they were to take it on the barbican.

"I have taken the liberty of selecting your wardrobe Your Majesty, I hope you find it well-suited," said Corinna.

"It is perfect, thank you but I will dress after breakfast."

Corinna was taken aback and gasped, "After breakfast Your Majesty? The King is joining you *for* breakfast!"

Veronica smiled. "Yes, it will be very nice," she replied, then realizing that Corinna was referring to her robe and bedclothes and that they were not appropriate clothing to dine with the King. "Well, he will have to get used to it, I loathe dressing before breakfast. After all, he is coming to *my* chamber."

"Yes, Your Majesty," replied Corinna bowing just as a knock was heard at the door.

Corinna opened the door as Veronica adjusted her robe, making sure she was covered and ran her fingers through her hair. After finding several snarls, she quickly ran to the bathroom as the King entered the chamber. Looking in the mirror she said quietly, "What are you thinking Veronica, your betrothed is meeting you for breakfast and you haven't even brushed your teeth?" She cupped her hand over her mouth to smell her breath and exclaimed, "Oh my!"

After dressing in the a cotton dress with white and gold embroidery that Corinna had picked out, she brushed her hair and teeth then made her way toward the barbican and her waiting guest as Corinna smiled. Stepping out on the east barbican that overlooked the falls, the King rose to greet her with a kiss on the lips and then her hand as he helped her sit. "You are devastating as always my Lady, I trust you slept well?"

"Oh, the best in all my life I think. Thank you. I could not be more comfortable. The castle is truly amazing, both in its reconstruction and placement. I ascended to the tower this morning. The countryside and even the village is right out of a fairytale—except that it is true," she said laughing.

The King smiled, remembering the evening he first introduced Veronica to Auctor, the King of the Dwarfs and when he was astounded that humans had both forgotten about fairies and that they were pathological liars. "Indeed it is," laughed the King before his countenance grew sober.

"What is it Your Majesty," asked Veronica, noticing the King's sudden change.

The King sighed heavily. "I have something I must tell you that brings me great agony."

Veronica playfully rolled her eyes trying to lighten the mood and said, "You have a wife and children in another kingdom you owe alimony to—I knew it!"

The King tried to smile, dreading the heartbreaking news he had to tell her on such a beautiful morning. But like opened wine, bad news is best served quickly before it becomes rancid and deadly. Just then, Jess walked out on the barbican and greeted the beautiful Veronica with a kiss on the cheek. "Good morning," he said while glancing at the King.

"Good morning, Your Grace, I was not aware you were joining us—but of course you are so welcomed," replied Veronica. "The wedding isn't until Sunday, and yet here you are all prepared. I suppose we could just get it over with," she said hoping to get a smile from the King but his heavy heart was not to be lifted.

"My dear," began the King. "I have some grave news I

must share with you that will undoubtedly make you suffer—but share it I must. Not only to free my mind of its heavy weight but so that you might adequately grieve."

Veronica's light spirits were now officially doused and she sat back fearing what news the King held. Whenever anyone addressed her as *dear*, she knew it usually meant something terrible had happened or was about to. Her mind raced through every possible packet of bad news she could think of in the few brief seconds of silence before the King continued. Her first thought was of Gus and that he had been killed or perhaps poor Shay, imprisoned in Norwich or maybe even the General. In that moment, she remembered all the times she worried about Matthew whenever he went off to battle and how he always returned—until he didn't. The subsequent days and months fearing his death were days she never wanted to relive. Then after concluding that no one was immune from death, not even her invisible Sir Matthew, she decided that it was death that the King needed to share—but she could never have guessed whose.

"What is it?" she finally asked. "I am already tormented with every piece of bad news I can imagine. Which one of our friends is dead?"

The King looked at Jess and then back at Veronica as his countenance fell even further. "Not one of our living friends, but he we thought was already dead," he said as tenderly as he could.

"What?" replied Veronica confused and growing angry as she tried to consider what the King meant.

The King reached out and took her hand as he continued. "Jess has joined us because the news I bear is also a confession."

Veronica was now growing afraid and she bit her trembling lip as the King squeezed her hand, trying to comfort her and give her strength. "I think it important that you first understand the circumstances."

Veronica nodded while fear ripped through her tormented soul as she fought the urge to imagine every possible deathly scenario.

After a long sigh, the King continued. "The night before the battle, the General ventured into your encampment. He was investigating the burning crosses and as you know, he discovered that the Hellhounds were about and that the crosses kept them to the shadows. However, on his way back he was met with the hounds and every man in his detachment was killed."

"And if His Majesty had not been there, he would most certainly been killed as well," interjected Jess.

The King nodded slowly looking at Jess and replied, "Indeed."

Jess reached over and put his arm around Veronica in preparation for what the King was now about to tell her but sensing something truly terrible was about to be laid upon her, she pushed her chair back and pulled her hand away from the King. There was only one scenario that she could imagine now that required such delicacy and she screamed in horror. "NO! It can't be—It isn't! I won't hear it—DAMN YOU, DAMN THE BOTH OF YOU!" as she burst into uncontrollable sobs.

The King got up and started to walk toward the other side of the table, trying to comfort her as he went.

"Get away from me! Get a-way!" she screamed as Corinna ran to her side.

"Veronica please," said Jess, "Let the King explain."

Veronica began sobbing out of control and was quickly becoming hysterical. She got up and ran to the barbican wall that overlooked the falls, getting as far away from the King as she could while Corinna followed after her. Leaning on the castle wall she wailed and shook as the thought of Matthew being a Hellhound ripped her heart and soul into pieces. She began mindlessly pounding the stone wall with her fists as she cried, opening up her barely closed wounds and they began to bleed again profusely. The King and Jess tried to approach but Corinna signaled them to stop and give them some space as well as time. She then placed her hand on Veronica's back as she too began to weep and whispered, "Oh Veronica." The only words she could utter before she too was overcome with grief.

Feeling Corinna's touch and hearing her voice, she quickly turned around and held onto her, still sobbing uncontrollably. There were no words Corinna could utter that could soothe such a wound, so she just held her trembling body tightly. She held her for a long while as her rent heart bled out and until Veronica had no more tears left. So violent was her emotional turmoil that the wound on her neck had also reopened and streamed down both of them, almost making its way to the floor. Veronica's strength had entirely left her, and as she was just about to collapse, Corinna signaled for the Chamberlin to assist them and they carried her back to her chamber.

The King and the Bishop both left, leaving Veronica's care to Corinna and her Chamberlin from Powis, two persons she loved and trusted—and that were not involved in any way with the heartbreaking news. With her strength gone and her heart broken again, she drifted into a dreamless sleep that was more like a coma and after many hours, she reluctantly opened her eyes to see her dear Corinna sitting on a chair with her head resting on the bed. Silently, Veronica reached down and touched her hair as a fresh tear rolled down her cheek. "Oh dear Corinna," she whispered.

Corinna sat up slowly and smiled whispering, "You are let living?"

Veronica nodded as several more tears left her sore and swollen eyes. "Somehow, I survive—though death is loads easier," she said as Corinna laughed slightly and replied, "I do believe you are right—for us both."

They lightly laughed mostly because their reservoirs of sorrow and grief were empty but still needing to release emotion, they laughed and held one another.

"How is my dear King and Jess?" Veronica asked after several quiet minutes.

Corinna sat back on her chair and sighed. "Oh, they are most-likely still sitting in the Drawing Room waiting for you to wake. The King has not left the castle not even for a minute. He is terribly vexed by your sorrow and, I must say he looks absolutely terrible. Veronica laughed slightly but grateful that her future husband was so tender and caring. "Will you please send him up?"

Corinna smiled, then nodded as she got up and squeezed her hand. Veronica watched her walk across the room and while turning her head, she felt a fresh bandage on her neck and then looked down at her hands. One was heavily bandaged and the other red and raw from pounding the rough castle wall. She sighed just as the King entered and rushed to her bedside, but before he could speak, Veronica placed her unbandage finger to his lips and said, "Shhh. I used to tell Gus that I was not made of glass, but alas, I find that I am. I am very broken I'm afraid."

The King sat on the side of her bed and brushed her hair from her face and whispered, "We are all broken my Lady."

Veronica looked into the King's eyes and continued, "I loved him William. I died that day he went missing. I never thought I would have to die twice, but this morning, I did."

"Or three times," said the King referring to the day she died in Gus's office back at the U.S. Senate and the both of them laughed lightly.

"Does it bother you—that I have so deeply loved another?"

The King thought for only a moment. "It would only bother me if you had never loved—I should think. You are a most loving and gracious woman. It is because you love, that I love you and I shall never be jealous of a memory; especially one so noble as Sir Matthew."

The King got up and walked around to the opposite side of the bed and laid down next to her, pulling her into his strong embrace. For a long while, neither of them spoke as their bonds of love and devotion sunk deeper, welding them together. The only sound was Veronica's stuttered-breathing as one does after sobbing for long periods. The evening sun was almost set and once again, the soothing amber rays of the Welsh late spring sun bathed the castle in warm gold light.

"You're sure he is dead then?" asked Veronica, feeling sufficiently brave to reopen the discussion.

The King thought very carefully before answering, not wanting to upset his soon to be bride for the second time in a single day and said, "Yes—very sure. I would explain the details but…"

"Please," replied Veronica.

Treading even slower and more carefully than before, he took a deep breath. "The General was perhaps less than eight feet from me and upon my approach, it looked up at me." He stopped to correct himself, apologizing and then said, "I mean, M—Matthew…"

Veronica padded the Kings chest as she laid upon it and said, "*It* is a good title. Surely the Matthew we knew had long since departed."

"I would agree. I only shot once but at that range, it was all that was needed. Nothing survives a ball at that close range I assure you."

"Where is he buried? Not that I have any burning desire to visit the grave, but…"

The King shook his head, "There is no grave. The Hellhounds it is said, leave no trace of their kills or their killed. When we went to bury the body it was gone as was the rest of the hounds and any sign that they were there at all."

Veronica sighed with relief. "It's probably just as well. Who else saw you shoot him?"

The King thought for a moment and wondered if he should tell her about the unknown men but considering he was talking to Veronica, he knew any deception would be short-term. Gently rubbing her head he sighed, "The General of course and Gus—there were also two other men I did not know. Why?"

Veronica was beyond exhausted and she spoke slowly with her eyes closed as she laid on the King's chest drifting in and out of consciousness. "Well, what if rumor spreads that you killed Matthew. No matter what you try and tell them, they will assume you did to capture and subdue me."

The King didn't reply as he rehashed in his mind once again the conversation he had had last night with Jess. He loathed the thought of killing a man because of what he knew, as did Jess, but before he could form an answer, Veronica sat up and said, "You didn't capture me—mind you. I surrendered. That's what needs to be spread throughout the Kingdom."

She then laid back down and snuggled into the King deeper and squeezed him tightly as she let out another deep and healing sigh. With all of her strength spent, she finally let herself slip into another coma-like sleep as she whispered almost unintelligibly, "I named my ship today…"

The King smiled, waiting for her to respond but there was none.

CHAPTER 2

THE WEDDING GIFT

Corinna always awoke early ever since she had been in service, but today she awoke even earlier and well before most of the castle staff. She made her way toward the kitchen, walking along the north wall that overlooked the falls, which wasn't the shortest route to the kitchen, but the view this early summer morning was spectacular and she took a deep breath as she paused to watch the river cascade over the falls. There was a light blue mist pushing into the Conwy estuary from the Irish Sea and in the pale blue of morning, she could see the workmen painting Veronica's ship in the only colors that could be produced in the post-Minimum era—light brown, red and black. Besides of course, gold-leaf, which they were using to paint the name of the ship on the stern and she strained to make out the letters *B-L-A-C.* She thought it rather odd but determined that they still had many more letters to paint.

The royal wedding was less than twenty-four hours away and as she walked, she mentally checked off her chore list and a made special note of the things she had yet to accomplish. The wedding was going to be performed at the St. Mary's Church in the center of the village, a twelfth century parish built during the reign of King Edward I and looking down into the outer ward, she saw the Archbishop making his way there to finalize the services with the local clergy. As she watched him walk, she thought to herself what a gentleman and great man he was and she very much enjoyed having him close by instead of far, far south in Canterbury.

Reaching the kitchen tower, she descended the narrow, winding staircase and after five dizzying revolutions, she entered the hot and busy kitchen. There were at least a dozen servants rushing about and numerous fires burning, each with several pots boiling and steaming. To the kitchen staff and the general hired help in the castle, Corinna was seen as a servant of high rank and someone who required proper titles and respect since she waited personally upon Veronica, the future Queen of England. When she entered the busy kitchen, everyone stopped what they were doing and acknowledged her presence with a bow.

"Good morning Miss," replied the head of the kitchen as she wiped her hands on her white apron which was already very dirty for being so early in the day. "Chamberlin Gilmore says you are going into market and can you fetch some ginger root? The Verte Sauce is plain terrible without it. Not fit for swine or beggar."

"Of course, how much will you be needing?" replied Corinna pleasantly.

"At least seven large roots, if you can find'em and that are not rotten. The merchant 'bout twenty paces inside the market usually 'as 'em, but he keeps the fresh one at the bottom of the cart mind you. 'Ere's forty-six Tallies…"

"Good heavens! That is certainly much more than I shall need—surely!" said Corinna surprised.

Tally Tokens was what the King and his household used to purchase from the peasants, which were small coins made of tin that the bearer could redeem for food and other supplies from the royal storehouses. It wasn't meant to be a full monetary system but it was quickly becoming the standard of exchange throughout England even though the only thing you could officially exchange them for was food, clothing and miscellaneous medical supplies. However, there was a rapidly-growing black market that accepted them for almost anything imaginable. Due to their wide value, both officially and unofficially, everyone eagerly accepted Tally Tokens in exchange for any product or service.

The head of the kitchen smiled and nodded, "Then you'll be bringin' me back some left-overs."

"Yes mum," replied Corinna respectfully as she picked up a deep wicker basket with two large handles, slid it over her arm and placed the tokens in her dress pocket. Before exiting the kitchen into the outer ward, she stopped and looked at her reflection in a large pan that hung over the table in the center of the room. The head of the kitchen smiled at her, knowing why she was fussing over her hair and as Corinna looked up and saw she was being observed, she smiled and walked out the door.

As she approached the west gate, her walk became slower and more dignified as she put on her best posture for a certain guard, Kelsey Blackett who once worked at The Grapes and whom she greatly fancied while she and Veronica lived in Powis Castle. As Corinna approached, her palms became sweaty with anticipation as her heart started pounding with yearning. From ten feet away, she looked at him, without looking at him, and saw him also stand a little taller, trying to clear his throat discreetly as he prepared to greet her.

"Ahem—beautiful good morning to you Miss Corinna,"

he said as the guard opposite him at the gate began to snicker.

Corinna blushed as she bowed her head, fighting to control a large smile that was forcing itself upon her. As she passed him, she reached out secretly and slid her finger across his chest on his metal breastplate, but due to her sweaty palms, the secret act of endearment made a loud, high-pitched squeak as Kelsey and Corinna both burst into laughter. The gate captain quickly turned his head to see what was the cause for the unacceptable outburst as Corinna quickly ran out the gate, holding back her laughter.

She made her way across the draw bridge and then turned down Rose Hill toward the open market on a large flat piece of ground that was once a commuter parking lot. Gone were the days of smooth, paved surfaces and most streets that were not made of cobble stone were now just black dirt, left over from the burning concrete during the Minimum. Whenever it rained, the black, inky soot that splashed up on boots, pants and dresses stuck to everything and was known as the murky muck, which was impossible to wash out. As she entered the market, she walked past several vendor carts who were selling fruit left over from the last growing season, but since it was now early June, they looked less than appetizing. She smiled graciously as she walked while the vendors waited for her to pass and then talked quietly amongst themselves, wondering who she was. Strangers were uncommon in any village in England, but especially a village as obscure and remote as Conwy. However, with the arrival of Veronica, the King and both of their households, the village had swelled by over a thousand, nearly doubling the previous population.

Most of the vendors paid her only mild attention until she

stopped to purchase the ginger root and paid for it with Tally Tokens. Taking the tallies out of her pocket, she counted out three and handed them to a cute, blonde-haired girl that didn't look over the age of thirteen. Her hair was parted into two braids and tied in the back with a single strap of leather and a spike of heather. It was a medieval hair style to be sure, but like most things medieval, it was very practical and kept one's hair smelling fresh and helped it stay clean since washing and bathing was such a chore. The girl's eyes opened wide as if she had just been given gold and she bowed in front of Corinna enthusiastically and said, "Thank you Miss!"

The attention of the surrounding market quickly focused on Corinna and every vendor then competed for her attention. Everyone knew that someone with tallies was from the Castle and they approached her, pushing their produce and wares in front of her, insisting that she purchase and pleading with her. Corinna was quickly overwhelmed and while she tried to be polite, the vendors pushed upon her all the more until she felt someone grab her arm and pull her backwards. In great alarm, she whirled around to find that Jess had come to her rescue. He was dressed in a brown monk-looking robe with a deep hood over his head but when the merchants realized that the Archbishop was in the market, it had a dousing effect on their heavy press and they receded back to their carts, still calling and pleading for her to purchase their goods.

"Thank you Your Grace, you are most kind to see a damsel in distress and slay the dragons about her. You are my hero," said Corinna in a benign, flirting way.

Jess laughed, "Dragons—perhaps not—but I can quiet a busy market on the right day as well as put a congregation right to sleep."

"Oh, Your Grace, you are a national treasure. What should we ever do if we were to lose the likes of you? God's great gain would be our undoing I should think."

Jess smiled and extended his arm to Corinna whereupon she gladly took it, patting it affectionately. As they walked through the market, Corinna stopped occasionally to inspect various handcrafts but then sat them back down with a frustrating sigh.

"What is it you are shopping for?" asked Jess finally, not wanting to interfere with a woman's shopping—a lesson he learned in the pre-Minimum world.

"I don't know to be quite honest. I wanted to give Her Majesty a gift but I am distraught. I suppose I thought I was going to the mall today but I see nothing that is worthy of such a gift from my heart."

Just as Jess was about to agree, he saw a man covering his cart and frantically trying to push it away and out of sight. "Wait—you there!" called Jess.

Hearing Jess call after him, the man was about to leave his cart and belongings but then considering it was the Archbishop, he stopped and turned around. Corinna and Jess walked over to the cart as the man knelt quietly with is head bowed not saying a word. Just as Jess was about to ask him why he was so unsettled, he pulled back the covering on the cart, then slowly looked at Corinna with a look of disbelief.

"Where did you get this?" asked Jess, as the man continued to kneel and stare down at the ground.

The man did not respond at first but then slowly looked up. "I am a sinner Your Grace, please have mercy and forgive me," he said.

"Very well, but the question remains my son, where did you find such treasure?"

Slowly and with great hesitation, the man replied quietly, "I found it in the castle whilst working last summer on the repairs."

Jess pulled the entire cover off the cart revealing dozens of artifacts including a longsword with a golden hilt, several scrolls of parchment, a dagger encrusted with rubies, pieces of armor and a long tube made from a small tree trunk. The wooden cylinder was about thirty inches long and had dried and cracked leather stoppers on each end. Curiously, Jess picked it up and inspected it. There was some form of writing carved into the tube that he did not recognize but the reason he was so intrigued was that it had several carvings of ravens along the sides and painted on both leather caps. There was also a leather strap that ran from top to bottom and looked like it had been designed to be worn over the shoulder like a quiver, but it certainly could not hold arrows, not with a cap on each end. All of the items in the cart appeared to be very ancient, certainly dating back to at least the tenth century but the tube he held in his hand was older, much older.

"Where did you find this?" asked Jess.

The man swallowed hard. "Under the well bridge at the center of the castle. It was in a lead box, sealed behind several cap stones. We only found them by accident when the small wall gave way."

Jess was about to open the tube and see what was inside but then quickly noticed that the eyes of the entire market were upon him and he graciously looked down at the man and bade him to rise. "Was there any more found other than what you have in your cart?"

"Only the lead box Your Grace. It is at my house. I swear to you I have sold nothing else," replied the man. "But of course, it is all yours to take to the King," he said smiling, trying to lighten the mood but when Jess did not respond he quickly added, "Free today—of course."

Jess was a man of great compassion and the look of humiliation and defeat on the man's face in front of the whole market was difficult for him and he reached into his pocket to pay him at least something for the treasures but he had nothing. He looked over at Corinna and asked, "I think I have found you the perfect gift for the Queen. There is nothing she loves more than history—she will be thrilled I assure you."

He then turned to the man and asked, "How much for the lot?"

The man stumbled in his speech, being wholly unprepared to sell the items, and to the Archbishop of all persons. "Um, I—a, five tallies?" he said sheepishly.

"Good-barmy man! Have you no sense of worth?" said Jess, turning to Corinna. "I am fresh out of tallies today, can you spot me?" he asked.

Corinna reached into her pocket and pulled out the tallies the kitchen gave her along with seven of her own. "I have," she stalled while she counted and then said, "fifty," and dumped them in Jess's out-stretched hand.

Jess then turned back to the man whose eyes were now as wide as goblets. "On behalf of God, I forgive you for stealing from the King, but since you have taken such care of the artifacts and kept them safe, I am willing to pay you for your protective services, as I'm sure the King would do the same." He put all the Tally Tokens in the man's hand but before he closed his fingers around the small fortune, Jess stopped him. "Ah-ah. There must be a punishment for your thievery," Jess said as he took back ten of the tallies, leaving the man with forty, which was still a great sum. The man started to look distressed but when he realized that he still had forty tallies, he bowed himself in front of the Archbishop, thanking him. Jess smiled and then bade the man to go forward and sin no more.

Jess and Corinna immediately made their way back to the castle with their treasure and as they crossed the drawbridge and were within the safety of the guards, Jess hastily picked up the tube. The leather cap was almost as firm as plastic and it cracked as Jess carefully but eagerly tried to pull it off.

"What's inside?" asked Corinna.

"I don't know but I'm guessing maps, or documents. Whatever it is, it was extremely important to hide away," replied Jess. As he pulled the leather cap away from the tube, it broke off in his hand, he sighed with frustration and then placed it in his pocket. He then peered inside the dark tube and saw what looked like a scroll. He looked up at Corinna puzzled and then reached his hand inside. The scroll rod was made of wood, which was perhaps normal, but the paper on the scroll was not paper at all, but cloth and to his great surprise, the cloth was damp not dry and brittle like anything would be that was over a thousand years old. He was about to pull it from the cylinder when he pulled his hand from the tube and said, "We should probably wait and open this inside."

Corinna nodded as Jess placed the tube back in the cart

and pushed it through the west gate. Corinna slowed a little and smiled at Kelsey as she passed and then ran after Jess who was already ten feet in front of her pushing the cart. Passing the kitchen, Corinna remembered the borrowed tallies and said nearly out of breath, "Your Grace, the tallies I gave you belonged to the kitchen."

Just then, the head of the kitchen saw Corinna and desperately needing the ginger root, she ran calling after her. Corinna finally convinced Jess to stop just long enough so that she could give her the root and to apologize for the missing tallies, promising that she would be reimbursed. Jess then turned to the head of the kitchen and asked, "Have you seen Her Majesty this morning?"

"Her Majesty is in the chapel, Your Grace," she replied with a slight bow.

Without another word, Jess pushed the cart over to the chapel that was across the courtyard from the kitchen and threw the doors wide. "Your Majesty, I have something you must see!" Then remembering that everything in the cart was actually a gift from Corinna, he retracted and said, "Actually, your dear Corinna has procured an amazing gift for you that I am very anxious for you to see."

Veronica was kneeling in prayer in the quiet solitude of the beautifully renovated medieval chapel and didn't speak or move for several minutes while Jess and Corinna waited quietly, catching their breath. Finally Veronica stood and walked to the back of the chapel, pulling the hood of her emerald green velvet cloak from off her head. Castles were terribly cold in the morning hours before the stone was warmed by the sun and she placed her hands inside her sleeves, shivering slightly and staring at the covered cart.

"Good morning Your Grace and dear Corinna. It appears

you two have been having some fun this morning?" said Veronica.

Corinna smiled as Jess replied, "Just so," giddy and anxious while forcing himself to refrain from pulling back the cover of the cart. "Forgive me Corinna, this gift is yours to give," he finally said, taking a step backwards.

Veronica looked at Corinna confused, not understanding the meaning nor purpose for the gift. Corinna then smiled and approached Veronica and hugged her. "It is a…" she paused. She was about to say it was a small gift but what was in the cart was anything but insignificant and she continued with better chosen words, "an incredible gift that His Grace and I happened upon in the market this morning—for your wedding, your Majesty, from me and the Archbishop."

Jess smiled in appreciation and approval but not being able to wait any longer, he pulled back the cover, revealing the historical contents and as Veronica gasped, he retrieved the tube and handed it to her, "I do not know what it contains but I peered inside and it appears to be a very curious document on a scroll."

Veronica took the tube from Jess, sat down on the last row of pews and looked inside. She then reached in and pulled it out. Jess's heart was pounding as was Corinna's but only because of all the hype the Archbishop was making over a seemingly simple cylinder of wood.

Ever since Jess found the ancient texts buried in the St. Martin churchyard, he had become an artifact junkie. The dozens of old documents and books found in the unmarked grave was the complete gnostic library that Rome had sought so desperately to destroy in the fifth century. With Gus and Veronica's help, they had translated the entire library which Jess had then used to rebuild an institution of faith that he refused to call a religion since the very definition of a religion was contrary to the advancement of knowledge. Religions had always been known as the steadfast pillar of so-called truth but the attainment of truth is a gradual process that had the potential to uproot any manmade organization. Therefore, the powerful religions before the Minimum suppressed new thought since the structure and leadership positions of religion was more important than the attainment of truth.

When Jess first felt the rolled cloth inside the tube, he imagined that it was perhaps the authentic shroud of Christ since the shroud of Turin that was supposed to be the actual burial shroud was proven to be a forgery back in the year 2019. Before the King had presented him a fragment of the true Cross, he believed all religious relics were bogus; meaningless ornaments used to manipulate ignorant parishioners. He still believed that most religious relics were forgeries, however there were some that were the real deal and wielded incredible power, just as the crushing of the Cross fragment ended the Sevren Valley battle a few days ago. As he anxiously waited for Veronica to withdraw the contents of the tube, he placed his hand into the pocket of his robe and felt the last few splinters of the Cross.

When Veronica removed the scroll, they learned it was not a scroll at all, nor a burial shroud but it appeared to be a banner that was wrapped around a very old-looking and very straight tree branch. The cloth was faded yellow and was wrapped around the branch at least a dozen times or more. Veronica stood up and slowly began to unroll it as she inspected it in minute detail, inch by inch as it rolled off the stick. The cloth appeared to be incredibly old but as Jess noticed, the cloth was not dry but somewhat moist and supple. As it came off the roller, she could see stains of all sizes and brightness on the yellow cloth, some that appeared to be blood and others that were certainly dirt. Whatever it was, she concluded that it has seen a lot of action and was of course, highly prized to be so hidden for so many years. With the banner unrolled four feet, there was still no insignia or symbol, only a pale yellow pennant. Then unrolling the last twelve inches, Veronica gasped and almost dropped the banner.

Jess jumped forward and caught the banner before it fell to the floor and held it as Veronica sat back down on the pew bewildered and amazed at what she saw. For several minutes she said nothing but just sat shaking her head. When she finally stood again she took the banner from Jess and turned it around so that he could see the front. Jess took several steps backwards so that he could get a better look at the full length of the banner and on the last twelve inches was an embroidered black raven. He stared at it for several minutes, lost to its meaning and at last said, "It's a banner with a raven on it?"

Veronica looked back at Jess incredulously as she shook her head, "You don't know what this is?"

Jess shrugged while Corinna shook her head and said, "No."

"I can't believe I'm going to say this—but this is the Raven Banner. THE Raven Banner!"

Jess and Corinna were still looking confused.

Veronica sighed. "Ragnar Lodbrok? Dane invasion, ninth century?"

"I know it," came a voice entering the chapel.

Everyone turned to see the King and they bowed respectfully, each uttering at varying intervals, "Your Grace," except Veronica who only bowed her head and kissed him.

The King had just come from court where he sat all morning listening to the grievances of the Agricultural Council; the lack of hands and supplies in Wales. He had called an hour recess and while walking to the inner court to find Veronica, he heard her in the chapel. "Good morning to you, my tomorrow-wife. Why are we discussing Ragnar Lodbrok?" he said.

Veronica held the banner high so the King could see it and after several seconds he looked back at her in amazement and asked, "Is this what I think it is? My hell, where ever did you get it?!"

Veronica smiled, being very excited that someone besides herself actually knew what it was—and appreciated its significance. "Dear Corinna and His Grace purchased it for me in the market. I swear, the things you can't find in the market these days."

The King was beyond amazed and as he and Veronica excitedly conversed about the ancient relic that was a supposed myth, the King asked enthusiastically, "I wonder if it really works?!"

Jess was now very tired of being in the dark and he finally asked, "Veronica dear, would you be so kind as to share with the class what you are talking about?"

Veronica laughed. "When the Danes invaded England, it was said that they carried with them a raven banner that was bewitched and if the raven was animated during the battle, the Vikings would win the day. It was terrifying to the English and many English forces fled before it, being so convinced that they could not prevail. But when the Vikings were finally put to flight, King Alfred stole the banner and marched it in front of the English armies. From that moment on, they never lost a battle and went on to vanquish the Danes from England forever—the only country to do so. The Vikings conquered all of Europe during that period, but not England. Archeologists never looked for the banner because, well let's face it, it was all myth and still might be. We have no way of knowing if it works. This may very well be the banner but I had always assumed that its animation was merely the result of the banner flapping in the breeze."

Veronica anxiously looked over the remaining items in the cart as Jess excitedly began taking out the remaining artifacts and sat them on a table at the rear of the chapel. He first took out the sword and then the rest of the items, saving the most strange for last. Handing the broken arrow to Veronica he exclaimed, "And the most bizarre of all, a worthless broken arrow."

Curious, Veronica took the arrow and inspected it for a few seconds then inspected the items on the table and asked, "You say all these were found together?"

"That is what we were told," replied Corinna.

"Then I think I know what this all is. They are tokens from a treaty and gaging from the looks of everything, I would guess sometime before the tenth century," said Veronica, setting the arrow on the table.

"What makes you so sure?" asked Jess and the King in unison.

"Well, the arrow was my first clue. A broken arrow like the

origin of the handshake, showed that there was no weapon between the two parties or that they held no weapon in their hands. Somewhere, whomever the treaty was with, is the other half of this arrow. The presence of the sword is, well, obvious."

"It is? How?" asked the King.

"If a war was long and terrible, it wasn't unheard of for the kings or generals to exchange weapons, again as a symbol that they are laying down their arms."

"But there are two weapons here and by the looks of them, they don't appear to be from the same forge," replied the King picking up the dagger. "This dagger's construction is completely different than the sword. I'm no weapon's expert but I'm betting the longsword and the dagger belonged to two different people from two different countries."

"Then why are they both in Conwy?" asked Veronica to herself just as Jess handed her the two scrolls from the cart.

"I'm betting these will shed some light," he said, handing them to Veronica.

Veronica carefully broke the wax seal on the largest scroll that was now almost like glass due to its ancient age, and as she bent it backwards, the seal shattered and fell to the floor. She expected to see elegant Old English calligraphy but there was nothing remotely close on the scroll. Unrolling it further and still not being able to discern the language, she rolled it out on the table and placed the sword on the edge to keep it from curling.

"What language is that?" asked Corinna.

Veronica slowly shook her head, "I'm not sure. My first thought was Gaelic but the runes have thrown me. I've never seen the two languages mixed, it's almost as if it was an intentional ruse."

"Two very obscure languages, combined—obscurely," commented the King.

Veronica broke the seal on the other scroll and unrolled it on the table beside the other. The smaller scroll was only about eighteen inches long and in Latin across the top it read, *Nos Septem.*

Everyone but Corinna, who couldn't read Latin said, "We are seven."

"Huh!," replied Jess in an epiphany.

"You say that as if it means something to you Your Grace," replied the King.

"I have no understanding but there is a rather curious grave at the church in the center of town that is covered with an iron grate with the inscription, *We are seven.*"

"Really?" replied Veronica, "Well, at least we know they are connected and that whatever these relics are tied to, they were not transported here for safe-keeping. Their significance is tied to Conwy and Wales specifically."

"Or at least it was seen as a good hiding place," suggested Jess.

The remainder of the scroll was like the other, a mixture of Gaelic and Runic and therefore untranslatable, at least for the moment. "Well, as interesting as all this is, I have a wedding to prepare for," said Jess as he bowed to take his leave, not considering the possibility that that the relics had anything to do with the present. "With no library on the premises, this cart of treasure should keep you quite busy since I know you will hardly rest until you have discovered and cataloged all its secrets."

Veronica smiled. "Thank you Your Grace, and thank you dear Corinna," replied Veronica as Corinna bowed and made her way toward the kitchen. Veronica collected the relics and carefully placed them in the cart as the King then pushed it toward the inner ward. Once inside the Great Room, Veronica placed all the artifacts on the large table in the center of the white fenrir rug and pulled up a chair. The King watched her for several minutes as she disappeared from the moment and immersed herself deeper and deeper into the scrolls until it became obvious that she was lost to the world around her and he smiled. "Well, I guess I shall return to court."

Veronica replied slightly above a mumble and said, "No thank you, I took breakfast already."

The King laughed and shut the door quietly behind him, leaving Veronica lost in her studies. As he approached the Great Hall, he saw Jess rushing toward the west gates, no doubt on his way to the Church, when he stopped and ran back calling, "Your Majesty!"

"Lest I forget, I have borrowed that which I cannot repay. Corinna owes the kitchen forty or fifty Tallies, would you mind terribly paying my debt to her?"

Feeling very well and jovial, the King replied, "Why, Jess—perhaps some time in a debtors prison will serve you well. How reckless—borrowing with no means to repay?"

Jess playfully extended his wrists so that he could be led away just as a rider burst through the outer gates, yelling, "I've a message for the King!"

The guards at the gate quickly lowered the portcullis and stood behind it, asking the peasant to identify himself and state his business. The rider was out of breath and obviously in great haste so the King and Jess walked over to the gate to see what all the excitement was about as the rider leaned over on his horse gasping. There was an arrow protruding out of his back with blood streaming down to his saddle and dripping onto the stone barbican but before he could speak his business, he fainted and fell to the ground. The King ordered for the portcullis to be raised and for the man to be brought into the castle. He was taken to the nearest enclosure which was the chapel, where he was laid on the rear table. After a few minutes, several maids from the kitchen entered and began dressing his wounds, stopping the flow of blood. As they busily worked, Jess and the King stood quietly, leaning against the last pew, studying the man and wondering where he was from. He was certainly not a member of the King's many armies marauding around the Kingdom at the moment but the dried salt on his britches suggested that he had come from the coast.

Both kitchen maids turned to look at Jess and the King with bewildered looks. They were not trained nurses or anything close to it. They knew how to cook and dress only small knife wounds as one frequently gets while preparing food but trying to remove an arrow was completely out of their depth. "How shall we get it out?" asked one of them, very insecurely and frightened almost in tears. Jess and the King walked over, looked at the arrow and the great amounts of blood streaming from the wound. They too did not have any experience with arrows stuck in the flesh and Jess slid his hand under the patient, feeling for a point protruding out his chest but felt none. He then turned to the King and suggested, "It appears to only be in the muscle, I don't believe it has entered the lung—I think."

The King then noticed that away from the wound was dried blood, looking as if the injury had happened hours ago and after inspecting the hole in his back further, he could see great amounts of swelling, suggesting infection. The King sighed, knowing that without antibiotics, the infection could not be stopped and the man would probably never wake. It seemed inhumane but since the King needed to know what message he held on his silent tongue, he reached down and broke off the arrow as far into the wound as he could and instructed the maids to simply stop the bleeding. This way, even though he would certainly die from infection, he could at least regain consciousness as his body produced enough blood to awaken. The maids nodded and began packing the wound with cayenne pepper and salt, two common kitchen spices that stop bleeding.

"Stay with him and notify me at once, no matter the hour, when he awakes," said the King.

Both maids nodded and curtsied as the King and Jess left the chapel and stepped out into the afternoon sun that was slowly fading behind dark clouds that were pushing in from the coast on a freshening breeze. The King's flag was flapping wildly, snapping in the stiff breeze atop the tower above the outer ward and looking up, Jess wondered at the latest turn of events. He concluded that the rider could only have one possible message and that was one of war. With his countenance falling, he turned to the King and said, "Whatever the message, it is bad news Your Majesty. I suggest you rally your forces and perhaps even create a press in the village to gather more men."

The King turned to Jess with resolve and iron beginning to flow through his veins and asked, "I wonder what the Raven Banner is doing at this moment?"

Excitedly but with apprehension, Jess nodded and they made their way to the Great Room where they found Veronica unmoved and still pouring over the scrolls, right where the King had left her. Not surprisingly, when they entered, Veronica didn't look up or even acknowledge their presence until the King walked up behind her and kissed her neck. Still without looking up she hummed with pleasure and reached behind her, feeling for him. The King had walked around the table to where the Raven Banner was and when Veronica could not feel him, she finally looked up to see the Banner being unrolled.

"What is it?" she asked. "And why do you have blood on your hands?"

The King looked down and inspected his hands, then at the Banner and back at Jess shaking his head. "Doesn't appear to be working," he said.

"You want to tell me what you boys are up to?" asked Veronica.

Jess then thought, unintentionally ignoring Veronica's question. "Wait, it's not working or it's not moving?"

"Both," replied the King.

"It very well might be working," Jess said. "It might just mean the battle—where ever or whatever it is, is not going to end well."

The King sat down the relic and then sat himself on the

edge of the table with a sigh, finally turning to Veronica. "A rider just came through the gates with an arrow in his back—he was frantic."

"Did he say why he had an arrow in his back?" asked Veronica slowly thinking it was a very important part of the story to leave out.

"He did not," replied the King, "He is unconscious at the moment—fainted from blood loss before he could relay his message. We then entrained the thought of the Raven Banner and that it might shed more light on the strange events—mostly out of childish curiosity. However, we would be none the wiser since the default state of the banner is motionless, is it not?."

"Ah," replied Jess, realizing his flawed reasoning.

Getting up and walking back to Veronica's side of the table, he placed his hands on her shoulders. "So, we wait and hope he awakes. It did appear that he had been riding for several hours, not days so we can probably assume the danger he encountered is local. We just don't know who, what or where."

Just then, Corinna entered the room and being surprised to find the King there, she quickly asked if Her Majesty would like a fire lit to take the chill off due to the high wind outside. Veronica nodded and thanked her. After the fire was roaring, the King and Jess sat as Veronica went back to her scrolls.

"Are you having any luck my dear," asked the King.

"Not yet. If only Ted were here. He is very well versed in medieval languages and has had some experience with runic languages as I remember. But…"

"Well, I'll have him brought at once," replied the King, then remembering that the Tower had been sacked his spirits sunk a little and he sighed. "No, I guess I won't. At least not until we know who sacked the Tower. I really hope it was your friends, then at least Ted might still be imprisoned. If it was the Celts, he is probably dead by now."

"Poor Ted," replied Veronica softly.

The King jumped to his feet after realizing his callousness and wrapped his arms around her. "I'm so sorry. That was terrible of me to say. Certainly there is a good chance he is alive."

"A chance perhaps but I don't think it is a good one," she replied.

"Forgive me Veronica, it is so easy to forget where we all came from and what has happened to our friends," replied the King as he stroked her hair. It was the first time the King had called her by her first name since before she was crowned Queen of Wales and the use caught her by surprise. She was amazed at how intimate her own first name was to her now, especially having gone so long without hearing it and she stood up and embraced the King, kissing him long and passionately, like she had never kissed him before. In response, the King held her tighter, pressing her small body against his as she quivered with yearning and passion to be with him. After several pleasurable moments, she released his lips and smiled, placing her hand on his cheek.

"I do love thee William," she said returning the intimate favor.

The King didn't respond as the light from the fire glistened in his watering eyes and he once again held her tightly, cherishing her beyond anything that he had ever loved. The use of his first name had the same effect on him, which is why traditionally no one addressed royalty by their first names. In fact, this tradition also trickled down to courting rules during the Victorian era where a male caller never addressed a woman by her first name until he was considered acceptable and desirable.

Just then Corinna entered the room and announced that the rider had awakened.

CHAPTER 3

WEDDINGS AND WAR

The King, Jess and Veronica rushed out of the inner ward Great Room and into the pouring rain toward the chapel. When they entered, they were greeted by Padrig, the Vicar of the castle chapel who had been attending to the injured man. He had been trying to keep his fever as low as possible by applying cold rags on his bare skin and refreshing them with the ones he had hanging outside in the rain. Consequently, the man was nearly naked and he shivered violently as new and colder rags were applied to his fever-burned skin. The chapel was aglow with dozens of candelabras and when the three most powerful persons in England entered, Padrig backed away from the patient and bowed. Upon seeing the King, the wounded man took a deep breath and tried to quickly speak with the same urgency as when he rode into the castle, as if he were resuming where he had left off. The King placed his hand on the man's chest, trying to calm him said, "Take your time son."

His voice was cracked and it took all the strength he had to inhale and expel the heavy air that would allow him to speak. The man nodded, paused for a moment and then swallowed hard before trying again. "They came from Holy Isle—killed an' burned everythin'." He coughed violently on top of his already violent shaking and he struggled to continue, as the King asked, "Who? Who came from Holy Island?"

The man tried to speak but once again, coughing overtook him and after several very hard ones, he began to spit up blood. The King rolled him on his side so he would not drown in his own blood and Veronica knelt down, telling him to try and whisper as she reassured him and caressed his shaking hands. After a few minutes and after more blood drained from his mouth, he told them that an army of great size had crossed over the Menai Strait, which was a very narrow piece of ocean less than a thousand feet wide that separated Llanddwyn Island from Wales. He described the army in such a way that made Veronica remember the terribleness Matthew had experienced at Holy Island and she exclaimed, "It's the hellhounds!"

"No! No!," coughed the man, "Celts!" as he started to seize and his eyes rolled into the back of his head. Veronica let go of his arm and held her hand to her mouth as the man shook for the last time, his lifeless body finally partaking of the peace that death is. Jess sighed deeply as he stepped forward and placed his fingers over his eyelids, shutting them while Padrig made the sign of the cross and provided last rites.

The King sat down on a pew and slowly rubbed his thumb over his bottom lip as he considered what the nameless man had told them. In his mind, he had supposed the Celts would advance into Northumbria where they already had a stronghold at Blackpool, west of the M6 but now it appeared he was caught between an army less than five miles to the south, an army in Blackpool to the north—not to mention the invasion in the south that had already taken the Tower. To make matters worse, the core of his army was over a hundred miles away, marching into Mercia with General Clancy to put down an uprising that might not even be. With the threat so close to Conwy, he determined that he had no choice but to ride to out to meet them and pray that Gus was holding his own in Northumbria. As for London, it would have to burn until they could understand what was happening in the north. He lightly pounded his fist on the back of the pew in front of him as he meticulously thought through every implication and as his thoughts drew closer to a conclusion, his pounding grew stronger and louder until he stood up. "I must have General Clancy and his army redirected here. He cannot go northwards, not now."

"But what of Gus?" asked Veronica, fearfully.

The King shook his head with frustration. "He will have to remain strong for at least a few more days. He does have over one thousand guns along the M6 and a force of nearly five-thousand. We shall have to pray for good fortune to rest upon Northumbria."

While the King was contemplating his next move, Jess stepped out of the chapel and summoned the King's Council. Just as the King was about to call the council himself, they walked through the doors and took a knee in front of him. The King immediately started doling out orders, sending a group of fast riders eastward to fetch the General and another north to inform Gus. He also wrote new orders for General Clancy in case there actually was an civil uprising in Mercia, he was to put it down with deadly force. He then sent another dispatch to London to ensure that he received news about who had taken the Tower. He knew that there were too many unanswered questions and he was certain he would make many mistakes, but he could not sit still and wait. He then ordered for every able man who did not belong to the castle guard to prepare for battle immediately and he formed a press to go into the village and surrounding countryside and press every able man and child over the age of fifteen to rally to the King's army the next day. As the chapel began to empty, his armor was brought and while he dressed, he turned to Veronica with sorrow in his eyes and sadness in his voice and said, "I so wanted a grand ceremony my Lady but, it is not be—at least not on Sunday."

In his full armor, he reached out, took her hand and led her to the alter at the front of the chapel. As his last order before riding into battle, he asked Jess to marry them. Veronica sighed with apprehension but then finally nodded in agreement. It wasn't the fairytale wedding she had dreamed of since she was a child, but she knew that she didn't live in a fairytale and that such stories were all lies anyway. This was raw, brutal and gristly real life where things seldom rolled the way she dream them, but she couldn't help from feeling wounded. She so wanted to at least have Gus present her who was the closest thing she had to family in the world and she had always dreamed of Gus giving her away even when she worked as his assistant in the U.S. Senate.

Jess then stepped forward and was just about to begin the make-shift ceremony when Veronica let go of the King's hand and raised it timidly, signaling for Jess to stop. "Can I please have Corinna fetched," she asked humbly as an involuntary tear rolled down her cheek.

The King, already feeling terrible for the unfortunate circumstances, could only nod as Padrig ran out of the chapel in search for Corinna. Ten minutes later, Corinna entered the chapel with a bouquet of wet wildflowers she had quickly picked along the side of the outer ward walls and she handed them to Veronica. Veronica smiled and hugged her affectionately, thanking her for the flowers as more tears fill both of their eyes. The King started to apologize but Veronica turned to him and placed her finger on his lips. "While I might be made of glass these days, I am not so frail as to not see the importance of this moment. England must be united—England is all the good the world has left."

The King smiled gratefully, held her tightly and was about to kiss her when Jess placed a Bible between their lips. "Good gracious, a kiss before the ceremony?!"

The King smiled weakly and then nodded as he stood up straight. Corinna ran a quick brush through Veronica's hair and straightened her dress, tying a gold sash around her waist that she had pulled from her pocket.

"Are we ready then?" asked Jess after Corinna stepped back.

"Yes, thank you," replied Veronica as she wiped the last tear from her cheek.

Jess performed the ceremony in Latin, which added a welcomed layer of formality and beauty to the urgent service. When it came time for the ring, the King realized he didn't have one and Veronica took the engagement ring off her finger and handed it to Corinna who then handed it to the King, which he took with an embarrassed smile and slid it back on Veronica's finger. Jess then tied their hands together with a sash he took from a curtain near the alter and completed the ceremony saying, "With praise be to God almighty for His mercy and His grace in blessing this nation with such as these two—the best in all the world, I seal you to one another as male and female, as Adam and Eve, as husband and wife, as loved and beloved, as King and Queen of England that the twain shall become one, uniting your souls and England, never to be broken, in Christ Jesus, amen. Now you may kiss your Queen, Your Majesty."

The King turned to face his Queen but before kissing her, he placed his hand under her chin, looked into her deep blue eyes and whispered, "I do also love thee, dear Veronica," as he leaned in and kissed her. In the stillness of the chapel and their long kiss, Veronica heard Corinna sniffing and wiping her tears while Padrig began singing a chanting-hymn in Latin, as a heavenly sacredness descended on the brief, but transcendent moment before her King and beloved husband walked out the door to war. Despite the rashness of the ceremony, it was surprisingly beautiful and Veronica sighed with adequate satisfaction as she thanked Jess by giving him a kiss on the cheek. Corinna then stepped forward to congratulate her and as they embraced, Veronica saw the corpse over Corinna's shoulder, still lying on the table at the back of the chapel and the urgency of the moment returned to her, as it did to everyone else. But before they left the chapel, Jess invited everyone to join with him around the alter while he invoked the blessings of heaven to be upon England, that right might prevail and that evil be vanquished completely in England. It was a mighty prayer that not only blessed everyone with comfort but armed them with power.

Jess had scarcely finished the prayer when Trevet, Veronica's former captain entered the room. He had been given control over the united army and announced to the King that the vanguard was assembled in the outer ward. Leaving the warmth and peace of the chapel, they were greeted by the pouring rain and the extremely imposing vanguard all dressed in full armor and when Trevet saw the King's hand still bound to Veronica's, he determined correctly that they had just been married and he raised his voice above the sound of the anxious army and the pounding rain and yelled, "Hail to the King and to Queen Veronica!"

The vanguard erupted into cheers as they yelled to the black night sky above them, "God save the King! God save the Queen!" The vanguard then all took a knee and bowed their heads in reverence as the King untied their hands and kissed her one last time. Veronica tried to be brave and even though she had only been married for a few short minutes, it had changed things, if not everything and her bottom lip began to tremble as she bid her husband good-bye. "You must come back to me! Do you hear me!" she yelled above the sound of the relentless rain. The King stepped into his stirrup and swung his leg over his saddle, without taking his eyes off her. He then placed his hand on her cheek and closed his eyes, burning the moment into his eternal memory and the feel of her tender skin in his hand. She looked up at her husband-King as more tears began to flow down her cheeks and then disappear into the rain on her face. The yearning moment could have lasted for hours and still been frustratingly short, but after what seem like only seconds, the King's touch left her cheek and the same hand that so lovingly caressed her, now gave the order for his vanguard to ride into battle.

Corinna and the Queen watched as the King rode through the gates followed by a hundred men who were then joined by a thousand more outside the castle. The sound of metal armor, weapons and horse hooves was deafening as it echoed off the walls and diminished by degrees as the last rider passed through the western gate. As the portcullis was lowered, Corinna was relieved to see Kelsey still standing at attention in front of it, he not having been assigned to ride with the King. But her heart sank for Veronica as once again, the man she loved was outside the gates, riding into the darkness toward an unknown foe. She knew the similarities between the night Matthew left and tonight were not lost on Veronica either and she put her arm around her, trying to console her and said, "He will come back Your Majesty, he is not riding to meet hellhounds and he rides with over a thousand men."

Veronica turned from blankly staring at the closed portcullis and tried to smile but her sorrow would not allow her to speak. After a few moments, she managed to nod her head as she tried to convince herself that Corinna was right but it was no use. This was the second time that the man she loved rode off into the night toward a vicious unknown army, leaving her alone with only her grief and worry. Over the past year, she had tried not to think about the night Matthew left and how terrible he was to her just before leaving. But for the first time since that fateful night, she allowed herself to be angry and she now resented him for how he had treated her. And then as memories always do, she recalled all the times he had offended her and all his episodes of juvenile arrogance returned to her mind like a magnet collecting iron out of the dust. At last, she finally convinced herself that tonight was nothing like the night Matthew left and she closed her eyes, clinging to the memory of the King touching her cheek, one of the most intimate and romantic moments of her life, made even more powerful since he afterwards rode into the darkness toward a murderous battle.

Even though it was July, the rain was cold and was accompanied by a stiff northwesterly wind blowing off the coast. As she stood in the outer ward shivering and clinging to the quickly fading memories of her husband, Corinna gently pulled her arm and suggested that they get out of the weather and next to a warm fire. Veronica nodded and they made their way toward the inner ward and the Great Room where they found a very grand fire burning and a quick but lavish meal prepared. Hearing of the private wedding, the kitchen staff hastily prepared a meal that was intended to imitate a wedding feast, even if the groom was not present. Smelling the freshly roasted mutton and potatoes, Veronica felt her stomach twist and knot, reminding her that she hadn't eaten since breakfast. She quickly moved the artifacts from the table and set them on the floor out of the way but seeing the lone plate on the table, her heart was pained and just as Corinna was about to leave the room she called after her. "Corinna, will you please stay with me tonight? I can't bear the thought of being alone on my wedding night."

"Of course, Your Majesty," replied Corinna bowing, resuming her very formal posture in front of the other servants. "I would be honored, I shall return momentarily after I change out of these wet clothes. Would you like some help changing Your Majesty?"

Veronica shook her head and told her she would prefer that they both just change quickly and sit for dinner. Corinna bowed once more and exited the room while Veronica rushed to her bed chamber, quickly showered, then put on her old Oxford sweats, the most comfortable clothes she owned. After pulling her hair into a single long ponytail, she returned to the Great Room to find Corinna waiting near the fire. All the kitchen staff had left the room, leaving only a single footman to wait on them. The room was quiet except for the cheerful fire and the sound of the rain hitting the French doors. Safe within the warmth and protective walls of Conwy Castle, her thoughts continually wondered after her husband who was riding away in the freezing rain wearing steel clothing toward a war. In the year after the Battle of the Thames, she had a suit of armor made for her which now hung near the fireplace in the Great Room. She had only worn it once and she was astounded at how cold it was. It was as if the armor sucked the coldest air particles from the room and expelled them into the suit, at least until the body had time to warm the steel cavity. With only that brief experience, she couldn't imagine how cold it must be for the King and all his men to be wearing it in the pouring rain while riding at a fast pace. The thought made her shiver.

"Are you all right Your Majesty?" asked Corinna.

Veronica sighed, "Yes, but it is not my well-being I am concerned about."

Corinna nodded and reached out to take her hand as Veronica said, "Thank you for staying with me." She squeezed Corinna's hand in return then said, "Isn't life a continual surprise? I didn't think I would be married until tomorrow, never thought I would be married to a King and then there is the wedding night. Never thought I would be spending it with you, and have a wedding feast with only two on the guest list—not that being with you is unpleasant dear Corinna."

Corinna smiled, "I shall not be offended if you would rather be in your wedding chamber with your husband than be with me Your Majesty. I would desire the same."

Corinna's comment made Veronica pause. According to custom and ancient law, a royal's attendants and maids were not allowed to marry until their mistress was married, which is why they were called *Ladies in Waiting*. She did not know how serious Corinna and Kelsey were but she wanted to ensure that Corinna knew she had her blessing to proceed. Setting her glass of Merlot on the table, she turned to Corinna and asked, "How are you and Kelsey these days?"

Corinna was surprised at her question and even more amazed that Veronica was concerned for her affairs when her own was a stew of uncertainly and fear. She swallowed and then smiled at the thought of her brave knight standing at the castle gate. "Thank you for asking Your Majesty," she replied formally due to the footman still in the room. She then released a frustrated sigh and continued, "We steal what moments we can." She then related the incident at the gate that morning when she ran her finger along his armor that possibly got him in trouble with the gate captain. They both laughed as did the footman behind him, though he concealed it.

As their laughter died, Veronica turned to her dear friend of many years and tenderly said, "I don't know if you were waiting for me to be married first, but I just need you to know, you have my blessing to marry him, if he ever ask."

Corinna was quiet for a few moments and in the ambient candlelight, Veronica could see her eyes watering. "Thank you Your Majesty," she replied. "He has indeed asked for my hand many times but I have refused it. Not because of any royal service etiquette—such policies were done away with in the eighteenth century, but because of my fear of what affect it would have on you."

"That is WONDERFUL! Wonderful that he has asked for your hand," exclaimed Veronica. "I am so happy for you—you must be married at once!"

Corinna was speechless and she stumbled verbally as she tried to first express her surprise and gratitude then her reluctance. "He has not mentioned it for some time, not since we left Powis Castle." A look of soberness came to her face as she continued, "I am very insecure as to what his desires are for me now. I know he does yet love me but…"

Veronica sat her serviette on the table after wiping her mouth and swallowing and said, "I shall go ask him his intention this very moment." She got up from the table and began making her way toward the door as Corinna tried to protest but she knew there was no stopping Veronica once she had that fire of determination in her eyes, so she just smiled and held her hand to her mouth.

As Veronica stepped through the inner gate, she looked up at the rain just as the footman placed her fenrir cloak over her shoulders and she pulled the hood over her head. After turning to thank him, she ran across the outer ward courtyard toward the western gate where two lone sentries were keeping guard. With her hood covering her head, the guards did not know who was approaching and they stepped in front of her path as Kelsey declared, "No one is to leave the castle tonight, by order of His Majesty."

Veronica ducked under the protective arch of the gate and pulled the fenrir hood off her head. The guards were completely unprepared to see the Queen out at such an hour and they politely but nervously protested that she please not leave the castle—at least not without an armed escort. "It isn't safe Your Majesty. We've no idea how far north the Celts have come and the King gave us direct orders on pain of death that you, especially, were not to leave the castle."

Veronica was at once astounded and irritated that the King would make such a stipulation concerning her—especially. She always resented any restrictions on her and whenever they were demanded, she wanted to do the exact opposite even if she had no previous desire to do the forbidden thing. Forgetting for a moment the reason she came to the gate in the first place, she demanded Kelsey that he open the gate.

"Um—Yer, I mean, Your Majesty, I must insist," replied Kelsey very frustrated and afraid.

Veronica stepped closer and whispered intently, "In case you have not heard, I am the Queen of bloody England. So unless you would like to be reassigned, I humbly implore that you open the gate."

Kelsey swallowed hard and looked to the other guard for courage. After as the opposite guard nodded, Kelsey gave the order to have the portcullis raised and shortly after the gate captain yelled down to inquire who was requesting the gates opened. Veronica stepped out from under the arch and glared.

"Your Majesty!" replied the captain to Veronica's unspoken reprimand. He was about to explain the King's order but he knew very well Veronica's disposition and just nodded and said, "Very well. Will you be needing an escort Your Majesty?"

"No," replied Veronica shaking her head and walking back under the arch. She then grabbed Kelsey by the arm and pulled him behind her out onto the barbican and yelled so that she could be heard over the pouring rain, "Do you yet love Corinna?"

Kelsey was beyond confused at this point, not being able to think clearly and before he could formulate an answer, he heard himself reply, "Corinna?"

Remembering the original goal of her mission, her anger subsided and she asked again with delicacy, "I know you have fancied my maid for quite some time and I even partially read one of your letters to her—quite by accident of course. But I know you loved her once and she has just told me that you asked for her hand."

Kelsey breathed a little easier upon hearing the Queen

change her tone from inquisition to inquiry and he smiled, "Ye—yes, I did. I do. I do love her—yes, ah-hm."

Veronica returned his smile and tenderly touched his cheek as she narrowed her eyes intently and asked, "Do you wish to marry her?"

Kelsey wasn't sure what the right answer was and the last thing he wanted was to upset the Queen or lose Corinna's favor. He also wasn't sure how much the Queen knew about his relationship with Corinna, or how close the Queen and Corinna really were. Corinna was always tight-lipped when it came to Veronica and never did she divulge anything personal about the Queen. It was of course obvious that the Queen knew something about his rebuffed wedding proposal and he therefore decided there was little advantage in withholding anything. However, the exact words were not forthcoming and he simply nodded.

"That is very well then," replied Veronica as she walked back through the gate and informed the gate captain that Kelsey would be needed in the chapel at the top of the hour. The captain acknowledged the order by relieving Kelsey as Veronica pulled the hood of her cloak back over her head and marched back toward the inner ward. When she entered the Great Room, Corinna was still frozen in the same position, her hand still covering her mouth. However, her eyes had changed from complete disbelief to great anticipation and as she watched Veronica enter the room and throw her cloak on the floor, her expression becoming painfully anxious. As Veronica took her seat, she patted Corinna's hand and said very matter-of-factly, "He yet loves you and wishes to marry you. He will meet us in the chapel at eleven."

Corinna was speechless and as the implications of what she had just heard sunk into her heart, she was afraid. Her fear was not from dread, but was the kind of fear that is felt when a long anticipated event is finally at hand. She looked back at Veronica and slowly started to shake her head. Veronica just smiled and patted her hand several more times. "Not to worry, this will be fun," she said as she took another long drink of her Merlot.

Corinna had never seen Veronica so unhinged before and watching her drink, not sip her wine as she usually did, she realized what was happening. "I believe you're drunk Your Majesty," she said laughing.

Veronica shook her head, thinking that Corinna's accusation was ridiculous. If she were indeed drunk, she would also be passed-out on the floor or vomiting. She had never been able to drink more than an ounce or two of alcohol without becoming ill and she was always careful not to drink beyond a dozen sips. However, when she looked down at her glass, the dark Merlot was almost gone and it was then she realized this was not her first glass. Was it her second, possibly even a third? She turned to Corinna confused and asked, "How many times has my glass been refilled?"

Corinna started to say that she did not know just as the footman volunteered, "I just filled it while you were out Your Majesty, you have just finished your fifth."

Corinna and Veronica both slowly turned to the footman who obviously had not been told about the Queen's intolerance to alcohol, but for whatever reason, she seemed to be tolerating it just fine and they both started laughing. "So this is what it's like to be drunk?" said Veronica finding the situation extremely funny. "I feel like I could stand up to the Celts myself. In fact, I think I will." She started to get up when Corinna grabbed hold of her arm and pulled her back to her seat.

"Your Majesty, bravery born of spirits always ends in bereavement. You are very drunk and I must insist you sit here with me," said Corinna between repressed bursts of laughter.

"But how? You know I can't drink," replied Veronica as her eyes glossed over and her head flopped to the right. "Besides, I feel—fine!"

Corinna laughed, "As you are supposed to Your Majesty, that is why they invented it."

A look of great excitement then came across Veronica's face and as she sat up straight in her chair, she placed her hand of Corinna's shoulder and said, "I have a grand idea!"

Corinna laughed as she took Veronica's hand off her shoulder and held it tightly. "One must be very careful with ideas when one is drunk, Your Majesty."

Corinna motioned for the footman to clear the glasses and to bring some coffee for the Queen and tea for herself. She thought it odd that while she only felt mildly affected by the Merlot after two glasses, she was certainly not drunk by any stretch. However, after only four and a half, Veronica couldn't see a hole in a ladder. She had never seen Veronica drink more than a few swallows in all the years she had known her and she couldn't help but feel responsible for the Queen's drunken state. But the real questions was, why she wasn't barfing. After the Minimum, everyone seemed to be able to drink more than they were able to previously and Corinna correctly assumed that the Minimum had equally affected her but she had never drank enough to know. She now hoped that like everyone else, the drunkenness would not last more than an hour or two.

After the footman returned, they both drank their tea and coffee in silence for their own separate reasons. Corinna was trembling over what was going to happen at eleven o'clock and Veronica was dealing with the onset of a quickly approaching hangover—as was customary. The trick with heavy drinking in the post-Minimum Era, was to pace one's self such that they never actually became drunk, but remained comfortably vinomadefied and thereby skipped the hangover episode. As the clock clicked toward the top of the hour and after several cups of coffee, Veronica was beginning to think a little clearer and she at last looked up at Corinna in horror and said, "I just asked Kelsey if he would marry you—tonight!"

"Yes you did," replied Corinna trying to smile. While she was pleased that she and Kelsey could at last be married, she was unsure of how Kelsey felt about the whole thing. The last thing she wanted was a wedding ordered by royal decree and the sorrow she tried to conceal was at last noticed by Veronica who was shaking her head in disbelief at what she had done.

"Dear Corinna, I shall go and give my apology to Kelsey," she said as she groaned with embarrassment. But just as she was about to stand and once again make her way to the gate, Corinna pulled her back to her chair and quietly said, "Wait."

Feeling clearer-minded by the minute but with her head pounding, Veronica tenderly looked into Corinna's eyes and took her hand. Corinna was obviously rethinking and second-guessing her heart, wondering if she should just go with it or put on the brakes and wait for Kelsey to step forward on his own. In her confused state, it was impossible to settle on a rational decision and she began to shake her head. "I don't know—maybe just... Oh—

perhaps I should just do it," she said, looking to Veronica for direction. Veronica didn't respond as she too struggled with what to do and just as the moment was about to get even more awkward, the footman stepped forward and said, "Begging both of your pardons, but may I make a suggestion?"

Veronica nodded with relief as Corinna replied, "Oh please."

The footman bowed respectfully knowing that he was very out of place to speak when not spoken too and after clearing his throat, he volunteered to speak with Kelsey and explain that the Queen expressed her deepest apologies and that she acted only out of love for her maid on top of a little too much Merlot. He then bowed to Corinna and continued, "If it pleases you, I shall then tell him that you do indeed want to be married but if he does not show at eleven, you shall not be sore."

Both Corinna and Veronica agreed that it was a good solution to the problem and as the footman disappeared out the door, Veronica led Corinna to her bed chamber where they got ready for the second wedding of the day, that is if Kelsey showed. Corinna was now sick with dread, wondering if Kelsey would make an appearance. In panic, she turned to Veronica with a tear in her eye and said, "What if he doesn't appear?"

Veronica was now almost sober and she was greatly pained at the mess she had created and how much grief it was causing Corinna. No matter what happened in the chapel in a few minutes, either event was equally distressing and unpleasant. If Kelsey showed, she would never know if he did so on his own desires and if he didn't show—that was the unthinkable. Veronica pulled Corinna into a tight embrace while she expressed again how sorry she was. She then placed her hand on her cheek and said, "Courage."

Corinna nodded but couldn't speak as was evident from her trembling chin. She turned to look at herself in the mirror and after tossing her hair slightly, she sighed and started to make her way out of the room.

"Miss Corinna Durst, you are not going to your wedding looking like that!" exclaimed Veronica.

Corinna walked back to the mirror, already forgetting how she looked a few seconds ago and shrugged. She owned only a half dozen dresses, all of which were servant-like so there was no point in changing one for the other and as for her hair, it was as good as it was going to get. She blew her bangs away from her eyes, making a raspberry sound with her lips while she shrugged. Veronica laughed and directed Corinna to have a seat and then walked into a deep closet adjoining her dressing area. After a few minutes, she returned with two beautiful dresses and held them up for Corinna to choose. One was mostly white and made of velvet. It had gold embroidery on the bodice with a deep violet skirt and white darts that elegantly flowed off the hipline, embroidered with more gold piping. The other was equally elegant but Corinna was completely taken with the other dress and she gasped in disbelief that Veronica would loan her one of her own dresses.

"I couldn't Your Majesty. I've never seen you wear it—it must be new!" exclaimed Corinna.

Veronica looked down at the white and violet dress as she set the other over the back of a chair. She held it up to her chin and looked in the mirror and then turned from side to side. "You're right, I have not worn it. I was going to wear it tomorrow," she said distantly, admiring the wearable work of art.

Tomorrow was supposed to be Veronica's wedding and Corinna shook her head defiantly, "No, no—I cannot wear your wedding dress Your Majesty!"

Veronica was lost for a moment as she gazed in the mirror, imagining herself walking down the aisle on Gus's arm. She then turned to Corinna, with her daydream still lingering behind her eyes and said, "It will never be worn—not by me at least." After one last look in the mirror, she handed the dress to Corinna but she refused. "I am so touched by your generosity but please, you needn't do this. I will not be sore over this no matter how it ends tonight."

Veronica smiled while she shook her head and replied, "That isn't why. I have apologized to you for what I have done, certainly that is adequate. I offer you this dress not out of guilt but love. Take it so that you may never forget my devotion and in case you still try to deny my gift, I order you as your Queen to take it and wear it."

Corinna then realized that Veronica was not loaning her the dress, but was giving it to her. She had never owned anything so beautiful, not even before the Minimum when clothing was so easy to obtain. She was again speechless as she slowly reached out her hand to take the dress but then instead of grabbing hold of it, she placed her hand to her mouth. Now that she was closer to the dress, she saw that it was encrusted with small crystals that followed the gold piping down the sleeves and encircled the elegantly hemmed, triangular cuffs. She was about to protest again but she remembered the royal order and she at last gave in. With a defeated sigh, she pulled her old dress over her head as Veronica then placed her never-to-be-worn, wedding dress over her and helped her arms through the sleeves. Veronica then knelt on the floor and pulled the skirt down, letting it elegantly flow around her just as Corinna would have done if she were dressing her. She deeply wanted to protest at having the Queen of England attending to her in such a manner, but she knew there was no use. Veronica was set on doting on her and nothing could change her mind. Another tear rolled from her eye as she admired herself in the mirror just as Veronica stood up, "Oh it looks so beautiful on you!" she said, covering her sadness over her rushed wedding three hours ago.

After brushing Corinna's hair and tying in a gold ribbon, the two of them rushed from the inner ward toward the chapel. The rain was still pouring relentlessly and Veronica held her large fenrir cloak over them both as they stepped over the deepest puddles. When they reached the chapel, Padrig was waiting for them and he held the door as they rushed in. The chapel was still warmly lit from Veronica's wedding hours before and they were both relieved to see that the corpse on the back table had been removed. After catching their breath, they made their way to the alter where Colton was standing with a bible in his hands and a large smile on his face.

"Oh Colton, I am so glad to see you have made it to Conwy. When did you arrive?" exclaimed Veronica.

"Just this evening as the Archbishop was riding out with the army—you will be pleased to know I was able to retrieve most of your library from Powis Your Majesty," he replied.

"I am most grateful to you Father. I am in dire need of it. I encountered some ancient documents since arriving that I cannot make any sense of, in fact I was wondering if…" Veronica cut herself short, remembering why she was there and she turned to Padrig and asked, "Please forgive me—what time is it?"

Padrig looked at the hour candle on the back table which was a specially made candle that took exactly one hour to burn. Hour candles had ten lines which marked each six minute interval and seeing that the third line had just melted away, Padrig replied, “About eighteen after eleven.”

Veronica slowly turned to face Corinna who was already in tears and said, “I’m so sorry Corinna, I didn’t realize how late it was.”

Corinna waved her hand and replied, “No, neither did I—but…”

Veronica turned to ask Colton if Kelsey had been there but before she could say a word, he shook his head. She then turned to comfort Corinna saying, “This means nothing. Since we have only just arrived, perhaps he was just waiting for us?”

Corinna knew Veronica was only trying to comfort her and while she was grateful for the effort, she couldn’t help but slowly push the emotional dagger into her own heart, convincing herself that she knew Kelsey had chosen not to make an appearance. She tried to keep her composure but it was growing more difficult by the minute and the longer she stood at the altar, the more she felt like a fool. The fact that she was dressed so elegantly only made the insult more lucid. She began to cry as she realized that there would be no going back to how things were, the playful courting and casual avoidance of marriage. And while she dearly wanted to marry Kelsey, she loved loving him and the tender relationship they shared. She concluded that it was over and seeing him in the castle now would just be awkward instead of joyous. Instead of going out of their way to see each other, they would find reasons not to pass by or even look at one another. A part of her wanted to be angry with Veronica but she knew that what she did was born out of concern for her even if that concern was lathered in alcohol.

She looked up again at the hour candle and saw that it was now half way burned, heralding even louder that Kelsey was not coming. She reasoned that one might be a little late to their own wedding but in her mind, thirty minutes was no longer late and it now signaled a forfeit. Not being able to take the humiliation a moment longer, she picked up the hem of her dress and began to walk to the back of the chapel just as she heard an armored guard approach the closed doors and stop. Just as she was about to turn to Veronica for an explanation, both of the chapel doors opened wide and in marched a column of twelve men dressed in full armor. They marched into the quiet and depressed chapel in a very dignified manner and after splitting into two columns, they stood on opposite sides of the aisle, hammering the ends of their halberds on the stone floor. The echo of their steel armor and the united hammer took several seconds to dissipate into the serenity of night but when it did, she saw the gate captain marching through the doors, escorting Kelsey behind him. The captain then took his place at the head of the columns as Kelsey passed by him. The column of knights saluted in unison with an arm to the chest making a powerful impression of respect and honor. Kelsey was dressed in his usual suit of armor, but it had obviously been washed and polished as it seemed to catch the light from every candle in the room.

As he approached Corinna, her tears of sorrow streamed into tears of joy and she rushed forward to embrace him. After a few minutes, they made their way to the altar as Veronica and the gate captain took their places on either side. Colton opened the Bible and was just about to read when Corinna reached out her hand and ran her finger across Kelsey's chest, making a familiar squeak as everyone except for the gate captain laughed.

CHAPTER 4

FIND THE KING

In a damp and hopeless dungeon under Norwich Castle, Shay rolled over onto his back in the darkness and reached under the rotting mattress to remove a rock that had disrupted his sleep. It was about the size of a baseball and as he held it in his hand, he remembered not only attending baseball games before the Minimum, but all of the other trivialities of life when mankind had leisure time to dispose of. He laughed within himself as he considered all the meaningless activities of the pre-Minimum world that were labeled as pastimes or things the world did to pass the excess time in their lives. The world was now so brutal and harsh that every waking minute was spent on either survival of one's self or the survival of another. Alone in the darkness, he had untold amounts of time to think, his only pastime, which pushed him to the edges of insanity. The most frustrating thoughts that spiraled in his mind was the passage of time and he struggled to determine how long he had actually been imprisoned. For the past several spans of time, he concluded it had been a least a month without a rescue attempt and he threw the stone baseball in the direction of his prison bars; at least in the direction he thought they were. In complete darkness, it was easy to forget the orientation of things but when the rock struck one of the iron bars, the memory of how things looked in the light returned to him and he watched a spark fly from the impact and fade as it fell to the ground.

The noise of stone striking iron echoed into the heavy darkness and he tried to remember the last time he heard any noise at all in the dungeon—a guard change, footsteps or even a breath in the darkness. He struggled to recall the last time he had eaten and while he was not offered meals at regular intervals, he concluded that it had been at least two days since he had been awakened with a finger tap, something the guard did every time he brought him food. In the first few days after his imprisonment, he interpreted the tapping as endearing, but as the days and weeks passed, he was sure he was mistaken and that the taps were condescending, but regardless of the intent, he resolved that it had been many days since had heard or seen anyone.

With a sigh, he staggered to his feet, his arms stretched out in front of him as he felt his way toward the bars of his cell and just when he was sure that he should have already felt them, a cold piece of iron slid between his fingers. After straining to see anything in the complete darkness of the dungeon, he started to call out, apprehensively at first and then growing louder and more urgent. After every call, he could only hear his own voice echo into the nothingness that swallowed both sound and hope. After numerous attempts to arouse anyone's attention, he made his way back to the mattress and after falling on his knees, he rolled over onto his back and sighed, still trying to determine how long it had been since he had eaten. Maybe it was more than two days, but if that were true, he wondered why he didn't feel hungry.

He awakened again after another unknown period of time and felt more fatigued than he could ever remember. As he drifted in and out of consciousness, he finally determined that his body no longer had the energy to remain coherent and that it must have been many more days than just two since he had eaten. He confirmed his hypothesis when he tried to roll onto this stomach and stand. He felt as if a heavy lead blanket was on top of him, making any movement difficult and then painful. Amidst his labored breathing from trying to roll over, he found it painful to even breathe and he concluded that he was dying. *So this is what it's like to starve to death,* he thought.

"This isn't so bad—so long as I don't move," he whispered. "I suppose I shall now just fall asleep and wake up in heaven."

Heaven? He thought as his consciousness faded in and out, wondering what it really meant. One's ideas of dying and heaven change greatly when the prospect of having definite knowledge about them both is imminent. He had been raised in a Christian home, but like most U.S. citizens in the years before the Minimum, it was a classification that held little real meaning and he could only remember attending church when his grandfather died. Beyond that, he had blurry memories of attending mass with his parents when he was very young. He had always assumed that heaven was a rather boring place where the pious worshiped God forever and ever. He shuttered, *I hope that isn't what is ahead for me,* he thought. *Surely that isn't heaven, more like hell where you can't die from boredom.*

He then heard a distant but strangely familiar laugh that started from silence and grew louder as if the volume was being turned up, "No, no, that's not at all what it's like Shai."

Gathering all his strength, he pushed off the mattress and rolled himself over, looking in the direction of the voice and called, "Grandfather?" Against the wall, he saw the first light he had seen in many days and he squinted from its painful glare. The light that began very dim, grew brighter and as his eyes adjusted, he saw his grandfather sitting on an unseen chair, looking as ghostly and young as he had back in Montana when he spent the night in an old military fort. The ghost stood up and knelt down next to Shay, then reached out his hand and tried to rub his head as a mortal might but Shay felt nothing.

"From the looks of things you might be joining me here on this side of the dungeon unless you get something to eat my boy," his grandfather said calmly.

"On this side?" asked Shay, still leaning on his shaking elbow.

His grandfather smiled as he continued to stroke his forehead, "We're all in this world together and we all need each other. Mortal man has no idea how much he is assisted by those who love him in the unseen world. And," he sighed, "he has no idea how much the spirits in the unseen world lament over our mortal flesh and blood—which is why I am here."

"Oh?" replied Shay, which was the only word his dying body would allow him to say as he laid back down with a thud.

His grandfather grieved within himself, stopped stroking Shay's head and then sat down next to him, folding his legs. "You are not going to die Shai, at least not today. The man you call the General is just now entering the city walls with a very large army. Sadly, he is killing anyone who will not support your King."

Shay sighed with relief and almost unintelligibly replied, "Finally! And why is that sad? They are the bloody buggers who put me in here."

The ghost sighed which sounded more like a lament and

Shay realized there was much he did not know about spirits and the unseen world. "I once thought as you do but what I didn't realize then and that you do not realize now, is that what we do to others, we do to God." He paused as if he were seeing something in his mind and after a long moment, he shook the vision from his head and continued, "Terrible, terrible." His mood then lightened somewhat and he smiled. "Your friend the General has a very well-developed talent for bloodshed I must say. There was a dreadful battle in Wales against your friend Veronica, but thankfully the Archbishop is fulfilling his calling in grand fashion."

"Veronica?! Why was he fighting Veronica?" he urgently asked using what seemed to be his last ounce of strength.

From four feet above him in the air where his grandfather had floated, he waved his hand over him which had an astonishing calming effect, forcing his heart to stop racing and his breathing to recede. After the blanket of peace covered him and after his grandfather could see that he was no longer alarmed, he replied, "She is fine and like all wars, it was a terrible mistake arising out of an equally terrible lack of clear mindedness—but there is another war that your friend the General is unaware of."

"And that is why you are here?"

"Partially," replied his grandfather, "My first mission in returning to mortality is to keep you breathing until the General walks down this corridor. The next is to tell you to light your bonfire flap the moment you are carried out of here." Shay had nearly forgotten that he had created a chain of bonfire signals or a flap network that were set on every prominent hill, castle and mountain along the northwestern frontier. When any one of them were lit, the next visible beacon would be lit in either direction and thereby alerting the next and the next until the entire country could be alerted to a Celtic attack. Everyone had guessed that the Celts would have invaded months ago and the news excited him. "We are being invaded then—at long last?!" he asked.

"Indeed," the ghost replied as he started to float backwards out of the cell. The light that surrounded his body started to fade and it appeared as if the light gathered in around him like a drain the further he floated backwards. Then just before he disappeared he concluded his visit with the words, "It's never too hopeless to be helpful Shai—remember this. England's hope resides with The Seven."

The light from the ghost was now almost gone as Shay struggled to stay awake and make sense of the last words he heard. As he strained to see the fading light, he saw a torch emanating from the same spot, growing brighter and approaching him from the end of the corridor.

"SHAY!" came a sound, which was the first noise his physical ears he had heard in many days, perhaps weeks and the effect was electrifying, providing him with the strength he needed to reply.

"HERE, I'm…" Shay coughed and struggled to continue. "I'm over here!" he finally said as his strength entirely left him. Then almost as if he were dreaming, he heard the rattle of the iron bars of his cell and then a very bright and very loud explosion as the General's men poured black powder into the hinges and ignited them. The door of his cell fell off its hinges and landed only inches from his face and he vaguely remembered someone picking him up and throwing him over their shoulder. The next thing he recalled was looking up at the grey sky and wisps of long narrow clouds streaking across the Norwich sky from the sea. The air was humid and full of life compared to the rancid decay of the dungeon and it alone gave him the strength to sit up and survey his surroundings. He was lying on a small cot in a make-shift field hospital outside the old Roman wall that once surrounded the entire city. To the east he could see several plumes of smoke rising from the town and the sound of war drifting through the relative stillness of the evening.

"Your Majesty!" came a voice from somewhere behind him but as he tried to see who it was, he felt his strength waning and he laid back down with a sigh. It was then he realized that the unknown person approaching was referring to himself, having almost completely forgotten that he was once the King of East Angles. He had only been in his new assignment for a few months before the riots broke-out in support of Queen Veronica and he soon thereafter found himself in the dungeon under his own Castle. He closed his eyes for a moment as he breathed in the healing air just as he felt a soft touch on his arm attended by an equally soft voice wondering if he were conscious, "Your Majesty?"

Shay didn't open his eyes due to his unbelievable exhaustion but replied, "Yes, I am conscious, just very tired."

He felt a soft hand on his forehead, feeling for a temperature and then slide behind his head lifting it up. "Please try to drink your Majesty. I can tell you've not had anything for several days," said his caretaker.

Shay slowly opened his eyes and saw the beaming face of a young woman in her late twenties smiling back at him, being very relieved that he was still conscious. She was of Asian descent but whether she was Japanese or Chinese he did not know, nor did it trouble him. She was like an angel and he smiled. She held a leather bag up to his lips as he drank down several large swallows which created a tingling sensation emanating from the back of his throat down to his stomach. Surprised at such a strange sensation, he began to cough as the woman lifted him up to a sitting position. "Slowly your Majesty. Small sips until your body is accustomed to having nourishment again," she said.

Looking into her blue eyes he smiled in between swallows and asked, "You seem quite the expert on starvation my dear. What is your tale?"

The woman blushed slightly but her demeanor quickly became professional and after she laid him back down she began to relate her tale as she took his pulse and attended to the sores on his arms and hips. "I was a medic on the HMS Dauntless that patrolled the Oman Gulf for several years during the Russian Wars and I became accustom to seeing and treating starvation. But if you're wondering how a Japanese woman becomes a member of the Royal Navy—well, that tale belongs to my parents and they are not here to tell it."

Shay laughed as much as he was able and asked, "So you don't know how you became a trained medic or how you enlisted?"

The woman smiled as she began to clean out an infected wound on his shoulder. "That part of my tale is rather dull and I ended up on a battleship in the usual way but as to why I am an English citizen by birth, that is the story I cannot tell. Only because I do not know it—both of my parents died when I was nine."

"I'm very sorry my dear," replied Shay sadly.

"Thank you your Majesty—but that was a very long time

ago in a very different world," she replied and then asked in surprise, "Do you not feel that?"

Shay casually looked at the bleeding wound she was cleaning with a small brush and then looked up at her as she continued. "You're not even wincing. Do you have any feeling in this arm?" she asked as she poked it in several places with a needle.

Shay shook his head as she stabbed his arm a little more aggressively and then shrugged. "Well, that will make this much more pleasant," she said as she proceeded to sew up the long cut on his shoulder with a sewing needle and cotton thread, drenched in wine. When she finished, she reached over and retrieved more wine and poured it over the stiches but just as before, Shay felt no pain nor even the sensation of liquid on his skin.

"Do you think the feeling will return?" he asked.

The woman shook her head. "I do not know. It appears that you are getting blood flow to your fingers so it must be some kind of nerve damage. Do you remember anything happening to your arm or shoulder?"

Shay thought a minute but before he could recall any coherent incident, he sat up in alarm. On top of the stone roof of the Norwich Cathedral, a fire was raging. However he wasn't afraid that the cathedral was on fire since he had placed a bonfire on the cathedral roof, it being the most elevated place in the area and since it was made of stone, there was no danger of igniting the building. He was only alarmed to see it lit but he then remembered his grandfather telling him to light the fires.

"Who lit the flap?" he asked earnestly.

His nurse only shook her head as she watched the fire and then after a few minutes turned to Shay and asked, "Are you certain it is burning? I mean, it doesn't really look like fire does it?"

Shay strained to see the fire more clearly and he determined that she might be right. There was certainly a bright light in the same place where the wood pile was supposed to be, but it was white, not yellow and red as a fire normally is. As they both studied the odd-looking flame, they could hear distant shouts as the bonfires on either side of the cathedral were lit and the flap was put into motion, alerting the north of England to the advancement of the Celts. Lying on his back, he continued to analyze the strangeness of the fire as his nurse disappeared into a large nearby tent for some food. After considering several possibilities, he sat up to look at the fire again but to his great surprise, it was gone and the wood still there unburnt. It then occurred to him what had happened and he laid back down and smiled.

The wheel of the supply wagon that carried Shay toward Wales, lodged itself into one of the many deep ruts that were common in the eastern countryside where almost all the paved streets had been destroyed. The wagon train of supplies was being escorted by over two thousand men—half of the combined army the General had amassed during his march to Norwich. The other half consisted of the Norwich rebels which the General forced into the King's service. The rebels were dispersed throughout the larger and more disciplined army so that they would be a minority and could not instigate an uprising. However, when most learned that the Celts were invading from the north, west and south, they soberly laid down their arms as well as their hatred for the King and joined the General. The few that resisted were hung for treason, which were less than fifty. In the urgency of the great war upon them, there was no time for a formal war trial and the traitors were hastily hung from the walls of Norwich castle and left to rot in the sun as a warning to any who questioned and defied the King.

The sudden stop awakened Shay from an insolvent sleep as he laid on the hard floorboards of the wagon covered with only a thin blanket. On the other side of the heavy canvas covering, he could hear frustrated voices as the soldiers deliberated over the best course of action to free the wheel. Amidst the widely varied opinions from men who were not at all experienced in horse and wagon travel, he heard a very gruff and blunt voice reprimanded the driver for veering into the rut-side of the road—something he had obviously been advised not to do. Shay rubbed his eyes, dispelling the remaining embers of sleep from his mind and crawled toward the front of the wagon and pulled back the canvas drop behind the driver who was apologizing repeatedly to the division commander. In the humid late summer afternoon, his driver was nearly drenched with sweat, so much that he wondered if it had recently rained but looking up at the nearly cloudless sky, the driver was obviously suffering terribly from both the weather and his size. He was a very large man, easily over twenty stone and wore a handmade hat made of straw that protected his bald head from the sun.

Without a word, Shay climbed over the back of the seat and sat next to the driver while the commander cut his reprimand short and bowed saying, "Good day Your Majesty, terribly sorry for the delay and the sorry skills of your driver. I shall have him removed presently. I have requested a replacement who at this moment coming from the rearward."

"That won't be necessary Commander," replied Shay, patting his driver's leg, "I am grateful to have been awakened from my ill-fated attempt at sleep."

The Commander saluted and then bowed as he acknowledged the King's wishes and walked to the rear of the wagon and began shouting out orders to the indecisive soldiers.

"Are you well enough to sit Your Majesty?" asked the driver, wiping his forehead with the sleeve of his very dirty shirt.

"Well enough, thank you," replied Shay as he smiled in an attempt to dispel the driver's obvious stress over the situation. "As I said, I was caught in a tempestuous cycle of delirium, dreaming the same ridiculousness repeatedly. So I thank you for from freeing me."

The driver smiled and slowly began to nod as he gradually accepted Shay's words as truth and not merely consolation. He then stared forward, holding onto the reins in his lap and said nothing as the awkwardness of the situation grew. Shay was still feeling a little hung-over from his nap, which only added to the uneasy moment, but after a few minutes, his driver turned to him and smiled without any reservation and then reached out and tapped his leg endearingly. Such a gesture was highly inappropriate between servants and royalty but Shay had spent most of his royal assignment behind bars and the expression was appreciated. But given the man's unsettled disposition over the circumstances, his touch was only a single finger, as if a full hand touch would have been too bold. Shay smiled and looked down at the driver's finger which was now on its fourth or fifth tap when he fully understood. He was actually tapping his leg with his ring and little fingers—

which together felt like a single finger—however those two fingers were the only two on his right hand and Shay looked up at the driver, first in alarm and then with compassion.

The driver slowly withdrew his hand to his lap and held onto the reins with the two fingers. His other hand appeared to have all five phalanges, but he was obviously right handed and the two fingers on his right hand were very callous, rough and swollen. Then without turning, the driver said apologetically, "Very sorry Your Majesty if I give offense."

Shay didn't respond due to his swirling thoughts as he was quickly reminded why the tap seemed familiar to him and he stumbled in his reply, trying to reassure his driver. "What? No, not at all. Think nothing of the sort. I only…" He paused, wondering how he should approach such a question while he was still arriving at a conclusion. "Did you… what I mean is…" Shay finally gave up on trying to be polite and asked, "Would you do me the honor of telling me your tale?"

His driver turned to Shay and nodded with a declining sigh, which he tried to hide with a smile and a wink, his very fat and full cheeks completely obscuring his face, leaving only small slits where his eye sockets were. Just then the wagon shook to the right as the men jacked up the heavy wagon. The driver quickly reached over to make sure His Majesty was secure in his seat with his two-fingered hand and then retracted once again to the security of his lap.

"My tale? It is a rather trite one I'm afraid," said the driver as he once again wiped sweat from his face but before he could continue, Shay reached out his right hand and said, "I'm Shay Naoki and you may address me as such if you wish."

The driver was startled and taken aback at such a gesture and he quickly retracted. "No—no I shouldn't, I cannot Your Majesty, I…"

"Then, only when we are alone and when you feel at ease," replied Shay.

The driver once again slowly nodded as he became more familiar with his King and began to see him as a man and possibly even a friend. He then looked down and saw that the King's right hand was still extended toward him and he struggled with what to do. An extended right hand is customarily responded with a right hand in a handshake, but with only two fingers on his right hand, he tried to extend his left hand whereupon Shay reached down and grasped his two-fingered hand and shook it. After several firm shakes, Shay released his hand and it fell to the wood seat with a thud.

"I'm Humphrey," replied the driver aghast, lifting his shoulder to his mouth, wiping away more sweat. "I am not an Englishman, I am originally from Ireland. My mother was American, my father Irish. They met online back in the day of the Transnet and after they married, me mum, moved to Ireland, Newcastle up on the Irish Sea, which is where I was raised."

"Odd, you do not sound Irish," replied Shay.

Humphrey laughed slightly as he shook his head. "Malory, me mum, never gained an accent either in all her years of livin' in Ireland. She and me dad split-up when I was 'bout ten and then me mum died when I was thirteen. Not knowen where me dad was, I became an award of the State and lived with an old man who lived on the coast—

guessin' no one else wanted a thirteen year-old problem. The man needed help with his fishing vessel since he was," Humphrey paused, "I never knew how old he was come to think of it," and he laughed. "He was very kind to me after a while, once I learnt how to work hard—not an easy learnin' for me back then. I spent the next twenty-five years fishing the Irish Sea, mostly alone since my guardian passed away when I was in my twenties." He raised his hand while he continued. "Which is how I lost me fingers. I am a drunk—but in my defense, most Irish sailors are." He paused as his mind wandered back to a menacing afternoon on the Irish Sea when dark clouds were pushing in from the north and he was awakened from a drunken coma by lightning. "I staggered to the rail to pull in me nets so they didn't act as a sea anchor and drag me boat to the depths, but I was too late. I was already healing almost to the rail so I reached for me knife and began cutting the ropes to free the boat. The rest is rather blurry, but needless to say, I survived and as the last of the ropes were cut, I somehow got my hand tangled up in the net and as the waves and storm carried away me net, they ripped away me fingers with them, excepting these two."

Shay was shaking his head in wonder and pity at Humphrey's tale just as the Commander reappeared and ordered the driver to steer the horses strongly to the right. Humphrey nodded as he shook the reins firmly and yelled, "Giddy-up then!" The two horses struggled to get any footing at first but after several small leaps and lots of protesting, they pulled the wagon out of the rut and onto the high side of the road as the jacks tipped over and the wagon landed on the hard ground creaking and groaning.

With the army once again heading west, Shay prompted Humphrey to continue his tale. "So where were you during the Minimum?" he asked.

"On the sea of course, bloody miracle that was. Everything in port was destroyed, as I would have been if I had been there. I suppose being a drunk has its virtues, eh?"

"Wait! The day you lost your fingers was the same day as the Minimum?" asked Shay incredulously.

"The same," replied Humphrey. "Though I didn't get back to land for several days after mind you. Me engines ran out of petrol sometime during the night and I thought I was a goner, with no steerage and all, bein' tossed about for several days. Not really sure how many days it was since I'm pretty sure I passed-out from blood loss, and rum—there were pools of it on the deck—blood that is. But it was probably the fact that I was so drunk that I was able to cut the bone fragments off with me wire cutters and wrap me hand—saltwater also probably helped any serious infection." Humphrey laughed as he considered his drunken good fortune. "Which is why I still drink too much some times since it saved me bloomin' life."

Shay smiled and nodded as Humphrey's laughter faded and for the better part of a quarter-mile, neither of them spoke. Finally, Humphrey continued as white cumulous clouds could be seen pushing in from the Irish Sea less than a ten miles to the west. "When I finally made landfall, it was in bloody Portugal, crashed up on the rocks near an old fortress and swam to shore, which is where the drink saved me life again!" he said laughing again. "I was nearly thirstin' to death as you can imagine, and I found some people who were taken refuge in an old castle who gave me rum—there bein' nothing else to drink in the world that was safe."

Shay turned to Humphrey with renewed interest in his story as it started to sound very familiar to someone else's tale he knew. "You were at Queijo Castle?" he asked.

"Yes, that was it. Couldn't remember the name after these few years, though not surprising considering how drunk I was, drinking only rum instead of water for a month," replied Humphrey.

"Then were you there when Veronica arrived?!"

Humphrey laughed. "Exactly so! Extraordinary woman that Veronica is," he replied excitedly. "I was one of only a handful that decided to sail with her. Course, I had no idea who she was or who she would become, but she was sailing to England and that was closer to getting me home than lying drunk on a Portugal beach." Humphrey sighed, placing a crescendo to his tale and concluded it by saying, "And the rest is history."

"Your tale is hardly trite my friend, quite extraordinary I must say. However, I must ask where you went after you arrived in England—if you don't mind my pry."

Humphrey didn't reply directly since he knew what Shay was trying to get him to divulge. They were a few hours from reaching the Welch coast to meet up with the King, so there was no sense in stalling. After he decided what to say, he continued but with apprehension, "If you are wondering if I supported Lady Veronica in her ascension to the throne, yes, I did support her."

Shay was a little irritated that Humphrey assumed Veronica wanted the throne and he took the opportunity to set him straight, "Lady Veronica did NOT seek the throne my friend, in fact she was willing to live her life in prison rather than dethrone the King."

With Shay wielding his authority in the midst of such a casual conversation, Humphrey quickly retracted as he remembered with whom he was speaking and said, "Of course Your Majesty, as you say."

Shay's authority derailed Humphrey's tale for several minutes but after he reassured Humphrey that he was not alone in erroneously thinking that Lady Veronica actively sought the crown, Humphrey continued. "I was of course trying to get back to Ireland to see what had become of me home and friends, but gettin' across the channel has been impossible. So, I tried my hand at farming when the Agricultural Council arrived in Norwich, but I didn't fare too well with it. I suppose my hands were meant for the sea not the soil."

"So what did you do?"

"Well, I assumed about the only occupation that was left, I became a guard at the castle. It was easy work if you don't mind the endless standing and abuse from the officers."

Humphrey had stopped sweating now that it was early evening and while he spoke, he ran his fingers over the top of his bald head as if he were combing hair that was no longer there. "Not everyone had it as easy, but I suppose the sea was a good teacher for a soldier."

"Really, how so?" asked Shay, enjoying the easy company and conversation with his new friend once again.

"When you're alone for days on end, only water in every direction, blue below you and blue above you, you finally figure out how to be at peace within your own thoughts. Standing looking at the same thing all day drives some soldiers looney. And as for the abusive officers…" Humphrey paused as if he were recalling a chilling memory and then sighed, "I know what fear is and what it means to look it in the face—officers aren't so scary." Humphrey then stood up and stretched, holding the reins in his mouth while he placed his hands on his lower back and grunted. "Although, I never had back pain until I started standing all day long." He then arched backwards as the sound of four or five vertebrae popped in his lower back and after a deep, cleansing breath, he sat down again and resumed his tale, the wooden seat protesting under his heavy frame. "But, after the riots started and you were imprisoned, I was assigned in the dungeon—I volunteered actually. I figured some walking about would help ease my back pain."

"Wait, you were in the dungeon? You didn't by chance bring me my food did you?"

Humphrey smiled and nodded, "As a matter of fact."

Shay looked at him incredulously, shaking his head and laughing, "What was with all the poking—tapping?"

Humphrey looked at him puzzled, not understanding at first what he was referring to but after a few seconds he realized what he was talking about. "I never poked you," he replied laughing as his belly shook. "I was trying to give you hope—you know, like an endearing, encouraging touch." He laughed again and repeated under his breath as he shook his breath, "Poking you."

"Now that I know what you were doing, I suppose I should thank you and let go of my irritation," replied Shay, laughing with him. "It sure felt like a poke."

Humphrey looked over at Shay and held up his two-fingered hand and smiled. "My apologies Your Majesty, I suppose my endearments were misinterpreted."

Shay smiled back at him, slightly nodding and placing his

hand on Humphrey's shoulder and said, "No apology necessary my friend. None at all. I thank you."

Neither man spoke for the better part of an hour, which would have made many men uncomfortable, but Shay had learned to be at complete ease with silence during his time in the dungeon and Humphrey of course had found peace in silence over the course of his life at sea. The sun was beginning to set before them in the west and from their vantage point atop the wagon, they could see that the first of the wagon train had reached their destination and had begun to fan out along the horizon. As their already slow pace slowed even more, Humphrey turned to Shay and waited for him to look back at him. After only a few seconds, Shay turned his head but before he could say anything, Humphrey looked him in the eye and said, "What they did to you was savagery. I'm very sorry Your Majesty, please know that I am your friend and your willing, steadfast subject—at your service."

Just then, Humphrey pulled hard on the reins and yelled, "Whoa there!" as he almost ran into the wagon directly in front of them which had stopped. Being so close behind, it was impossible to see what the problem was up ahead and when no orders were forthcoming, Humphrey and Shay climbed down and began walking to the forward. A few hundred yards ahead, they could see the army standing on the crest of a hill but no one was advancing beyond it and they correctly assumed that whatever they were looking at, was incredible enough to stop everyone in their tracks. However, when they came up behind the quiet army, the incredulous sight before them was beyond human expression.

From the top of the hill, Shay could see the ocean a half-mile away but the earth between him and the sea was an unbroken mound of bodies. The ground could hardly be seen, so great was the slaughter and where there was earth between the dead, it was drenched with blood. Not only was it the bodies of men, but horses, hundreds of them and a surprising number of women. From the odor, the battle had ended many days ago, the ravens and vultures desecrating it as if it had been a landfill.

With his shirt pulled up over his nose, Shay walked out onto the silent battlefield, stepping over bodies, slowly picking a narrow path through the carnage. Most of the bodies had been dismembered and mutilated after they had fallen dead, in a most abhorrent and brutal manner, as if it wasn't enough to only kill. After he had walked several yards, he realized that there were no Celts among the dead, only Englishmen. Shay looked around with fearful astonishment, wondering what could have possibly happened and he wondered what kind of army could so completely destroy the other that they lose not a single man?

As Shay looked back at his army still standing motionless on the hill with all eyes upon him, he realized that he was the highest ranking officer and that they were all looking to him for orders. General Clancy had gone north to assist Gus in Northumbria and his orders were to march to Wales and support the King and Veronica. His heart then sank into his blood-soaked boots as he realized it was the King's army lying dead all around him and the King himself was certainly among them. He then groaned out-loud and fell to his knees with his face in his hands. He knew that Veronica's iron will would have forced herself into the battle, despite the King's or anyone else's forbidding. He knew the next gristly task before him was to scour the battlefield and search for the King and Queen. The thought of finding either of them sickened him and he leaned forward on his hands and knees and vomited, while he wept.

After several long minutes, he felt a finger on his back—two of them—that started to tap. Looking up, he saw Humphrey with tears in his eyes also, trying to find words that might bring his new friend comfort but there were none. Humphrey helped him get to his feet and then with his oversized frame, held him very tightly. Humphrey was awkwardly large like his ill-sense of social norms and after a few moments too long, Shay began to tap Humphrey on the back saying, “I need air my very large friend.”

Humphrey released him and looked down smiling, still saying nothing. Shay didn’t realize until that moment how incredibly large Humphrey was. He knew he was very heavy but he was also very tall, over six and a half feet, truly a gentle giant. “Thank you,” replied Shay, “Not only for allowing me a breath, but for your kindness.”

Humphrey smiled even bigger, causing his cheeks to nearly close his eyes. Then as if he knew the dread in his friend’s heart he said, “I’ll help you find them.”

“Again, I thank you,” replied Shay as he turned and yelled to his army, “FIND THE KING!”

CHAPTER 5

THE LIST

Shay stood knee-deep on the Welch coast, staring across the Irish Sea and into nothingness as the crimson waves churned the bodies of his countrymen. Three days of picking through the dead, trying to identify any body part that might have once belonged to the King had not only proved fruitless, but stretched the grit of every man. The abhorrent task leached away every man's desire to eat and now that they had reached the sea with the search completed, they were without strength and desire. However, some had grown so accustomed to handling the dead that they sat collapsed among them, completely depleted of physical strength and passion. In a different medieval time, the task might have been less taxing on the mind and heart, but for a body of soldiers who were once dentists, businessmen, laborers and other comparably gentile professions, it was bankrupting to the very soul.

As Shay tried to clear his mind and focus on his next move, an arm washed up against his leg and he noticed it had a ring and he picked up the detached limb inspecting it. The King had always worn a platinum band with an inserted row of rubies but after closer inspection, the ring on the lifeless finger was only yellow gold and he carelessly tossed it back into the sea just as Riley, his captain, approached from the beach.

"All detachments have reported Your Majesty," he said

flatly. "His Majesty the King is not among the dead in this above-ground graveyard—judging from what we can see anyway."

Shay slowly turned in the surf, dislodging his feet out of the soft sand saying, "Thank you Riley. We should be grateful I suppose but I don't think I could feel joy today even if Jesus himself appeared." Shay walked slowly out of the surf, found a small clearing in the bodies and sat down on the red sand. He silently motioned for Riley to join him and the two sat for several minutes staring at the sea where the red water turned purple further out to sea and then blue.

"Perhaps he has been taken prisoner?" said Riley breaking the surreal silence.

Shay turned and shook his head. "Unlikely. I mean, look around. Prisoners are only valuable if they can be used for leverage. The Celts have no desire nor apparent need for prisoners. They have come to destroy and take complete control with no negotiation."

Riley nodded reluctantly, "You are right of course. But…"

"I hate to be the pessimist but according to the General, the King was meeting the Celts here," said Shay interrupting. "So either he escaped or most-likely, his body was so mutilated, we could not recognize it."

Riley nodded again, concluding that the situation was as grim as it seemed and he then asked Shay if he intended to bury the bodies. Shay shook his head, "It would be the right thing to do but I don't think we can afford the luxury. By the looks of things, the Celts did not retreat back from where they came. I saw tracks of an immense force leading northward."

"As did I," replied Riley.

"Did you notice any women in your search?" asked Shay, shifting the conversation.

"A few, why?"

"I don't have any evidence other than my own experience but I think there was a very good chance the Queen was here. She's not one to miss a fight as you may or may not know," replied Shay.

Riley became a little more sober on top of being already extremely so and he replied with a trembling voice mostly due to his fatigue but also due to the fact that he was once Matthew's Number One and a friend of Lady Veronica's. "That would be most—unbearable, the most dastardly thought I can think. I simply cannot bring myself to accept it."

They both sat in silence as the heavy implications of their losses settled upon them while Shay tried to devise their next move. It was his duty to follow the trail of the Celts northward, but moving a two-thousand man army was anything but stealth. If he were to stand any chance at all against the Celts, it would have to be by surprise and that meant leading a small and greatly inferior force. Then as if Riley were reading Shay's mind, he turned and asked, "What is your plan Your Majesty?"

Shay slowly got to his feet and tried wiping his hands on his trousers but it was of little use. He, like every other man in the army, was covered from neck to foot in blood and he at last gave up and turned to Riley and replied, "We have to chase the Celts northward even though it may be akin to chasing an adder into its nest. I would like you to choose fifty of your bravest and follow me. We can't bring the entire army since it would be impossible to conceal our presence and frankly, when I come upon them I don't want to be seen—not until I have a plan first."

"Very wise Your Majesty. And what of the army?" replied Riley.

"Have them retreat northward slightly just beyond the battlefield and set-up camp and begin digging a mass grave. The Celts will not come looking for them among the dead. However, give them strict orders to not make any fires, absolutely none, not even for cooking. Right now, what we need more than anything is information but since I have no idea how long it will be before we get it, I can't have one of England's only surviving armies announcing their position to an enemy who could be anywhere."

Riley nodded, "Very well."

"Have your men ready to move within the hour," concluded Shay, as he turned and made his way back to his wagon where he was very happy to have a change of clothes and for the first time in three days, get something to eat. When he arrived, Humphrey greeted him with a full smile as he sat eating a piece of hard bread. He was wearing only underwear, having removed his blood-soaked clothes the moment he got to the wagon and from his sitting position on the ground, it appeared he had not moved, not even to redress. When he saw Shay, he struggled to his knees and reached through the wagon canvas, retrieved a large piece of bread and handed it to Shay. Shay hastily bit off two large mouthfuls and then as if following protocol, sat his bread on the wagon rail, pulled off his shirt and pants and with a sigh, sat down next to Humphrey in the shade of the wagon. Stale bread was not the most nutritious food available but it was readily accessible and he didn't have the strength to seek or cook anything else. Besides, his detachment was moving out in under an hour and he concluded that a heavier meal would have to wait until later in the day when he could fill on salted beef and beans.

Shay leaned his head back against the wagon wheel and closed his eyes for a moment but shortly thereafter, Humphrey tapped him on the shoulder, waking him. Riley and his fifty were ready to march and Shay staggered to his feet, his familiar fatigue from the dungeon returning to him.

"I didn't realize we were traveling so light," said Riley upon seeing Shay in only his underwear.

Shay smiled weakly as he reached out and took the clothing Humphrey had retrieved from the wagon and quickly dressed in a pair of heavy cotton trousers and an off-white shirt with laces up the front instead of buttons. Clothing in England after the Minimum was the most valuable commodity after food and to have more than a single change was rare, something only the privileged or lucky owned. Even though Shay was officially the King of East Angles, he traveled more like one of his captains with little baggage and no attendants. He was also relatively unknown to his subjects since he had spent most of his rein in captivity, which was just fine with Shay. When he was designated King of East Angles, he only did so with the pretense that it would be a temporary installment, until the Celtic wars were over. All of the royal assignments in the heptarchy were given to members of the privy council, the purest Anglo-Saxon blood, but of all the heptarchy kings, Shay was perhaps the most unsuited for leadership and he struggled under the heavy crown on his head. Things might have gone differently for Shay had the country not rioted in favor of Lady Veronica and had the Celts not invaded. But such as things were, Humphrey was the closest thing Shay had to an attendant and he gladly stepped into the role, having attended to Shay as best he could while he was withering away under Norwich Castle.

By the time Shay was dressed, Humphrey had saddled up one of the horses from the wagon and had it ready to ride. He handed the reins to Shay and then offered his clasped hands as a foot up. Shay was already fond of Humphrey due to their long ride together and the past three days on the battlefield, but seeing him serve so genuinely endeared him even more. Shay nodded and smiled as he stepped into Humphrey's hands and swung his leg over the saddle. Handing him the reins, Humphrey then slid the only musket into his saddle scabbard and then reached into the wagon and retrieved his longsword. Firearms of any sort were very rare since manufacturing in England had not reached the proficiency necessary to produce them, so the only firearms available were antiques from the seventeenth and eighteenth centuries. Cannons on the other hand, were much easier to produce since the machining requirements were less demanding and England had manufactured them in great quantity. Shay's army alone had over one-hundred pieces and every occupied fortress in the Kingdom was equally well-equipped, which gave Shay hope that they would find Conwy Castle unmolested.

Shay lightly flanked his horse and pulled on the reins to face the detachment Riley had assembled. The small force was arrayed in a very orderly fashion, sitting at attention on their mounts with Riley sitting before them on Matthew's old percheron. Riley was a very large man, much like Matthew and he commanded a powerful, but also quiet respect from his men. Most of the men he had chosen were former members of the Ravenguard and had served under Matthew. They were men who knew what it took to be victorious in battle, not only because they had won so many, but had also known great defeat.

As Shay surveyed Riley's choice, he was pleased and confident that he had chosen wisely and as he approached them, they all quietly drew their swords in respect and pointed them toward the sky. The sound of fifty-one longswords being pull from their scabbards was powerful, even more so than if any words had been spoken. In the fervent silence, with the points of cold steel contrasted against the dark clouds, Shay closed his eyes and prayed. Like most in the post-Minimum world, Shay had a new faith in God, brought about by the overall difficulty of life and the fact that he had actually conversed with the world of spirits, or at least one of them, and it was to this spirit which he prayed. The words of his grandfather whilst he was in the Norwich dungeon, returned to his mind often, especially during the last three days, sorting through the dead. He wondered greatly at how the world of spirits are very much aware of what is happening in mortality and even more incredulously, that they cared.

Shay had had many difficult times throughout his life but his grandfather or anyone else for that matter, had never appeared to him. However, in comparison to the savage trials since the sun had nearly forsaken the earth, his previous hardships were tame and even trivial. *Maybe that's why?* he thought. As he sat atop his horse before some of the bravest men alive, he had an epiphany. Many of the changes in the world of man and beast seemed to be nothing more than evolutionary adaptions even the spiritual strength like the changes in Jess. While he reasoned that the ability for mortals to see spirits was heightened because of the Minimum—as his grandfather explained—this did not explain why, only how.

"They care about us," Shay said under his breath as the

epiphany came full circle in his mind. He slowly began to nod as he felt a burning within him confirm the realization that mortal man is not alone on this earth and when life becomes sufficiently satanic and harrowing, the veil of heaven is thinned, evening the playing field against evil.

Shay raised his sword in honor of the loyal and brave-hearted men in front him and he struggled with what he might say to them. After a few moments of silence, he concluded that there was nothing to be said and he lowered his sword and slid it into the scabbard. The men then also quietly sheathed their swords and looked onwards with quiet, but iron-determination. Every man knew that in all practicality, they just might be the last English army since after every defeat, the Celts grew stronger and England grew weaker. Shay then rode past the detachment northward toward Conwy Castle as the men fell in behind him, single file on the narrow trail. After the first few hundred yards of their journey, he turned in his saddle to look behind him. Following close was Riley and then the fifty, their armor looking cold and menacing under the dark sky. Far behind the procession of steel was Humphrey, driving a single horse-drawn wagon which carried surplus weapons, powder, ball and food.

The overland journey to Conwy Castle was just over thirty miles northeast, which under normal conditions, a horseman might make the journey in less than a day's travel, but between the beach and Conwy lay Gwydyr Forest. The ancient Welch forest of Gwydyr was a mountainous region containing numerous streams and other natural obstacles, not to mention, fenrir, wolves and other wild animals, which slowed their progress greatly. However, both Riley and Shay determined that it was still faster than trying to go around. By the time daylight was gone, they had only made it as far as a Llyn Dinas, a small lake less than three miles into the forest but it was teeming with fish and once they crafted a net out of a worn blanket, they all ate their fill of freshwater eel and pike while their horses filled on the abundant summer grass.

With a satisfied and very full belly, Riley fastened his sword around his waist and made his way toward the camp perimeter to relieve one of his men who had been standing watch since their arrival at sundown. Shay had organized the watches into fifths so that ten men would only have to stand guard for an hour a half and then get some well-needed sleep. Guards were placed approximately every twenty yards around the encampment and those who were sleeping, gathered around the supply wagon at the center of camp where Shay, their King slept.

Just as Riley approached his post, a light rain began to fall and being so far from the light of the campfire, Riley called out, "Long live the King of East Angles." It wasn't the most encrypted code-greeting but since humans were scarce this deep into the forest, the only real threat was that of fenrir and stray harbingers and since neither of them could speak, the greeting was deemed adequate. But as Riley reached the post, he could not find the man he was to replace. He turned to face the flicker of the fire to see if he had veered too far to the right or left, but he was sure he was in the right place. He then heard footsteps approaching him quickly through the tall grass and before he could turnaround, he felt a cold blade press up against his neck and he froze.

"State your business—very slowly and quietly," came a voice behind the dagger in almost a whisper.

Riley knew his men kept all of their blades razor sharp and as he replied, he was very careful not to move or even swallow. "I've come to relieve you, you shameless bugger," he said indignantly, but the man did not immediately lower his blade. Instead, he leaned forward and whispered in his ear, "We are not alone out here Sir."

The man then slowly lowered the blade against his throat and apologized so quietly that Riley could hardly make out what he was saying. "What makes you so sure?" he asked.

"The body lying over there near the thicket," he replied pointing.

Riley looked at the man in alarm and then hurried over to the place where he had pointed, which was a cluster of small trees with about three feet of underbrush not far from the lakeshore. When he approached the spot, it was impossible to make out anything on the ground in the dark, so he shuffled his feet slowly as he moved forward, anticipating at any moment to stub into something, but after feeling his way several feet he found nothing. He turned to make his way back to the opening of the thicket and saw the silhouette of the soldier against the distant fire, pointing several feet to his left. Once he was standing over the body, he could see the outline of a man lying face-down in the grass, not moving.

"Did you kill him?" asked Riley.

"Not sure really. I was standin' right here takin' a leek and he came up from behind. I pretended not to hear him, though he was as noisy as a woman bathing in a river. When he was near enough for a blade, I came around and struck him with the hilt of my sword. He lays where he fell and after I tied his hands, I stood here waitin' for him to come too—which is why I didn't hear you call out—assuming you did."

"Indeed I did. Well done soldier. How long has he been out?" asked Riley as he knelt down to take his pulse.

"Maybe ten, fifteen."

Riley couldn't find a pulse at first but after several tires, he found one, very weak but he was alive. "Help me get him into camp and we'll tie him to the wagon wheel. You did very well to keep him alive. This might just be the break we are looking for."

"As I surmised Sir," replied the man as they each took and arm and drug the intruder toward the fire and the center of camp.

Once the prisoner was secured, Riley assembled his men and informed them of the potential for more Celtic scouts like the one they had just captured. He then doubled the guard around the camp and went to wake Shay.

"Your Majesty," whispered Riley, pulling back the canvas cover of the wagon.

Shay sat up with a shot. "What is it? I'm not asleep, 'er not too much anyway."

"We've captured a Celtic scout and I have him tied to the wheel," replied Riley sounding very eager.

"Fantastic! Has he spoken at all? Though I'm guessing these Celts would die rather than talk," said Shay as he climbed out of the wagon.

"No talking yet, he is still unconscious, though I assume you are correct based upon the destruction they leave."

Shay and Riley walked around to where the Celt was tied, the wheel nearest to the fire which was still brightly burning. In the flickering light, Shay was still rubbing sleep from his eyes as he stood in front of the prisoner, surprised that he looked—normal. In every age, from playgrounds to battlefields, enemies have always been demonized so that hatred and cruelty toward them could be justified. After three days of combing through the Celt's handiwork, Shay and the rest of his army were sure that they were fighting the devil himself, but now that he was face-to-face with one, the mental image of his enemy was shattered. He was just like they were except for his poor clothing and lack of armor. Then he fell to his knees in astonishment.

"I—I know who this is!" he said in complete disbelief.

"Your Majesty?" questioned Riley.

Shay slowly looked up and said, "This is Senator Schyuler."

"Who?" replied Riley as he knelt down next to Shay.

"Theodore Schyuler—my friend from Washington!"

Riley slowly began to nod as Shay reached over to untie him but before he was able, Riley grabbed his arm and pulled him back. "At last report, Ted was being held in the Tower for treason," Riley said still holding firmly to Shay's arm.

Shay indignantly pulled away and retorted, "What? No he wasn't, he was a royal prisoner in Maidstone. I saw him there! Besides, whatever he is or guilty of, he is hardly dangerous."

Riley sighed. Shay was not aware of Ted's move to the Tower nor his confession to Gus that he was working with Toprak and Riley related to him all that had happened to his friend while he was imprisoned. Shay was shocked but still could not believe Ted was guilty of such a thing and he repeatedly shook his head. "Surely you are mistaken, you don't know him. Not like I do."

"It's true Shay. All of it," said Ted as he moaned and came too.

Shay was speechless and for several minutes he sat staring into Ted's eyes as if he were frozen, while the truth about his friend sunk into his heart.

Ted's voice was horse and broken and after clearing his throat, he replied, "I'm sorry, but I assure you I am not here to harm you in any way. Ask the man who knocked me on the head, I came unarmed."

Shay looked up at Riley for confirmation of Ted's words but Riley didn't know and didn't think to ask the soldier who apprehended him. But as he thought, he didn't remember seeing any weapons on the ground and the soldier didn't mention any either. There was a chance that Ted was telling the truth and he replied to Shay with a shrug then said, "Perhaps."

Ted looked terrible. He had a three-inch beard that was soaked with blood due to the blow to his head and his clothing was threadbare and filthy, which was why Shay did not recognize him immediately. It was obvious he had not bathed for many weeks or even months and given the state of his worn-out shoes, he had been traveling for quite some time and had traversed many miles. Seeing Ted, his long-time friend and Senator from the State of Nebraska in such a state was more than Shay could take.

"Good hell!" he exclaimed as he reached over and cut the ropes off his feet and then his hands. "He is surrounded by fifty men and in his state, he couldn't over-power a stuffed girl."

Ted rubbed his wrists as he thanked Shay and then felt his head where he had been knocked to the ground. It was still producing an unhealthy flow of bright-red blood and just as Shay was about to call for a field kit, Humphrey knelt down beside him with a large smile and began cleaning up the wound. Shay was over-joyed at seeing Ted after all that had happened to them, both of them having been imprisoned and now chasing a Celtic army many times their size, a tear rolled down his cheek. "Seeing you brings me more happiness than you can imagine Ted."

Ted opened his eyes and smiled as he reached out to touch Shay's hand. "I can't tell you how happy I am to hear you say that brother. My reception around the Kingdom hasn't been all that great lately."

Whatever Ted had actually done was still up for debate in Shay's mind and probably to everyone else in the Kingdom, including Riley. Everything from his forced residency in Maidstone to his alleged imprisonment in the Tower of London made no sense. Ted, while sometimes a heavy drinker, was certainly not a traitor. Whatever it was all about, Shay determined that it could wait until morning after Ted had had a good night's rest and a hardy meal. He assured Ted that he need not worry for his safety whilst in his company and that he would be treated with dignity and respect—upon his orders.

Ted shook his head. "There isn't time Shay. You shouldn't have even stopped for the night."

"What are you talking about?" asked Riley, moving in closer.

Ted sighed deeply. There was so much to tell but before

he could even begin, he knew he first had to tell them how he arrived in Wales before they would trust what he knew. After all, he was a traitor and he did not blame Riley or anyone else for treating him like one. While he made his way to Norwich looking for Shay and then to Wales, he was extremely surprised at how ignorant everyone was about the facts of the invasion and how terribly unprepared they were for what was coming. While he was in the Tower, he was certain that the King knew what was going on, due to their many talks in his cell above the Tower Green and the King's know-all attitude. But after escaping, he realized that the King didn't have any idea and he hoped that at least Jess knew since the war they were about to come head-to-head with was between what good was left in the world and all of hell. After traveling the three-hundred and eighty miles to find Shay, he was convinced that no one knew the truth.

Ted cleared his throat and tried to swallow. "Could you spare some water?"

Humphrey handed Shay a leather bag and he held it to Ted's lips. After drinking all he could, he reluctantly began his tale with a sigh. "It's all true what they say about me Shay, and for what it's worth, I'm sorry. I got caught up with a woman who looked like Nicole and I may have done some things that lead to the attempt to exhume Professor Moran's bones but at the time I was not aware of their plan, I assure you."

Shay and Riley both nodded. "Yes, I had heard that," replied Shay.

"But, as it turns out, it wasn't a woman who looked like Nicole, it was Nicole," Ted said.

"What?! But, how did she—where did she go after the

Battle of the Thames?" replied Shay in disbelief, leaning in closer so that he could not misunderstand a single word.

"That I don't know. I suppose it's no secret that I was in love with her and in my sad state in Dover, I was just glad to see her and be with her again. But looking back now, she had changed. How, I'm not really sure except to say that she was just, darker."

"Was that before or after you were *assigned* to the Maidstone Castle?" asked Shay.

"Oh, long before. The King and Gus placed me in Maidstone for safe-keeping after the Moran incident and I had been there just over a year I think when Jess, Matthew and Veronica arrived one night in the rain—that was a good night," said Ted smiling. "But it quickly turned ugly and though I can't blame Matthew and the King, they assumed I orchestrated the whole thing."

"What whole thing?" asked Shay.

Ted shook his head and laughed slightly. "Have you been under a rock Shay? I'm talking about the whole fenrir incident."

Shay looked back at Ted with sympathetic eyes nodding, "Yes, I have been under a very large rock called Norwich Castle. I was a prisoner there for several months. At last report, you were the forced regent of Maidstone, which is how Gus put it to me when last I saw him on his trip southward to meet with the King, just before the riots broke out."

"I'm so sorry, I didn't know," replied Ted. "It appears we have much in common."

"Except he didn't betray the Crown! He was imprisoned for supporting it," interjected Riley.

Ted raised his hands in the sign of a truce. "OK, fair enough, fair enough. That isn't what I meant, but at any rate, where was I?"

"Fenrir," replied Riley unenthusiastically.

"Oh right," said Ted in a downward tone as he became more sober. "That night was the next time I saw Nicole. She came to my chamber after everyone had gone to bed and amidst other things, said that she desperately needed my help. She said that Horsa had returned and that he knew Jess was a guest in my castle."

"Horsa!" exclaimed Shay and Riley at the same time while Humphrey looked at them both in confused alarm.

"Yes, but it gets worse I'm afraid," replied Ted.

"Worse? How? Horsa now has an eviler twin?" said Riley flippantly.

Ted thought for a moment, considering Riley's comment and replied, "Yes actually—well, of sorts anyway. But I'll get to that in a moment. Nicole came clean that night and told me she had always hated Veronica and all the events of the Battle of the Thames, how her ship never engaged in the battle."

Shay was in shock. "She threw the entire battle because she didn't like Veronica? Are you friggin' kidding me?" he said vehemently.

"Well, yes, but not how you're probably thinking. Horsa boarded the *Euterpe* sometime before leaving port, which explains the confusion onboard that Veronica observed and why the *Euterpe* never engaged in the battle."

"So let me guess, when you were in Maidstone, she said that unless you turned over Veronica, Horsa would kill her," said Riley.

Ted was getting a little irritated with Riley but he couldn't blame him and he continued with a sigh. "She said that Horsa would either have Veronica or Jess and that it was my choice. I resisted of course and told her that he would have neither. Which is when Horsa walked through the door of my bed chamber. I had never seen him up-close before and there are nights that I wish I hadn't. I never believed in evil until I saw him that night, standing there in my moonlit room over seven feet tall, frighteningly massive and dark as the night. I don't recall what he said, I just remember thinking that we were all dead, no matter if we did what he asked or not."

"Wait. Horsa asked for your permission? The Horsa I know kills for the thrill and takes whatever he wants," said Riley disbelieving everything Ted had said so far.

Ted nodded, "That is the Horsa we both know. When I think back on that night, I think Nicole and Horsa were trying to craft some kind of Toprak initiation by making me a part of Jess's capture. After all, that's how gangs and thugs work—get you to do something terrible and you become hostage to their secret. But beyond that, with all the armed soldiers at the castle and Matthew, I don't think Horsa could have taken Jess on his own. So, feeling like I had no choice, I walked with Horsa downstairs to show him where Matthew was sleeping and where he could find Jess, except Jess was not there. That's when Matthew leaped from the shadows and attacked Horsa, surprising us both but mostly Horsa. And that's when Horsa changed into a fenrir and crashed through the front doors."

"He changed—into a fenrir," replied Riley unconvinced while Shay and Humphrey were transfixed.

"I assure you, that is the truth as everyone there will attest. He is more than a man. After that night, I believe he commands the devil himself."

Shay was amazed with Ted's story, but he was more concerned with Horsa's plans and why he wanted Jess specifically. He and everyone else in the King's Privy Council knew why Toprak wanted Veronica, even if it was a little ridiculous, thinking that she was somehow a blood relative to the Saxon Princess Ronnie. But he had never known Toprak to be strategic in the Post-minimum era, just brutal. He raised his hand to stop Riley from questioning Ted's story any further and asked, "Why Jess?"

"Well, Toprak obviously sees him as a threat and according to Nicole, he is second on their list."

"They have a list?" asked Humphrey, feeling a little like he was listening to a ghost story at a camp-out.

Ted smiled slightly and replied, "Yeah, but you're probably not in the top ten, though we're all on it somewhere I imagine." Ted shifted his weight onto his left side and began rubbing his back as he continued, "As I figure it, Jess is the best person I know. When you think of it like that, it makes sense, but hearing how desperately he needed to know where Matt was that night, he must be number three."

Ted was becoming anxious to hurry through the preliminaries so that he could tell Shay the really important news and he resumed his dialogue at a little faster pace.

"So, Matthew took me to the Tower and that's when Gus and I talked for days on end in the dark. It's because of Gus that I'm here really. Sitting in the Tower dungeon, I lost hope and eventually convinced myself that I deserved to be there. From that point, it was easy to just stop caring—about anything."

"I'm glad you had Gus and that the King allowed him to visit you so freely," said Shay.

Ted laughed slightly under his breath. "I guess you could call it a visit. At the time, I really thought he was a prisoner like me. As I look back on it, it was rather odd that he would have a cell right next to mine."

"What, Gus was imprisoned too?" asked Shay, not believing it possible.

Riley shook his head. "No, Your Majesty. He was only there to extract information from Ted about Toprak. I'll explain later."

Ted looked at Shay and smiled, "Your Majesty. I had forgotten, congratulations."

Shay waved his hand signaling that it was nothing and motioned for him to continue. Ted nodded as his disposition changed, becoming more intense and contrite. "No one knows this in the north, but Toprak landed at Dover just over a month ago and have marched as far as London. They have taken the city—what's left of it anyway—and the Tower of course. They freed me when they arrived and for a time, I was one of them."

"How Ted? How could you do that?" asked Shay, heartbroken.

"I had given up, especially when the King told me that Gus had been beheaded for treason—but he wasn't," he quickly added before Shay could respond in horror. "It was a ruse, and it worked very well on me. There had been beheadings in the Tower mind you, just not Gus. From my cell above the Green, I could see the severed heads, but their faces were turned away from me, deliberately. Even after I was released and free to move about the Tower, I couldn't bring myself to look at them. It was during that time I learned a great deal about Toprak's plans, which is why I'm here."

"So we're supposed to believe you've just had a change of heart and that you are now here to warn us? How do we know you're not still in Horsa's saddlebag?" interjected Riley.

Ted looked Riley in the eye intently and replied, "You don't I suppose. But when the King told me that Gus's head was on a spike outside my window, any hope I had left me and I no longer cared what happened to me. Then when Toprak entered the Tower, I was impartial and the more I learned of their plans, the more I believed England didn't have a prayer. They've been gathering their army from around the world the last three years and they have a massive operation in Ireland, where in Ireland I'm not sure."

Riley and Shay could hardly believe what they were hearing and Riley for the first time asked Ted for clarification without being condescending. "You mean we are not pursuing a Celtic army? And the army that defeated the Ravenguard at Holy Isle was Toprak?"

"That is what I'm saying," replied Ted.

"Stop, wait a minute," said Shay turning to Riley.

"Matthew said the army that defeated the Ravenguard at Holy Island was Celtic."

Before Shay finished speaking, Riley had already began to shake his head. "No, no that isn't what he said. I was there when we were licking our wounds the night before we rallied. He only said that because of their banners and the unknown language they spoke—but the officially accepted name of our new enemy came about because Jess suggested that what Matthew saw and heard sounded Celtic, and it stuck. Why would we assume it was Toprak? We had every reason to believe they were rotting at the bottom of the Thames. Besides, they came from Ireland, which was the last ancient Celtic stronghold."

Riley was becoming more heated by the minute and Ted recognized it was because he was feeling out of control with the situation and as the commander of the army, he was operating with gross misinformation. Ted nodded as he listened to Riley's explanation and then resumed his tale. "As such, your triumph over them the following day put Horsa in a very bad lather. That was the day he realized he had to disband the Ravenguard and kill Matthew if he was going to be successful." Ted had not heard if Horsa had in fact accomplished this goal to kill Matthew but as he turned to look at Shay, both he and Riley nodded.

Ted looked down at the ground with dread. "That makes things terribly worse. I had hoped Matthew was with his Ravenguard in Northumbria. Toprak was supposed to advance there as well," replied Ted and for a long while, no one spoke, each man reeling over what they had just heard. Then as if Shay's soliloquy had made a complete revolution, he looked up and asked quietly, "So what changed your mind—why are you here?"

"I finally got brave and looked at the heads on the Tower Green and discovered that none of them belonged to Gus. That was when I figured out that Gus was only sitting in the dungeon to give me hope and of course to learn what I knew about Toprak—which wasn't much at the time. The last time the King visited me, he asked me to consider my friends and what side they were fighting on but at the time I didn't care since I figured it was just a matter of time before we all were dead. Every day I spent in the confidence of Toprak, I couldn't stop thinking about our damn committee in the Senate and how Toprak was so fully in charge—ready to destroy my friends."

Ted paused as he recounted the last month, his escape and search for Shay, while Riley stood up, still trying to come to grips with what he had just learned about Toprak. Ted then took a deep breath and said, "It does matter what side we're on—even if that side is ultimately destroyed."

Shay looked up from his deep thoughts a little surprised and asked, "So, you don't think we can win?"

Ted slowly shook his head, then stared at the dirt and said, "I don't."

CHAPTER 6

THE LONE DANCER

As daylight broke, Shay and his small detachment had already put several miles behind them on their way to Conwy Castle in the north of Wales where they hoped to find Queen Veronica alive. Shortly after he and Riley learned that Toprak had once again invaded England and that the Celts were only a figment of everyone's collective imagination, Shay dispatched Riley back to the beach while he pushed on to Conwy. Riley was ordered to quickly prepare the army for a rapid march northward, following the old A498 motorway, which they hoped would quicken their pace. Marching overland with the small detachment on horseback was rather painless, but to advance a two-thousand man army and a sizeable baggage train in the same manner was foolhardy. Even though much of the old roadway had been broken up, it still traversed the forest following the lowest river valleys, which Riley assumed would make things easier and therefore faster.

The rain that had begun to fall after dinner the night before, continued to drizzle down upon Shay and his fifty men. It wasn't a down-pour, just a constant, soaking mist that is typical of the Welsh mountains in the late summer which made the ground more muddy and colder by the hour. Just after mid-day, they approached a vine-covered building with smoke rising from its chimney and Shay ordered the company to stop. Most of the men were accustomed to riding long distances, but on this, his second day in the saddle, Shay was painfully aware that he was not and he needed a break. The two-hundred year-old building appeared be an inn, or at least had been at one time during its existence but regardless of what it was now, it was large enough to accommodate fifty-two cold and wet men and Shay slid off his mount and knocked on the door.

There was no immediate answer but while he was dismounting, he was sure that he heard voices coming from inside. A shiver shot down his back as he considered the possibility of Toprak soldiers being inside and he slowly drew his sword trying not to make a sound. Following Shay's lead, all of his men did the same as they stood by the side of their mounts, prepared for an ambush. After a few long minutes, Shay determined that who or whatever was inside, must be as alarmed and cautious as they were and he stepped back from the door and called out, "We come in the name of the King, seeking shelter only!"

From behind one of the dark windows, Shay saw a curtain move and for a brief moment, the face of a child appeared in one of the square panes before it was quickly pulled away. He then heard the bolt on the door being worked followed by the sharp creek of it opening a small crack. When the door did not open any further, he reached into the crack and pushed the door wide, still being prepared for an attack. His guard was quickly put down when he saw only an elderly couple with fear in their eyes and a four year-old girl in their arms. They were huddled together next to a grand stone fireplace surrounded by elegant hardwood, which convinced Shay that the building was indeed an old English inn and that the occupants were probably alone. But as he stepped inside, he saw the little girl's eyes look at something behind the door and he stopped. Slowly raising his sword and pointing it at the door he said, "I wouldn't try to be clever."

A man in his thirties slowly stepped out from behind the door and dropped his weapon, a useless doubled-barreled shotgun. Shay lowered his sword as the man raised his hands and walked over to the fireplace to join the others. There was an awkward pause until Shay finally sheathed his sword and extended his hand to the elderly gentleman and said, "My name is Shay. Me and my men are on the King's errand and we are very much in need of a reprieve from the weather and perhaps a cup of tea."

"Cledwyn," replied the man as he reached out to take Shay's hand. "You are welcome of course but I'm afraid there is no tea."

Shay smiled and shook the hands of his wife and the middle-aged man, thanking them for their hospitality and waving to the little girl who was now hiding behind the legs of Cledwyn. "We have supplies enough and would not think of imposing you in any way, except for the warmth of your fire," said Shay as his men began approaching the door. As Shay turned to motion it was safe to enter, he noticed his muddy footprints on the spotless hardwood floor and he told his men to stop and remove their boots before entering, which was no easy task since they were all clad in full armor but after several more minutes in the rain and amidst much clattering and clanging, they returned in stocking feet and took a seat at the many empty tables in the large room. The last person through the door was Humphry who was carrying a large basket containing tea leaves. He also had a pot slung over his shoulder and what looked like a half side of salted beef under his arm. When he was halfway across the floor he noticed that everyone else had removed their shoes and he stopped where he was, unsure of what to do. He started to walk back to the door but the load he was carrying was growing heavier by the second and he desperately needed to set it down.

“Carry-on then,” said Shay, talking off his wet shirt and wiping up his and Humphrey’s muddy tracks.

The old woman was uncomfortable with a stranger cleaning her floor and with his own shirt for heaven sake—especially after he had been so kind and considerate. She started to protest but her husband held her arm and shook his head. Cledwyn was easily in his eighties and epitomized the proverbial wise man of the woods. He had a long snow-white beard that was braided at the end and a scar under his left eye that ran diagonally toward his mouth. His nose was beet-red from a life time of ale and from the smell of the room, he was also a pipe smoker. Shay watched as he whispered in his wife’s ear, telling her to help Humphrey with his preparations. The two of them disappeared into the kitchen and Shay walked over and sat down on the end of a bench near the fire as he thanked Cledwyn again.

There wasn’t much talking among the soldiers as they dried their face and hands but the room was surprisingly loud due to the clattering of armor. Some of the men were helping each other remove the more cumbersome pieces while others were content to just lean against the walls, having only removed their helmets and tried to sleep. Before long, Humphrey returned with his pot full of steaming tea and the man’s wife brought a platter of cold beef. The feeling in the inn was still somewhat tense but as the tea was drank, the mood softened and Cledwyn came and sat down next to Shay and Ted.

“Where are you boys from?” he asked, Shay finding it a little humorous that he referred to them as boys when they were nearly forty. But considering how old he was, they were merely boys.

"America," replied Ted flippantly with a tired voice before Shay could speak.

If there was one thing Shay hated about being an American, it was American brash and he looked at Ted with disgust and slapped him on the chest saying, "What are you doing, huh?"

Ted shrugged as Shay apologized. "Forgive my friend here. He doesn't get out much and the first time I do he embarrasses me—honestly," he said shaking his head before he continued. "Seriously, we are Americans but only us two. We have come from Norwich seeking…"

"On a private matter for the King," interjected Ted, thinking that it would be best if they didn't publicize their mission.

Shay turned to Ted wondering what he was doing as Ted shook his head slightly with the look on his face that said *shut your mouth!* Shay was not accustomed to war and all the rules of intrigue but once he realized the potential danger, a look of enlightenment came to his face and nodding, he turned back to the old man and asked, "Have you seen any other army move through these parts recently?"

The old man looked up just as the middle aged man approached the table and replied for him. "Rumor says that a large army was seen traveling along the sea not long ago."

"Can you give us any idea how long ago that was?" asked Ted.

The man shrugged. "It's just a rumor. We don't venture far from this valley except for hunting," he said forcing himself to sound uninterested.

"I suppose it's possible that they came through here and we missed them," said the old man trying to be helpful.

Shay turned to face the old man who was still sitting at the table across from him and shook his head. "Not this army. We can tell they haven't been though here."

"How?" asked the middle-aged man.

"You're alive," replied Ted without emotion.

"It's the Celts isn't it?" said the old man. "You're tracking the Celts, that's what yer doin'."

Before Shay could respond again, Ted quickly said, "That's it. We are tracking the Celts. You are very shrewd."

Both the old man and the younger one knew Ted was being rude and they wrote it off as an American problem and from then on tried to ignore him and only talk to Shay. However, the conversation became strained and after a while Shay announced to his men that they would be moving out within the hour as he poured himself one last cup of tea from the fresh pot Humphrey had just brought to the table. As he raised his cup, he noticed out of the corner of his eye, the old man shaking his head at the younger man who had just returned to the room with the little girl who very much wanted to see the knights in their armor. There was something odd about them from the moment they entered the inn. It was understandable that they might be afraid but even after they knew they were on the King's errand, they still acted afraid.

"What is it?" asked Shay, acknowledging Cledwyn and the middle-aged man's secret dialogue.

Both men looked at each other for several intense moments, continuing their dialogue with only their eyes until the younger one turned to Shay and said, "We have a devil." His words caused the entire room to become quiet and they all waited for him to continue as the old man looked out the window shaking his head.

"What did you say?" asked Ted.

"We, we have captured a—a devil. What should we do with it?" replied the man.

Ted stood up and drew Shay's sword from its sheath that was lying on the table and said, "Show me."

The man led Ted and Shay out of the inn and to a small stone building that was once used as a smokehouse. As such, it had no windows and the door was barricaded with tree branches and large stones. Whatever was inside, it was extremely obvious that it was dangerous. As they approached, the man began to whisper, "I found it in here one morning eating my dog and when it saw me, it came rushing at me and I shut it in. Most of the time it is quiet unless it hears something."

Ted walked over and swung Shay's sword over his head, striking the door, hoping to wake whatever was inside but nothing came from behind the door. "It usually wakes, sometimes when I just walk by," said the man feeling stupid. "It has been a few days though, perhaps it's dead."

Ted waited for a few seconds longer and then began removing the large branches wedged against the door just as a loud scream was heard that turned into a deep, guttural growl, "AHHHHHH-OHH-RRRG!" It was unlike anything Shay had ever heard and he turned to Ted with a look of horror just as something hit the door, almost breaking through it. To Shay's surprise, Ted was not alarmed at all, in fact he thought he saw him laughing with amusement.

"What is that?" asked Shay, his pulse racing.

Ted smiled, "That my dear Shay, is a *dancer*."

"A what?" asked Shay as the man moved further way, getting ready to run.

Ted thrust the sword into the ground and began moving away the larger branches. "A dancer. It's the new and improved way Toprak makes harbingers these days. Although, they're not exactly like the harbingers we used to know and love. Make no mistake, these buggers have a terrible attitude and love to eat raw flesh right off the bone but they can't be used as a communication device."

Shay didn't need to ask how he came to have such knowledge but what he desperately wanted to know was what in the hell he was doing now. "Surely I'm mistaken, but it looks like you are going to let it out," he said taking a few steps backwards.

"I am," Ted said with a smile still on his face. "Don't worry, I'm pretty sure I can stop it before it gets too far."

"I'm not feeling a lot of confidence in your plan Ted," replied Shay as the man behind him nodded in agreement.

Ted removed all the branches and was bracing his shoulder against the largest boulder with little success when he asked Shay to come give him a hand. Shay timidly approached the door and then bent down just as the dancer violently hit the door again and screamed. Ted quickly leaned up against the door to ensure it did not escape before he was ready and after a few minutes, all was quiet again and they resumed the work of removing the stones. There was one last, large branch that secured the door and Ted quietly motioned for Shay to stand several yards away but directly in front of the door so that the dancer would be distracted with killing him instead of noticing Ted at the side of the door.

"I would feel much better doing that if you had said you *knew* you could kill it instead of being pretty sure," whispered Shay.

Ted laughed once under his breath and walked over to where Shay was standing and said quietly, "These dancers are not very bright—evil—but they're all foam and no beer. Now—you get enough foam together and you'd have a problem on your hands but one by itself, we can just blow it off." Ted then put his hand on Shay's shoulder and asked, "We good to go?"

Shay slowly nodded, putting his complete trust in Ted and swallowed hard. The middle-aged man was standing near the door of the inn, ready to run inside if he needed too. Ted was standing at the side of the door with his sword ready and he looked to Shay one last time before kicking away the branch. Shay nodded and watched Ted kick the branch and then quickly move away as if he had just kicked a hornet's nest.

Nothing.

Ted slammed his sword against the door with a loud crack as the dancer came bursting through it. Just as Ted said, it came rushing out as if its hair was on fire, completely ignoring Ted with its focus only on Shay, the first thing it saw. The dancer had only advanced three feet out of the smokehouse when Ted swung his sword through its path and connected with it on the neck. The velocity of the sharp sword and the speed of the dancer caused the blade to effortlessly cut all the way through its neck, bones and all, and its head flew behind it as it ran. However, like a chicken without its head, it only got a few feet before it collapsed and bled out.

The scene was horrific but Ted seemed to be amused by it all and Shay correctly assumed that he had certainly seen much more than he had told. Sorting through the massacre on the beach had sufficiently numbed Shay's sensitivities to enable him to pick up the severed head and place it near the dancer's neck so that he could get a better look. The dancer appeared to be a male in his twenties and was completely naked except for a tattered shirt and one sock. What was most peculiar was the steel ring that was pierced through his right wrist and seem to serve no purpose. He was filthy beyond belief with maggots crawling through his hair and Shay looked down at his own hands in alarm realizing that he had just picked up its head. Not having anything to wipe his hands on, he stood over the dancer with his hands extended, being careful not to touch anything, especially himself.

"Pretty huh?" said Ted. "That's how they grow them these days. This guy was just like you and me a fortnight ago."

"He was my brother," came a voice from behind them as the middle-aged man walked over and stood next to the body. "I never had a good look at it until now. Everyone assumed he had died—he had the St. Vitus."

"I'm so sorry," said Shay. "There was no healing him you understand. Perhaps we can we help you bury him?"

The man quietly shook his head as tears pooled in his eyes,

rendering him unable to speak. Shay didn't know what else to say and while he wanted all of his men to see the dancer, he decided against it and after taking his sword out of Ted's hand, he turned and walked back towards the inn. Just as he had ordered, all of his men were ready to ride and were waiting for him on the street in front of the inn. The door was still open and he stuck his head inside to thank their hosts one last time. When the old woman saw Shay, she ran and fell to her knees several feet before him, thanking him for killing the devil. The old man who was standing near the fire, exchanged a pregnant glance with Shay and he at last understood. No one but the old man knew the dancer's identity and he silently thanked Shay for not disclosing his secret to the little girl or the old woman. As he was about to turn and walk out the door, the little girl peered around the door at him smiling, finally getting brave enough to approach him.

Shay smiled as he knelt down on one knee and said, "Hey, there you are. Are you finally going to be my friend?" The little girl quickly ducked behind the door again and then reappeared with a weak smile. She had long brown hair, a round face and very fair complexion. When she smiled, her eyes danced with excitement that forced Shay to smile in return. "Aren't you a delight! I'm the King of East Angles, but you can call me Shay. What is your name?"

He saw the old man out of the corner of his eye making hand gestures but he didn't catch what it was since he was so focused on the beautiful child in front of him. When he turned to look at the old man, he saw that he was desperately cautioning him not to speak to the child, but he then realized what was going on. The dancer behind the inn was her father and Shay's heart sank as tears began to whelm up in pity for the poor girl's loss, though she was obviously not aware. Shay discretely wiped his eyes before tears fully formed and turned back to the child, forcing a smile.

"Mille," the little girl replied.

"Mille, that is a beautiful name and I should say it suits you wonderfully. Do you know what Mille means?"

The little girl slowly shook her head, still beaming.

"Mille is a very old English name that means; gentle strength—which is what you are to me, dear Mille. Thank you for letting us visit you today."

Mille left the security of the door and approached Shay, placing her hands in his lap and leaning on his knee then in excitement said, "My da is coming home!"

Shay could no longer hold back the wall of emotion he was restraining and tears freely flowed down his cheeks. "That is WONDERFUL!" was all he could say without his voice cracking.

When Mille saw his tears, she began to back away slightly and Shay reached out to hold her. "No, hey it's OK. I'm only crying because I'm so happy for you. Do you live here with your nana and granddad?"

Mille's smile returned and she nodded excitedly.

"You are a very lucky girl," Shay said wiping his eyes again and wishing he could protect the child from the harsh reality of the world that was as close as the backyard. He reached into his riding cloak and retrieved a bag of tallies that amounted to a modest fortune for a commoner and he reached into the bag and handed one to Mille, "This is for you, keep it safe OK?"

Mille's smile turned into sheer excitement as she took the token and held it tightly in her fist. Shay then handed the remainder of the tokens to the old woman who had joined her husband at the fireplace as he thanked them both for their hospitality to strangers. He then made his way out the door and to his small band of warriors who were still waiting patiently on their mounts, having observed the whole interchange between their King and Mille. Without a word, he soberly gave the signal to ride and he gave the lead to the Commander while he and Ted followed behind. The weather was unchanged except the roads were muddier and they kept to the tall grass as much as they could so that the horses did not become fatigued.

Shay and Ted didn't speak as they normally did while riding, but Ted knew why and he didn't try to bring up trivial subjects or pry into what he was feeling as a woman might. Even though a woman was what he probably needed, it was still the man-code in the Post-minimum age to keep one's darkest feelings to one's self and they rode along for several hours without a sound between them. It wasn't until they reached another large lake somewhere near the headwaters of the Conwy river, that the heavy silence was broken. The sun was starting to set, causing the temperatures to drop to a surprisingly low level for late summer and the clouds descended, casting a thin fog along the mountain valleys they traversed. As they skirted the lakeshore, they saw the Commander waiting for them on the roadside, having told the men to continue on while he asked the King when and where they would stop for the night.

"We will not be stopping Commander, not tonight. We must press on to Conwy without delay," replied Shay.

The Commander didn't respond directly but after a slight delay, he saluted and said, "As you wish Your Grace," and rode to the front announcing the King's wishes as he rode past Humphrey and the rest of the men.

After Shay's silence was broken, it somehow made it easier to at last speak his thoughts and he leaned forward in his saddle stretching his back. "I know you don't believe we can, but we MUST win this," Shay finally said. "I have never been more determined in anything and nothing is more important to the world than this war, this moment."

Ted didn't respond, mostly because he still truly believed they didn't have a prayer and not knowing what else to do, he nodded as Shay continued. "Have you ever wondered what it was like to be at the signing of the Declaration of Independence, or at D-day—pivotal moments of history, like moments before the crucifixion of Christ?" Shay waited for Ted to respond but he still said nothing. "We're there Ted! This is it. And unless we win, this moment will be lost from history forever. Toprak will not record what we stood for or that we even tried, only their victory will be recorded and we will become nothing. All of our suffering and all of the blood we let into this English soil will be nothing. Mille's suffering and a million other Mille's will be nothing. All of our suffering will only be validated and reverenced if we win."

Ted finally nodded with some conviction but he still could not bring himself to share in Shay's optimism or determination. However, Shay's faith was contagious and instead of only seeing himself as a martyr, destined to die with the rest of the good-guys, he found himself searching his knowledge about Toprak, trying to find ways that they might gain an advantage. Little did he know, Shay was also reviewing everything he had ever known about Toprak in his mind—and had been since leaving the inn—trying to predict their motivations and their next move. However, Shay's concentration was continually interrupted with visions of Mille and her disfigured and beheaded father lying in the yard. He finally gave in to his determined thoughts and focused on the bizarre events at the inn, Mille and Toprak's creation of harbinger warriors. What he did know about harbingers was all Pre-Minimum knowledge and according to Ted, Toprak no longer used them in the same way nor were they able to create them like they once did. But no matter how they were created or used, the thought that kept haunting him was all the innocent people Toprak used and destroyed to further their agenda. He then remembered the middle-aged man saying his brother had the St.—something, but he could not recall the conversation clearly now and he turned to Ted and asked, "How do they make them?"

"Harbingers? I'm not sure I can explain how, but I know the sequence of events," replied Ted as he pulled the hood of his riding cloak up over his head in an attempt to keep warm. "Well," Ted paused, collecting his thoughts and then finally concluding that no matter how he said it, it was going sound ridiculous so he continued. "They collect the emptors from just about anywhere, which I always thought was strange. Out of a group of ten, for example, they might only draw away one, then in another village, nine, it always seemed very random to me."

"Emptor?" asked Shay.

"Oh, sorry, that's what Nicole called them. Basically it's people who were pre-disposed to be consumed, which is rather curious when you think about it. An emptor is someone who purchases something. I always wondered what they bought—but it may also just be a meaningless term. As I mentioned, the mechanics of the whole process were never shared with me but when the emptors were drawn away, they became diseased, but not like any disease I ever saw."

"Oh, the St. Vitus!" cried Shay, remembering.

"Is that what they call it in England? Nicole called it the Rehearsal, which pretty accurately describes the process." Ted then also remembered the middle-aged man at the inn and replied, "That's what he must have been talking about. I wonder why they call it the St. Vitus?" Ted then thought for a moment, drawing upon his degree in medieval history and eventually, like Veronica, he put the pieces together and exclaimed, "That's incredible!"

"What is?" asked Shay.

"The St. Vitus Dance was a type of plague during the medieval period—mostly—where those who contracted it would dance for days on end, being quite out of their minds and from what I can remember, they had a terrible hatred for the clergy."

Shay was aghast, "You're kidding!"

"No, I'm not," replied Ted as he thought deeper, connecting the dots between history and the Toprak rehearsals. "Wow, to assume that Hengist and Horsa are stupid is a massive mistake. Somehow, they must have figured out the cause of the disease, or—perhaps the St. Vitus Dance is, like everything else Toprak takes advantage of, just another effect of the Minimum on humans that they leverage."

"So this Toprak rehearsal is a dance—of sorts?" asked Shay, still trying to wrap his head around the harbinger-ization process.

"Well, you could call it that but it is grotesque in the extreme. There is music, which is what gets things moving, then the Emptors progress from a rigorous dance to self-abuse and even mutilation, twisting and contorting their bodies in ways that seem impossible. By the time they reach that stage, they are quite out of their minds of course and they would then do whatever they are commanded to do. But they don't get to that point in a single rehearsal. It takes at least four or five. One rehearsal I saw an Emptor eat the hand off another, who didn't seem the least affected by it."

"Once effected, do the Emptors display symptoms continuously? In the case of the dancer at the inn, it appeared he could sit quietly," asked Shay.

"They can, at least until they hear the music and they then have no choice but to dance. That was Nicole's duty from what I gathered, to conduct rehearsals, mostly in the south, but Toprak apparently perfected their methods in Ireland—I'm guessing they have untold numbers of harbingers there."

"I think you mean here—now," Shay interrupted.

Ted nodded. "Right. But once the rehearsal is complete, for all intents, they are harbingers, hell-bent on killing whatever is in front of them. When it's dark and quiet, they're like a bird in a covered cage and they go into a coma-like state—eyes and mouth wide open, barely breathing—very creepy. Which what was happening in the smokehouse. When it was quiet, he just sat there in the dark. He was most certainly beyond the rehearsal stage."

"How can Toprak control them sufficiently to move them from one place to another if they are so—crazed?" Shay asked as he shook the rain from the hood of his cloak.

"Not sure if you noticed, but the harbinger at the inn had

an iron ring through his wrist," Ted replied.

"Yes, I saw it."

"They can only be controlled by force, physical or mental, and they chain them together using the ring and lead them about like animals. It is very common for harbingers to kill one another, but they have so many Shay, so many—they can afford to lose a few hundred here and there."

"Wait," said Shay, coming to a realization. "If the harbinger at the inn had a ring, then he was already—I guess you could say, employed as a war harbinger. Is that accurate?"

"It is—I was just thinking the same thing, but the strange thing is, how did he get loose. I mean, he didn't tear the ring from his wrist—which I've seen happen before. Maybe he was left behind?"

Shay thought for a moment, and it then occurred to him that perhaps all harbingers were not equal. "Maybe he fled the battlefield. The inn was only about four miles from the beach, certainly within walking distance. Maybe he remembered who he was."

Ted considered the thought but he had seen a lot of harbingers and not a one of them had a non-violent thought, to say nothing of knowing who or where they were. But, it was the only plausible explanation for now and he replied with a shrug and said, "Maybe."

Looking up, Shay saw his Commander waiting along the roadside for him and he realized it had been several hours since they last talked and they must have traveled over five miles, he also realized that he was very hungry.

"Your Majesty, we are just coming up on Rowen and the men are worn. May I suggest we pause for breakfast and a brief rest before entering Conwy," said the Commander.

"How far-off is Conway Commander?" asked Shay.

"Just under two miles I believe Your Majesty."

"Very well Commander. Stop at the next most convenient place for a small fire, hopefully somewhere we can get out of this damn rain."

The Commander thanked Shay, saluted and then disappeared into the fog toward the front of the detachment. England was the only place Shay had ever been where it could rain and be foggy at the same time, something unheard of elsewhere in the world and he cursed under his breath while drawing in his cloak tighter. He then turned to Ted and asked, "Quickly before we stop and no longer have our privacy, did you ever learn how Toprak is able to control the harbingers? What does history say about the St. Vitus Dancers, were they controlled by someone?"

Ted sighed, not wanting to talk about Toprak's evil ability to control things. It was the very reason he believed that nothing could prevail over them but, it was probably time Shay understood what he was facing since there was a very good chance that before noon tomorrow, he would experience it first-hand. "Let me preface what I am about to tell you that it may make you lose hope," Ted said as he looked over at Shay, waiting for a response.

Without hesitation, Shay nodded soberly and said, "To borrow one of Veronica's favorite lines, 'I'm not made of glass' Theodore. I would rather swallow the barb wire of truth than suffocate on the sweet aroma of ignorance."

Ted smiled as he thought about Veronica. She was truly an amazing woman and he wondered at how she had emerged from Gus's young, attractive intern to a pillar of society, the Queen, who gave even himself and Shay strength as they rode through Gwydyr Forest toward an uncertain dawn. "Nicole and I spent a lot of time together in Dover, always at night…"

"Nice!" interjected Shay.

"No, not like that—well, not always like that anyway. She had to stay out of sight of course so we would meet at the Belle Pub and then end up at the castle. Looking back on it now, I can see I was being played. Toprak needed information about In Spem and especially Jess, Matthew, Gus—hell everybody. It goes back to the whole Anglo-Saxon blood thing, which every member of In Spem has as you know. I'm sorry Shay but I certainly told her more than I should have. I was in a bad place and—I have a drinking problem and I broke my ten year sobriety, in a very bad way."

Shay nodded. "I knew about your alcohol thing, everybody does. Everyone on the committee that is. Gus confided in all of us after he made that public drunkenness charge go away for you. But before you think him impertinent, he thought it important that we support you in your sobriety."

Shay's words surprised Ted. He had always thought everyone would think less of him but as he reflected, their knowledge about it didn't change anything, in fact, they supported him without judgment. These were his true friends and he shuttered within himself at how he almost betrayed all of them to, quite literally, the devil. Knowing that his friends knew about his darkest secret was liberating like going to confession and he took courage.

"Horsa is the power behind Toprak, but I'm sure you guessed that."

"Power perhaps but I had always thought Hengist was the brains," said Shay.

"That was probably true before, but Horsa is not to be denied his rites. That's R-I-T-E not R-I-G-H-T. He is, as I mentioned, very evil. Nicole says that during the Russian wars, he found someone who taught him magic of the darkest sort. She claimed that there are degrees of skill and that each degree requires the accomplishment of darker and darker deeds. Each degree is marked on his right palm by a deep scar, after all five degrees are attained, they combine to make an inverted five-point star—and it's true, I've seen it. She says Horsa was reluctant to complete the last degree since there is no easy return from it, but it apparently happened in Vancouver and thousands of people died during the deed—all at once."

"All at once?" Shay asked, amazed and inwardly terrified.

"That's what I was told and from what I have seen Horsa do, I am compelled to believe it. Through the power that he wields, he is able to control the harbingers, though only when they are within a certain proximity from what I understand." Ted paused and then shook his head in amazement, recalling more about the history of St. Vitus plague. "In the dark ages, they believed that the cause of the St. Vitus Dance was the devil—of course—and that he controlled them. The coincident similarities are uncanny!"

"Maybe they're not coincidences," said Shay, thinking out loud and then changing the course of the discussion. "Go back to the control thing. What happens when Horsa doesn't have proximal control over them, are they freed?"

"No, not hardly. The diagnosis of harbinger is a terminal one. The harbinger at the inn was rogue and you saw how it was hell-bent on killing anything it laid eyes on. All Horsa does is channel and direct their aggression, which seems to be a common theme in everything thing he does."

The detachment had stopped a hundred yards ahead under a roof fragment of an old barn and when they arrived, Shay dismounted and told Ted to stay where he was. Shay wanted to continue their conversation out of earshot of his men and he walked over to the small fire and returned with two cups of tea and bread. The tea was healing on such a cold morning and for a few minutes, they were quiet, warming their hands on the sides of their pewter cups. Then speaking softly, Shay asked, "What else can Horsa do?"

Ted looked around to make sure they were alone and then stepped a little closer and said, "You heard about the shape-mutation in Maidstone. A fenrir is only one of many forms he can assume, however he can only take on a dark shape, such as a fenrir."

Shay blew across the top of his cup, sending steam up over his head as he asked, "What constitutes a dark shape?"

"Anything can be dark when it is animated with evil intent, even, if not especially, man." Ted then pointed to the eastern skyline in amazement which made Shay turn to see that it was a deep, violent orange signaling the rising of the sun. As it continued to rise, it illuminated a long, thin, blood red cloud. It was spectacular and caused everyone to pause from their tea and take notice. Conwy was less than two hours north of their position and after his long talk with Ted during their night ride, he was completely afraid of what he would find there. It was one thing to purse a ferocious army, but to purse one that wielded such surreal power as Toprak's was, well futile and he wondered if he had made a mistake in following Toprak to Conwy. He had only fifty men and while they were among the best England had, they would be insignificant in the face of Horsa and his harbinger army.

CHAPTER 7

THE SEVEN

Shay's detachment rode single file through the Conwy Upper Gate, making their way toward the Castle at the opposite end of the walled village. The streets were deserted with not even the sound of a distant dog barking, just the lonely wind blowing off the north sea. Shay led his long procession of armed men down the narrow streets as the sound of hoofs on cobblestones echoed off the walls of the medieval buildings, certainly loud enough to arouse attention, but the further they progressed into the village, the quieter it became and the thinner their hope.

At every turn, Shay desperately clung to his fragile faith, hoping that the village had taken refuge in the castle and that they would find them all safe with the Queen or at worst, besieged by Toprak. With every step, he convinced himself that would be the best he could hope for and he could then wait for Riley to return with the remainder of the army and give Toprak flight. When they came closer to the castle, Shay had so completely convinced himself that he was right, he drew his sword, certain that at any moment they would see war harbingers in the streets. He then raised his hand, silently ordering the detachment to stop as the sound of hooves dissipated between the empty buildings. With his hand still raised, he listened for the sound of an enemy army, but there was nothing. He turned his head several times trying to ascertain if the sound he heard were distant voices or just the mournful wind sowing the seeds of hopelessness.

With apprehension, Shay dismounted and silently motioned for Ted and his Commander to follow him and they made their way toward the Castle. They hadn't progressed far when they began to see blackened and chard buildings, the evidence of a great fire that, from the smell, was less than a few days old. However, as they walked further, every building was progressively more chard until everything including the cobblestones under their feet were black and covered in ash.

The Commander, who had been previously stationed at Conwy during its reconstruction, motioned that the Castle was on the next block and Shay, with his hope nearly extinguished, nodded and peered around the corner. Just as the Commander had said, Conwy Castle stood just beyond their secluded position. Its majestic towers pushed upwards into the sky, powerful and intimidating just as it had for nearly five hundred years but as his eyes followed the outline of the walls downward, the nightmare he envisioned and feared all night while talking to Ted was unfolding. Not having ever been to Conwy Castle, he first thought the fortress was made of black stone, but it quickly became apparent that, like the rest of the village, it had fallen into the hands of a very great and massive fire.

As he scanned the wasted scene from the Castle mound, down to where he was standing, everything was charcoal, not even a single blade of grass broke the black landscape. He then stopped breathing when he realized that the ashes surrounding the castle consisted of mostly bodies, black skeletons, heaped upon the earth as far as he could see. He slowly turned from the diabolic scene and sank to his knees. There was at last, no hope left in his soul and he knew that whoever was in Conwy was certainly dead, including Veronica. Whatever happened here was brutal and extremely thorough, a Toprak signature, ensuring nothing was left alive, not even a stray dog. From Shay's response, Ted and the Commander didn't need to look to know what he had seen, but when they stepped out into the street, they were speechless. The dark and threatening skies above Conwy threw an even heavier shroud over an already burdensome scene as they progressed through the ashes toward the Castle.

Ted lifted his cloak over his mouth to avoid breathing the rancid black dust and carefully guided his horse through the mounds of bodies, picking his way as best he could, trying not to step on the black bones that shattered under their horses hooves. The slaughter was immense and as they came to the entrance of the Castle, the detachment dismounted and began scouting for alternate ways into the castle since everything that was made of wood, like the drawbridge, was consumed. The Commander approached the entrance where Shay and Ted were standing and without a word, threw a grappling hook over the castle wall, swung on the rope across the wide ditch, then threw the line back to Shay.

Once inside, the scene was the same. Everything that could be burned was, which included every living thing. As they passed the stables, Ted noticed that Toprak hadn't even taken the horses as plunder, their black skeletons lying in a heap where they stood in their stalls. The only thing they found within the castle walls was ash, bodies, black stone and the bones of a single harbinger, which was identifiable by the iron ring between its radius and ulna bones in the wrist. The further Shay progressed into the castle, the more angry he became until he saw something shine in the ashes near the inner ward gates. Picking it up, the growing rage within him became complete as he held in his hands, the golden crown of the Queen, found near the harbinger bones. The thought of what happened in the very place where he now stood was more than he could bear and in torment, he picked up the harbinger skull and threw it, shattering it against the wall as he cried, "DAMN YOU HORSA!" He then fell to his knees and wept with Veronica's crown in his hands.

The thought of the Queen dead was defeating in the extreme for everyone, but none more than Shay and Ted, who had lost a woman they adored and had known more fully than anyone except for maybe Gus. It was the second time in three days Shay had arrived too late and found himself mourning among the remains that Toprak left in their wake. A heavy blanket of powerlessness fell upon the entire detachment, robbing them of all hope which was manifest in their collective, strangled silence. For Shay, his sorrow and defeat quickly gave way to anger and with incensed rage, he stood up and began kicking the harbinger remains in front of him, cursing all of Toprak, vowing to kill every last one of them. He continued to kick the charred bones until they were scarcely more than powder. Ted then walked over and wrapped his arms tightly around his friend.

For several hours, the only sound in the Castle and surrounding country was the howling wind that mourned the loss of the city and the country's Queen. In the late afternoon, the dark clouds began to drop their rain again and the Commander ordered for a canopy to be erected within the walls where the chapel once stood since it provided the best break from the wind. Ted and Shay sat with their backs against the wall mostly in silence, punctuated with laments of disbelief.

"It's not enough to just kill for Toprak is it?" cursed Shay.

"*Evil is as evil does*, as Jess always said. They must humiliate, desecrate and spit on God," replied Ted.

After another long span of silence, Ted placed his hand on Shay's shoulder and asked, "You going to be OK brother?"

Shay took a deep breath and shuttered as he let it out, "I'm breathing but I don't know why. Are any of us going to be OK after this?"

From where Ted was sitting, he could see out in to the outer ward of the castle and he thought he could see more signs of harbingers in the ashes and he at last concluded that he wasn't imagining it. He slowly got to his feet with a grunt, not because of physical fatigue but from emotional devastation, and he walked out into the courtyard. His suspicion was right and he easily collected a dozen or more iron rings out of the ashes within a six foot radius. As he stood in the rain, looking at the collection in his hands, it finally occurred to him why there were so many harbingers among the dead and why everything was burned beyond recognition. He slowly turned and walked back to the canopy and dropped the iron rings at Shay's feet and said, "Most of the bodies in the ashes are harbingers, not Englishmen. In fact, it appears that for every one of ours, there are at least twenty of them."

Shay looked up at Ted confused. "What does that mean? It doesn't make any sense."

"Actually it does, if you understand Toprak." Ted said as he sat back down next to Shay, picking up an iron ring and turning it several times in his fingers, almost as if it was something familiar to him. "This was a harbinger ignition."

"A what?" asked Shay, "They ignite too?"

"Yes, but not on their own. Nicole briefly mentioned it

once but then refused to say anything more about it. I got the feeling she had said more than she should have and at the time, not trying to gather information about Toprak, I forgot about it," Ted paused, "You're going to be very displeased with me but, after what I tell you, I think you will agree it is meaningless."

Shay looked at Ted in disbelief shaking his head, wondering how he could have so completely betrayed all of them and he prepared himself for more bad news.

"I'm sorry but I mentioned to Nicole that we had created a mixture of gun powder that would ignite."

"You what?!" asked Shay, incensed at Ted's stupidity.

"I didn't give her the formula mind you, because she told me that Toprak didn't need gun powder."

Shay raised his hands and shook them in frustration. "Are you a moron! Just the fact that Toprak now knows we can produce powder at will is dangerous enough!"

Ted was trying to be humble and repentant but Shay's anger irritated him and he retorted, "It's no big surprise buddy, they knew we had it at the Battle of the Thames."

"Yes, but that was three years ago and right after the fall of the Minimum. We needed Toprak to think that we just got lucky and found some old powder. It was paramount that they not know we could make the stuff. What the hell Ted?!"

Ted didn't reply and just looked down at his feet as he pulled his knees up to his chest and concluded that Shay was right. Toprak's knowledge of the powder would allow them to be prepared for it, which could have certainly accounted for the complete rout of the army on the beach and now Conwy.

"We had hoped that the guns along the M6 wall would be a great surprise but that party will never happen now. The Toprak army that was here has in all likelihood, continued to Northumbria to hem Gus in on two sides, giving him only one retreat, northward—which is a dead end once they get to Scotland." Shay shook his head in disgust and said, "Powder was our only hope. I can see now why you didn't have any."

After a few minutes of heavy silence, Shay pulled his dagger from his belt and stabbed it into the stone floor between them, wedging the blade into the crumbling mortar and said, "It's time you came clean Ted. I need to know what you have betrayed to your beloved Nicole—and everything she told you, though I doubt her tongue was as loose as yours."

Ted was once again penitent and he replied quietly, "That's it I swear."

"Not hardly, you've yet to explain what a damn harbinger ignition is!"

"Except for that," Ted said apologetically. "When I asked why Toprak didn't need gun powder, she said Horsa could ignite a harbinger at any time and that it was much more effective than a single ball powered by gun powder. In fact, she laughed when she told me as if gun powder was a pathetic second to what Horsa could do."

Shay pointed to the surrounding Castle and replied sarcastically, "Have you looked around? I'd say she was on to something."

Ted nodded humbly with a sigh.

"So, it's not bad enough that they are all hell-crazy, now every one of them is a potential bomb. That's bloody fantastic!"

Shay was beyond frustrated and for the first time, he understood why Gus and the King had imprisoned him. He did believe Ted was sorry for what he had done but he couldn't ignore the heavy toll he had brought upon the Kingdom and if it had been anyone else, he might have already been hung for his crimes.

Just then the Commander approached and saluted respectfully saying, "Your Majesty."

Before responding, Shay got to his feet and took several steps away from Ted mostly out of frustration than anything else, but he also didn't want him to hear what the Commander had to say just in case it was sensitive. Shay was at a difficult crossroads and he was unsure of what to do. He believed Ted could be trusted to do the right thing in battle like he did at the inn, but what concerned Shay the most was how the army would receive him. The night Ted arrived in camp at Gwynant Lake, he vouched for him and it was only his word that kept the detachment from hanging him. Riley would be in Conwy with two-thousand men tomorrow and he didn't know if he could ensure his safety if he was not right by Ted's side. With this heavy burden, Shay finally nodded for the Commander to continue.

"As you requested, we have completed our sweep of the village and found no survivors except for possibly within the church. Every door is bolted and despite our attempts to arouse the inhabitants, we neither saw nor heard anything. I commanded that the doors should not be forced without your approval."

"Thank you Commander," replied Shay as he motioned for him to walk with him. They walked out of the burned-out chapel toward the courtyard and into the rain that had backed off to a light drizzle. When Shay was sure they were out of earshot of Ted, he said, "Select three men to attend us to the church, then place a guard of six at the moat entrance and two on every tower." Shay then leaned in and whispered, "The remainder can get some rest in the chapel, but I want a very close and discrete eye on Ted at all times. He is not to go anywhere unattended. I will tell him that I have ordered a guard to be about his person for his safety but it is more for our safety and the safety of the Kingdom. Is this clear?"

The Commander nodded with satisfaction, pleased that Shay had finally come to his senses about his friend and he smiled. "It shall be done Your Majesty," he said, saluting.

Shay made his way back to the chapel to find Ted helping himself to a cup of tea from the make-shift kitchen Humphrey had set-up at the front of the burned-out chapel, using the alter as a table. When Ted saw Shay approach, he asked him if he would like a cup, but Shay shook his head. "I'm riding out to investigate the church in the center of the village. It apparently didn't sustain much fire damage and every door is bolted fast from the inside. We may find some survivors."

"Oh, I'll go with you," replied Ted, setting his empty cup on the alter and pulling his cloak up over his shoulders.

Shay placed his hand on Ted's forearm, stopping him from putting on his cloak and shook his head. "I really need you to stay put—for your safety and mine."

Ted looked at Shay in surprise, unsure of what he meant exactly but for the first time, he saw Shay as the commander of a small and very well-trained army and he decided to not push the issue. Ted raised his hands in the air as if he were at the point of a sword and replied somewhat irritated, "OK! Fine."

Shay almost responded but then decided there was nothing left to say. He looked at Ted for a few seconds longer then shook his head and sighed just as the Commander motioned they were ready to ride.

The church was just beyond the blast zone and compared to the black landscape around the castle, the green grass of the grounds was startlingly beautiful and Shay and his men dismounted in the churchyard then made their way to the nearest door. Just as the Commander had said, it was bolted from the inside and despite their long pounding, there was no response. They made their way around the church, trying every door and peering into windows, but it truly appeared that there was no one inside.

"There must be," said Shay. "The doors are bolted from the inside. Unless—they are now dead," he added as he thought through the most-obvious scenario.

Shay took several steps back and motioned for the Commander to break down the door but after several attempts, the door remained secure, since it was made from three-inch solid oak. All four men then tried together, but it was no use and the Commander determined that unless they had a battering ram, they would not gain entry. They then began searching the churchyard for anything that could double for a battering ram, or at least a crowbar, and Shay spotted a strange grave that was enclosed with iron bars. The church was at least twelfth century and Shay reasoned that the iron just might be rusted enough to pull apart and be used as a crowbar, but when he reached the grave, he froze. The iron enclosure stood about three feet off the ground but it was more than just a fence. It was completely enclosed over the top and all sides as if it were meant to keep something from getting out. But what made the hair on Shay's neck and arms stand on end was the inscription on the grave—only three words, *We are seven.*

The iron enclosure was very secure and must have been buried deep in the ground since Shay could not lift it, even with all his strength. He then noticed that there wasn't a gravestone inside the enclosure and even though the grass grew healthily around the enclosure, it didn't grow inside it. The enclosure had seven iron crosses along the top and was unmistakably built to keep something in. But despite all that, the most startling thing about it was the inscription—resonating with the words of his grandfather who said, "The hope of England resides with The Seven." Shay knew it was not a mere coincidence and that whatever his grandfather meant, it had everything to do with this grave, making it more important than ever to access the church and find the burial records or someone who knew more about it.

While he was staring in disbelief, two of the men walked up behind him and began to comment on the strange grave, but after several random comments, he determined that they knew nothing and he decided that for now, he would keep what he knew a secret. Shay then saw the Commander walking toward the door with a rod from the churchyard fence and began prying at it, with some success. They all returned to the door and watched the Commander pry away the wood near the jamb and eventually revealed the bolt. He then ordered everyone to push against the door while he pried the bold backwards and after the count of three, the door swung open and the three soldiers fell on their faces inside the dark church.

With less than an hour of daylight remaining, Shay stepped inside behind the three men who had just gotten up off the floor and were in the process of lighting torches. The church was extremely quiet and if anyone was inside, they were certainly hiding, unsure of who had just broken in. The Commander handed a torch to Shay and they all walked into the chapel as the other three men were ordered to spread out around the King in the event of an ambush or similar surprise. The light from their torches danced off the high ceilings, casting long shadows into the dark corners and from what Shay could see, the church was completely empty.

"Hello? Is there anyone here?" Shay finally yelled. "We are here in the name of the King. You need not be afraid." His words echoed off the stone walls and reverberated down the dark corridors and then returned, creating an eerie playback as if something had yelled them back in a bewitched tone. The Commander drew his sword and the other three men quickly followed as they made their way toward the furthest corners of the church. If there were anyone lurking in the darkness after they had the opportunity to announce themselves, they were most-likely unfriendly and Shay drew his sword as well and followed behind his men. After thirty minutes, they had explored every inch of the church and had found no one, which explained why no one responded, but it didn't explain how the doors became locked from the inside. Then the Commander discovered something that explained all three.

"Your Majesty," he called from the front of the chapel, illuminating the crucifix with his torch.

Shay walked from the back of the chapel and after reaching the spot where the Commander stood, he looked up to see the priest hanging from a rope by the neck. The locked doors and the ladder leaning up against the crucifix provided enough evidence to suggest that the priest had committed suicide. Judging by the grotesque break of his neck, the Commander determined that he had climbed the ladder, then up the crucifix itself before jumping, leaving his broken body to hang next to the crucified Jesus.

"Cut him down," said Shay with a sigh. "And before we are tempted to judge him, let us remember he most-likely saw hell-fire, damnation and the devil outside these windows last night."

The Commander and the other three men found some shovels in the gardener's shed behind the church and while Shay looked for a record book in the church office, they buried the priest in the churchyard. There were many record books on the shelves and after thumbing through them all, Shay grabbed the oldest one and made his way out to the graveyard and joined his men. They were just packing down the mound when he walked up behind them and he offered a short but respectful prayer on the grave, asking for God's forgiveness on behalf of the priest who chose to take his own life rather than have it burned in the fires of hell. As they mounted up, the Commander noticed Shay trying to conceal the record book in his cloak but said nothing.

When they returned to the Castle, everything appeared to be in fine order especially since Humphrey had cooked their first full meal in days and Shay, Ted and the Commander sat down to a thick beef stew, hard bread and ale. Humphrey had created a table out of two barrels and some planks he found down near the river and several small crates that were not consumed in the fire to sit on. While the rest of the men ate in shifts, Shay tried on several occasions to lighten the mood between he and Ted but without success. It wasn't until all the men had eaten and only he and Ted were left at the table with a nearly extinguished fat candle between them. Shay had nearly given up trying to talk to Ted but from out of the silence, Ted finally said, "I don't blame you, I want you to know. I would have done the same. Though, it still hurts that I don't have your trust."

Shay nodded with a slight smile of relief. "Thank you Ted. I might have over-reacted after hearing about the harbinger thing. It just seemed like for every hope, Toprak had a remedy for it."

"And indeed they do," replied Ted defeated.

"Except for Jess, and…" Shay stopped himself from saying anything about The Seven and didn't finish his sentence, which made Ted curious what he was going to say.

"Jess and what?" he asked.

"Did you hear about the battle between the King, Gus and Veronica?" Shay said, changing the subject.

Ted looked at Shay a little sideways, knowing that he had intentionally derailed their conversation, but following his lead he replied, "I… think I remember Nicole saying something about Veronica getting lucky again and something about Jess. I was eaves-dropping of course, they did not tell me directly. Whatever it was that Jess did, it put Horsa in pretty good lather and earned him a spot on the Toprak most abhorrent list."

Shay looked back at Ted surprised. "I should think you are their most abhorrent, you certainly know enough to be a liability—something Toprak doesn't usually have."

“I suppose,” replied Ted. “But they know I’m no threat. I’m not extraordinary in any way and they truly believe that it doesn’t matter if the King and all of England knows their plans and capabilities. Besides, they currently believe that I’m out of my mind right now.”

“What do you mean?”

Ted held out his arm and pushed his sleeve up to his elbow. He then held it near the candle. Shay leaned over and saw a round and very deep wound in Ted wrist that looked as if it had only just stopped bleeding. Ted then turned his wrist over to reveal an identical wound on the back and Shay looked up at Ted in disbelief.

“I was never a harbinger,” Ted said before Shay had a chance to scold him again.

“When I learned that Gus was not dead, I started to plan my escape but Nicole figured something was not right with me and began asking questions. She also followed me and saw that I was investigating the exits to the Tower and when she asked me about it, I of course denied it. I then decided that I would just hide in the dancer barracks and then just walk out the front gate when they were deployed. It almost worked but Horsa saw that something wasn’t right with me and once he learned who I was, he had Nicole put a ring in my wrist. Horsa’s plan was to make me a dancer but…” Ted stopped and quickly realized that he couldn’t tell Shay how he really escaped and still gain his trust. The truth was, Nicole secreted him in with the morning dancer deployment the night before and then made sure Horsa was distracted when they marched chained together through the gates. Nicole claimed that she would simply tell Horsa that she actually turned him into a dancer. He knew that Shay would never understand his relationship with Nicole, so he made up an alternate conclusion to his tale before Shay thought his short pause was suspect.

Shay stared at Ted in disbelief at what he had suffered and he slowly began to think that he might be able to trust him after all. Despite everything, Ted was an Anglo-Saxon, even if he were the weakest blood in council—something Ted did not know—and that had to account for something. He looked down at Ted's wrist again, thinking of the unimaginable pain he must have been in as he related what happened at Wales and the war against Veronica. He couldn't provide any details since what he knew about it, he had heard from General Clancy.

"That now makes sense why Horsa is so preoccupied with Jess," replied Ted, shaking his head in awe and for the first time finding a sliver of hope. "Maybe we do have a chance. I believed that only Toprak could command the supernatural. Although, history says that the good guys don't always win."

Shay paused, struggling whether or not he should tell Ted about the conversation with his grandfather, but he at last concluded that since Veronica was most-likely dead, Ted was the Kingdom's foremost expert on medieval history. If The Seven truly was England's hope, he had no choice but to trust Ted since it appeared that destiny had brought him to the grave in the churchyard and they didn't have any time to lose. Shay looked around the table to see if anyone were close enough to hear their conversation and discovered six soldiers keeping an eye on Ted, just as he had ordered.

"You men are relieved," he called, as they saluted and disappeared into the darkness of the castle, no doubt to get some rest, as a hazy, full moon was rising above the eastern walls, shining through the clouds. He then turned to Ted in earnest and said, "I am not ready to trust you, but against my better judgment, I have no choice since I desperately need your help."

Ted looked back in surprise and wondered what he could possibly say that would relieve Shay's anxiety concerning him but he could think of nothing profound so he placed his hand on Shay's forearm and said, "You certainly can. Perhaps this is just the thing that will allow me to prove it."

Shay nodded slowly and began to speak. "I have reason to believe that what I am about to tell you is the very thing that will allow us to defeat Toprak once and for all." But before he continued, he looked Ted in the eye, hoping he would not find a traitor. It was a risky and very difficult decision but he reasoned once again that time was ticking away on England and he took a deep breath. "I saw my grandfather again when I was imprisoned in Norwich and we spoke."

Ted wasn't at all surprised at Shay seeing a ghost since the paranormal was normal these days and he just nodded as if it was the most common thing in the world.

"He told me that the hope of England resides with The Seven," said Shay as he then sat back and waited for Ted to have an epiphany as if he had just lit a fuse.

Ted stared back at Shay thinking that he had missed something, but when Shay didn't say anything more, he replied confused, "The Seven? What is that? I'm getting the feeling like that should mean something to me and I'm feeling a little stupid."

Of course this isn't going to be easy, Shay thought as he leaned forward and began to whisper. "I have no idea what it means but while at the church tonight, I came across a grave. It was covered with an iron cage, but with no tombstone. The only inscription was a simple wooden plaque that read, *We are Seven.*

Shay could see Ted's mind now running a hundred miles an hour as he dug through everything he knew about Welsh history. His mental research was only broken when he stopped to ask the age of the church and other clarifying details, but to Shay's dismay, Ted finally turned and said, "I have no idea what it means."

Shay then pulled the burial record from under his cloak and set it on the table near the candle. After a brief explanation, he began turning the pages of the medieval book, looking for anything that referenced the odd grave, but after turning the last page, neither of them found anything remotely helpful. Ted sighed in frustration and apologized that he was not much help and he closed the book, rubbing his hand over the worn leather cover in deep thought. He then noticed that the cover seemed to be embossed—rather odd for a book of its age—but lifting his hand, he couldn't see any leatherwork on the cover, nor even a title. He felt the cover again, this time pressing down harder and following the edges of the embossing. He could feel the edges of a rectangle and as he pushed on one edge, it moved under the leather cover. He pulled the book toward him and with his knife, made a long cut at edge of the cover and then shook it until the rectangular object fell out. Due to Ted's brisk shaking, the object fell off the table and onto the dark floor but after feeling around, he picked it up and placed it under the light of the candle. It appeared to be an over-sized playing card until Ted turned it over and dropped it on the table after he saw what it was—a Seven of Swords Tarot card.

CHAPTER 8

THE ASHES OF CONWY

Riley dismounted and stretched his legs while he waited for the scouting party to return. A mudslide had covered the A470 roadway just past Roman Bridge cutting off their passage northward. The slide caused the swollen river to cut a new course, digging a thirty foot deep trench across the narrow canyon. If they could not get passage, they would be forced to backtrack a half-day's journey and then go overland on a more northeastern course to Conwy, similar to the direction Shay had taken two days earlier. His journey to Conwy had already taken a full day longer than anticipated due to the ugly weather and the deep mud that was over eighteen inches in some places.

He walked over to the edge of the ravine and looked down at the wild water below, becoming mesmerized as he watched it cut deeper into the countryside, churning up white foam from the depths of the earth. Looking to his left, there was a small waterfall that cascaded down a shallow outcropping of granite. It ran clear unlike all the other rivers and streams he had encountered over the past few days and he walked toward it while removing his gloves. He filled his cupped hands and lifted them to his nose, smelling for a sweet, woodsy scent, which would indicate the presence of natural menthol—poison. After taking in several deep breaths, he concluded the water was safe and he refilled his hands several times, enjoying the sensation of the cold water down his throat. Throwing the last handful on his face, he dried his hands on his cloak as he studied a curious flower growing near the waterfall. It was sprouting from a vine that looked to be bindweed, but the flower was orange instead of white and it became darker orange toward the center until at the pistols it was blood red. He reached over, plucked the flower and held it to his nose. To his surprise, it had a sharp, spicy smell that reminded him of a cologne he used to wear in a different world before the Minimum. He smiled and placed the flower in his cloak pocket just as the scouting team returned.

"We picked along for at least a quarter mile and conditions only got worse Sir," said the leader of the party. "We may pass with just the men, but never with horse and wagons."

"Well, we'll need those," Riley replied flippantly. "We'd best beat a retreat southwards where the ruins were and then march overland due northeast. With any luck—if we can manage luck today—we should connect with the old A489, which is the path His Majesty took. If we would have just followed in his tracks we'd have made better time."

The members of the scouting party all saluted and began making their way back the main body of the army several hundred yards away as Riley climbed back on his horse mumbling under his breath about their terrible luck and the bitch that hindsight was. Moving a two-thousand man army was painfully slow and as he waited at the rearward for things to get under way, it reminded him of sitting in traffic on the old A12 motorway during his commute from Stratford to Romford every day. For the first time in years, he thought about his former life, when the world was tame and a man could purse his passions at leisure. For a moment, he closed his eyes and could smell once again the heavy chlorine in the air as he always did when he walked into the Aquatics Centre for work. He smiled slightly as he opened his eyes, remembering how much he enjoyed coaching Olympic athletes, and how much he also loved swimming. He had been an Olympic Silver medalist for England in the 2038 Games but since the Minimum, he had only been in water deep enough to swim in once.

An hour later, the rearward finally started to move and he lightly flanked his horse forward, falling in behind the supply wagons. Just past the Roman ruins, a half-mile ahead, he could see a sizable hill and he broke from the formation and rode to the top so that he could get a better lay of the forest. From the top, he could see for at least ten miles and to his relief, he saw the trail that once was the old A498 less than three miles away. He sat for a long time watching the slow, winding snake that was his army, make their way through the Afon River valley and he again thought about swimming, once his only passion in life. In his early college years, he was told that while he was a good swimmer, he would never be great due to his body shape and size. Back then, he was six foot-three and nearly 15 stone, much larger than the other swimmers but he was determined to be great, probably because he was told he couldn't. He remembered being featured on the front page of the newspaper after he had won silver with the headline, *The strongest swimmer alive.* Early on in his Olympic training, his coach drilled into him that he was slower than all the other athletes, which only meant he had to be stronger than all the others. He spent almost as much time in the weight room as he did in the water and consequently when he stood on the blocks before a race, he was a daunting opponent, at six-three and 18 stone of pure aquatic muscle. Where the other swimmers glided through the water, he charged through it with a slash and burn mentality, creating rapids of white water that crashed into the other swimming lanes, a common complaint from competitors who had to swim next to him.

Since the Minimum, his tale was like most, simply trying to get by and survive in a brutal and unforgiving world. At the time of the Minimum destruction, he was at the Centre as usual and he found protection in the water as the building collapsed and burned around him. He was stuck in the water for two days when he finally accepted that no rescue was coming and he began climbing out of the rubble. He was surprised at his strength, even after not eating for two days and he couldn't figure why his swim trunks were so ill-fitting. Like Sir Matthew, the old commander of the Ravenguard, the Minimum had greatly increased his strength and he now stood six-ten and a massive 22 stone.

He reached down and smelled the flower in his pocket again and breathed out slowly, enjoying the memories it brought. Just then, breaking his daydream, his percheron became spooked and jumped forward, causing him to almost lose his balance. As he turned to see what the alarm was, he saw five grey wolves approaching a very easy meal—him. He was about to draw his sword but now that they had both seen each other, the wolves kept their distance—at least for now—and he decided he would be better off to return to the company and he made his way down off the hill and fell in near the middle of the formation.

It wasn't long before they reached the old road that was now only dirt and mud, the concrete and asphalt having been destroyed like the rest of it in the world, but it still made their progress easier, which also meant faster. Being back with his medieval army and the clattering of armor and steel, his remembrances of his former life were truly like a dream of some make-believe land where there was ample food and no war. If he had not lived it, he would consider such memories mere fantasy and a distracting reverie. Why today of all days was he wandering through the visions of his past? Taking a cleansing breath in an attempt to also clear his mind, he looked up and saw an old inn where two roads met and as he drew closer, he could see a man on the side of the road, waving the army on and crossing himself. He turned his horse so that he could be on the side closest to the man as he once again smelled the fragrant flower in his pocket. He pulled it out, realizing that it was the familiar fragrance of the flower that had him falling down memory lane and causing him to drown in the memories of his former career. He was leading an army of two thousand men into battle and on top of everything else, nostalgia was a complication he didn't need. After one last smell, he was about to throw the flower in the mud when he saw a little girl holding onto the man's leg who appeared to be middle-aged. When the little girl saw him, excitement came to her face as if she knew him but as he drew closer, she must have realized she was mistaken and her expression became more sober. When he finally came alongside, he stopped as the army behind him continued their march. Due to the massive size of his horse, the girl was only as tall as his stirrup and he leaned off his saddle to hand her the flower.

"A flower for the most beautiful princess I have seen this whole day," said Riley smiling.

The little girl lit up once again with excitement as she reached out to take the flower—the second time within a week, a knight had given her a gift. Fumbling slightly, she carefully transferred what looked like a coin from one hand to the other and then took the flower. She was obviously very taken with the grand march of the army past her home and especially that one of them would present her with a gift. With a little prompting from the man next to her, she forced a dignified posture, bowed and said, "Thank you kind Sir."

Riley laughed at the unexpected response from a child so young and replied, "Your charm is indeed more powerful than this whole army."

With less than a mile to go before reaching the upper Conwy gate, he rode to the front so that he could slow their progress and send his scouts ahead to discover what was waiting for them within the walls. It was dark before the scouting party returned and Riley saw them coming from a distance, watching their torches growing brighter. He assumed that their lit torches could only mean that all was well and before they even arrived, he ordered the army to move, while he rode out to meet the scouts.

"Is all well in Conwy?" he called out when he was within shouting distance. The look on their faces was difficult to discern and when he came alongside them he asked again, "You found everything well I take it?"

"As well as hell," replied the leader. "The village is deserted, I doubt there is anything living in it but when we saw light from the castle, we made our way there and found the East Angles King and his men—but that is all."

"That is all? What do you mean?" asked Riley now concerned.

"The Commander met us at the ditch and told us that darkness was all that was left of the once great village and Castle of Conwy. He says that Toprak burned everything to stubble—they found nothing alive."

Riley's heart sank. Given the Queen's powerful disposition and her fire in battle, he never once considered that Conwy would be sacked and for several minutes he couldn't speak as the great defeat settled into him as if he were drowning. His heavy thoughts were finally interrupted when one of the scouts asked, "Sir, surely the Commander is mistaken. This was the work of the Celts, not Toprak." The scout was noticeably afraid of the possibility and he laughed nervously and said scoffing, "Toprak, like that could happen."

Riley was never one to sugar coat anything, which was probably the result of a brutally honest swimming coach who never gave him an inch that he didn't earn with his own sweat and blood. He slowly looked up into the eyes of the scout and replied, "It happened and it is now our sacred duty to avenge it. It appears Toprak is back."

Making their way through the village, Riley could smell the heavy smoke still emanating from the ashes and when he came to the Castle walls, he might have wept having seen it before in its glorious renovation, but his thirst for revenge over powered his sorrows and he grit his teeth harder. The last time he was in the Castle was just after the King's marriage to Veronica and he remembered seeing her kiss her husband good-bye in the rain, for the first and last time. In his mind, he remembered how she looked, determined, brave and ever-beautiful. Allowing his heart this privileged memory, a defiant tear finally forced itself down his cheek as his internal mourning grew to a crescendo, while his outward rage exploded into his blood stream. With a single leap, he cleared the wide ditch as adrenaline pulsated through his massive frame, seeking a violent release, which he found in the form of an un-suspecting sentry standing at the gate. Unable to control his rage, he yelled at the top of his lungs and connected his fist with the face of the soldier, knocking him off his feet and throwing him ten yards into the castle keep, unconscious.

Following the sound of voices echoing through the empty

halls, he eventually made his way to the door of the chapel where he found Shay and Ted quietly conversing about the Tarot card—something they had done every night for the past three nights waiting for Riley to arrive. There were also a dozen soldiers sitting around a small fire near the make-shift kitchen laughing and drinking more ale than they should have. When they saw their Captain standing in the doorway, they quickly became sober and stood at attention. The sudden silence in the chapel caused Shay and Ted to pause their discussion and turn around. As they did, they saw Riley's formable frame filling the doorway with a look of great displeasure and a dangerous disposition.

"Comfy are we? So content to only sit whilst our enemy distances themselves from us?" said Riley in a raised and murderous tone.

The men around the fire weren't sure what to say or do, but they figured leaving the chapel, pretending they had somewhere to go was a good move so they saluted and left. Shay sighed and nodded in agreement with Riley, remembering how tormented he was when he first entered the Castle and he motioned for him to sit and have a drink. Shay slid the Tarot card into his cloak as he poured the Captain a cup of ale. Riley sat down with a heavy thud, too tired and irritated to be friendly.

"We've all been where you are when we first entered the Castle—so beside ourselves we couldn't think. But we had the advantage of not having a powerful enough army to purse and we were inclined to stay put and wait for you. An activity that probably saved us from further losses," said Shay calmly.

Riley was about to accuse him of being a coward but then remembered he was talking to the King of East Angles, he forced a slight nod then took a drink.

"It would appear that your suspicion about the Queen is the same as ours, but we believe we have confirmed the worst," Shay said, placing Veronica's crown on the table. "We found it near the inner ward gate, the entire Castle is once again a ruin."

Riley was still too angry to speak rationally and for several minutes he focused on his ale while Shay shared all they knew about the return of Toprak, their potential size and the harbinger ignition. He intentionally left out the discussion of The Seven and the grave, not because he didn't trust Riley, but he didn't want him to know that he had shared something so important with Ted. Instead, he launched into a discussion about where Toprak had gone and what their next move would be just as Riley finished his ale and slammed his pewter cup on the table. He wiped his mouth on his sleeve and then rubbed his hands over his face as he let out a long sigh. "What have you been able to learn about Toprak's direction?" he said focusing on Shay and noticeably ignoring Ted.

The slight was not lost on Shay but he pretended not to notice. "Over the last two days, I sent men into the countryside in every direction, looking for tracks but we have found none, not even with all this mud. I have concluded that all of his war-harbingers were killed in the ignition and he left alone, or with only a small number. Still, there are no tracks leaving to the east or the south, not even a party of one."

"He didn't leave on foot," replied Riley. "He sailed. That's how they retreated from Holy Island after we finally routed them. What about the Queen's ship? I'm guessing it was burned."

Shay looked at Ted and then back at Riley and said, "I was not aware that the Queen had a ship. It is not docked in the river at any rate. What sort of ship was it?"

Riley leaned forward, placing his elbows on the table. "It was a first-rate ship of the line, I forget the number but around a hundred guns and complement of three-hundred men. It was armed to the hilt last I saw it. They were just painting the name on her."

"So it wasn't something we could have missed then?" asked Shay.

Riley shook his head.

"Then maybe Veronica escaped!" exclaimed Ted.

Riley already disliked Ted and hearing him be disrespectful to the Queen—a woman he adored—by calling her by her first name, he reached over and grabbed Ted's arm and stabbed his dagger into the table next to it. "Living or dead, you will show respect to the crown of England!" he said looking into Ted's eyes and gripping his arm tighter. "She is Her Majesty, the Queen, even for the sorry likes of a red-handed traitor like you!"

Shay was stunned at Riley's fierce loyalty and after a brief shocked pause, he placed his hand on of Riley's, patting it. "It's nothing personal Captain. It's still hard for those of us who knew her so well, so many years ago to refer to her correctly. We shall try harder. I assure you, he meant no disrespect."

Riley released his grip and threw Ted's arm back at him as if it were unattached, still glaring at him. He then turned to Shay, once again, intentionally ignoring Ted and said, "I'm sure Toprak claimed the ship for a prize. Given the state of the world, I'm certain there is no equal."

Ted started to shake his head in disagreement, but was slow to speak until Shay and Riley turned to him. "I've never known Toprak to take any spoils from a battle. They destroy."

"Biz-yok," said Shay, remembering the Toprak war cheer before going into battle at the General's ranch in Montana.

"Biz-yok?" asked Riley.

"It's a long story, but we were saved once by Toprak in America and before they rode out to face our enemy, the United States army, Horsa's troops roared *Biz-yok,*" replied Shay.

"It means 'we destroy' in Turkish," added Ted.

Shay shook his head, still in disbelief after all these years over the absolute carnage in the General's pasture. "And they certainly did destroy that night—every last man was killed at least twice—complete desecration."

"If what you say is true about Toprak and if there truly is not a wreck at the bottom of the river, the Queen might still be alive," said Riley with the first glimmer of hope in his voice since arriving.

"Well, that remains to be seen. We did not know to look for a sunken ship in the river," replied Ted, dampening Riley's optimism.

Shay looked upward at the night sky and quietly said, "Please God let their not be a ship at the bottom of that river."

With the roof destroyed, the stars shown down upon the Castle with the bright streak of the Milky Way slicing across the sky while a lazy late summer moon was barely visible above the eastern walls. The night was warmer than it had been the last few nights, now that the storm had abated and the winds shifted eastward, blowing out to sea.

When the morning broke, Shay, Riley and Ted made their way down the rocky beach of the estuary and progressed toward the inlet where the Conwy River flowed into the Irish Sea, the place where the Queen anchored her ship in four fathoms of water. At the end of the peninsula where a thick grove of trees grew down to the water, the Queen tethered her pinnace to a small dock less than twenty feet long. Riley had escorted her there several times so he knew its precise location and when they reached it, they were all dismayed to see her pinnace still securely tied to it.

"She could have swam to the ship," said Ted, trying to revive hope. "How far out was she anchored?"

Riley walked to the end of the dock, staring at the place where the Queen's ship once stood and said, "Fifty yards. Certainly a swimmable distance for even an average swimmer, but not in a dress."

Shay laughed slightly, thinking about how practical Veronica had always been and said, "A dress would not have stopped her. The Veron…" He paused and corrected himself, "The Queen I know would swim naked if it meant beating Toprak. She has certainly never stood on principle nor pageantry as long as I have known her."

"How long *have* you known her?" asked Riley, longing to hear more about the Queen from her closest friends.

Shay looked at Ted for validation as he thought. "Let's see.

Four, five. Yes, five years, perhaps five and a half. We all met her at the same time when Gus hired her as his summer intern, we were all immediately very taken with her."

Riley nodded with a distant look and then pulled off his shirt and sat down on the end of the dock, slipping off his boots. He then stripped down to the skin and dove in, leaving Shay and Ted wondering what he was doing. They watched as he swam further and further out, amazed at not only his speed, but also the rapids he created with every stroke. Then after he was out about fifty yards, he stopped while treading water and after a deep breath, he dove strait down.

"What is it?" asked Shay, responding to Ted's quiet huff.

"Oh, nothing. Just analyzing one of the many idioms in the English language."

"Honestly Ted, between you and Veronica, your minds never stop." Shay laughed at himself, "I was just thinking how the clouds look like a pony."

After a short pause, Shay asked, "What *is* an idiom anyway?" trying to keep his mind off the very real prospect that Veronica's ship was at the bottom of the Conwy River.

"Well, the word *idiom* is Latin, meaning special property but the specific idiom I was trying to remember the origin of was the term *red-handed.*

"As in, caught red-handed?" Asked Shay.

"Yes. We all use idioms but sadly most people are not even aware of what they mean anymore. For example, to be *caught red-handed* meant you still had blood on your hands when you were discovered killing someone. I believe the term originated in Scotland if I'm not mistaken—1430's during the reign of James I."

Shay was just about to say what a random thought that was until he remembered Riley accusing him of being a red-handed traitor last night. "Ted, I'm sure Riley didn't mean to suggest that you had anything to do with the sacking of Conwy and the," Shay choked slightly, "the death of Veronica."

Ted got to his feet and scanned the area where Riley dove down starting to be concerned that he hadn't surfaced. "Oh, I know. Like I said, most people mindlessly repeat their favorite phrases without considering their true meaning," Ted replied waving his hand as if it was nothing.

Shay and Ted did not know Riley's tale nor did they know that they were watching the second fastest swimmer in the world but they were starting to be concerned. They waited for another two long minutes before he finally broke through the surface, spitting water out of his mouth and not appearing to be out of breath. "Good news! There's no sign of wreckage on the bottom," he yelled before swimming back.

When he reached the dock, Ted extended his hand, offering to pull him out of the water and onto the dock but Riley refused. He swam several feet away and held onto the dock, preparing to pull himself out but Ted stepped in front, blocking him.

"I'm not what you think I am and I'm certainly not your red-handed enemy," he said with his hand extended showing that his hand was not red.

Riley tried to ignore him again as he moved to another place on the dock but Ted persistently stood in his way, insisting that Riley hear him. "I didn't choose Toprak, they chose me. They led me to believe that all my friends were dead, or would be soon and that I could do nothing to help them. Even the King led me to believe you were all soon dead. When I saw your grief and anger last night, it reminded me of myself, except I didn't have my friends around me to build hope. I finally concluded that what I did didn't matter—until I learned that Gus was alive. When I learned that, I figured everything else they told me was also a lie, which is when I fled. I already died for my friends once and I would do it again without a thought," Ted said while continuously extending his hand in friendship.

Riley finally looked up and slowly extended his hand while Ted pulled him onto the dock. Riley rolled onto his back, staring up at the blue sky and for several minutes he was lost in his own thoughts. He had forgotten how much he loved to swim and he couldn't help but wonder what his time was, certainly slower than his average. He then sat up and while reaching for his pants, he said, "There's more good news. The Queen," he stopped as he just thought of another possibility and then continued. "or whoever sailed away in the Queen's ship, cut the cables. Both anchors are sitting on the bottom and one of them was dragged for about thirty yards. Whoever sailed out of here did so in great haste."

"For now, I'm going to believe it was V… the Queen who sailed that ship," said Ted. "I have to believe it."

Riley looked at Ted and nodded slowly while putting on his boots and said, "Agreed."

Returning to the Castle, the Commander, who was Riley's

number one, met them at the ditch where the draw bridge used to be and saluted. "We shall be ready to move within the hour Captain."

"Very well Commander. See that a mount is made ready for Theodore here. He rides with myself and the King," replied Riley as the Commander saluted again and disappeared into the castle keep.

Ted smiled but Riley was not looking at him. He was standing on the edge of the ditch marveling that he jumped it the night before and he reached for the rope and swung across, followed Ted and Shay. When they walked into the chapel, they saw Humphrey packing up the last of the kitchen and he bowed, acknowledging the presence of the King and presenting the three men with the last of the morning tea. While they stood around the smoldering fire that was more smoke than flame, Shay asked Riley, "So, where are we going?"

Riley bowed apologetically and replied, "Forgive me Your Majesty. I had planned to tell you but the Commander spoke out of turn."

Shay ensured Riley that it was nothing and that he completely trusted his leadership. "I'm just wondering how much to pack," he said trying to lighten the mood.

"What I meant to tell you was the directions the General gave me when we rode out of here a fortnight ago. He said that if the unthinkable happened—which is has, to march with whatever army I had to Northumbria. He sees Northumbria as a vital prize for the Celts, or Toprak rather, that cannot be lost. I trust his strategy completely."

"As do I," said Shay and Ted nearly simultaneously.

"I suggest we ride near the coast so that we can watch the sea for Toprak ships—and God willing, the Queen—also heading that direction. Both Toprak and the Queen certainly know that we have an army there," said Ted feeling part of the command for the first time.

Riley nodded. "Perhaps just off the coast. If we see ships, we don't want them to see us," he said as he dumped the last of his tea into the smoking fire and then walked out of the chapel. Shay wasn't accustomed to having a servant looking after him and when he went to pack his personal belongings, he found that Humphrey had not only packed them, but had already taken them to his wagon.

While they waited for Ted to collect his scant belongings, Humphrey began piping on a pan pipe. He was surprisingly accomplished at it and the tranquil sound echoed through the quickly emptying castle, placing a benediction on the terribleness that had happened there.

With spare time on his hands, he sat down on the table with his feet on a crate and pulled the Tarot card from his pocket and studied it for the first time in the daylight. He held it up to the sun to see if there were anything escribed on it, or invisible writing but he saw nothing. From all appearances it was a typical playing card, which is what Tarot cards were originally created for, a game. It was only the subsequent generations that turned them into divination tools and mystery. On the front there was a hand painted figure of a man carrying five swords, with two stuck in the ground behind him. He appeared to be a knight, a soldier, maybe a squire—or a thief. Regardless, he wondered how the card was tied to the grave, as there certainly was a connection. He then wondered if he should leave someone here to protect the grave but then quickly determined that if Toprak hadn't seen fit to destroy it, it was probably safe and secure—secure through obscurity.

He returned to studying the card while enjoying Humphry's piping when he noticed something. He licked his thumb and tried to wipe away what he thought was a red smudge but when the stain remained, he concluded it must be a deliberate coloring of the card. Holding it at arm's length he was now certain of what the coloring was—the sword bearer had red hands.

Just then, out of the corner of his eye he saw Ted attempting to dance to the panpipe but the closer he watched, it appeared to be more of an involuntary twitch and he considered that maybe he was experiencing the effects of his ill-treatment while in the Tower, at least until Humphrey stopped playing and he resumed his normal posture and turned around and said, "I think I know what the significance of Seven is!" Just as Riley returned to the chapel ordering everyone to move out.

CHAPTER 9

HIGH TREASON

Jess stepped out on to the steel steps that lead up to the second level entrance of Peveril Castle and watched a small detachment of soldiers make their way across Hope Valley toward him. The soldiers had been away for a little over a week at the King's request to search for Gus and his army that were supposed to be defending the M6 near Blackpool. Peveril Castle was little more than a ruin, but it provided a secluded hiding place with several covered rooms to keep the late summer rain out. While the ruin was technically considered a Norman Castle built deep in the Derbyshire forest in 1176, it was the size of a royal hunting lodge, scarcely big enough for the King and the thirty-seven men that had escaped the routing on the beach in Wales. When Jess saw that the battle was lost, he insisted that the King flee with as many men as possible to a secluded place and then reunite with Gus. The King was an important chess piece in Toprak's game of war and Jess believed that so long as he was alive, there was hope for England, even if the King didn't share his optimism.

For the number of lives lost in Wales, the battle was incredibly quick and decisive. The King had never heard or read of any battle throughout all of English history where so many were cut down so quickly. They met what they thought was a Celtic army during the early morning hours near the channel that separated Wales and Holy Island, after marching all night from Conwy in the rain. They quickly realized after the first wave, that their enemy was not human and that they were terribly unprepared for the invasion. The advance was so swift that it was impossible to strategize, divert or even retreat. Every effort of every soldier was engaged in defense and it seemed that the enemy was everywhere at once, every man defending himself.

Even Jess wielded a sword while struggling to call for divine intervention. It wasn't until he fell to the ground after a sword sliced through his robes and into his thigh that he was able to call upon heaven while he lay among the dead. As he looked up into the grey clouds that seemed to block his supplication, he struggled with what he could possibly pray for. His lack of faith in the face of such absolute destruction would not permit him to pray for increased strength since he believed that nothing wholesome, man or beast could fight as the enemy did. The King's pitiful soldiers were cut down like stoic trees, hardly aware of what hit them, to say nothing of defending themselves and many were dead before their bodies hit the ground. Others lay gasping on mounds of corpses, drowning in their own blood until they fainted or bled-out.

As the dead began to fall upon him, he finally summoned sufficient faith to believe that the dense fog pushing in from the sea was divinely sent which reduced visibility to less than four feet. He then pushed the draining corpses off him and hobbled to where he last saw the King. With the help of his personal guard, they were able to disappear into the clouds that rested upon the battlefield. As they retreated eastwards, they were lucky enough to secure horses that had fled during the battle and they disappeared into Gwydyr Forrest in full retreat, but alive.

Once they were out of immediate danger, the King saw to Jess's wound personally, stitching it up with a blood-soaked thread from his tattered robe and then led them toward Northumbria, keeping to the forests and traveling from twilight to twilight, using the vail of darkness to their advantage. As they rode, the King relentlessly evaluated and reevaluated the war that had finally come to his Kingdom. Everything he thought he knew about the invasion he had to assume was wrong since there was no such thing as a Celtic army. After facing the devil-army, it was unmistakably clear that Toprak was his enemy. True to form, Toprak flawlessly executed a strategy that had been years in the making, hidden from everyone. That meant harbingers were probably everywhere. It also meant that there was no guarantee that Gus's army would be along the M6 barrier where they were supposed to be, so he sent scouting parties into the north to find Gus and to the south to Norwich, hoping to find the General and an English army that was still alive. Over the last four years, he and all of England had been deceived in believing that a Celtic force was making advances, but that was mostly because everyone wanted to believe Hengist and Horsa were dead.

On the dirt floor, the King had drawn the outline of England and over the last several days, had been marking the placement and advances of all the Toprak events he suspected over the last four years. He started with Toprak's defeat on the Thames and progressed up to the time when he was routed in Wales. While he still had many questions, a Toprak strategy started to emerge and he realized his Kingdom was being invaded on three sides. With his hands clasped behind his back, he walked in circles around his war map, struggling with a hundred *what if's* and a thousand *then what's*. With Wales already sacked, it was imperative to unite with Gus and then determine the state of the General's army, wherever it was. It greatly pained him that for now, he would have to let London burn, which was exactly Toprak's plan. As he continued to analyze Toprak's strategy, the more he began to get a glimpse of why they had invaded where they did and he was continually amazed at the precise timing of things. With modern communication, their coordination would have been obvious, but without it, he couldn't imagine how they did it. Looking back down at his map, he realized he had forgotten to mark the very first Toprak invasion on Holy Island in Wales where the Ravenguard was beaten but then rallied. He then took a step back and wondered why Wales was so important to Toprak. They had invaded there twice, once being refused, which explained the massive force the second time and then it occurred to him—Veronica. They were still pursuing her and still attempting to recreate history.

With Veronica's memory once again revived and burning within his heart, he stared out the western window toward Wales, wondering where she was, hoping that the force he sent northward at the same time he fled to the east had been successful in retrieving her. Never had the lack of modern communication been so painful to live without and never in all the time he had known Veronica did he miss her so terribly. If he were any other man, he might have spent his days in self-loathing and cursing himself for leaving her so ill-protected in Conwy, but he knew such cyclonic thoughts were destructive and he preferred to focus on her rescue. He uttered a silent prayer for her safety as he always did when thinking about her—which was often. Breaking his concentration on his beloved wife, Jess entered the small keep announcing the arrival of the scouting party.

"Your Majesty, the northern party will be here momentarily. I have counted their numbers during their approach and all are accounted for," said Jess walking toward the King, being careful not to step on the map.

It took the King several seconds to respond as he finished his prayer but he finally turned and replied, "Thank you Jess, I pray they bring encouraging news."

Jess knew where the King's mind went whenever he looked toward the west but there was nothing he could say to bring him comfort and despite all his own prayers and supplication to God, he still did not know if Veronica was alive. Just then, footsteps were heard on the metal stairs behind them. Before the approaching soldier could kneel, the King bade him to skip the formalities and report. The soldier thanked him with a bow and after placing his helmet on the floor, he proceeded. "Your Grace, we did find the army of Northumbria—or rather they found us, but not at the M6 line. They have been pushed back as far as Woodsome, which is where we met with them after they saw us coming from their look-out on Castle Hill."

The King and Jess were exuberant and began asking questions in rapid order with the soldier answering them as quick as he could. "Yes, we did meet with the King of Northumbria and he sends his best greetings. He was very relieved to hear you were well especially after we told him of the rout in Wales—and he was also very pleased to hear you are well Your Grace," he said nodding to Jess.

"What do you know of their losses?" asked the King.

"They were met with a similarly terrible force along the M6 as we were but just as they were about to make the ultimate sacrifice and storm the enemy line, General Clancy arrived with a force of nearly three thousand," said the soldier as the King and Jess interrupted him.

"Oh, praise be given!"

The soldier nodded, "Yes Your Grace, Your Majesty. The

General ordered a full retreat and they are at this moment planning their revenge and your presence."

"Thank you, your service and your report is very well. Very well indeed," replied the King. "We shall depart at once for Woodsome." He then turned to Jess and asked, "Have we had any news of the Norwich party?"

"None Your Majesty," replied Jess.

The King paused and then shook his head. "We cannot wait, things such as they are, we must ride. Leave for them a message written in Latin just in case any war-harbingers have followed us here. I'm certain the hateful things cannot read Latin if they can read at all. We shall just have to pray that Horsa or Hengist is not with them," the King said as he began destroying the dirt-drawn map on the floor.

As the King and the only remaining men from his army prepared to ride, Jess shut the iron gate to the small castle and wrapped a piece of titrate around one of the bars, tying it with another thread he pulled from his robe. He then turned and made his way down the winding steps to his waiting mount, a tired grey mare who turned and neighed at his approach. "I'm sorry girl but we must ride once more, though not so far, nor as fast," he said as he stroked her mane and neck. He then placed his foot in the stirrup with a grunt, pain searing down his leg, while pulling himself into the saddle and then flanked her forward.

After the onslaught of the Minimum when crops failed, vegetation now grew much faster than they once did in

England and many of the destroyed towns and cities were already partially buried under dense forests, especially in the North. The Woodsome forest—as it was now called—covered farmlands that once spanned the countryside from Castle Hill to Doncaster and the roads that previously cut through that area were impassible with a cart. The English Oak and Black Poplar trees that used to be plentiful in the Kingdom were once again dense and thriving amidst a healthy underbrush that provided the perfect hiding place for a large army. Equally perfect was the Tower atop Castle Hill that was built in 1899 to commemorate Queen Victoria's rein and was one-hundred six feet high—high enough to see an invasion from almost one-hundred miles away.

Castle Hill had been used as a watch tower and military stronghold for over a thousand years, including World War II and the reason was obvious. As the King and his small army made their way through the Holm River valley four miles way, their spotting was announced from the Victoria Tower, sending a rider down off the hill to Woodsome Hall where Gus and the General made their military HQ. Woodsome Hall was over five hundred years old made of native, grey English stone and had been beautifully maintained over the years by Lord Dartmouth. It overlooked the Farnley Valley, which had been turned into a golf club in modern times but it was now over-grown by the thick Woodsome Forest, making the Hall the only manmade structure amidst a sea of trees in over a hundred miles.

When Gus and the General fled before the Toprak harbingers, they could see the Hall from the top of Castle Hill and determined right away that the combination of thick forests and the Hall was the perfect place to lick their wounds and prepare for hell another day. The surrounding forest had grown so thick that they had to cut their way into the Hall, it being too dense to pull any wagons through.

When the King and Jess arrived at Woodsome Hall, their horses were taken to the stables and they were escorted inside by very disciplined soldiers who spoke only if necessary and then very matter-of-factly. Even the soldiers who stood guard never even blinked as the King passed, they just stood taller and clicked their heels together as they saluted. Not since leaving Buckingham Palace had he observed such impressive military discipline and he turned to Jess but before he could mention it, Jess nodded, confirming the same observation. They were escorted into the great hall, which was equivalent to a modern-day living room, except that it was designated for only entertaining guests. At the far end of the hall was a very large fireplace but contained only a small fire. From what they could see in the fading light, the walls had eight-foot wainscoting as was typical for the period, the building having been preserved in the same state for over five hundred years.

As they walked into the room, a hunched-over figure in front of the fire wearing a black riding cloak struggled to see who had entered but he soon became animated when he saw his guests.

"Your Majesty!" called Gus as he struggled to get to his feet. "How absolutely wonderful it is to see you! We had heard nothing from Wales but feared the absolute worst after we discovered that the so-called Celts along the M6 was indeed Toprak."

"We have had our share of war–harbingers as well I'm afraid," replied the King as he embraced Gus.

For a moment, Gus and Jess stared at one another from across the room neither saying a word as the miles and years rushed together until at last Jess walked over and embraced his long-time friend and mentor. Their firm embrace lasted several minutes as they expressed their deep gratitude to each other and to God that they were both alive. When their embrace was finally broken, Gus stumbled while he tried to regain his balance looking very old and tired.

"You appear to be much worse for wear my old friend," said Jess as he grabbed hold of Gus's arm and helped him to his chair in front of the fire.

"Only just," replied Gus. "I took a sword point under my right lung and my medic thinks it pierced my liver—thankfully those can grow back together."

"I too am worse for wear," said Jess sitting down and pulling up his rope to show Gus the soaked bandage around his thigh. "Thankfully His Majesty is a surprisingly good flesh seamstress and I am very pleased to report he is still in one piece with only a minor scrape or two—bloody miracle I believe considering the losses we took in Wales."

Gus sighed upon hearing the bad news and asked, "How many did you lose?"

"All, excepting the thirty or so who escaped with us. It is a miracle I was not hurt and I have you to thank for that Your Grace," replied the King and then appropriately added, "and God."

Jess and the King related to Gus all that had happened in Wales, the marriage, the war, the escape and their journey to Woodsome. Gus was delighted to hear of the marriage and that Veronica had submitted willingly and lovingly, something that was very important to him as if he were her grandfather. But as the tale progressed, Gus's joy quickly turned into great concern when he learned that they did not know Veronica's condition or the men who were sent to fetch her. Just then the General entered the room with a torch and walked over to the fireplace where they were all seated. He slid the torch between the balusters of the balcony rail above them, adding a much needed light to the room and then sat down with a heavy sigh. He then respectfully but silently nodded a greeting to the King and Jess with something heavy on his mind.

Gus knew what the General was laboring under since he knew from where he had just come and after a long pause he enquired what it was he had found. The General leaned forward, placed his forearms on his knees and said while staring into the fire, "They have scarcely moved beyond the M6 with most of their supplies still west of it. The fact that they didn't purse us in flight only means one thing."

"Which is what?" asked the King.

"They're waiting for something."

Gus began to nod. "Well let's face it, they know we have gone east and we couldn't go too far since in less than one hundred miles we run into another ocean. Which makes me wonder, where is Shay in all this?"

"Yes, where is Shay?" asked the King, hoping he was not still in Norwich dungeon.

"No, last I knew he was safe," replied the General. "As you requested, I liberated him and his faithful men. Those who were not faithful marched with me and I taught them discipline."

The King began to smile and nod. "I noticed your very impressive discipline on our way in. Only at Buckingham have I seen anything equal."

"It only takes one hanging before the rest fall in line," replied the General with no emotion and then continued. "I sent His Majesty Shay and at least two thousand back to Wales to assist you. I'm guessing you did not see him or…"

"No, we did not see him, though we made it a point to only travel at night and then only through the most dense forests," replied Jess dispelling the General's thought that Shay had been killed.

"However, just like at the M6, there is a good chance that Toprak stayed put and Shay may have marched right into them," suggested Gus soberly.

Everyone nodded as they accepted the possible scenario while the King sighed in frustration. "I have been trying to determine how Toprak has been able to guess our every move and the only conclusion I have is that we have been betrayed."

"By whom?" asked Jess.

"Ted," replied the King as Jess and Gus exchanged a nervous glance. "The knowledge he had about the organization of the heptarchy and the distribution of forces explains why Toprak knows and how they so perfectly dissected us. I'm sorry gentlemen but we should have hung him in Dover."

Ted was a very tender and sore subject for everyone but none perhaps more than Gus. For a few long awkward moments, no one spoke until Jess resumed the previous conversation. "You could have still turned to the north or the south, it doesn't make sense that they did not purse."

"No," replied the General shaking his head. "They know that we know about the sack of London and that we would never position ourselves between two armies. Our only retreat is north—if we decide a full retreat is wise."

"So why not cut off our route northwards?" asked Gus.

The General was deep in thought as he continued to stare into the fire, his military genius exploring every angle and after a few minutes he responded slowly, "It's as if…" he paused trying to make sense of his premature conclusion before verbally committing to it. "It's as if they are creating a diversion. They know we can't communicate between our armies, but I wonder what they could accomplish by making us flee into the interior?"

Just then, a soldier entered the back of the room announcing the King of East Angles, which at first took everyone by surprise, unsure of what it meant. Then when the dots connected, they all jumped up to see Shay walking into the great hall looking extremely tired. The reunion between Gus, Jess and Shay was pleasing and might have been even joyful had not the circumstances been so grim. An extra chair was brought from another room for Shay but before he sat, he requested that they bring one more chair. Gus looked at Shay a little puzzled wondering who could possibly be joining them when Shay said, "You'll never guess who I ran into."

Everyone looked at Shay and then each other shaking their heads confused. Ted was waiting outside the hall so that his announcement could be a surprise but the surprise that awaited him was not at all what he or Shay expected. Just before Shay announced his surprise, Jess had guessed it and raised his hand to stop him but it was too late.

"Ted!" exclaimed Shay as Ted walked into the back of the room.

Ted's timing couldn't have been more terrible as the King had only just talked about hanging him and as he made his way toward the fireplace, the King ordered the guards to seize him, which they did by knocking him to the floor with the hilt of their swords landing him unconscious. To everyone but the King, Ted was a beloved friend and seeing him dragged out of the room to be bound was difficult to watch, especially since his appearance was intended as a joyful surprise not an abhorrent one.

Shay began to protest but Gus stopped him by placing his hand on his shoulder and shaking his head. Gus had seen the King's swift justice when it came to traitors at the Tower of London and now that it was rather obvious Ted had betrayed his plans to Toprak, death would be close behind. There might be a time to plead for Ted's life but now wasn't it. The room became deathly quiet, only the sound of the fire could be heard and everyone nervously sat back trying to remember what they were talking about and where they left off so that they might relieve the tension in the room.

Jess recalled first that they were just discussing why Toprak would drive them into the interior of the island and he said, "The answer to why they want us inland, lies in what's on the coast that they could possibly want."

"Or need," said the King, his voice trembling slightly from the rush of anger. "They want Veronica."

The General was confused since he did not know about Hengist's infatuation with her and his insistence that she was the true Anglo-Saxon heir to the throne of England—a direct descendent of the Princess Ronnie—and in order to legitimize his ascension, he needed to marry her. But after Jess explained Toprak's plans he was dumbfounded.

"You mean to tell me that they are acting out some historical passion play? That's absurd!" he said getting up to pace and ease his frustration over the discussion and Ted's incarceration. "If that's the case, we don't need to worry about her safety."

"Only her honor," replied Gus quietly and like a protective parent.

Though no one said it, they were all worried for Veronica, their dear friend and Queen. While it did appear that Hengist needed Veronica alive, they didn't know if that meant alive and well or just alive. Before the conversation continued, Shay told the group about their trip to Conwy Castle after they searched for the King among the bodies on the beach and that they found the Castle completely torched with not a living soul left.

"But that's not all," said Shay reluctantly. "The most terrible is how the Castle came to be torched."

Everyone looked at Shay waiting for him to continue. He paused thinking how he could paint Ted in the best light possible and also let the King know how valuable Ted's information about Toprak had been. "Ted noticed that the ashes contained hundreds and maybe thousands of harbingers. That's when he told me about Horsa's ability to ignite harbingers in a type of explosion. I know how it sounds, I thought the same thing, but it is true I assure you. Why he destroyed his own army I couldn't say except for maybe wanting to send a message."

The General continued to pace as Shay spoke, trying to place the pieces of Toprak's strategy together. "So, Hengist wants Veronica for his Queen and they attack Wales and Northumbria at nearly the same time—at least close enough so that two English armies are preoccupied. Why not just nick her when she is out on a walk? I mean, seriously! In attacking, they have played their hand whereas before, we still thought they were the bloody Celts! Not only that, to do that ignition thing, I would have saved that for the grand finale."

"Evil is as evil does," said Jess quietly.

"What do you mean by that?" asked the General, frustrated.

Jess had always been a little intimidated by General Clancy. Not only was he a large man but he was as brash as he was powerful and being a military man through and through, explaining good and evil to him was sometimes futile unless you could explain the stratagem. But for the first time, Jess turned to him without restraint and said, "Toprak is unlike any army you have ever faced General. They not only have hell-crazy soldiers—that double for grenades apparently—they are at the very core, evil. That pure evil causes them to do things that are neither rational, strategic or logical. I believe they showed their hand for no other reason than to *show their hand.* They want us to know what waits in the dark for every Englishman and with that fear, they will then grind our faces in it and afterwards, dismember and spit upon the endless mounds of our dead. It's not enough to win. It's not enough to kill every last one of us. They must do it all knowing that fear first bled from our eyes before they drink it and piss on our corpses."

As usual, Jess painted a vivid picture using only words and the illustration settled harshly upon everyone but none more than Shay who had seen so much death and carnage in the Toprak wake. For the General, Toprak tactics were so foreign and backwards from what he was used to and he couldn't get his head around why a general would kill his own soldiers to turn a battle, it made no sense.

"It does if you understand where Toprak soldiers come from," said Shay. "They don't have to worry about preserving their armies, they know they have ample to take England—enough mindless soldiers to burn—and if they can do it with horror, they will."

"So all the blood in Wales and along the M6 was only a prelude to set the mood?" asked the General still frustrated.

"It would appear so," replied Jess. "But not without value of course. If they can make us tremble and shrink under our fear, the battle is more than half won before they even get serious. Fear is a terrible thing. It not only robs us of the ability to act, but it actually begins to kill you physically due to all the negative energy it attracts."

"So in a sense, every moment any of us or our men spend being afraid, Toprak is prevailing?" asked Shay.

"Just so," replied Jess.

The General was a little irritated with the discussion of fear as if they were sharing their feelings at a slumber party. He had experienced fear most of his life but had learned to manage it and he retorted to Shay and Jess directly. "Fear is part of the package, gentlemen. You either learn how to ignore it and perform your duty or you're dead. Not from pent-up negative energy, but from a sword through your neck."

Jess smiled and looked the General in the eye and asked,

"So you're not afraid?"

Without hesitation or even blinking the General quickly replied, "Certainly not!."

Jess was able to look into a man's soul and sense things about them that they were not even aware of and as he looked deep into the General's eyes, he truly could not see any fear cowering in some small corner of his heart. After a few seconds Jess laughed slightly with amazement. "You truly are not afraid my friend. Extraordinary!" he said as he shook his head in disbelief. He looked around the room and could sense varying levels of fear from everyone but the General. He then got to his feet and limped around the room while everyone watched in silence. As he circled the chairs, he seemed to be flicking his fingers and mumbling but no one could hear or understand what he was saying or doing. He then stopped near the fireplace and looked as if he were mentally gathering something in front of him. Whether he could see something before him or if he were just imagining it, no one knew but after a few seconds, he closed his eyes and waved his hands above the heads of everyone seated three times and then did the same over his own. He never outwardly spoke but at the moment he waved his hands over them, everyone felt a rush of relief including the General as if a blade had just been removed from their sides. Gus and the King gasped in surprise and small tear rolled down Shay's cheek, expressing the unspeakable words of a relieved soul. Shockingly, the General was the most affected and he almost collapsed in his chair and then slowly regained his sitting position laughing with pure joy while his eyes filled with tears.

"What the hell!" exclaimed the General, genuinely surprised beyond belief as everyone else voiced similar expressions of amazement.

Jess smiled humbly as he returned to his chair while they all asked him what he had done. "Call it the devil or negative energy, it hides within us even when we insist it does not. Much like sweeping a room, I dusted the fear from your hearts and the relief you feel is all the evidence you need to know that fear robs a man of his strength and resolve."

The General was still reeling from the inexplicable reprieve he was experiencing, amazed that he could have harbored so much fear when his conscious mind was not aware of any of it. Jess was equally amazed with the General's relief and turning to him he said, "My friend, you are extraordinary, truly. There are not many men alive who can control fear as you do. Your relief was great because the amount of entombed fear within you was also great." He then turned to the group and said, "It is a temporary relief however. Fear can always find its way back into your hearts but it will be of your choosing."

Everyone continued to express their profound relief as Jess attempted to place their council of war back on the rails. "Let us know discuss Toprak without fear—at least for now."

Their discussions of Toprak and how to defeat them drew out long into the night until they were all sleeping where they sat in front of a fire that was also extinguished. Gus was the first wake as the morning sun streaked across his face through the obscured fifteenth century glass window and he sat without moving trying to make sense of a voice he heard outside the Hall. Looking around the room he noticed that the King's chair was empty and once he awoke more completely, he realized that the voice outside belonged to the him. Staggering to his feet, he made his way out the front doors and stepped onto the grand porch to see the King directing two soldiers as they threw a rope over a high branch and then tied a noose. Even though Ted was guilty, if it had been anyone else, Gus would be in complete agreement with the King's justice, but this was Ted, his long-time and very dear friend. He knew that the King had beheaded two men in the Tower for much less and even though he had not prepared a defense, he cleared his throat, attracting the attention of the King.

The King turned around to find Gus standing on the porch with his hands behind his back, waiting for an explanation. He had hoped to discuss the hanging with Gus and his friends before actually going through with it and he realized how the scene must have looked, as if he were going to complete the deed before they awoke, which was not his plan. "Guiscard, it was never my plan to hang your friend without a war trial. However, we both know Ted is as guilty as the day is long," he said as he stepped onto the porch.

Gus nodded. "That knowledge doesn't make me feel any different about it."

"I understand, but I simply can't write him up and place it in his file," said the King as he sat down on the porch wall.

"Agreed but…" replied Gus interrupting as the King raised his hand signaling that he had not finished what he was going to say.

"I will stay his execution if there is value in keeping him alive. I'm very sorry Gus but he being a longtime friend and Senator of the old United States will not be sufficient. I am greatly pained but surely you must see the necessity of my actions. Dead men can no longer tell their tales to Toprak."

Gus nodded slowly as Jess and Shay stepped out onto the

porch, having heard the entire conversation from within the Hall. Despite the fact that Ted was their close friend, they still could not think of a valid reason to stay his execution and they each took a seat on the porch wall as Ted was brought around from the stables where he had been bound all night. The guards stood him before the King in the tall grass with his hands still tied behind his back. He looked up at the King humbly and then back down at his feet, refusing to look at his friends. He did not want to pretend that his crimes were not worthy of death, nor did he want to appeal to his friends on the basis of friendship alone. He had betrayed them all whilst in Nicole's company and before he had even escaped from her, he vowed he would willingly die for treason, so long as he could clear his conscience and perhaps save his friends with the knowledge he now had about Toprak. Staring down at his feet, it appeared that his vow was being realized and he waited for the King to pass his sentence while he wondered if any of his former colleagues could find sufficient value to stay his fate.

The King looked around to see if everyone was ready to begin just as the General came around the building after tending to some early morning business. The King then stood before the porch and started the proceedings. "Gentlemen, I have no distinction in standing before you under such abhorrent circumstances, but grim as they are, we are at war and Theodore Schyuler has been accused of treason. According to the articles or war, the punishment of such is death by beheading or hanging. Under the circumstances, I have chosen hanging unless there be any who prefer the alternative."

No one looked around, since it was mutually understood that hanging would be preferred if he were found guilty and the King continued. "I have requested General Clancy to judge the evidence since he is perhaps the most experienced in such matters and he is also perhaps the least biased."

The General gave Gus a quick, powerless look before he was seen by the King as Gus nodded back just as quickly, letting him know that he understood and that he didn't blame him. After the King's introduction, the General stepped forward and began the war trial. He had conducted such a trial before in Guyana back in '37 when he was a new general but the task then was nothing like the emotionally-charged one in front of him now. He had no idea how the English traditionally conducted such trials so he just proceeded like a U.S. General would and with as little emotion as he was able.

"Theodore Schyuler, you have been accused of high treason and therefore an enemy to the Crown of England. If you are found guilty by this assembly, it has been unanimously decided that you shall hang by the neck for the determined period." The General then turned to Ted and asked, "How do you plead?"

Ted looked up and calmly replied, "I am guilty without excuse."

Ted's reply was not what he was expecting and he stumbled on his words as he asked if anyone present desired to speak on the accused's behalf. Everyone desired to speak but no one could offer anything concreate to save him. Their biggest counter argument was that he was their friend and after several long and very painful minutes, everyone began to slowly shake their heads. When no one spoke, Ted raised his head to find that none of his friends would look at him. It was at that moment the thrust of his fate completely fell upon him and he slowly bowed his head and waited for the next words.

"Is there no one?" asked the General incredulously while everyone looked back at him powerless. With a deep sigh, the General then said with great reluctance, "Theodore Schyuler, a council of your peers has found you guilty of high treason and you are therefore condemned to hang by the neck immediately following this trial. Have you anything to say in your defense and before God?"

Ted looked up again at his friends and then turned to the General resigned and defeated saying, "No, I do not."

The General had seen Ted only one other time so defeated and that was in Virginia when he shot him in the foot to test his resolve. At that time, Washington D.C. was filled with traitors and Toprak pawns and he had to be sure Ted was on his side and he made Ted believe that he was about to die. As Ted laid on the ground looking up at him, he remembered him having the pitiful look of an innocent man who was resigned to his fate—the same look he saw today. The difference today however was the fact that he could not stay his execution.

"Damn-it!, swore the General before he motioned the guards to lead him away. Almost as reluctantly, the two guards each grabbed an arm and walked Ted over to the gibbet as everyone looked on in horror. Since there was no platform, Ted was ordered to mount a horse and without complaint or any hesitation, he placed his foot in the stirrup while the guards helped him to the saddle. As they led the horse under the noose, Ted couldn't bring himself to turn and look at his friends and he wondered if they were watching or if the scene was too abhorrent. He tried to imagine if he would watch one of them hang, just as the noose was placed over his head and tightened around his neck.

Whatever normal formalities there should have been at this

point were skipped so that the gristly deed could just be over with. Closing his eyes, the King gave the nod and the guard led the horse forward as Ted swung off its back and began kicking in the air.

CHAPTER 10

THE PEARL RAIN

"Begin the count," said the King unenthusiastically as if he had said it a million times before. "Cut him down after seven."

No one, not even the King could bring themselves to watch Ted swing back and forth as his spasmodic kicking become slower. Jess turned to Gus and asked quietly but loud enough for Shay to hear, "What does he mean, cut him down after seven?"

"After seven minutes and if the prisoner is still struggling, they are cut down as a show that the King has mercy even on the condemned," replied Gus.

"So there is still hope for Ted?!" asked Jess quietly but with hope in his voice.

Gus shook his head, "Certainly not. The neck is cut, not the rope. It's a mercy killing meant to end the suffering."

The significance of seven, thought Shay as he remembered Ted saying those exact words as they were leaving Conwy but never asked him to explain. In that moment he realized that Ted might have solved the riddle of The Seven and the secret to England's salvation—certainly something worthy of preserving his life. In mortal alarm for his friend's life, he jumped to his feet and ran toward Ted while drawing his sword, something no one expected especially the two soldiers who were busy counting. As he came within eight feet of Ted's swinging body, one of the soldiers rushed toward him, clumsily trying to draw his sword. For the first time since college where Shay had only earned a brown belt in judo, he instinctively ducked sideways as he leaped into the air and then swung around with his leg extended, toes pointed, finishing in a powerful wheel kick that knocked the soldier to the ground unconscious. After lightly touching the ground, he then jumped an amazing four feet in the air, spinning, while his sword sliced the rope in two causing Ted to fall to the ground. He then threw his sword behind him and ran to loosen the noose but he was met by the other soldier who appeared more determined. Like before and without hardly thinking, Shay grabbed hold of the soldier and with a following foot sweep, landed him on his back followed by a strong blow to his head. He then loosened the noose while Ted struggled to regain his breath—he was alive.

Everyone was shocked that Shay could be so bold and against the Kings orders, to say nothing of his very impressive and deadly skills. It was a side no one had ever seen of Shay—including Shay himself—and while he attended to Ted, everyone watched in silence, secretly relieved—everyone except for the King. At first he didn't know what to do but once he concluded that his justice was being denied, he walked over and drew his sword, placing it under Shay's chin. Shay at first didn't move, being incensed at the King's determination but as the King began to draw upward pressure, Shay slowly stood. As far as the King knew, Shay was also committing treason in trying to save a traitor and Shay would have spoken first before acting but Ted's life was in the balance with only seconds to spare. Standing at the point of the King's sword, with pressure increasing and slowly drawing blood,

Shay quickly reached out and grabbed the raw blade with his bare hand and twisted it from the King's grasp then pointed it back at him. The King was both incensed and startled as he slowly took several steps away from his own sword. Shay then threw the sword behind him and out of the reach of the King while blood ran down his fingers and dripped into the dirt.

Watching the entire sequence of events unfold, the General determined that Shay, who was normally very even-keeled, had good reasons for what he did. A reason that would legitimately save Ted's life but with tensions so high and with more soldiers drawing their weapons, he stepped forward with his own sword drawn. Standing behind the King, he motioned for Gus to draw his sword and accompany him. Seeing the General and Gus positioned for checkmate caused the approaching soldiers to stop while the situation grew more tense by the second.

As clear as non-verbal communication would allow, the General intimated to Gus that he was not threatening the King, but was ensuring that themoment did not spiral into mayhem. With things back within a thin measure of control and after Shay determined that Ted would in fact live, he turned to the small crowd around him that was increasing in size, but before he spoke, he struggled where he should begin. No one but he and Ted knew about The Seven and now was not the place or time to divulge such important knowledge with so many ears present. He knew he had to say something with sufficient weight that would at least cause everyone to put away their weapons until he could explain in detail, so he raised his hands to show a cease-fire as the profusion of blood from his hand ran down his arm.

"Forgive me, but I had to act quickly. These men shall revive momentarily, surely I am the most wounded here," said Shay as he looked down at Ted and apologized. "I'm sorry my friend. You and I have a secret and I was slow to remember it."

Ted couldn't speak and was still laboring to fill is bloodstream once again with oxygen but he smiled gratefully and managed to say in a hoarse voice, "You've have saved me twice."

Shay wasn't sure what he meant but then remembered how Riley wanted to execute him when he first found their camp in the forest. He nodded at Ted, acknowledging that he understood and resumed explaining himself. "I know, on very good authority, something that will allow us to turn the Toprak tide in the world but it is still a riddle and quite a dark enigma. I came upon it while in Norwich and while you may disapprove, I shared it with only Ted."

"You shared something such as that with someone you knew was a traitor?!" exclaimed the King.

"Please, your Majesty, please hear what I have to say, but not here. From what I have learned from Ted—which has been a great deal—this is our only hope. After I share it with you, I think you will agree that his knowledge of the former medieval age will be paramount, especially since Ver…" he stopped to correct himself, "the Queen's life and location is unknown."

The King stared at Shay for several minutes as his soliloquy finally allowed him to agree and he at last nodded in frustration then said, "Very well. Let us hear what you have to say and I shall judge if it is worthy."

The sheathing of many swords was then heard, relieving the tension with the sound as Jess and Shay helped Ted get to his feet. The General commanded the surrounding soldiers to return to their posts around Woodsome Hall and commanded them to not let anyone pass for any reason unless they brought news of Toprak advancing. Alone again, the only remaining body of the privy council gathered on the porch in the late morning sun to weigh what Shay had to say. They laid Ted on a several riding cloaks that had been removed due to the warm weather and encouraged him to drink while Shay presented his ghost story. For the King's benefit, Shay related the events of his first sighting of his grandfather in Montana and Gus validated the story, setting the stage for his experience in the dungeon.

"He appeared again, just before I was rescued by the General and frankly, he kept me alive. Among other things, he encouraged me to stay positive and hopeful but before he departed, he told me that the hope of England rested with The Seven."

"THE seven," inquired Gus.

Shay nodded. "Yes. Of course at the time it meant nothing to me, and still doesn't hold much value, but in the Conwy churchyard, there is a grave that has the inscription…"

"We are seven," interrupted the King.

"Exactly! You know what it means then?" asked Shay excitedly.

"No, I'm afraid I don't. It is a medieval grave to be sure, but it is one of those pieces of English history that has been lost. I've often wondered if it is nothing more than a publicity stunt to lure visitors to Wales. But, perhaps there is a burial record at the church?" wondered the King.

"I thought the same and I did find a book for the correct

century, but I could find no record contained in it, though I could have missed it since my Latin and Old English isn't as sharp as Ted's. However, we did find this in the sleve," Shay said holding up the Tarot card.

The King stood up and took the card and examined it carefully, holding it to the light and then edge-wise. It was certainly an authentic medieval playing card, no forgery, but its meaning was lost on him and he handed it to Gus while Shay continued. "Ted and I concluded that the co-incidence of the Seven of Swords in the record for same time period was not mere coincidence. We discussed it a little at the time but we did not have the privacy required to delve too deep and just as we left Conwy, Ted told me he thought he knew the meaning of it, but we never had a moment alone to discuss it. It wasn't until I heard Jess ask Gus about the seven count that I remembered our cut-short conversation."

Reluctantly, the King began to nod and then said, "You have done wisely Shay. However, we will now have to wait until he can speak."

"I can speak," replied Ted as he struggled to his feet and leaned on the porch wall. "I don't suppose I have to tell you that the number seven is a very reverenced number in the world of numerology and many other religious sects. But none of that made any sense until I remembered that Pythagoras believed numbers actually had souls and magical powers associated with them."

Gus began to nod in agreement without looking up, still studying the Tarot card. He then had a small epiphany and said, "Why swords? The connection to the number seven is obvious, but as I recall, there is a Seven of Cups and other suits in a Tarot deck. The swords must be significant and I don't think it a stretch in light of what your ghost said that it relates to war."

"That is probably the outcome or end result," replied Ted. "but according to Pythagoras, seven was the most holy of all numbers. He referred to seven as the Septad, seven contained in one—which is what I happened upon when I mentioned it to you in the chapel Shay."

The mention of the chapel at Conway cast a heavy blanket over the King and he was visibly disturbed when he thought of its destruction and the memories it held for him, but it went unnoticed by everyone except Ted.

"Did he refer to seven as the Septad, or THE Septad?" asked Jess.

Ted thought for a moment but didn't know the answer. "I don't know, but if he called it THE Septad—well, that really means something then doesn't it. The connection between The Seven, The Septad and the We are seven grave is no co-incidence." Ted stood up and leaned over, trying to un-stretch his back as he continued the Pythagoras discussion. "He also separated numbers into male and female as well as light and dark. Seven or The Septad was holy because it was seven in one, the collective balance and all the potential power in the universe."

The General was lost on such deep philosophy, as was most everyone else with the possible exception of Gus and Jess, and he said with a hint of frustration in his voice, "What does that even mean?"

Ted wasn't through and he raised his hand to calm the General. "Let me explain. The numbers one through three represented each of the three heavenly spheres and numbers four through seven the major elements of earth. Three plus four of course equals seven, the meeting place of heaven and earth. No matter how you look at it, what we are dealing with here is total power, add the swords and I think you could even say, total destruction—or total protection depending on how you look at it."

Always the tactical thinker, the General shook his head and sighed. "But what is it! Sounds like we know the theory behind The Seven, but we're no closer to discovering it or controlling it."

"I wouldn't say that," replied Jess calmly as he walked with his hands behind his back, deep in thought. He placed his hands in the pockets of his robe and felt the last remaining fragments of the Cross that he always kept with him as he walked the length of the porch and then turned around and stopped. "What I was able to do in Wales was not dissimilar to what our friend Pythagoras described. Certainly there was a meeting of heavenly power and earth, though not anywhere near the scale he described, but I wonder…" He paused, returning to his thoughts and he walked the length of the porch again before he stopped in front of Shay and said, "I need to get back to Conwy and see that grave."

Shay looked at Ted and then the King for a response. As he figured, Conway was destroyed and there would be no reason for Toprak to return to it, making it a rather safe trip. After a moment of silence, the King finally agreed but insisted that they travel the same route he took while fleeing Wales and that they travel only at night—with at least a dozen men.

"Actually, Your Majesty," replied Jess. "I agree with Shay, that there would be no reason for Toprak to return to a graveyard, especially if they have captured Veronica. We could travel much lighter, quiet and quicker if just myself, Shay and Ted went. That is if you can ride Ted?"

Ted nodded, "I'll be fine I think."

Gus was about to protest but traveling with a larger group was probably only an illusion of protection since the King was so completely overpowered and his own army was pushed back from the M6 with many casualties. Jess was probably right, or at least not wrong and he nodded, agreeing with his plan.

"I suggest you leave at once, while the evening is waning and the weather willing," said the King. "By the time you reach the Holm Valley, it will be nightfall and you can continue straight on. With any luck you could make Peveril Castle by morning and stay the day there. As for us, we will stay put until you return."

"Very well Your Majesty," replied Jess with a bow as Shay followed him into Woodsome Hall to collect their gear and Ted made his way to the stables to ready their horses. While throwing a saddle over Jess's grey mare, the King entered the stable alone and announced his presence by clearing his throat. Surprised, Ted looked over the back of the horse to see the King and he wanted to say something flippant but decided against it. The King took a few moments before he spoke but when he did, he was surprisingly sober and more personable than he had even seen him.

"I've never had to face a man that I had killed before and I have to say I am without words—nor are there any words designed for such a purpose," said the King. "I can't be sorry for what I did nor why I did it, but my heart is wounded because I did. I am at a great loss at how to frame this incident in my mind."

Ted walked around the mare and leaned against the railing

that surrounded the stall and said in a hoarse voice, "Let me make it easier for you. I betrayed you. You can hang that from your rope without a sound from me. When you left me in the Tower believing Gus was dead, I lost all hope and I didn't think anything mattered. What I learned of Toprak during those months, I truly didn't believe England had a chance and it was only a matter of time before—well, before there was no more resistance. Then after Horsa sacked the Tower and I discovered Gus's head was not on one of those spikes, I knew I had to escape, even if that meant I was beheaded for treason by you. I only wanted to be on the right side of things, even if my head eventually found its way in a basket."

The King was pacified if not impressed and as Ted resumed his labors, he extended his empty hand, showing that he had no weapon in it, which was the origin of the handshake, a symbol of peace between two men. Ted looked down at the King's hand a little surprised then slowly extended his and they shook firmly.

After seeing Jess, Ted and Shay off, the King ordered his own horse saddled up and he made his way northward for no other reason than to be alone with his thoughts and hopefully find his way out of them. He loathed wielding such a brutal hand and since the beheadings in the Tower, he fear he was not only having to do it more often but that he was also becoming desensitized to it. As he rode, he became more and more alarmed at the thought that he had almost hung Ted. In a terrifying, uncontrolled daydream, he saw Veronica swinging from the rope instead of Ted and he gasped out loud as he shook the vision from his mind. Just as he was about to entertain that he was perhaps going mad, he remembered learning about nymphs and how they could seduce a man in any way they pleased.

Nymphs were of course part of the mythology of ancient England but given the fact that he had just legitimately stayed Ted's execution because of a ghost story, fantasy was reality now and he struggled to remember the lore of nymphs. He first remembered of course that they were female-like spirits who inhabited mountains and forests and could sexually seduce a man, similar to the mermaid lore. Like the mermaids, they could be either benevolent or evil but unlike the mermaid, they had the required hardware that would enable human intimacy, resulting in immortal offspring. Struggling to remember more about the nature of nymphs, he thought he saw something move in the underbrush, something that looked like a woman. After clearing his head again, he remembered that they could also bring peace and resolution to the troubled mind which is why even in the modern age, humankind has always sought refuge in nature to clear their head and even connect with God. He closed his eyes and against his modern, rational mind, he prayed to the nymphs of the forest to come to his aid and help him find his way out of the terrible wars that were soon to descend upon his kingdom.

After the sun had set and there was no more daylight to allow any more work to be done, Gus entered the great hall and sat down at the table with a grunt, his wound still providing plenty of discomfort. Across from him sat the King, who had not waited to start eating and as Gus poured himself a cup of ale, the General walked in to join them. Nightfall was already an hour old and the three men hoped that Jess, Shay and Ted were now at Holm Valley, nearly safe in the forest. Gus pulled a large piece of meat from the platter in the center of the table and not having any utensils, he began pulling the meat off the bone with his fingers and then gave up and raised it to his mouth chewing the meat from the bone.

"What is this?" he asked, being pleasantly surprised at the flavor.

The King was slow to respond, having been very quiet the whole day since the near hanging that morning and he snickered, finding it slightly amusing that Gus didn't recognize the taste. "Pork," he replied.

Gus and the General both looked at the King confused as Gus said, "I wasn't aware that we had any aposeptic pork, only beef."

"It's not aposeptic. It's fresh. I went on a ride this afternoon down to the river and was approached by a wild boar of all things."

Both Gus and the General knew that most wild animals these days were much larger than they had previously been and they were astounded that he was not hurt. "How did you ever kill it?" asked the General.

"Well, I can't claim the kill. I was not alone of course and the four guards who attended me did the job—bloody mess it was. The animal was at least five feet from head to hoof and tusks like your arm. In fact, that's one of them by the fire," replied the King getting up to show them.

It was unlike any animal horn the General had ever seen. It was spiraled and curved in nearly a half circle with a razor sharp tip. Holding it closer to the candle he saw that the tusk was grey and dark purple that twisted around in offsetting colors. "Extraordinary!" he said, handing it to Gus, but before he reach up and take it, a soldier ran into the hall and yelling, "War-harbingers!"

The three men looked at each other for only a very brief second before jumping to their feet and rushing out the door. Stepping out into the cool night, they heard the ill wind of panic spreading through the camp and as they ran to the stables, they found their mounts waiting for them, along with their armor bearers standing at attention. After only wasting time for their breastplates and weapons, they quickly mounted and sped toward the look-out post on Castle Hill. When they arrived, their disciplined army was already forming a line on top of the hill as Riley and the other captains rode the length of the line on horseback, preparing the faint-hearted soldiers while shouting orders for the attack. At Riley's command, three soldiers stepped forward to take the horses as General Clancy, the King and Gus ran up the stone steps to the top of Victoria Tower and looked westward with great foreboding.

"Just there along the horizon Your Majesty," said the watch commander as he handed the King his looking glass.

The King looked to the western horizon beginning in the north where the soldier had pointed and then slowly scanned the rolling hills that bordered along the M6 as far south as he could see. He slowly lowered the glass with a heavy sigh and handed it to the General but said nothing.

"Bloody hell," said the General, still looking through the glass. "Are there really that many people left on earth?"

The advancing army seemed as numerous as the stars above their heads in the moonless night and after Gus saw for himself, he turned and looked down on their meager army of roughly five-thousand standing in fear, certain that death was waiting for them on the other side of the hill. Gus then put the glass back up to his eye and scanned the southern borders towards Holm Valley, hoping to see any sign of Jess, Shay and Ted, but it was too dark and too far to see anything resembling three lone men on horses.

"How are you holding up?" Jess asked Ted as they crossed a small brook and made their way into the protective darkness of the forest.

"I'll survive. Who knew hanging would be so painful," he replied trying to ease Jess and Shay's shame in letting him swing on the rope. Since they left Woodsome that afternoon, they had repeatedly told him how sorry they were for everything, not just the hanging but also the imprisonment and after five hours of riding, they had reconciled their differences. However, the last hour was spent mostly in silence, having run out of things to talk about and they each focused on their mission and what dangers awaited them in the forest.

"Did you and the King see any fenrir when you traveled this wood?" Shay asked Jess.

Jess shook his head. "No, but that's probably because we traveled his leg during the day and evening, never at night. However, we did spend several nights at Peveril Castle and never heard any—whatever that's worth."

"I've been thinking about that," said Ted. "Peveril Castle is actually out of our way. I think we'd make much better time if we rode due west from our current position."

Neither Jess or Shay spoke for a few minutes as they considered the implications. There were many dangerous considerations but none more poignant than Toprak. Fenrir, while nasty and usually deadly, were not the threat they once were, not since Matthew had taught everyone how to kill them, which was accomplished by a longsword through the eyeball. The stalled response convinced Ted that Jess and Shay needed more convincing and as they came to a clearing, he rode up alongside Jess.

"The most dangerous thing in the world tonight is an unaccounted for Toprak army. I think we will be safer if we get in and out of Conwy as fast as we can and then get back to the army," he said as Shay joined them. Ted always thought twice before sharing what he knew about Toprak since it was usually received poorly and with heavy suspicion but after a few more minutes of silence he continued. "There is no moon tonight gentlemen. It's nights like these…"

"That the hellhounds come out," interrupted Jess.

"So you've heard?" replied Ted.

"I spent many an evening with Veronica in Wales listening to their hateful cries emanating from the moors—trying to comfort her. Not sure if you heard but that's what did Matthew in," said Jess with great sorrow in his voice. "Lord how we miss him and could sure use him now."

"Yes, I had heard that, but…" Ted hesitated again, unsure if he should continue but then forced the words, "Matthew's not dead."

Jess and Shay both pulled on their reins, stopping their horses and then stared at Ted incredulously. "What did you say?" they replied nearly at the same time.

"The hellhounds don't kill, well, not usually. That's not their purpose."

"They have a purpose?" asked Shay intently.

"Everything to do with Toprak does," Ted replied somewhat casually as he tried to un-stretch his neck, something he was never quite able to do.

"Holy hell Ted! The hounds are Toprak too? Is there anything in England that doesn't bloody answer to Horsa? I suppose you're going to tell me that the St. Vitus is Toprak too?!" exclaimed Jess angrily.

Ted looked Jess in the eye and with great regret he nodded and said, "Yes, the dancers also are Toprak. They do seem to hold every card I'm loath to say. As for the hellhounds, they are in a sense, harbingers, though they look and act differently on moonless nights. They are what I guess you could call reapers, and the final deed that turns dancers into harbingers—from which there is no return, excepting for your intercession Jess, of course. There's no telling where Matthew is, but if we do find him, there is hope for sure."

Jess began shaking his head, wishing he could share in Ted's optimism, but Matthew was dead and he flanked his horse forward as he replied, "Matthew's dead Ted. The King shot him at point-blank range the night before the battle against Veronica."

"What?" asked Ted. "Are you sure? I mean, how was anyone able to recognize him. Harbingers don't usually look anything like the host and," Ted paused trying to make sense of what Jess just told him, but he couldn't. "From what I understand that's rather impossible—for him to become a harbinger I mean. Before the Minimum and early on, sure that was possible with only a single bite, but not now, which is why Toprak needed the dancers. Was Matthew ever a dancer?"

"No," replied Jess.

"Matthew's dead Ted! There is no coming back from a ball through your chest," replied Shay with irritation in his raised voice.

Suddenly, Ted stopped and raised his hand, signaling everyone to stop and be quiet. In the darkness, the natural sounds of the forest seemed to fade into a heavy silence as Jess and Shay waited and wondered what Ted had heard or seen. Following Ted's lead, everyone froze as they waited and waited. Ted wasn't sure if he smelt the rancid trail of a hellhound or if he had just imagined it since they were just talking about them, but if they were surrounded, he knew the next one to move would lose. With his hand still raised, he allowed himself to take a breath and he opened his mouth just a crack, then slowly sucked in oxygen. After filling his lungs, he held it so that he could absorb every last ounce before letting it go. The forest was so quiet that the only thing he could hear was his pulse throbbing in his ears and as he slowly released his breath, his horse became spooked and neighed. Then as if he had tripped an alarm, he saw the red glow of countless hellhound eyes in the darkness, followed by their curdling screams, "AHHHHHH-OHH-RRRG!"

"Move!" yelled Ted as he thrust his heels into his horse's side and leaped forward in an all-out sprint while drawing his sword. He didn't look behind but he could hear the hoofs of Jess and Shay's horses following closely as he prepared for a legion of hellhounds to appear. On cue, one leaped toward him from the left and he threw his sword in the air, catching it in his opposite hand and beheaded it without breaking stride. The headless body fell to the ground, tripping up several other hounds just as he saw the wide clearing they were riding through end. Once inside the forest again, it would be an easier task to defend themselves due to the dense foliage but the closer they got, they couldn't see an entrance. Before them was only thick trees and underbrush as high as their saddles, prohibiting access for a man on a horse, especially at full speed. The three of them pulled hard on their reins just in time to keep from crashing into the natural wall and they then turned about to watch the hellhounds rapidly close the short distance between them. There was nowhere to go, and literally nothing to do against a number so large. It was impossible to count in the darkness but there appeared to be thousands of them, overkill for only three men, but if Toprak had a motto besides Biz-yok, it was certainly overkill. The only thing to do was stare at one another in disbelief, which is what they did. After a few seconds, Jess climbed off his mare and faced the approaching wall of hellhounds, then knelt on the ground.

Ted and Shay watched in horror as the hounds drew closer and closer. They both knew Jess was praying but that was the last thing there was time for and they drew their swords across their chests in a defensive position. With the hellhounds less than fifty yards away, Jess slowly got to his feet and after looking toward heaven, he reached into his saddlebag and pulled out a small piece of flint and after gathering up a handful of dry grass, he knelt down with his knife and began striking the bar of flint as if he were trying to start a fire.

"They are not detoured by fire Jess, you're wasting your time!" yelled Ted.

Jess appeared unsure of what he was doing, almost as if he were making it up moment by moment and as he struck the flint one last time, the spark ignited the dry weeds which quickly turned into a robust flame. Even though Ted knew the fire would not slow down the hounds, he still took several steps backwards, placing the small fire between them and the press of certain death. Unsure of what to do next, Jess stood up and after placing his hands in his pockets, he felt the Cross fragments again and threw them into the fire, in desperation.

White fire shot from the small flame as the sky cracked above the forest canopy and a pearlescent hail rained down. The fire exploded through the possessed army leveling them to the ground as they howled out in a single evil chorus, unable to rise. When the pearl rain hit their grotesque bodies, they cried out as it burned deep into their flesh, every drop like a hot dagger. The scene was beyond description, and Ted and Shay coward behind Jess, afraid that the rain would destroy them also, but to their surprise, it was only wet on their skin. Between the fire and the pearl rain, the forest was illuminated like a ballpark for the brief few seconds it took to destroy the several thousand hellhounds Horsa had led to capture the three Anglo-Saxons he happened upon while in-route to Castle Hill.

Horsa, who had been watching the entire scene, couldn't believe his luck to find three Anglos all in one place and practically giftwrapped, but he was dumbfounded at what he had just witnessed and he dared not step out into the rain. After the howls and screams ceased, Jess fell on his knees exhausted as he saw Horsa disappear into the darkness on the opposite side of the clearing.

As they surveyed the scene before them in disbelief, Shay walked past the small flame that was now almost extinguished on his way to inspect the hellhound that was closest to them and after a quick look, he turned and said, "They're dwarfs."

"Dwarfs?" asked Jess as he slowly made his way toward Shay.

With the hellhound possession dispelled, they resembled their former selves and just as Shay had observed, they were dwarfs, all of them. Jess began to shake his head in disgust and then anger. "That's why they have so damn many of them. They have enslaved all of the dwarfs in Ireland."

Jess and Shay both looked at Ted for confirmation but he just shrugged and said, "I didn't know."

Jess sighed as he surveyed the terrible loss of life and then said, "We have to get out of this forest."

"Well, it's not like Toprak has another hellhound pack waiting in the wings—at least not tonight," said Shay.

Jess started to make his way to his horse and then turned to Shay and said, "Hellhounds, perhaps not, but they did not come alone."

"What do you mean they didn't come alone, what else did you see?" asked Ted.

"Not what but whom. Horsa is here," Jess replied as he pulled his hood over his head and then looked at Ted and said, "and Nicole."

CHAPTER 11

BLOOD-MEMORY

Horsa stared in disbelief as he watched the three Anglo-Saxons disappear into the protection of the midnight forest. While he waited for the pearl rain to subside, he cursed himself for his arrogance and for terribly under estimating Jess. He and Hengist knew Jess might be a potential barrier to their plans but never on the level or scale of what he had just witnessed. Jess had always been very devout and pious but nothing they observed about him suggested that such religious observances gave him any real power and he wondered how the Bishop could have grown so strong without his notice. What he had just witnessed not only completely defeated him and twenty-five hundred hellhounds, but it was equally as powerful and complete as his harbinger ignition. That kind of power had the potential to defeat Toprak if left unchecked and he determined that Jess's capture could not wait until next year as he and his brother had planned. Exactly where the three were going he wasn't sure, but there wasn't time to return to Ireland for more harbingers or a council with his brother. This was a job he would have to do himself, and with the power Jess now had, it would be a delicate chess game where Jess would have to be placed in a situation where he would willing give himself up.

With the pearl rain reduced to only a drizzle, he stood and looked around for Nicole who was right behind him at the start of the attack but not seeing her, he made his way back to their horses. The wet leaves of the underbrush burned his hands like acid so he raised and placed them on his head. When he approached the horses, he saw Nicole sitting atop her mount waiting with a startled look. She then gasped with relief and said, "For a second I thought you were being marched out of the forest by sword point."

Horsa wasn't amused. With his hands still on top of his head, he walked over and looked her in the eye even though she was sitting on her horse. Horsa was a massive man and as he drew near, he struck Nicole with the back of his hand, knocking her from her horse and throwing her ten feet into the brush unconscious.

"Don't lie to me bitch!" said Horsa as he picked up her limp body and threw her over her own saddle. He then walked over and picked up his reins off the ground, finding that they were still in the cold, dead hands of his servant—a dwarf harbinger who had apparently died from the rain. With disgust he picked up the lifeless heap with one hand and threw it into the forest. He then tied Nicole's horse behind his own and began making his way westward, following the trail of the Anglo-Saxons.

Just before daybreak, Nicole slowly sat up in her saddle, having been unconscious and in a deep sleep since they left the forest. The last thing she remembered was being knocked from her horse and since she knew why, she said nothing to Horsa. After she allowed Ted to escape from the tower, she told Horsa that she sent him to a dancer camp, but now that he had seen him, it was an obvious, but partial lie. They were approaching Hogshead Wood in the lowlands outside Chester and she determined that they were tracking Ted, Jess and Shay. If she allowed herself, she might begin to recall warm memories of crossing the Atlantic with the three of them but she quickly shifted her thoughts to less pleasant things which put her mind at ease. She rarely thought about those days anymore since they didn't serve any beneficial purpose. She had always been a survivor, aligning herself with whatever side appeared to have the advantage, just like when she made an alliance with the man who both protected and abused her on the *Euterpe* before Gus arrived. After Matthew killed him, she sailed with Gus and his friends to England. Now that she was with Toprak, she saw her life as nothing more than a continual alignment with those who had the best odds of winning. Ted once accused her of having no moral compass but as she saw it, it would be immoral to not do everything in one's power to win. In her mind, defeat was the greatest immorality and it disgusted her that so many in the world surrendered to it.

As they rode, neither of them spoke since everything that needed to be said had been by the back of Horsa's authoritative hand. Over the years she had learned that that was Horsa's way. He was not a man of great words and everything he did was brutally direct. The back of his hand was equivalent to another man's angry rant for hours, or days of the silent treatment and she much preferred Horsa's manner—swift, direct and nothing more needing to be said. There was no mistaking how he felt and the fact that she was still alive meant that he forgave her. She reached up to feel the swelling bruise that covered the right side of her face from her eye down to her chin but quickly lowered her hand when she saw Horsa finally turn to her and speak. "They're returning to Conwy," he said as he dismounted and bent down to pick a handful of buckhorn, a bitter but edible berry.

"Why? There's nothing left, not even their precious Queen," replied Nicole in an embittered tone.

Horsa continued to kneel as he chewed and spit, deep in thought. Whatever they were after in Conwy, it was important enough to risk all of their lives. It was also urgent enough that they traveled very light, without any additional soldiers for protection. He then stood up and threw the remaining berries in his hand on the ground and said, "What do you think your boyfriend is looking for in a burned-out city?"

Nicole rode over to where Horsa was standing and grabbed hold of his long hair, turning his face toward her. She then leaned over and kissed him violently, then with passion as she caressed his beard. After she released his lips, she pushed him away and said, "You know I only slept with him for his secrets. Knowing the Senator, he's probably chasing a medieval myth he remembered from college—dragging his precious friends into the heap."

Horsa shook his head. "Jess is no ewe. He's the leader of this expedition. Whatever it is they are chasing, I can't allow them to find it." He stared out over the shallow valley below them and watched the Anglos make their way westward, completely ignorant of his presence. "What are you after Bishop?" he whispered, leaning on his saddle.

Nicole had never seen Horsa take Ted and his friends so seriously nor had she seen him so unsettled. Whenever he wanted something, he always just took it. She was certain that Jess and his friends could not withstand Horsa for even a moment in battle, yet here he was, timidly watching and scheming his attack. The more she watched him, the more humored she became until she laughed out loud and said, "Just ride down there and claim your prize for hell's sake! What are you afraid of?"

Horsa slowly turned around with a slight smile that quickly faded. "There is only one thing that scares me in this world and I first saw it in a mirror—the thought of meeting myself in battle. Last night I looked into that mirror," Horsa said as he became lost again in his own thoughts, staring blankly across the valley. "I always thought

Guiscard was the one we had to watch. According to the professor, his blood was the purest in the world but the Bishop's must be purer still—which is why I can't just kill him."

"I don't' understand," said Nicole, believing that Horsa's solution to everything was death.

"I can't kill him no more than Veronica could kill me the last time we met. Before my fifth mark perhaps she could have, but not now. Men like us must suffer more than simple death," replied Horsa soberly as he continued to stare at Jess making his way across the valley.

Nicole shook her head, still unconvinced. "You mean to tell me that your sword piercing through those blessed, brown robes wouldn't kill him?"

Finally breaking his concentration, Horsa mounted his horse and replied, "Perhaps. I just have to be sure. Our plans demand it." He flanked his horse forward and slowly made his way off the hill as he called back to Nicole who was still watching Jess, "You coming Afet?"

Afet was the name of a Turkish woman Horsa had loved during the Russian Wars that never returned his affections. He forced her to travel with him as he and his brother cut their way across Turkmenistan until she was brutally murdered—skinned alive and hung on a tree outside his tent. It was assumed that her countrymen did it since Horsa forced her not to wear her veil, he having loved her long black hair that fell down to her waist. Oddly enough, considering Horsa's rough exterior, it was something he never got over and in his quiet moments, Nicole knew he still dreamed about her. When Horsa first laid eyes on Nicole, he thought she looked exactly like Afet, despite her blonde hair. The name *Afet* meant, devastatingly beautiful in Turkish, and Nicole took it as a compliment, not being jealous of a memory. Afet was the most endearing term Horsa had for Nicole and whenever he used it, she could be assured that everything was well between them so she smiled and replied, "Right behind you my Lord."

The best of two days were spent following the three men who rode in the open valleys below them, following the rivers that eventually emptied into the large Conwy River, then to the sea and the castle. While their journey was relatively easy, Nicole and Horsa had to ride at nearly double their pace since they kept to the highlands, traversing the hilly terrain and fording countless streams. Jess, Shay and Ted never stopped again on their journey to rest and subsequently neither did Horsa. Late in the second day, Nicole was having difficulty keeping up with Horsa's inexhaustible strength and he at length placed her in front of him on his horse while she slept in his arms and he towed her horse behind.

Nicole was a rather delicate creature when compared to Horsa. She stood only five foot, four inches on her tip-toes and weighed just under eight stone. In his arms, Horsa was more of a giant than a mere man. Like Matthew, Riley and many others, the Minimum had transformed them into mighty men of war as if nature had stepped in to ensure the survival of the human species. Four years after the onset of the Minimum, Horsa was now over seven foot and weighed well over twenty-three stone. Nicole's petite body resting before him and cradled in his left arm was almost an afterthought as they traversed the countryside. Leaping over a small brook, Nicole stirred slightly and nuzzled back into Horsa's massive bicep before nodding off again. There were few things she enjoyed more than being in Horsa's dangerous embrace, an embrace that was like a double-edged sword wielding both fear and security. It was perpetual ecstasy to be coddled by a man so powerful who was able to crush her tender body, but instead secretly cherished it. It was as if her body calmed the violent warrior she had seen cut down hundreds in battle and it was the ever-possibility of an easy death in his embrace that satisfied her like no other man she had ever loved. Even though she had never heard Horsa tell her he loved her, right now the lion was a refuge for the lamb which rendered any possible endearing words powerless.

In the fading light, the sun slowly set behind the Conwy village walls as Horsa watched Jess and his companions enter through the south gate and disappear inside the ancient fortress. He had been following at a safe distance until they reached the Gyffin River less than a mile from the village where he settled into an elevated vantage point that allowed him to observe their ultimate destination. To his surprise, they did not make their way to the castle, but it appeared they turned left once inside the walls where he could not see them any longer. He surveyed the surrounding countryside trying to determine the place that would give him visible access beyond the walls and while there were several prominent hills around the village, he concluded that they were too far away in the event he needed to act quickly. He finally concluded that the southern garrison along the wall would provide both a front row seat to the happenings in the village and seclusion.

Crossing the Gyffin, he guided his horse toward the garrison he had seen from the hillside and the closer he got, the more he was convinced that he had made a good decision. The garrison was positioned on a gently rising hill along the ancient wall, providing both pivotal observation and protection from the view of the Anglos and the weather. From the time he fought his first battle in Wales against Matthew and his Ravenguard, he had rarely experienced Wales without clouds or violent rain and it appeared that tonight would be no exception. Grey clouds were pushing in from the coast, making the evening much darker than it really was and creating perfect conditions for surveillance. Ugly weather was distracting for most people, which allowed for closer and more aggressive observation than would have been possible under a clear sky. Reaching the wall, he climbed off his horse and pulled Nicole up over his shoulder as she squoze his neck, waking.

"Wow, that was quick," she said as a child might who had slept during a long car ride.

Horsa sat her down without a word as he drew his dagger and then stepped over to the wall. While Nicole secured the horses, he wedged his blade into the crumbling mortar and quickly removed one stone after another, creating foot and hand holds along a crevice where the garrison met the tall walls. With his makeshift steps completed, he threw bags over his shoulder and bent down, motioning Nicole to climb up on his back. She placed one foot on his weapon belt, then jumped up and grabbed hold of his shoulders while wrapping her arms around his neck. Horsa scaled the wall with little effort, then peered over the top to make sure they were not being observed. In the dark village below, he couldn't see any signs of life in the deserted streets. It appeared just as he had left it, black and desolate. He waited a few minutes more to be sure they were alone and then in a single motion, he grabbed Nicole by her thin waist and swung her over the top of the wall.

The village walls like the castle itself, were in ruins but the largest barbican where they had ascended was mostly intact, containing a solid battlement and a partially covered retreat below. All of the dark grey stone that faced north was covered with an emerald moss, as was most everything in Wales, except where the stone was black and charred from the harbinger ignition. Crouching down behind the wall atop the battlement, Horsa could see the faint outline of the castle in the last light of the day, the dark towers nearly invisible against the menacing sky. Every last bit of light had fled from the village below him so he studied the darkness for any signs of light and listened intently for movement, but there was nothing. Wherever the three Anglos were, they were secluded somewhere within the walls and being very careful, obviously thinking that they had escaped unobserved.

"Do you ever wonder what this place must have been like in its heyday?" whispered Nicole, waxing a little nostalgic in her medieval surroundings and sitting atop one of the greatest preserved wall cities in the world.

The furthest thing from Horsa's mind at that moment was sentimental nonsense surrounding the darkest and most brutal period in history, where modern so-called historians, invented stories of chivalrous knights rescuing helpless damsels in an emerald forest. The thought of such stupidity made him angry and he smirked at the thought, but since there was nothing to be observed in the village, he turned and leaned up against the shallow wall with a sigh, deciding he would give Nicole an honest history lesson.

"I don't have to wonder what it was like, I know what it was like," he replied.

Nicole was amused and she laughed. "You do, do you? Please enlighten me," she said as she crouched behind the wall next to him.

"What you're sitting on was among the most terrifying things in that age. It represented everything that was wrong with the world—oppression, caste, poverty and privilege for a few. Those were the positive things. For the rest of the kingdom it meant injustice, torture and agonizing death." As Horsa continued, his words become slower and his tone distant as if he were recalling a very old memory. "The modern world before the Minimum was an illusion that hid the realities of life. The reality that power belongs to only those who can physically wield it and where the weak are rightfully subdued—and if not subdued, destroyed. But even with all of its horror, it was an honest time. Men's tongues didn't fight battles or win wars back then. Offenses were revenged swiftly, with mortal force when necessary and there was no such thing as something as ridiculous as passive-aggression—only aggression. There were no courts to hide behind, no slippery laws to protect the flatterers." Horsa leaned his head back on the wall as he reminisced. "In all its horror, there's no denying it was a beautiful time, but not for the reasons history tells you." He then shook his head with amusement and laughed, "Oh but how it smelled!"

Nicole leaned forward and looked at Horsa incredulously, shocked to hear him speak so matter-of-factly about events over eight-hundred years ago as if he had been there. "How would you know how it smelled?" she asked shaking her head, sure she was being made a fool.

Horsa was still caught-up in his reminiscence with his eyes looking toward the dark sky like he was watching a movie. After a few minutes he slowly turned to Nicole and said smiling, "Because I was there."

Nicole had seen Horsa do a lot of unbelievable things but accepting that he had lived for hundreds of years was pushing her belief system and she rolled her eyes and sat back up against the wall shaking her head. Horsa began to laugh but smothered it, fearing he was too loud then continued in a softer tone. "I suppose I have left a lot of dots unconnected for you, but I am surprised you have not connected them yourself." He lifted himself up to peer over the wall, making sure he wasn't missing anything down below and then resumed. "You did not become a new soul the day you were born, nor were you ever, in the devil's name, created equal to everyone else in the world. Haven't you wondered why world power remains in the same hands, the same families, century after endless century—even in America? If you traced the genealogy of the American Presidents, you would find an uncanny connection to the same ancestors. But beyond that, the real power in America was not with the office of the President, it was the corporations. The wealth and power of the world since the dawn of time has always been and remains in the same hands."

"What are you talking about?" replied Nicole more confused than ever as she wondered what world power and blood-genealogy had to do with him being eight-hundred years old.

Horsa's smile intimated that he was getting to his point and he continued as if he were about to share a great secret. "I wasn't the only one who was there. You were too."

Nicole laughed, "No—no, I assure you, I wasn't."

Horsa looked deep into Nicole's eyes and for several minutes said nothing while turning his head several times as if he were searching for something. He then rubbed the five-point star scare on his palm, something he did anytime he called upon dark power. A big smile then came to his face as he began to nod. "Yes, you were there—I should perhaps be more watchful of you from now on however."

After another peek over the wall, Horsa settled in to relate one of Toprak's greatest secrets and sources of power—something he could now do since he had seen Nicole's blood-memory and he was confident he was among his own. Nicole's confusion had no voice as she sat waiting for Horsa to explain himself or at least tell her that he was having a go at her but the look on his face was not playful and he turned to her with intensity.

"You have been alive for many a millennia but you are only conscious of the moments since your birth—or at least that's how it is with most. But every pivotal moment of your ancestry is within you, making you who you are. You cannot escape it, you cannot change it, you cannot ignore it. It effects everything you do and how you do it. Everything from your clothing to the men you love and hate."

From the look on Nicole's face and the involuntary shaking of her head, he knew she wasn't buying what he was selling, so he decided he would prove it. "Tell me. Why did you spurn your Senator boyfriend after you milked every last ounce of useable information out of him? How could you passionately kiss him, sleep with him, and then turn him out? Even more, how could you turn on your friends and align yourself with their enemies so easily?"

Nicole couldn't provide Horsa with an answer no matter how hard she tried to unravel her motivations. "I don't know, I guess I—I don't know, I just decided," she said feeling stupid.

"You did it because you have done it before. In fact, you were famous for it once. You should be proud," replied Horsa, sounding like a pleased mentor.

"How do you know?" asked Nicole a little concerned due

to Horsa's confidence.

"Your ancestor's deeds are recorded in your bones, just as their blood is still pulsating through your body at this very moment. Professor Moran called it blood-memory. It's the marrow that produces blood cells and the marrow in one's bones has always been synonymous with strength and vitality has it not? And fittingly so. The memory in our marrow infuses into our blood and therefore every cell of our body."

"And who do you speak of in my past?" asked Nicole now completely vested in the conversation.

"Well, it would take months if not years to unravel all of it, which is why Hengist and I retained the professor for so long. But the strongest memory in your past emanates from none other than Judith the Cunning."

"Who?" replied Nicole wondering if this was someone she should know. She had never heard Horsa wax so intellectual nor profess to be an expert in anything except death and she stared in amazement as she listened to him expound upon her own history.

"Judith was a medieval woman renowned for her cunning. It is said that she even beheaded a prince in her book *The Sword of Judith,* you should read it sometime."

"What, you've read it?"

"No, but you should. I'm certain you will find yourself in it—like looking in a mirror. In fact, the more you learn about your ancestors, the more you will learn about yourself and the more you will be surprisingly, unsurprised. But, I'm being ridiculous."

Nicole's fascination turned to rage as she realized Horsa was having a go at her and just as she was about to slap him, he caught her arm before it connected with his face. "See, there she is. Judith is with us still," he laughed, "What I meant was, I was being ridiculous for suggesting that you read—not that you can't. There's just a faster and eminently more efficient way to know it."

Horsa got to his knees and faced Nicole looking sober and serious. "This must be of your own willingness, for it will change you."

"Change me how—what are you talking about?" asked Nicole feeling uneasy and a little afraid.

"Your eyes will no longer be clouded with the death of your ancestors."

"Is that all?" Nicole interrupted, laughing nervously.

Horsa smiled as he shook his head with eagerness. "You will become more powerful than you have ever dreamed. Knowing one's past does that."

Nicole looked down at the ancient stonework of the battlement and wondered what Horsa could possibly be talking about as she trembled slightly with fear. "Do I have to…" she asked as she made a cutting movement across her palm thinking that he was suggesting that she cut a demonic inverted star on her hand—from which she knew there was no return.

"No, nothing so grim," he replied, taking her trembling hands in his. "You will just have knowledge—knowledge is power. Let's just say your eyes will be opened."

Her rational mind was screaming that this was all a stupid

joke while something else inside her was drawing her toward it. It was at once terrifying and yet somehow her heart's desire. It reminded her of the first time she tried 'shrooms in college at the coaxing of her then lover and how desire and fear battled for control. After a few minutes, just as she did in college, she looked up at her lover and nodded.

Horsa's quiet nod for some reason unsettled her even more and just as horror swept through her, he made a single cut on her palm and then squoze it hard with his hand containing the star scar, causing blood to ooze from the wound. He then held his hand above her head and motioned for her to look skyward. She was now beyond afraid and as she watched black clouds stream across the forbidding sky, a tear of fear rolled down her cheek while she bit her lip to keep from crying out. Just then, Horsa tightened his grip on her bleeding hand almost to the point of breaking bones, causing her tight lips to burst. She cried out in agony and terror just as a drop of her own blood fell from their clasped hands and into her eye that was wide with fear.

The black sky above her head cracked turning everything in the world red as it seemed to revolve around her in slow motion, the eons of earth passing through her mind accompanied with the sensation of falling and a dagger being thrust into her breast. Then one-by-one, but nearly instantaneously, doors in her mind were violently torn open, reacquainting herself with herself and facets of her being that were unknown but not altogether foreign. She then saw Horsa sitting atop the battlement in the rain, holding her lifeless body in his arms as she fell toward him, the speed of her descent growing faster and faster until she opened her eyes in his lap. While the rain fell on her face, she looked up at Horsa as he smiled and tenderly brushed back her blond hair from her face. Within seconds of being aware of where she was and what had just happened, she felt a power whelm up from seemingly every cell in her body, causing her to clinch her fists and shake as if molten iron were being shot into her bloodstream. Horsa knew what was to follow and he held onto her delicate body while she arched backwards and screamed as if she were being ripped apart.

Several minutes after the echo of her torment faded beyond the stone walls, she opened her eyes, finding herself still in Horsa's arms and he still tenderly stroking her head. As she slowly tried to sit up, her new disposition finally entered her conscious mind, crossing the blood-brain barrier like a powerful drug and she shot up with excitement. Compared to the mental prison she was in just moments before, she felt like she could fly and Horsa, remembering the feeling, held tightly to her just in case she tried to jump from the tower. The vastness of mind she felt could not be expressed as her excited intellect sped faster than her lips could utter, resulting in whimpers and gasps. She finally gave up on speaking all together and jumped into Horsa's arms, squeezing him tightly in a thankful embrace.

Horsa held her small body in his arms as the rain continued to pour down, both of them enjoying the moment of enlightenment as if she had been blind since birth, and in essence, she had been. Just then, Horsa saw the light of a lantern near the center of the village in the churchyard, the Anglos at long last making their presence known. Breaking their embrace, they both watched the light, knowing what it meant and that the time to move was now. Horsa slid his dagger under his belt then turned and offered his hand to Nicole but to his surprise, she already had one leg over the wall. She looked at him and shook her head, wondering if he were serious, then lowered herself as far as her arms would allow and then completed the descent with a backflip, landing firmly on ground with both feet. Horsa smiled and shook his head as he leaped from the tower, landing next to her and said, “I could get used to that Afet.”

CHAPTER 12

TO CAPTURE A BISHOP

Jess held a lantern high above his head as he slowly turned in a circle, scanning the dark graveyard with dread and trying to discover the source of the scream they had just heard. Shay and Ted were standing by his side with swords drawn, waiting for something terrible to leap out from the shadows but they saw nothing as the rain pelted down upon them. When they heard the scream, they were all in the basement of the ancient church, searching for clues. that would help them unravel the mystery of the *We Are Seven* grave. So far, their hunt had not revealed anything substantial, but they did find a long forgotten crypt in the east end of the basement. They were just about to sweep away the centuries of dirt and dust when they heard the horrific sound.

"Let's at least circle the grounds once," said Jess as he pulled a dagger from his cloak and began walking toward the bell tower.

Shay and Ted nodded and followed closely behind the lantern within the illuminated circular illusion of safety. The tombstones seemed twice as numerous in the dark and at least three times more sinister, their tall shadows casting ghostly images across the wet ground. As they made their way along the north side of the church, they walked along a narrow path that lead out to an alley and from there, to the river. Before they reached the alley, they would take a small footpath on the right that would lead them back to the church, but before they got to the path, they heard a noise somewhere in the darkness of the alley. Ted heard it first and just as he was about to alert the others, Jess lowered his lamp and blew out the flame. They were standing in the most expansive area of the churchyard with nowhere to hide and without the light of the lantern nor the moon, there was nowhere to run, so they all crouched down, trying to make themselves disappear as they listened.

There was definitely something in the alley less than one-hundred yards ahead of them, but they couldn't name the sound until Ted whispered in Shay's ear, "Fenrir."

Shay looked back at Ted in alarm as he nodded. He then leaned forward and shared with Jess, Ted's discovery. The few times Shay had seen a fenrir, it was charging and running toward him but Ted had observed them in a more peaceable state while feeding, which is how he recognized the sound—heavy shuffling footsteps and deep, hollow fanning. There was no question that a fenrir had better night vision than humans, making an attack fatal if it caught their scent. Ted lifted his head to ascertain if they were up or downwind from the beast and felt a slight breeze pass his face, right toward the fenrir which made him wonder why they had not been discovered. It then occurred to him that the heavy rain doused their scent before it traveled more than several feet—at least that was his guess and he decided to not push their luck.

He tapped Jess on the back and then quietly led the way back to the church in the wet darkness. On a night like tonight, with no moon, no stars and no manmade light, it was complete blackness like the depths of a cave where objects could not be seen, only felt. Consequently, Ted felt his way around the tombstones in the direction he last remembered seeing the church, crawling headlong into several stones. After he was sure he should have already run into the church, he made a sharp right turn in an attempt to backtrack just as his head bumped into iron bars. He remembered their being an iron gate at the entrance of the church but as he felt the bars in front of him, they terminated at about waist height.

"What is it?" asked Jess, wondering why Ted had stopped.

He was just about to say that he had taken a wrong turn when Shay realized where they were—the grave of The Seven.

"This is the grave," said Shay.

"THE Grave?" asked Jess.

"Yes," replied Shay as he moved to one side.

Jess felt the stout bars surrounding the grave and then reached inside the enclosure, but as he felt around he felt nothing—not even the bare earth. The further he reached downward, the more astounded he became as he could still not feel the ground. It was as if the grave was open and he turned in surprise as Ted crawled up next to him.

"So, the grave is open?" he said in alarm.

"What—no, it isn't," replied Shay.

"Well, it is now!"

Shay and Ted both reached inside the iron enclosure with apprehension, trying not to think too heavily about reaching inside a medieval grave in a dark graveyard.

"Your dreaming Jess, the ground is as solid as it is wet," replied Ted.

It was impossible to have any kind of meaningful conversation given the heavy rain and the fact that a fenrir might be tracking them, so Jess determined he might as well be sure and he reached his hand into the enclosure again. He lowered his arm downward as far as he could until his shoulder wedged in between the bars and then felt around. There was nothing except… He stopped and turned his hand over several times to be sure and then concluded he was right. Pushing up from the grave was warmth much warmer than the wet, night air at the surface, but why? He then thought he touched something but he wasn't sure. Did he just imagine it or did he touch the grave wall? To be sure, he felt around for the side of the grave and found it many inches away from where his hand was, which made his hair stand on end. Just as he was about to withdraw, he found the courage to feel for the touch one more time and he made a broad sweep through the grave as far as he could reach but felt nothing. The situation was perfect for anyone's imagination to run wild and he finally determined that his was getting the best of him.

Just then the familiar sound of an angry fenrir somewhere in the darkness announced it was drawing closer and they all jumped to their feet and ran in the direction they believed the church was. Running blind, they hoped their collective sense of direction was accurate and that they would reach the safety of the stone walls of the church before the fenrir did. Nothing distorts time and space as does complete darkness and just as Jess was sure he should have reached the church, he crashed over a gravestone that upended him at the knees and he fell face first on the other side. There was no time for an accounting of his injuries and he jumped up again but after only several steps, he ran headlong into the church, knocking him on his back. Rolling onto his knees, he crawled around to the door he knew was only a few feet to his left, finding Ted and Shay already there and they pulled him inside.

Jess limped over to a small table at the back of the chapel and lit a candle while Ted and Shay bolted the door. After they caught their breath, they began removing their wet clothes until Shay exclaimed, "Jess, your arm!"

Thinking Shay was referring to his run-in with the tombstone, he looked down and was surprised to see that his arm was covered in blood from his shoulder to his fingertips. "What happened, were you attacked?" asked Ted rushing over to inspect his wounds.

"No, I don't think so," replied Jess confused, pulling off his drenched robe and throwing it in a heavy heap on the floor.

Ted examined Jess's shoulder for wounds but found none, except for a gash on his knee and forehead, both of which were not serious enough to cause much bleeding. Jess picked up his wet robe and began wiping off his arm as he secretly observed Shay quickly wiping blood from his own hand before Ted saw it. Catching Jess's glance, Shay motioned for Jess to keep quiet until they could speak privately. Jess quickly nodded but not before Ted noticed the unspoken dialogue that excluded him.

"What? What are you guys talking about—besides me that is?" asked Ted mildly irritated but waiting for the conclusion of the joke. "That wasn't really blood was it? What are you playing at? Ha, ha, joke's on me is it?"

Shay took a deep sigh and then bit his lower lip, wondering what to say. Unknown to Jess and Ted, he did not feel the solid earth when he reached inside the grave. Like Jess, the grave was most certainly open and the fact that Ted's hand was not covered in blood proved the grave was closed to him. Shay knew Ted already felt like an outsider and the last thing he wanted to do was alienate him further on the outside of things but Shay could see no way around the truth. Jess and Shay both looked at each other, waiting for the other to explain but just as the pause was getting painful, Shay volunteered.

"Ted. No, we are not having a-go at you. It's just that…"

Ted began to roll his eyes, "Oh, never mind. I get it. I STILL can't be trusted."

"NO!" exclaimed Shay and Jess at the same time.

"It's just that—I couldn't feel the ground inside the grave either," said Shay, stopping the runaway train that was Ted's sensitive feelings about his loyalty. "Knowing you were the only one to whom the grave was closed to—well, I didn't know what it meant—and still don't. If I knew any secret in this moment I would surely tell you Ted. I…" Shay paused and pointed to Jess, "We trust you."

Ted sighed and then abruptly laughed.

"What's funny?" asked Jess.

"Well, you both assume that the grave being open to you is a good thing. I mean, it is after all a grave. Maybe I'm the only one who isn't going to die tonight." Ted laughed again trying to dispel the mood and lighten the strained relationship between he and two of his best friends. His laughter echoed off the stone walls and then into silence, their effect not changing the underlying mood in the chapel. The reason the grave was closed to Ted was obvious to everyone including Ted and just as he was about to describe the elephant in the room, Jess spoke. "That isn't accurate Ted."

Ted and Shay both looked at Jess confused.

"What you were about to say—the reason why you felt solid earth. The real truth is we don't know what all this means. Hell, you could be right. Maybe you are the only survivor tonight."

Ted smiled weakly but inwardly he knew he was locked out because of his betrayal and he knew his friends knew it also; at least until Shay caught-up with the silent conversation running underneath the spoken one.

"What?—Wait, Ted, no! Certainly what happened at the Tower has nothing to do with any of this and that ISN'T what we were thinking."

Jess confirmed Shay's words with a nod though he was deep in thought just as he noticed a patch of blood on the underside of his wrist. Studying it a little closer, he lifted it to his mouth and dabbed the spot on his tongue and slowly processed the taste.

Well?" asked Ted, anxious for the result. "Is it blood or ketchup?"

Jess was confused with the taste and assuming he didn't get a large enough sample, he licked the entire spot, saturating his taste buds and waited. "Hmm, not ketchup—not anything. It has no more taste than water."

"What do you think it was?" asked Shay.

"No idea, none whatsoever," replied Jess, whipping the

remainder of the missed blood off his arm.

"Oh—I meant the scream we heard that got us outside in the first place."

Jess and Ted had almost forgotten due to all the excitement and Ted laughed lightly and said, "No idea, none whatsoever." Jess however appeared sullen.

"What is it Jess?" Shay asked.

"It was certainly human and a woman. What if it was Veronica? What if she *was* here and you missed her somehow in your search and Toprak has now come back to find and finish her?" said Jess.

Ted seemed to be the only one thinking rationally and he shook his head insisting that it was impossible. "We searched every inch of the castle and the city. We even searched the bottom of the river. She was not here and we didn't find any bones that were a possible match either. I'm certain she either fled in her ship to safety or is a Toprak prisoner. Either way, she is probably safe."

"Unless…" Jess replied.

"Unless what?" asked Shay.

"Unless she is terribly wounded and bleeding out somewhere, hoping we come find her."

Ted sighed with frustration. "That is possible Jess of course, but given the day and the hour, such defeated talk is pointless. Let's focus our energy on hope."

Jess sighed, "You're right, you're right. I am two days without sleep and as the adrenaline abates from our scare,

I am ready to collapse. Let's get some rest and start in the morning. One seldom, if ever, finds answers in the dark."

Shay and Ted agreed and they all found a pew near the back of the chapel and tried to get comfortable. Jess removed his brown robe and began rolling it up to form a pillow but in doing so, he felt the shape of a small leather-bound book stuck in one of the pockets that he found in the crypt earlier. In the dim light he wasn't sure of its contents but it appeared to be a medieval procedure manual for the clergy and he placed it back in the pocket so that he would not forget it in the morning. He had always wondered how the modern church differed from its predecessor but even if it contained nothing important, he figured it would make interesting reading especially since books were so scarce in the modern world.

As he rolled onto his side, it wasn't long before Ted could hear snores from his companions while he suffered with insomnia. Ever since he went with Nicole to watch a dancer encampment, he found it difficult to sleep and some nights, he didn't ever nod off. He took a deep sigh and tried to focus on his breathing, something he learned to do at the Senate when he need to grab a quick nap. He found if he rolled his eyes backwards and took a shallow breath and then held it for several seconds, it reduced his heart rate and induced sleep. However, after several attempts, he sat up in frustration just as he saw the faint outline of a face in the obscured glass of the window. He shook his head wondering if perhaps he was asleep but concluded he was not and he laid back down and then rolled quietly off the pew onto the floor. He knew the visual dynamics of night did not allow for clear vision into a dark building from the outside so he was certain who or whatever was outside did not see him—that is if it wasn't all his imagination.

He crawled on his hands and knees to the back wall then slowly stood up and carefully inspected every window in the chapel. There was a very good chance that the obscured, centuries old glass only made him think he saw something but he also knew Horsa and that he would not be easily defeated, especially after such a crushing and humiliating blow. He knew Horsa and Nicole in all probability had followed them to Conwy but he didn't want to worry his friends unnecessarily so he said nothing and just kept an eye out for signs of their presence—this being the first sign. Any chance of sleep now had completely left him and after a thorough sweep of the chapel, he took a pew next to his two sleeping friends and placed his sword in his lap, determining that being right next to them was the best place to be in the event of an attack since he could both alert and protect them in an instant.

As the hazy sunlight began to illuminate the eastern sky, Ted reached down into his bag and pulled out a tattered copy of *The Sword of Judith,* a medieval manuscript he found in Dover castle. It was a certified work of medieval fiction in the pre-Minimum world, but now he wasn't so sure. He had read it several times, mostly because it was the only book he owned and he had to satisfy his insatiable hunger to read. Besides that, he found it amusing how much Judith reminded him of Nicole.

"Good morning your Grace," said Ted as Jess sat up rubbing his eyes.

"Have you not slept?" asked Jess as he slowly got to his feet and stretched.

"No," I figured someone should keep a vigil just in case.

Jess nodded, "Thank you for doing that. You must be

completely fagged. Are you sure you don't need to sleep?"

"I'll be fine for at least one more day, but tomorrow it's your turn," replied Ted as he licked his finger and turned a page.

"Did I hear correctly that you didn't sleep?" asked Shay coming to life.

Ted just shook his head, then set his sword on the floor and returned to his reading. The rain was only just starting to subside as the sun struggled to break through the clouds, casting a silver light through the stained glass, causing Jess to wax transcendent.

"How beautiful this sacred building is," he said looking around the chapel in the light of day. "I am always astounded when I consider the events of these ancient buildings and the sacrifice it was to even build them. We had no frame of reference for such things in the Pre-Minimum world. We can imagine it now, but before we had no idea what a sacrifice it was to work on a building for a hundred years or more—incredible! The secrets these old churches must hold." He then turned to Shay directly and asked, "Speaking of secrets, did you by chance search the hidden compartment under the inner ward of the castle for Veronica?"

"I didn't know such thing existed," replied Shay as Ted put down his book.

"Well, if she was in there, from what you say, she would be dead from the heat of the harbinger ignition, but just for the sake of being thorough, we should make sure there isn't a body under there. When we first arrived in Conwy, the construction crew found several artifacts inside," said Jess as he felt his cloak to see if it were dry.

"Very well, let's check that out in the daylight and then return here and finish our exploration of the crypt," said Shay as he opened the door and looked up at the sky. "Looks as though we have a clear weather window at least for the next few hours."

Ted nervously stepped in front of Shay, quickly surveying the churchyard, afraid that Horsa might be waiting for them but he only saw the illuminated wet grass as it sparkled in the sunlight. Despite the fact that he wasn't sure if what he saw in the window last night was real, he determined that he had better tell his friends lest they assume they were safe.

"Um, there was a reason I stayed up last night," began Ted as they made their way across the churchyard. "I was having a bout of insomnia and when I sat up, I thought I saw a face in the chapel window. I discretely checked them all and kept a solid watch for several hours but I never saw it again."

Jess smiled. "Well, thank you again Ted," he said just as they reached the large iron gate of the church where they had tied their horses and he froze. "Where the hell are the they?" he asked, scanning the area.

Ted and Shay shook their heads as they also tried to see if they had wandered off in the storm. "Do you think the fenrir got them?" asked Shay.

"No, fenrir only eat humans," replied Jess flippantly. "Or, I think that's all they eat," he added turning to Ted.

Ted shook his head and then shrugged. "It's unlikely but possible I guess. Nicole said that they only feed on humans and dead things. Besides, there doesn't seem to any carnage in the area."

Jess sighed as he tried to remain positive. "Well, I guess they've run off."

"Or…" said Ted as Shay and Jess looked at him, waiting for him to continue.

Ted didn't want to be accused of withholding information again and he took a deep breath before sharing his bad news. "I'm pretty sure we were followed here. After what you did to Horsa and his war harbingers, he will not be so easily defeated and I have never known a man as hell-bent for revenge. I'm sorry I didn't share my fears with you sooner."

Shay laughed with a single huff. "Well that's no secret. We all assumed that, right? Did you see something that you're not tell us?"

"Only what I just told you—you both seem so calm and I didn't want to destroy your moment of bliss," replied Ted.

Jess nodded. "Bliss maybe, but that was only inside the church. I suggest we get to the castle and back as quick as possible." Jess then paused and asked, "What are you staring at?"

"Your hand Jess, look at it," replied Ted.

Jess casually glanced down at his right hand and then held it up for a better look in the daylight.

"Whatever was in that grave, it stains something fantastic," said Ted.

Jess's hand was blood red from the tips of his fingers to

his wrist, but as he pulled up his sleeve, he saw his skin was indelibly red clear to his shoulder.

"Are you well?" asked Ted. "It almost looks like you are bruised or that you are bleeding internally. Do you feel pain?"

Jess shrugged as he rolled his arm over several times, "No. No pain whatsoever. Not even tender."

He pushed his sleeve down and suggested that they check-out the well and get back to the church as fast as they could—then get out of Conwy all together. As they hurried their pace, Shay secretly inspected his hand that he placed in the grave and his too was red up to his wrist as if it were tattooed.

They made their way down Castle Street towards the blackened district where the harbinger ignition turned everything to charcoal and as they turned onto the Square Shay paused. This was the very spot where he had learned that Conwy had been sacked and when he first feared Veronica was dead. Swallowing hard, he forced one foot in front of the other just as Ted stopped dead in his tracks.

"Horsa is here," he said as he caught his breath.

"How do you know?" asked Jess.

"The horses. He took the horses. I know mine for sure was tied too tight for a struggling horse to free itself," Ted replied as he resumed walking but at a slower pace.

Shay drew his sword and slowly turned around as Jess and Ted did the same. The village was as quiet as it was black, not even the relentless Welsh wind was blowing and they determined that they had best make a run for it. They were only a few hundred yards from the castle and when they reached the moat, out of breath, they each took turns swinging across on the rope that Shay's commander had placed there several weeks ago. The castle appeared just as they had left it, except for maybe there was less ash on the ground, it having been washed away with the nearly continual rain in Wales. Jess walked across the outer ward toward the gates leading to Veronica's living quarters where the trapdoor was discovered and upon reaching it, he pulled up on the iron ring as it broke off in his hand. Shay knelt down and began wiping away the dirt and ash from around the edges, discovering that several large stones had been wedged into the cracks, too tight to be removed with fingers. Just as Shay looked for a lever, Ted was approaching with an eight-foot piece of iron that had once supported the roof and he rammed it into the crack, causing the brittle door to cave in.

Jess peered through the small opening as Shay and Ted began removing the remaining pieces of the door. The first thing Jess looked for was a body and as the light expanded with the removal of the door, he sighed in relief. The area under the trapdoor was the site of an ancient well but had a small compartment that looked just large enough for a man to crawl through. It was impossible to know just how far it went in due to the lack of adequate lighting but according to the workmen who found the artifacts, it was just an alcove.

"See anything?" asked Shay.

Jess stuck his head lower into the hole, trying to let his eyes grow accustomed to the darkness but finally lifted himself up and said, "No, it's just too dark. I didn't think to bring a lamp, it being daylight and all."

"You never did say what the workmen found," said Ted.

"Well," replied Jess, sitting on the edge of the well. "They found the raven banner that Veronica believed belonged to Ragnar's army and…"

"No kidding!" exclaimed Ted. "I wonder if it works?"

Jess nodded. "So did we, I suppose it does," he replied without going into the reasons why he believed it. "And a longsword and a few other rather meaningless items. Where they are now is anyone's guess however."

Shay shook his head. "It doesn't seem to make sense. Now if it were seven swords—well, then we'd really have something."

"It is possible that the site was plundered over the years. Maybe there were seven swords once," suggested Ted taking a look inside the hole.

Shay was frustrated. "Even if there were—what the hell would it mean. It would just add one more piece to the mystery," he said as he stood up.

"It sure looks like it goes deeper into the side," said Ted. "How about you two lower me down and I'll check it out?"

Jess wasn't sure. "I don't know Ted. If we had a rope, maybe. That well looks like it goes all the way to hell—there would be no getting you out," he replied as he looked inside the hole again.

Ted reached out his hand to Jess and said, "Here, take my hand, I'm sure I'll be fine. It's only five feet to the entrance. Besides, we don't have all day—who knows what time we really have."

Reluctantly, Jess took hold of his hand as Shay came over to help. Ted stepped into the dark hole and tried to brace his foot along the side but due to the moss-covered stones, he slipped, nearly causing him to fall into oblivion. Jess and Shay quickly grabbed him tighter as his feet dangled in the darkness and they slowly lowered him so that he could reach the opening of the alcove. With his heart pounding, he touched the mossy edge with his toes and tested it for stability and then slowly put more weight and faith in his decision. Once he was safely standing on ledge, he slowly let go and slid inside.

Once his eyes grew accustomed to the darkness, he could tell that it wasn't a simple alcove at all but a tunnel that extended under the castle and perhaps much, much further. It was barely tall enough to crawl through and once he was more comfortable with his surroundings, he crept inside a little further, making sure that the floor was solid. Feeling his way, he felt something cold and hard in front of him and the more he blindly inspected it, he was convinced that it was a sword—many of them.

"Well?" asked Shay just as Ted was about to tell them what he had found.

"I found more swords," he replied.

"Really, how many. Are they longswords?" asked Jess.

"I'm not sure, let me hand them up," Ted said as he handed up the first one.

It looked identical to the other sword that came from the well as did all the others, four in all.

"It appears you have your wish Shay," said Ted yelling

from the tunnel. "But there are only five, counting the one Veronica hopefully still has—and we're none the wiser just as you predicted."

Ted crawled several more yards into the tunnel but it was futile to go any further without a light and he made his way back and yelled, "There's nothing more to see without a light—lend a hand?"

Neither Jess or Shay replied and after a few long seconds, Ted become a little irritated. "Um—hello up there. Anyone care to pull this rabbit out of a hole?"

Just then a hand grabbed his and jerked him violently out of the tunnel and into the bright sunlight while he dangled in mid-air. Abruptly coming from the darkness into daylight, he couldn't see anything except blurry, painful shapes and as he closed his eyes, he wondered what the devil was going on. He didn't have to wonder for long as he then heard a deep laugh that stabbed him with fear.

"Look, I'm magic. I just pulled a rabbit from a hole!" the voice said, finding great humor in his own joke. "Oh—my mistake. Forgive me Father. It's not a rabbit but I got the hole right, it's an asshole!" said Horsa taunting Jess and throwing Ted against a wall several yards away. The impact with the wall nearly knocked Ted unconscious but with his eyesight returning to him, he rolled onto his hands and knees as Jess and Shay helped him get up.

Horsa was standing several yards in front of them looking very pleased and giddy as he always did just before he was about to kill something. He then noticed Nicole pointing a sword at Jess and Shay which explained why they were so silent and stiff. The situation was as terrible as he could have imagined, Horsa holding all the cards with no retreat. They had their backs to the chapel and Horsa stood in the way of any hope of escape and he knew it as he laughed and derided them. With his faculties now completely about him, Ted saw Nicole approaching him out of the corner of his eye but he didn't want to look at her and she apparently knew it. As she approached, her sword caught the bright sunlight and it was among the most incredible weapons he had ever seen. It was made of the finest polished steel with a golden hilt and as she placed it under his chin, he saw that rubies had been encrusted in the handle. For several minutes she continued to press the blade against his skin as its razor-sharp edge slowly drew blood and greatly increased her enjoyment at watching him sweat. She then lowered her blade and kissed him on the lips.

"Good morning Senator. You're looking fetching," she said pleasantly, which didn't match her demeanor.

Ted couldn't place it but there was something very different about Nicole but it wasn't necessarily her actions. He had seen her be cold and cunning while tormenting her victims but it was as if she were more intense and dark. He then thought. For a Toprak ambush, it was progressing rather slowly. Everyone was still alive and he didn't think he was imagining it but Horsa appeared to be uninterested or at best, distracted. Perhaps he was waiting for his harbingers to arrive but if they were anywhere near, they couldn't be heard, which they always were, sometimes from miles away. However, his concern over the stalled assault was quickly remedied as Nicole pointed her blade at Jess.

"What's so important in Conwy Father that you just couldn't stay away?" she asked while pushing her sword into his abdomen but stopping before it harmed him.

Jess didn't respond. He stood silently as if he were praying—and knowing Jess, he probably was. Ted then realized that if there was going to be an escape, it would have to be due to Jess's piety. When Jess didn't answer, Nicole moved on to Shay as she dragged her sword across Jess's chest, cutting his robes.

"How about you… I forget your name," she said laughing. "I guess you just don't make that deep of an impression. Maybe I can help you with that." She raised her sword up under his chin while she enjoyed his trembling and then lowered it to his shoulder, just under his collarbone and slowly pushed the blade all the way out his back. Shay's whole body began to shake as he fought to stay standing, refusing to fall or even make a sound.

"My! Aren't you a surprise," she said as she twisted the blade inside the wound slightly. "Don't you think my Lord," she called to Horsa.

Horsa smiled but from his tone he was obviously disinterested. "Indeed," he replied just above a whisper as he studied Shay's red hand and then turned to inspect the others. When he saw Jess's hand, he quickly turned to look at Ted but when he saw that both of his hands were white, he shook his head, reaffirming in his mind that Ted was as worthless as he was uninteresting. Then, breaking his concentration, he turned to Nicole and replied again in his usual tone, "Indeed!" as he spit a buckhorn seed on the ground casually as if Nicole were picking wildflowers. Whatever was going to happen, this interrogation was certainly a prelude and Horsa for now was content to let Nicole play with their captives like a huntsman lets his hounds have the first kill of the day.

"Please Nicole, don't," said Ted feeling powerless and doing everything he could to help Shay, which wasn't much.

Nicole turned at looked at Ted with eyes cold as steel and glared. It was then he realized what was different about her. There had always been a gentleness about her, even behind her cruelty, but now it was as if her soul was black. She ruthlessly pulled her sword from Shay's shoulder and walked toward Ted as Shay at last broke and yelled out in pain on the ground.

"Aren't you the brave one all of a sudden," she said, pointing her blade in Ted's face.

Ted instinctively raised his hand to stop her sword from hitting his face and the blade cut into his arm.

"Perhaps you would like to spill your guts about what's going on here, or I could spill them for you," she said as she tapped his raised hands with her sword, cutting them each time.

"What's happened to you?" Ted said under his breath and shaking his head.

Nicole glared into Ted's eyes for several painful seconds and then slowly began to shake her head. "You know nothing about me Senator." She then quickly lowered her sword, cutting off his thumb.

As Ted yelled out in agony and quickly wrapped his hand in his shirt, she turned to the three of them incensed and yelled, "What side of ignorant-hell did you wake up on this morning Senators! Does it look like I'm conducting a congressional hearing?! I will hear your answers now or you all start losing body parts!" she yelled while Horsa laughed.

Jess struggled to clear his mind and reengage with the power he felt in the forest but whether it was due to his friends bleeding in agony or whether he just lacked the power of mind he did not know. But the harder he tried, the more desperate and frustrated he became until he at last realized there wasn't going to be a deliverance or miracle this time. Angry with himself, backed up by his anger with Horsa, he began to tremble as he considered the very real reality that they were all probably going to die—at least until he remembered the Toprak list and that Toprak always did what they did according to some grand plan. Considering what he did in the forest, he correctly assumed that Horsa must be here for him, which also accounted for the fact that he was the only one that was unharmed at this point.

As Jess saw it, his friends would continue loosing body parts until Nicole and Horsa got the answers they wanted or until Horsa tired of the game Nicole was playing. He realized that sometimes life was like the game of chess and that the pain of losing a bishop is sometimes required to save the King. So with desperate resolve, he stepped forward and without a sound, knelt before Horsa and bared his neck.

The last thing he heard was Horsa's guttural laugh and the words, "The bishop is inspired!"

CHAPTER 13

CENTENARY CAMPS

Nicole and Horsa stood above Jess's body as he lay unconscious on top of the ashes that carpeted the destroyed castle. For several minutes Nicole and Horsa didn't speak. Nicole assumed that Horsa would immediately kill him now that he was completely in his power but after a few more minutes of inaction, she pointed her sword at Jess's heart and said, "I can do the honor if you like."

Horsa slowly shook his head, obviously deep in thought and after a few moments he looked down at her and replied, "No, he must be conscious and aware of his demise, it's the only way."

"Actually there are many ways to kill a man my love, all of them yielding the same result," said Nicole as she sheathed her sword.

"Not this one. If we're not careful, he'll just come back and I hate having to do anything twice," he said as he turned and looked at Ted and Shay.

"What shall we do with them?" asked Nicole having completely given up on the pretend interrogation.

"I think we should give them a fifteen minute head start before we call for the hounds," replied Horsa and when neither Ted or Shay moved, Horsa yelled, "Release the Harbingers!".

Ted jumped to his feet and rushed over to help Shay get up and they ran out of the castle as fast as their wounded bodies could move, realizing that Jess had sacrificed himself for their escape.

After watching the Senators scramble and laughing at the sight, Nicole sighed with satisfaction and walked over to inspect the pile of swords Ted had pulled from the tunnel and asked, "What manner of death do you suggest then?" continued Nicole, as she picked up a rusted sword to inspected it.

Horsa finally broke his concentration and faced Nicole. "Aren't you the inquisitive, conniving bitch these days?" he said amused. "He must be killed with ceremony—as I must be, but if you think I would share such a thing with you, you forget I know what you're made of these days."

Nicole's brash-bravery was difficult for Horsa to get used to but he also loved her new confidence and cruel dishonesty, so long as it was within his control. Feeling empowered at Horsa's slight display of insecurity, she walked over and placed her hand on his cheek and smiled. "Feeling a little insecure are we—what would your brother say?"

Horsa had worried that one day Nicole's new confidence would need to be checked, but he didn't think it would be today, so soon after her blood-memory. Like disciplining a harbinger, Horsa cruelly grabbed Nicole's arm and quickly flipped her on her back then stepped on her throat while he drew his sword. With the point under her chin, he looked into her steel-blue eyes but said nothing, his quick and deadly actions doing all the talking. He wanted this moment to be remembered so that the lesson would never be forgotten and to ensure it, he nicked the razor point of his sword just below her jawbone on her neck, enough to leave a scar. To his surprise, Nicole didn't flinch or even cry out as she certainly would have yesterday. She just stared up at him with a soft defiance as blood started to ooze from the wound which appeared to be deeper than Horsa had intended. She continued to stare up at him with retreat in her eyes, but not defeat, and when it appeared that they understood one another, he sheathed his sword and then extended his hand. After getting to her feet but still without emotion, she kissed him on the lips and then retracted slowly as blood ran down her neck.

With her unbroken stare still locked on him, the Welsh wind began to whisper through the castle ruins, gently blowing her blond hair across her face as she stood firm and immovable as a statue. Through the unspoken dialogue, she had conceded to her Lord's superiority but Horsa knew deep within her was an unconquerable core that would not yield and was as deadly as venom if bitten. With her blood now soaking into her velvet dress without the least display of emotion, her dangerous beauty bewitched him and he at last had to turn away to keep her from entering his heart where she could increase her power over him. In the silence of the burned-out castle, the sun was beginning to cast eastern shadows, signaling its descent in the afternoon sky and Horsa looked up, noting the time was half-past the noon hour.

He planned to rendezvous with his ship that was anchored in Shell Bay, five miles to the north before nightfall, which meant he needed to start heading that direction. Shaking his head in an attempt to also shake his heart, he walked over to Jess, who was still unconscious and wondered how he could keep him from waking during their journey. He needed to keep him incapacitated as long as possible, but how? Binding him would be no use since it was his spirit he needed to subdue and he then remembered a dark procedure he had seen performed by his mentor, but one that he had never attempted. He walked back over to Nicole who was still staring into space as if she were made of stone and with his hand that contained the pentagram-scar, he tenderly slid it up her chest to her neck, catching a small handful of blood. He then held it over Jess and let it drip from his hand and onto his forehead as if to cover his third eye—which is the spiritual eye.

"What manner of magic is that?" asked Nicole, walking over to see her blood being put to good use.

Horsa waited a few minutes before responding and then kicked Jess, testing his magic. When he didn't stir, he replied, "That should keep him incapacitated until we get back to Saxonice and at least until I determine what to do with him."

"I thought we were heading to the M6. It's already the new moon, making us two days late."

Horsa shook his head. While her newly honed manipulation skills were undoubtedly as sharp as his sword, she was still no military genius and he laughed. "Unless you have an army tucked in your bosom, we won't be much help. Besides, the invasion on Woodsome was only a taunt, meant to stop any advance and instill fear—the most powerful weapon. We will return at the next no moon and finish up the Woodsome job. Now that we have their Bishop, checkmate will be rather simple."

With little effort, Horsa picked up Jess and threw him over his shoulder and began making his way out of the castle ward when he stopped and turned to look at the pile of rusted swords. What value the swords held he could only guess but he knew there were all kinds of medieval legends that had pretended power, some of them real and others, if not most, were foolishness.

"What do you think they are for?" asked Nicole, picking one up and brandishing it in the air.

"They're certainly of no use in battle. There must be some other purpose or value. It's probably nothing but just to be sure…" Horsa walked over and kicked all the swords back into the well, their metallic ring echoing into nothingness and then finishing with a splash at the bottom.

Nicole nodded in agreement and as Horsa walked away, she threw the last sword spiraling in the air and watched it disappear into the darkness, waiting for the splash. Due to the great depth, she waited longer than anticipated but then thought she finally heard it splash at the same time Horsa called her, addressing her as Afet. She then picked up her own sword, sheathed it and casually followed Horsa out of the castle, down to the river where their horses were grazing. As Horsa secured Jess on one of the horses he had stolen the night before at the church, Nicole turned to him deep in thought and asked, "Why do you suppose the Bishop was unable to…" Nicole stalled and tried to find the words that would describe what she saw Jess do and for the lack of a better word she said, "Conjure? I mean, what was the difference between today and two nights ago in the forest?"

Horsa shrugged. "I am completely unaware of the power he wields," he replied, assuming that Jess possessed unearthly powers as he did, completely unware of the secret of the Cross he carried. "Regardless, he will certainly revive and rise to the crisis eventually—I would, which is why he must be removed from the chessboard before he does," Horsa said as he mounted his percheron and turned downriver.

A mile to the east, the Conwy grew almost a half mile wide, making it traversable on horseback and after fording the river, they turned and made their way northward where Horsa's newly built ship, the *Bizyok*, was anchored in a hidden cove at the base of a cliff. The *Bizyok* was only eighty feet, two masts and no guns. She wasn't designed to be a battleship, her only purpose was to transport dwarf harbinger troops from Ireland. Toprak had built a dozen just like her and they could efficiently move ten thousand harbingers over a forty-eight hour period from Saxonice to England—something that was about to happen at the next no moon.

After their defeat on the Thames four years ago, Hengist, Horsa and Nicole had retreated to the Isle of Man where they quickly subdued the few remaining residents while they perfected their new method of creating harbingers. Once the entire island was under their control, they invaded Ireland with under one-hundred harbingers and were surprised to find it inhabited by dwarfs. They quickly realized that a dwarf-harbinger was at least twice as powerful as a human-harbinger, their raw aggression being more like that of a wolf than a man and when they landed the first pack in Wales just over a year ago, Horsa was delighted to hear that the English referred to them as hellhounds—a most fitting name.

In less than six months, Horsa and Nicole had enslaved the majority of the dwarves in Ireland since they had a natural inclination to dance and make merry, which played perfectly into the St. Vitus Dance plague. At the height of the capture, Horsa had caused the great St. Patrick's Cathedral to roar with flames while twenty-thousand dwarves danced grotesquely long into the night and into the captivity of Toprak. Horsa estimated that they now had around seventy-thousand mature war-harbingers running wild on the emerald isle, only needing to hear the rancid sound that called them to dance where they were then pierced with an iron ring in their wrist and hauled off to Saxonice, the new name Hengist had given to the Isle of Man.

Saxonice was now the official world headquarters for Toprak and after they had built several ships, Horsa and Nicole sailed first to Belarus and then to Morocco to collect their scattered armies and supplies. Due to the devastation they saw everywhere they went, people approached their ships by the hundreds, pleading that they be allowed to join Toprak and pledging unfailing loyalty. Once back on Saxonice, the volunteers were evaluated and segregated on their strength of mind and might. Those that failed at both, were harbinger-ized and assigned to the dwarf detachment that was used as fodder in harbinger ignition at Conwy Castle. The rest were taught how to command the war-harbingers and were made captains and other lower ranks over the new and vicious Toprak army, each one eventually reporting to Horsa. Saxonice was also used to stage the waves of invasion forces that were planned for England at the next no moon cycle—the war-harbingers time of greatest aggression. At this moment there were approximately thirty-thousand harbingers on the island and as the moon waned, their hateful cries could be heard as far away as Wales, as they anticipated the night of the month.

It was almost twilight by the time Horsa reached Shell Bay and the last remaining sliver of sun cast a silver light through the clouds and across the grey sea under his ship that was riding on the tide. In the fading light, the ship's hands raised the Toprak colors, signaling that they acknowledged their Lord's unmistakable silhouette atop of the cliffs, a massive man on an equally massive horse that instantly shot fear into their hearts. Within a few minutes, he saw four men in a pinnace rowing to shore to retrieve him just as several lanterns were seen on board in the quarters reserved for the Lord of the army, the hands preparing for his arrival. Before descending down the steep trail that lead to a narrow inlet where the pinnace would land, Horsa turned to Nicole who was directly behind the horse that carried Jess. She had pulled the hood of her black riding cloak over her head due to the cold northern wind that swept over the cliffs and when she looked up at Horsa in the fading light, he only saw her steel eyes set behind her soft porcelain skin peering from the darkness of her hood. The surreal silver light radiated from her face and electrified her blue eyes as she tenderly looked back at him, surrendering her body and heart, but her spirit locked away in a fortress deep within her. Perhaps it was because he wanted what he could not have, knowing that Nicole was not completely his, he was consumed with her and when he didn't speak for being lost in her beauty, she nodded respectfully and said, "My Lord."

The cut on her neck had stopped bleeding but the smudged streak remained and was visible through the opening in her cloak. As every woman knows when she is being admired, Horsa's silent glance betrayed him, giving Nicole the power of the moment and she breathed deeply, adding to Horsa's fantasy then said, "The tide awaits my Lord."

After a few lingering seconds under her spell, Horsa regained his power, turned and made his way down the cliff to the pinnace that was now resting on the beach with the oarsmen standing by with lanterns. Once on the rocky beach, the high cliffs above them amplified the crashing surf, making it difficult to converse. As Horsa approached, the men saluted and then bowed respectfully before taking control of the horses and assisting Nicole on board. Horsa carried Jess to the pinnace as if he were a mere satchel and tossed him in the bottom, then walked to the bow and began pushing it off the sand into the rising tide. Once in knee-deep water, he climbed aboard as the oarsmen rowed them to the waiting ship, the sea growing more rough by the minute.

"Hoist the sails but don't draw them until the horses are on board," yelled Nicole as she stepped over the rail, taking control of the ship. "But don't let them flap—and loose the anchor. This tide is going to rip us apart if we don't hurry!"

"Yes Madame Captain," yelled back the captain's Mate as he called all hands on deck just as a stiff wind blew across the bow, blowing Nicole's hood off her head.

"Madame, you are injured!" yelled the Mate so that he could be heard above the wind.

Nicole waved him off in such a way that told him she thought it was a trifle and he went back to his work of preparing the ship. She then walked back to the helm and after noting the direction of the current, she turned to watch the horses being hoisted on board and after the last one touched the cargo hold floor, the Mate gave the order for the sails to be drawn. Nicole guessed that the wind was around twenty knots and once the sails were tight, the ship lunged forward while the young timbers creaked and groaned under the sudden pressure of a full spread of sail. She took a deep, clearing breath as the ship caught up to the wind, which made it appear that the wind had nearly stopped but the truth was, they were now moving at almost the same speed making the night fair and pleasant on deck. There were few things Nicole loved more than sailing and as she set a north easterly course, she thought about the many times she had circumnavigated the globe on the *Euterpe* before the Minimum. Then like now, life never changed on the sea and it was like returning home no matter where she was in the world or what age.

"Madame Captain, tea and vodka?" asked the steward holding out a tray with a single cup on it.

"Have you served Lord Horsa?" she asked as she reached out to take it.

"Yes Madame," he replied with a bow. "Just now."

Nicole took a sip and slowly swallowed as she closed her eyes. "Thank you," she said with her eyes still closed and waiting for the pleasant wash to reach her mind. "At what hour were the men piped to dinner?"

"Eighteen hundred Madame, as ordered," he replied. "I am warming dinner at this moment. Will you be dining with his Lordship this evening?"

Nicole downed the last of her tea and set it back on the tray. "No, none for me tonight, please send my regrets to my Lord and tell him the sea is to blame. Our approach on this side of Saxonice with this swell has me concerned."

"Very well Madame. I shall relay your regrets," replied the steward with a bow and then turned to walk away until Nicole called after him.

"Please do bring me a warm towel," she said as the steward bowed once again and disappeared below decks. Within minutes, he reappeared holding a rolled towel on a tray accompanied with his respectful bow. Nicole thanked him as she unrolled the towel and placed it over her face, his footsteps fading into the distance. After wiping her face, she washed the blood from her neck and stared at the stain on the towel for a few minutes before throwing it overboard, vowing to never allow Horsa to draw her blood again.

Four hours away on the island of Saxonice, the changing of the harbinger guard was in process, a generally uneventful and mundane routine but not tonight. Just over a thousand harbingers had arrived from Ireland that afternoon in preparation for the next no moon invasion, making the usual duty burdensome. All harbinger transports had their share of problems but this particular dispatch was the worst in recent memory. The biggest problem with any harbinger transport was the chaining, where they were linked together through their wrist rings in groups of a hundred, called a Centenary. It made controlling and directing them easier but there was always one or two who attacked the other harbingers on either side and if not put down, they would incite the entire group, making it impossible to regain control. The only option in such a deteriorated situation was to kill the entire Centenary—which infuriated Horsa. It was therefore commanded that any single harbinger causing problems should be immediately killed before they infected the entire centenary.

Once landed, each Centenary was arrayed in a straight line and secured to the ground with four-foot stakes at each end so that if fighting did break out, the problem harbinger could be quickly identified and disposed of. At the beginning of the second watch, there was already three Centenaries with a dead harbinger somewhere in the line and the night watch was just beginning.

"Twelfth guard block reporting sir," said a short and stocky soldier, saluting.

"It's about time you buggers got here," replied the commander. "We've been bitch-flogged all evening—worst transport I've even seen."

"We were detained at the docks sir, equally terrible down there. Came as soon as we could sir," replied the soldier.

"Never mind then, I suppose you've come at a good time. Things are pretty quiet for the time being, but you'll need to keep a close eye on the western-most Centenaries. I've seen enough of these unstable ones to know that we'll probably put at least one more down tonight," said the commander as he picked up his sword and secured it around his waist.

"Very well commander," replied the soldier nodding. "What chain number is this problem harbinger?"

The commander thought for a moment, trying to remember but in the chaos of the evening, the Centenaries all blurred together and he finally swore and replied, "I don't remember, but you can't miss him, he's the big, dumb one. If it were my choice I would have killed him already just to be rid of the liability, but Lord Horsa orders are only if they harm the others as you know."

The soldier nodded in agreement and then saluted as the commander left, wishing him luck. The wide-open hills near Dreemskerry lent themselves very well to the staking out of harbinger Centenaries but the absence of dwellings also meant that the guard assignment was under the open and most often, wet sky. Consequently, Centenary Duty was the least desirable of all posts in the Toprak army and every soldier abhorred their twenty-four hour assignment there. Each Centenary detail consisted of seven soldiers, with one designated as the commander. Before the newly-arrived detail settled into the watch, they conducted their required walk-through before returning to the canvas canopy that at least kept the rain off their heads. As they progressed through the camp, it appeared that the harbingers were finally acclimating to their chaining and preparing for sleep, except for the fifth Centenary. The fifth was still very alive with intermittent howling, that then excited the other nearby Centenary. The commander lowered his torch so that he could see the faces of the harbingers as he walked the line, searching for the big, dumb one, when halfway down the line he stopped and gasped.

Most harbingers these days were dwarfs, but it was obvious that this particular harbinger was human, but not just human, it was massive and compared to the dwarves, it was a giant. He was crouched over on bent knees like an ape but even then, it was at least four or five feet high and the commander estimated that at full height, it was probably close to seven feet. It was nearly naked and the sparse rags it wore only accentuated his ripped and massive muscles that were crossed with protruding and pulsating veins. After a hard swallow, the commander started to step backwards as if he had discovered an asp but just then, the massive harbinger looked up. Right away, he knew there was something different about it, more than just its size. Its eyes were clear, not glazed like other harbingers and its movements were relatively graceful, though obviously painful. As he looked into its eyes, the commander convinced himself that this particular harbinger wasn't fully baked, something that happened from time to time for reasons no one understood. It was as if they awoke while under anesthesia and the only thing that could be done was to kill the poor thing. But as he took a step closer with his torch, the harbinger lunged forward with a low, guttural growl and bit him on the arm, removing a chunk of flesh. It then jerked the chain that ran through the ring on his wrist so hard that it flung the remaining harbingers between itself and the stake several feet in the air, pulling it from the ground.

As the commander held his arm, several guards quickly seized the end of the chain to prevent any escapes while another clubbed the large harbinger over the head, knocking it unconscious.

"You all right?" asked the soldier with the club.

The commander spit on the large, lifeless harbinger and sighed. "I'll live—though I'll probably die of rabies in a fortnight." He removed his hand to inspect the wound and saw that it was not a clean bite. There was a flap of skin, attached to muscle, three inches wide that dangled from his arm and he carefully fitted it back into place and said, "I suppose it will mend nicely."

"Shall I behead the half-baked bastard?" asked the soldier, drawing his sword.

"No," replied the commander.

"No?" asked several men at the same time incredulously.

"No, there is something right odd about this one and I'm certain Lord Horsa will want to see for himself when he hears of it in my report. Remove him from the chaining and bring him to the canopy where we can keep an eye on him," replied the commander as he walked away.

Removing a harbinger from a chaining was difficult and tedious work since every harbinger removed had to be staked individually and then placed back in the line in the same order so that the disruption could be minimized. Confusion and disruption was one of the switches that caused harbingers to respond so deadly in battle and therefore it was critical not to introduce too much change within a Centenary until they reached the battlefield. Several hours later, the guards finally approached the canopy with the large harbinger.

"That's creative," exclaimed the commander upon seeing the large harbinger being dragged behind a horse.

"It was the only way sir, it was far too heavy for the two of us," replied one of the men laughing as he started to remove the chain from the harbinger's wrist.

"Wait! Leave it chained to the horse, that way if it gives us any more trouble we can use the horse's strength to our advantage," said the commander as the soldier nodded and then looked toward the sea.

"What do you suppose it is?" he asked.

The commander turned to see what the man was looking at and about a half mile off shore there was a light, a single lamp, approaching from the south.

"A ship, but why I wonder?" replied the commander. "I was not aware of any dispatches tonight, nor has the army ever landed harbingers at night."

They both watched the light bob up and down on the tide as it drew closer until the commander ordered a rider down to the beach to discover who it was. As the rider disappeared into the darkness, the large harbinger groaned and tried to roll over but the commander quickly attached a shackle to its ankle and stretched it to a tree. He then led the horse forward so that the harbinger was completely stretched out, removing any opportunity for a repeat performance. The make-shift rack made it very angry and it started to groan and then growl which made the commander uneasy. However, he figured all he had to do was draw the chains tighter and he led the horse forward a few more inches, causing the harbinger cry out even louder.

Even though harbingers seldom understood English, the commander yelled above the howling and said, "Calm yourself bitch and I will ease the chains."

"Go to hell!" replied the harbinger which completely unsettled the commander and he fell backwards in shock. While it wasn't uncommon for a harbinger to understand a verbal command, he had never heard one respond or least of all, speak. Whatever was happening with this particular harbinger, he concluded that it would only get worse and cost lives so he determined that he had better just kill the damn thing. Getting to his feet, he drew his sword and walked toward it as it thrashed in the tight chains, its groans and howls growing louder and more horrifying. As he raised his sword, it quickly turned its head and upon seeing it about to fall, he yelled out like a man that caused the commander to pause just long enough for the harbinger to muster the strength to jerk on his chains in a final attempt to preserve its own life, which was also something unique to this harbinger. Most were so completely out of mind that they neither cared for their own lives or the lives of others.

In complete disbelief, the commander watched the horse jerked off its feet and flung several feet backwards as the chain finally broke from the saddle. The harbinger was free except for the shackle that was attached to the tree but before the commander could run, the harbinger swung the chain attached to his wrist and caught him by the neck. Struggling to get free, the harbinger pulled the commander closer and he began calling desperately for help, hoping the remaining soldiers would hear him but it was too late. He was now lying at the massive harbinger's feet as it towered above him. Oddly, the harbinger paused slightly as if it had a conscience—something no other harbinger had—before it raised its foot to crush his neck. To his great surprise and even greater relief, the harbinger looked as if it were becoming dizzy and began shaking it's head. Whatever was happening, it made it terribly angry and it began stomping its feet indiscriminately, trying to find the commander's neck, but in vain. The commander quickly rolled away and as he got to his feet, he saw Horsa running toward him almost as angry as the harbinger. Without hesitation, Horsa rushed towards the harbinger and grabbed it by the hair, then thrust his palm against its forehead, his palm containing the pentagram scar. The effect was devastating. The harbinger released an unearthly scream as if it were being scorched with fire until it fell silent and lifeless on the ground in a heap.

"What the hell is this harbinger doing here!" yelled Horsa turning to the commander.

"My Lord," he replied, falling to his knees. "Begging your great pardon, but he was here when I took over the command at nineteen-hundred."

"Why isn't he part of a chaining?" he demanded.

Still on his knees, he pled with Horsa to not be angry as he tried to explain. "The previous guard said he had been a problem since arriving and after he took a bite of my arm, we took him out of the chaining. Pleading for your forgiveness my Lord, we should have just killed him I see now."

After realizing that this unforgivable error did not belong to the Commander, Horsa became more calm and he bade him to rise. "Had you killed him, I would have killed you," he said as he rolled the harbinger over with his foot.

"Which is precisely why I didn't my Lord," replied the commander with renewed hope. "I noticed there was something not right with it and just before your rescue—which I eternally thank you for—it spoke."

Horsa turned in surprise and asked, "It spoke?" with alarm in his voice.

"Yes my Lord," replied the commander, pleased with himself that Horsa was interested in what he said.

"What did it say?"

The commander stuttered for a few seconds while he tried to recall the exact words. "Um, let's see it was—um, go—yes, Go to hell—that was it, I'm quite sure."

Horsa laughed with amusement but then quickly returned to his irritated mood. With a sigh, he looked northward toward the church in the large graveyard on the hill, the only structure in the area and said, "Drag it to the church and lock him inside. Take all your men with you and I will take the watch myself until the next guard arrives. Whoever is responsible for bringing this harbinger to Saxonice will learn how to Dance."

CHAPTER 14

BLOOD ATONEMENT

With a torch in one hand and the reins in another, the Commander led a horse carrying the oversized harbinger into the darkness toward the graveyard that surrounded the old church on the hill above the harbinger stakeout. A light mist was pushing in from the sea that was only a few hundred yards to the east and it grew heavier the higher up the hill he walked. The continual wet was something he never got used to, not even after the last three years he had spent in Saxonice and he let the reins slide up to his elbow, cringing as they scrapped past the bite, then flipped his collar to cover his bare neck.

There was a sliver crescent moon hanging in the western sky, that appeared only momentarily as the clouds of mist blew inland, affording very little light. Looking toward the church, he saw the faint light of a torch flicker near the western end where he believed the front doors were located and he wondered what it meant. As far as he knew, he and his men were the only ones on the island except for the guard stationed at Toprak HQ located in the old Peel Castle on the opposite side of the island where Hengist could effectively oversee the war operations on Saxonice and the harbinger colony in Ireland. He watched the torchlight disappear and then reemerge as he continued his ascent and he concluded that whoever was at the church was walking in and out, perhaps preparing the makeshift prison for the oddly special harbinger.

As he approached the doors, he heard a voice ask from within the dark church say, "What's this about?"

"Official business," replied the Commander, trying to sound authoritative. "Lord Horsa wants this bugger imprisoned in the church."

A black figure stepped through the open doors and by the light of his torch he could tell he was a sailor, no doubt from the *Bizyok* that had just docked at Maughold Head, the harbinger deployment port on the island.

"The more the merrier I suppose," replied the sailor as he walked past the commander to see what he was dragging. He assumed the bugger he referred to was a trouble harbinger or perhaps an unfortunate soldier who had displeased Horsa, but the sheer size of what he saw startled him and he jumped backwards exclaiming, "What the hell is that?"

"The biggest damned harbinger there ever was!" replied the commander with pride as if he had bagged it himself. "This one is special to his Lord for some reason, which is why we just didn't kill it when it acted like it was in pentacode."

"So it's alive?"

"Indeed!" replied the commander laughing slightly and then growing sober as he began wondering how he was going to get the harbinger inside the church.

Perceiving his dilemma, the sailor waved his hand, stopping the commander from unchaining the harbinger and then led the horse through the church doors, dragging the massive harbinger behind it as its head cracked against one of the stone pillars that framed the doorway. Once inside, they removed the chains that were fastened to the saddle and looped through the harbinger's wrist ring.

"Who's that?" asked the commander, noticing another body on the floor.

"I haven't a clue actually. Lord Horsa found him," replied the sailor.

"Is HE alive?"

"I think so," replied the sailor pausing and then shaking his head. "Are you certain his Lord wanted these two together? I mean, if this harbinger is as bad as you say it is, he'll have this one's bones picked clean before sunup."

The commander laughed as he turned to walk out saying, "That's most-likely his plan. Whoever that poor bastard is, he must be on Horsa's most detested list."

After leading the horse out of the church, the Commander bolted the doors and then looked downhill to see if his men were on their way. "I will have several joining me shortly, so you need not stay," he said, giving the sailor leave.

"I've been at my post for a fortnight—I wasn't planning on staying anyway," he replied already several yards into the graveyard on his way back to the *Bizyok*.

The old parish church, which was now a Toprak prison, dated back to the fifth century. It was a solid structure with small windows that were covered with iron bars, installed sometime in the last hundred years, making it a the perfect prison. Due to its many improvements and renovations over the past fifteen-hundred years, the Minimum fires had destroyed everything about the church that was once beautiful and consequently, it was an empty shell with four walls and a nearly intact roof. The floor was half stone, half dirt, which meant it was mostly mud due to the continual rain on the island. It sat amidst a five acre, densely packed graveyard that added to the sinister night as the commander looked around for his men. From the vantage point of the hill, he could see several torches making their way toward him and he began walking around the building to ensure that every window was secure. He was certain that if the harbinger escaped, he and all his men would not be able to subdue it without killing it so he needed to be sure there was no escape. Once he was satisfied, he found a prominent tombstone near the front doors, sat down and made himself comfortable.

Inside the church, Jess was slowly regaining consciousness as he first became aware of his aching head, a throbbing hematoma from Horsa's blow in addition to the careless transport to—wherever he was. He slowly opened his eyes but due to the meager moonlight and the darkness of the building, he could see nothing, not even the muddy ground he was laying on. Rolling onto his back, he looked up at the sky, thinking he was still somehow miraculously alive in the ruins of Conwy Castle but as his eyes grew accustomed to the darkness, he sensed he was in a damp and secure enclosure, evidenced by the stale air that carried the scent of mold. As he rehearsed in his mind the events he last remembered, where he was quickly became meaningless, as he considered why he was still alive and what had happened to Shay and Ted. Rolling onto his side in an effort to raise himself up, he became aware of uncountable body aches and open wounds all over his legs from the knee down, the result of being dragged instead of carried to his dungeon. Looking across the room, he could make out a dim light that framed several windows along the eastern wall and he was surprised to learn just how large his prison cell was. Mostly out of habit, said a silent prayer for Shay and Ted, hoping they were safe just as he remembered the hopeless moment of his capture. The fear and desperation of that moment when the only hope for any of them was his surrender returned to his memory and with heavy dread in his heart, he sank back down on the floor with a sigh. Groaning within himself, he lamented his failure, his inability to use the Cross to save them since there were no more fragments left as a tear burned out of the corner of his eye.

"Oh God, where art thou?" he whispered.

For several hours, he laid on his back motionless as he took a thorough inventory of his past sins, asking once again for forgiveness and pleading that God would turn away his wrath and deliver his friends and England a second time from evil—Toprak. While in his retrospective frame of mind, he couldn't help from mentally wandering through the hell that had descended on his life and the entire world since that summer afternoon in Washington when Gus and Veronica were shot in their Senate Offices. He rarely thought about such things since the memory of life before the Minimum only served to depress the reality of the world in which he now lived but in his weakened and defeated state, he gave in to his grief and mourned the loss of the world and the rise of absolute evil in the form of Hengist, Horsa—and now Nicole. Never in his life did he feel more alone and more hope-stricken. Not only was he without friends, but for the first time in his life, he felt that God had even abandoned him and his loneliness sank deeper into the abyss of his soul, that dark place everyone has but few ever face. That abyss where one stands alone, stripped, painfully naked, devoid of mental rationale, emotional covering, excuses, self-myths; forced to gaze into the dreaded, black mirror, into his own nothingness, where all certainties are abandoned. In that moment of transcendent dread, time ceased to exist as he wandered through his empty soul, discovering and then rediscovering—nothing.

“I am nothing and will ever be,” he exclaimed with barely a whisper from his lips but inwardly bawling out to God.

There was no reply, no comfort and no signs, only the silent, black mirror demanding a decision, a choice, the only thing that is discernable within the obsidian frame. In this darkest of all nights, he was alone; more alone than he had ever been—absolute loneliness, devoid of the companionship of any person; mortal or spirit. For the span of time that seemed as if it could have been many days, he lay as if he were dead, paralyzed, waiting for death or a sign as to what he should do, feel or even think. Deep inside the abyss, he at last wandered upon a passage of faintly illuminated passage he had translated from the ancient records he discovered in the St. Martin churchyard that dripped hope into his heart and as he pulled on the thread of memory, he exclaimed, “That’s it! That’s what The Seven means!” Jess didn’t realize he was speaking louder than a whisper, perhaps much louder and he heard the noise of movement to his right—he was not alone in his dungeon and he froze.

“Shay, Ted, is that you?” Jess whispered with fear returning to his heart.

When there was no immediate response, he wondered if he had imagined the sound and then he heard someone or something sigh and rollover. But then after several minutes of silence, he placed his hands behind his head and said, “Sounds like it’s just you and me God.”

Silence prevailed once again in the dungeon and just as he convinced himself that he really didn’t hear anything, his dark peace was broken by a voice from the grave that said, "Jess—is that you?"

Jess shot up and looked around despite the fact that he knew he would not be able to see anything. Not only was he alarmed to hear a voice, but it was a voice he knew. A voice he knew very well and one that did not belong to Shay or Ted.

"Matthew?" he said at last, timidly.

The darkness didn't respond again but Jess thought he could hear someone sniffing and the unmistakable sound of tears followed by a humble reply, "You couldn't possibly know how glorious it is to hear your voice Jess. I have been in hell," Matthew said sobbing.

"I think I know something of hell but to find you alive and well is the greatest of any blessing in this moment—how great God is!" replied Jess as he crawled in the direction of Matthew's voice.

"Alive, but not very well my brother," said Matthew just as he felt Jess's hand touch his arm and they embraced. "I've been trapped as a harbinger."

Jess endearingly rubbed Matthew's back and replied, "But you are certainly a harbinger no longer."

"Sadly I am," he replied, breaking their embrace. "I'm not like most harbingers you've known. I didn't understand it at first but for whatever reason, when Horsa is at some distance from me, I return to myself—though not nearly so much as I feel right now. The moment he returns, I am his," Matthew sighed. "Thankfully I don't remember much when I am, but the things I do remember," he groaned, "I would that God destroy me for the heinous deeds I have done."

Matthew looked nothing like the harbingers or hellhounds he saw in the forest and after considering it, he remembered Moran explaining how harbinger's were made and he replied, "Professor Moran said that Anglo-Saxons couldn't be made harbingers. Your Anglo blood is as red as mine brother, how is this possible?"

"Clearly he was mistaken," replied Matthew. "But even if he were correct back then, things are different now. Believe me, I've spent endless nights in the most horrific dungeons wondering how I got there while being wracked with unbelievable pain as I returned to myself again and again. The last thing I remembered was calling the Ravenguard together outside Powis Castle to go investigate the—howling."

"The hellhounds?"

"Yes, that's right—hellhounds. I had forgotten. The next thing I can remember now after that night was waking up with an iron ring in my wrist, chained to hundreds of other poor bastards like me."

"Oh Matthew, I'm so sorry! Everyone of course believed you to be dead and Veroni…" Jess stopped himself before launching into a full-blown discussion about Veronica and in an instant, he saw in his mind the mountains of heartache and tears she had shed at Matthew's death. Then there was the battle in Wales, her marriage to the King and the current crisis of her missing with no clues to her whereabouts or even if she was alive. Before he could recover and change the subject, he heard Matthew take a deep sigh.

"Veronica, Veronica… I used to say her name out loud

over and over—it made me feel closer to her oddly enough and it was the only thing that kept me alive I think—still does. How is she Jess," he said with great sorrow in his voice. "Tell me everything you know about her."

Jess had placed himself in an impossible situation. How could he tell Matthew that she was married to the King and quite possibly carrying his child. Telling Matthew the truth in the current circumstance was out of the question but he also knew he couldn't lie so he resolved to be as vague as possible. The truth could wait for another time when the entire events of this terrible year could be explained and when he could understand the impossible situation Veronica was placed in. He was sure Matthew could accept Veronica's marriage once he learned how it kept England from tearing apart but he knew Matthew would be destroyed if he knew the King adored her and that she returned his love.

"She is, well—Veronica," Jess said laughing slightly, motivated by nervousness. "Last I saw her she was resolute, defiant, brave and of course beautiful beyond compare. The most incredible woman I ever saw."

"Indeed," replied Matthew with the sound of a smile. "When did you see her last?"

Jess sighed. It appeared he would have to tell more than he wanted and he replied first with a preface, "Matthew, a lot has happened in England since you've been gone and I wish to God they were pleasant. Besides the civil war…"

"What!" exclaimed Matthew, interrupting.

Jess nodded though no one could see. "Yes. Thankfully it was resolved before too many lives were lost and it ended with the King still on the throne—glory be to God. There were some painful compromises but the Kingdom is intact. Shortly thereafter, Toprak invaded Wales—twice and… well, Veronica is missing at the moment, Matthew."

"Missing? Holy hell, Jess—how—who is searching for her?!"

Jess's voice began to shake, he not wanting to break Matthew's heart but if he were to break it, he would choose the hammer of her disappearance rather than the hammer of her marriage. "No one at the moment, brother. Gus, Clancy and the King are holed-up in Northumbria with a Toprak force pinning them in just passed the M6 and Shay and Ted are…" he paused realizing that he didn't know where they were either and he sighed. "I don't know where they are." Jess could see where the conversation was going and he desperately tried to change its course. "Do you remember anything about the night you left?"

"Not much, just rallying the men and listening to the local lore—which I of course thought was ridiculous at the time."

"You don't remember speaking to Veronica before you left?" Jess asked, very encouraged.

Matthew thought hard for several moments then shook his head, "No—did I?"

Jess sighed with relief, "I'm so grateful to hear that!"

"Why did I do something stupid?"

"This will be hard to hear but you should know," Jess began. "She desperately wanted you to stay within the castle walls but you were hell-bent on riding out that night.

When she forbid you leave," Jess swallowed, "you cursed her and before marching out to your death—so she thought—you told her that she was not your Queen, only Gus's bitch."

Matthew didn't respond but the sound of his tears more than adequately expressed the pains of his broken heart. Jess placed his hand on Matthew's back to try and consul him but there was no comfort.

"That was the hardest thing about your death for Veronica. I believe I convinced her that you were not in your right mind somehow and that you could never be so cruel."

Matthew sniffed. "Thank you for that," he replied with rage building. "I vowed more times than I can count, that if God freed me I would throw Horsa and all Toprak back into the hell from whence they came, but when Horsa returns, I can never resist him. Maybe if I felt like I do tonight I may be able, I feel almost normal."

After Jess didn't respond for several minutes Matthew asked, "You still with me Father?"

"Yes, my apologies—just thinking. It appears that you were already affected before you chased the hellhounds that night, but how can that be? Had you any interactions with harbingers, Horsa or even Nicole before that time? What about Folkestone?"

Matthew shook his head, "No, I'm sure I didn't."

"What about the battle on Holy Island? You received many wounds from what I remember."

"Wounds, I had plenty but" Matthew paused, "are you

telling me that that was a harbinger army on Holy Island and not the Celts?"

"Yes, we were all deceived and made Toprak fools," replied Jess, turning to see the first light of the orange sun illuminating the eastern sky.

Matthew sighed again, becoming overwhelmed with bad news. "Have you not any good news? How is Morgan?" Matthew stopped, thought for a moment and then gasped. "Morgan! That's how it happened! Do you remember how I found him?"

Jess nodded.

"When I was placing him in the wagon, he convulsed, rose up and bit my ear. I thought nothing of it at the time but as far as I know, that was the first and only time I had blood contact with a harbinger. But that makes no sense since many of my men have been bitten but didn't turn."

"Wow, that was so long ago, the incubation period must be tremendous—at least for Anglos," replied Jess. "The bite victims I have seen, do display disorientation and mind-fog but never change into a harbinger. However, the bite does explain your dissonance that night and, well, the Dance must have done the rest."

"The Dance?" asked Matthew.

Nodding, Jess continued, "Yes, Ted is our resident expert on how harbingers are made these days,"

"Ted—who let him out of prison?!" exclaimed Matthew remembering that he had placed him in the Tower.

"That's a long story and one that can wait," said Jess with a sigh, "but Toprak is able to turn almost anyone using the Dance these days."

"Wait—by the Dance you mean like what we saw in Folkestone?" Matthew replied, his memories flooding back to him.

"Indeed. They have enslaved tens of thousands in the world, some from England but I would guess less than a few hundred. We believe the attack on Holy Island was only a Toprak dress rehearsal. They attacked again, crossing the causeway into west Wales and completely routed the King's army there. Only he and I escaped with a few dozen men. The Toprak army then marched on Conwy, where Veronica had moved just before she was m…" Jess stopped and quickly tried to think of a recovery word that began with the letter "M", that would keep him from talking about Veronica's marriage.

"Before she what?" asked Matthew when Jess didn't continue fast enough.

"Before she went—missing," he lied. "With the King's army destroyed, it was at least a week before Shay and Riley reached the castle, they having just come from the civil war in Norwich. When they entered the castle walls, everything had been burned—there was nothing left."

"And Veronica was for sure there when Toprak invaded?"

"We believe so, yes, but a very thorough search was made and I promise you, there was no sign of her, Colton or Corinna in the castle, the town or the surrounding countryside. I understand they even dragged the river but found nothing." Jess wanted so badly to give Matthew hope and encouragement but there was sadly none to be had. They both sat in the morning light that bathed their prison in orange light as silence passed between them for several long minutes until Jess quietly said, "England has really missed you Matthew. We have needed you so badly—ever so badly."

Matthew staggered to his feet and replied with defeat, "I'm of no use to anybody. Once Horsa returns I will most-likely kill you."

Jess was not defeated even though he didn't have a plan or even a guess of how they would escape but there was one thing he did know and that was fate had brought them together and he replied hopeful, which didn't match the words he spoke. "I'm certain that is Horsa's plan—for you to kill me."

"You sound eerily OK with that," marveled Matthew.

"I am," replied Jess, getting to his feet. "If that be God's will, then so eternally be it—but I don't think that is his plan today."

"No?"

"No," replied Jess as he reached inside his robe and pulled out the small book he had taken from the Conwy Church. "Our meeting is not accidental and nor is the fact that I have this."

"A book?—Oh, that should help," replied Matthew sarcastically.

Jess smiled, recognizing Matthew's flippant personality for the first time and said, "Welcome back."

Matthew shook his head in amazement as he walked to the window. "I don't think I've felt this good—nor so much like myself since—I can't remember. Horsa must be very far away," he concluded.

"Or..." said Jess turning slowly, observing the room. "It's because you're in a church."

Matthew looked around and concluded Jess was right about the building but in his mind, buildings were nothing more than stone, mortar and wood. Out of the corner of his eye, he saw Jess trying to get to his feet and he turned to him and said, "No, it's you."

It had always been hard for Jess to accept a transcendent compliment but like decrepit buildings, without a bright spirit they were just empty shells and he replied humbly, "Perhaps," and then changed the subject. "Do you remembered what happened to the members of the Ravenguard that followed you that night?"

"I remember nothing, only coming too in a dungeon. How long that was after that night I have no idea," Matthew replied as he considered for the first time that he didn't know what month or even what year it was. "How long have I been gone—what is today's date?"

"Matthew..." replied Jess, pausing as Matthew turned from the window. "Today is September third."

But before Jess could continue Matthew interjected, "SEPTEMBER?! I've been gone four months?!" he exclaimed remembering that Veronica moved to Powis Castle in early May. "Veronica has probably married the King by now!"

Jess was stunned into dumbness, powerless to respond, looking back at him blankly as he wondered at his words and why he would say such a thing. Not only had he been missing much longer than four months, he also appeared to know the very thing he had been trying so hard to conceal.

When Jess was slow to respond, Matthew scoffed, "I'm kidding. I think I know Veronica better than that."

"Matthew—you've been missing for much longer than that."

Matthew's eyes narrowed and he became extremely sober as he waited for Jess to continue. "For everyone in England, you've been dead a year and four months," said Jess shaking his head with pity and sorrow.

Matthew was speechless. After several seconds of terrible wonder, he slowly collapsed on the floor, devastated. "I've been a harbinger for sixteen months," he said incredulously, shaking his head. "I can't believe it. I suppose it's a blessing, but—sixteen bloody months!"

"I'm sorry," replied Jess, the only words coming to his mind over Matthew's terrible losses. Then after several painful minutes he finally mustered the courage to ask, "Why did you worry that Veronica had married the King?"

"Just immature jealousy," he replied shaking his head, feeling ridiculous. "I once felt intimidated watching them one evening at Kensington when they were having an intellectual discussion about some fine point of English history. They were conversing in Latin which I didn't understand at the time and I read much more into it than I should have—though it was always in the back of my mind."

Just then they heard voices from outside the church and they both fell to the muddy floor, pretending they were still unconscious while they listened to the changing of their guards. They had no idea how many guards were outside during the night but they heard a commanding voice order the number tripled and for every man to be alert. Jess began to wonder if the voice was none other than Horsa himself and when he looked at Matthew for confirmation, he saw him rolling on his back groaning, Horsa's influence making its presence known. As Jess stared in horror, for a brief moment, he caught Matthew's eye and saw that he was still Matthew, not a harbinger. He was fighting the takeover with all his might as he groaned and his body jerked involuntarily. Lost in his frightful focus on Matthew, he was startled to hear the doors being opened and he quickly rolled on his stomach. With one eye partially opened, he saw several sets of feet pass by, completely ignoring him and stand over Matthew, watching while he suffered under Horsa's gaze. After several minutes, the men turned and walked out of the church as Horsa said, "That should bind him for another day at least, but if there is any disturbance, send a rider immediately."

The Commander of the watch clicked his heels and saluted as another bolted the doors. The voices grew more distant over the next few minutes but Jess waited for another thirty just to be sure they would not be interrupted and he leaned on his elbow to see how Matthew was recovering. His back was toward him and he wasn't moving so Jess carefully looked around the church to make sure he wasn't being observed through the windows and quietly crawled over. Just before he reached out to touch him, Matthew said, "I'm alive—though it feels barely so. If you weren't here I'm certain I would be in my harbinger state for at least a day as Horsa said."

"Well then we don't have any time to lose do we?" said Jess as he pulled out the medieval book from his cloak.

Matthew rolled over and looked up at Jess with glossy eyes. "What did you have in mind—you're going to read to me?"

Jess smiled, enjoying once again Matthew's personality that was pushing up from within. "I'm going to heal you—God willing."

"Well, I've seen you do it before so I have every confidence," replied Matthew.

"Your case is different than the others. I already tried to bless you last night but Horsa still has his claws in you it appears, which is why I am consulting this book."

"What book is that?" Matthew asked slowly pulling himself into a sitting position.

Jess closed the book and showed him the cover. "It's a medieval clergy manual of sorts, it's called Gregory the Great's Pastoral Care. The church still printed similar books up to before the Minimum and I am of course very familiar with their modern contents, but direction on extreme demon exorcism was removed from the manual centuries ago. When I found the book, I kept it just for its novelty but as I mentioned, God knew what purpose it would have."

"So what do you think, do I have any hope?"

With a look of confusion, Jess thumbed through several pages and then looked up. "Well, I'm a little confused with the terminology and with some of the words—it's written in a mixture of Latin and Old English, but I believe in your extreme case we must use blood atonement."

"Blood what?" asked Matthew as he tried to get on his feet.

"That's what has me confused. I am of course aware what blood atonement is, but I've never heard of it being an ordinance," replied Jess searching for an index or glossary in the back of the manual. After a few minutes he gave up and placed his finger in the book and closed it. "Blood atonement is a requirement for forgiveness of the most terrible sins. It basically states that the blood of the sinner is required for restitution and eventual forgiveness, but I struggle with how to apply it in this situation."

"So, it's like blood-letting? I cut my wrist and drain a few pints as if purging a disease?"

Jess smiled for a brief moment but then shook his head. "Not exactly. A few pints will not do, all of it is required."

"Oh," replied Matthew soberly.

Jess opened the manual and began reading out loud, translating the Old English words into Latin, hoping Matthew might have the insight he lacked but after only several sentences, it became clear as reading aloud sometimes does, and he thought to himself, *The blood of a worthy soul atoning for the misfortune of another.*

Jess sat the book down and looked up at Matthew who was peering through the crack in the door and said with conviction, "I understand now—and I understand why I am here and why we are in a church. God is both mysterious in his ways and perfect in his plans." Jess got up and walked to the front of the chapel and stood before a stone altar that was crumbling with age and sighed. As he knelt down, Matthew walked to the opposite side and following Jess's lead, he also knelt.

"What do I have to do?" he asked, placing his hands on the altar.

Jess looked into his eyes intently and said, "Accept what I am about to do for you and commit to be the best man you can be until your dying breath." With that, Jess reached inside his robe and retrieved a short dagger and pushed its sharp blade into both of his palms as Matthew looked on in horror. He then clasped them together and began to pray for Matthew, his blood streaming down his arms and bathing the altar.

CHAPTER 15

GOLIATH VERSES GOLIATH

Jess's voice progressively became quieter as his utterances grew more poignant and determined, until only his lips moved, as if the words were too sacred to be heard by mortal ears. Finally, with his blood draining off the alter and pooling around his feet on the stone floor, Jess's lips stopped moving and he collapsed, falling backwards just as Matthew opened his eyes to see if he were still praying. Matthew called out his name, perhaps louder than he should have, and rushed to revive him. From the opposite side of the alter, he was unaware of just how much blood Jess had lost and he tore out the seam from Jess's robe and wrapped it around the gaping wounds on his hands. He then put his ear to his chest and was relieved to hear his transcendent heart still beating, but only just. His breath was so faint that it could barely be felt on the back of his hand and he lifted his nearly lifeless body onto his lap and wondered what could be done. In another age he would have been given a transfusion and liquids, but in this medieval age, he feared all he could do was watch the most holy man he knew, die. While a transfusion was impossible, he began looking around for water, no matter how rancid, to try and revive him and if not too putrid, give him drink.

At the far end of the chapel, below a missing section of roof was a puddle that appeared to be several inches deep. He picked up Jess's limp body and carried him over to the pool where he carefully dipped his hand into the cold water and poured it on his forehead. After three or four handfuls, Jess shook his head slightly and opened his eyes for a very brief moment, smiled weakly and closed them again, exhausted. Matthew feared that the blood atonement ritual required Jess to give his life, something he only thought about after the ritual had begun and he took a deep sigh of relief as he looked up through the hole in the roof, thanking God. He wondered if Jess truly meant to give his life as a ransom but now that he was alive, did that mean the atonement was void? Seeing Jess so near death on his behalf was tormenting and he vowed he would gladly go back to being a harbinger for the rest of his life, rather than have his friend lay down his life for his.

"Can you take some water?" Matthew whispered.

Jess slowly responded with a very slight nod and Matthew scooped up some water from the puddle, being careful not to disturb the pool so that the water might be as pure as possible. Placing it to his lips Matthew whispered, "Please God, if there ever was holy water, I pray his may be it."

Jess was only able to manage a few shallow swallows before becoming too exhausted. Matthew leaned against the wall with Jess cradled in his lap, every few minutes checking his pulse but before he knew it, he found himself waking from a deep sleep. In alarm, he reached down and placed his hand on Jess's neck and to his relief, his pulse was not only there, but it was stronger. Wondering how long he had been asleep, he looked up at the largest window in the church that faced east and noted that the shadows were growing long, which meant it was at least five or six in the evening. He had been asleep for at least three hours and it was then that he realized he felt his strength completely returned and his mind more clear than he could ever remember. Just then Jess shifted in his lap and opened his eyes.

"I think it worked!" Matthew said quietly but with excitement.

Jess smiled as if he already knew.

As Matthew held more water to Jess's lips, they heard voices outside the church that sounded more urgent than the usual idle chatter that they had grown accustom to hearing and Matthew listened intently before reaching for more water. Based upon the excitement, something unexpected was happening and after he provided enough water for Jess to have his fill, he quietly got up and walked over and peered through the crack in doors. In the churchyard, the commander had set up a make-shift camp and a fresh fire was burning in preparation for the cool evening ahead. He also saw a soldier dismounting and after saluting, informed the commander that Lord Horsa was on his way back from Peel Castle and that he would be here within the hour.

"That's bloody well with me," replied the commander, "I've had enough babysitting."

Matthew looked down at Jess in alarm. If they were going to escape, they had less than an hour to make a plan and execute it since their chances of success were much greater with Horsa out of the picture.

"Are you well enough to travel?" Matthew asked with hope in his voice.

Jess nodded and tried to smile as he replied in a very weak whisper, "God willing."

Matthew paced back and forth from the doors to the red

alter trying to formulate a plan, estimating that there were at least twenty men surrounding the church, which he didn't see as a problem except that he would be carrying Jess. *Twenty men, yes*, he thought, *but not with one hand behind my back*. He had to find a way to escape unnoticed but as he walked to the large stained-glass window, he determined that the building was completely surrounded. Fighting would be the only way. He strategized that he might be able to kill or otherwise subdue all the soldiers, then retrieve Jess and flee to the Maughold Docks. From there, they could either hide and wait for a poorly-manned ship or take one by force. It wasn't the best plan he had ever come up with, but it was all there was time for and he knelt next to Jess and told him how their escape would play out.

When he finished, Jess smiled, squoze his hand and nodded saying, "I've seen you do it before so I have every confidence."

The rapid twist of fate made Matthew pause. Just hours before, his life was in Jess's hands and now Jess was in his. With fierce determination, he looked down soberly and said, "I won't fail you Father. You have saved my life, and I shall save yours—I swear before God."

Jess's expression turned sorrowful rather than hopeful and he intently looked into Matthew's eyes and replied, "Be careful you don't promise that which is contrary."

"Contrary! Contrary to whom? I will bring you back to England, even if I have to go through or around God to do it!"

Jess shook his head and then took a hard, dry swallow, "Matthew, hear this."

"Save your strength Father, you needn't worry," interrupted Matthew not wanting to entertain failure.

Jess grabbed hold of Matthew's arm with all the strength he could muster and said, "MATTHEW—If you have to choose between me or England, choose England. England is all the good that is left in the world."

Matthew tried to write off Jess's words as nothing more than the effects of blood loss but as he shook his head, Jess grabbed his arm again and looked at him sternly until he finally nodded.

"Besides, if Horsa wanted me dead, I would already be so don't you think?" said Jess with a voice of encouragement.

"There are worse things than death Father," replied Matthew with a sigh.

"True enough," Jess nodded. "Among them is knowing that I was the reason the captain of the Ravenguard never returned to avenge England."

Acting in such haste, Matthew couldn't help but feel foolish but there wasn't time to allow his plan to settle and gel in his mind and he walked again to the front doors to take a head count. There were at least ten men settling in around the fire and as he peered out the windows around the church, he counted nearly thirty in all—too many to fight all at once. What he needed was a sieve that could effectively meter the assailants like a small opening or… He walked to the large stain-glass window behind the alter and cupped his hands around his eyes and peered out one of the more transparent sections. There didn't appear to be bars on the outside of the medieval glass window, unlike all the others and with time ticking, he backed up several yards and took a deep breath.

After assuring Jess once again that he would not forget him, he said, "Forgive me Father," and he ran as fast as he could toward the seven-foot stain-glass window that was over a thousand years old. Using the alter as a launching block, he jumped up on it and leaped at full speed, diving through the ancient glass. As old buildings settle over time, the windows come under increased pressure and as Matthew's enormous frame came in contact with the glass, it exploded, first making a loud bang, then a crash as the razor shards shot from the frame. He saw that there were three guards, on his way to the ground; one to his right and two on the left. Just as he hit, he noted that the guard's sword to his right was closest to him and as his hands touched the dirt, he did a complete summersault, rolling to his feet.

All three guards were stunned by the sudden noise and he quickly pulled the sword from the lone guard's belt before he was aware what had just happened. He figured he had less than thirty seconds before the other guards would be rounding the building and he killed the first guard immediately, thrusting his own sword into his gut up to the hilt. Out of the corner of his eye, he saw the other two guards running toward him and he kicked the lifeless soldier in their direction as he withdrew his sword from its gut and spun around. With a broad sweep, he first knocked both guard's out-stretched swords to the ground, then at the same time as he thrust his sword through one man's neck, he knocked the other unconscious with his fist. He hesitated for just a moment as he looked at the unconscious guard but then quickly concluded that a dead man could not purse him later and he thrust his sword through his heart. He then collected several daggers before he ran behind a large gravestone and waited for the others to arrive.

Finding the three dead guards and the shattered window, the commander knew right away what had happened and assuming that Matthew was still a harbinger, or at least harbinger-like, he ordered for his men to spread out.

Matthew laughed to himself and whispered, "Perfect."

He could hear the soldier's footsteps dissipate in all directions as he sat patiently, waiting to be discovered as a child does when playing hide and seek. It took the soldiers much longer than it would have taken a child to find him but a single soldier finally rounded the large gravestone and gasped in surprise. Taking advantage of the soldiers gaping mouth, he smiled and said flippantly, "Aw, you found me," as he threw a dagger into the soldier's chest.

Just then, he heard someone yell, "There he is!"

He stood up and quickly surveyed the graveyard, noting where all the soldiers were and planned his strategy as they all ran to kill him. With the soldiers all spread out, it ensured that they reached him in a nearly perfect meter and he began cutting them down as they came until there were less than five or six left. Seeing that they were no match for the massive harbinger that appeared to be in his right mind, they backed away toward the front of the church where they had horses and a speedy escape. As he casually followed them, he smiled, remembering how much he loved winning in battle and he hated to admit it, but his time as a harbinger had made him much more agile. Not surprising, when he rounded the front of the church, he saw the men riding off on their horses but just as he was about to retrieve Jess, he saw them returning even faster than they left. The look on their faces was one of panic and they timidly dismounted then reluctantly drew their swords, but didn't advance. The reason for their forced valor quickly became apparent as Horsa made his way into the churchyard atop his massive percheron. He had never fought Horsa but from all reports and after watching him when he was a harbinger, he knew that any distractions flittering about would be death so he quickly advanced upon the six men who appeared to be like deer caught in headlights and cut them all down before Horsa dismounted.

Horsa didn't appear to be in any alarm or hurry as he casually removed his riding gloves and then withdrew his sword from the saddle scabbard with a yawn. He then took one step forward and knocked the mud from his boots with his sword one-by-one before looking up at Matthew and tossed his sword from hand-to-hand.

"You're looking much like yourself today Matthew," said Horsa as he spit buckhorn seeds.

Without a word, Matthew took several steps backwards and bent down to retrieve a second sword from the hands of one of the dead soldiers without taking his eyes off Horsa.

"How is it that you are yourself?" Horsa said, casually walking toward him.

Despite every effort to resist, Matthew betrayed Jess and looked toward the church and seeing his glance, Horsa replied with anger. "That damn Bishop! He has cost me greatly, but not for much longer. My brother and I have something very special planned. Too bad you won't be around."

Horsa then brandished his sword several times in the air and finally looked as if he were mildly serious about his fight with Matthew. He was either unconcerned with Matthew's skill and strength as a fighter or he was very concerned and was just playing the casual fool to unsettle him. Either way, the truth was, two of the strongest and mightiest warriors in the world were about to cross swords—a Goliath verses Goliath—where there would not be any lucky stone shots, only steel against steel, wielded by perhaps two of the most powerful men to ever live. If there was an advantage for either man, it fell in Horsa's favor since his sword was fifty inches long, four inches wide and weighed a massive hundred ten pounds, a giant of a sword made for a giant. The swords Matthew held in both hands were standard issue weapons, made for standard men and they were like blades of grass in comparison.

Matthew continued to walk backwards as Horsa approached, waiting for an aggressive opportunity and he bumped up against the only tree that stood in the churchyard. As he bowed under a low-hanging branch and took several sidesteps, he halfway anticipated Horsa to change into a fenrir but knowing there would be a moon tonight, it unfortunately prohibited him from doing so. Having killed so many fenrir over the years, he preferred facing one instead of Horsa. Fenrir were slower and didn't wield a sword, to say nothing of being able to throw blue fire from their palm. Horsa took a step closer as he cut away the branches with one swing of his massive sword, severing wood larger than his arm and laughing.

"It's too bad really, to have to kill my best harbinger. I feel as if I'm putting-down a prized stallion. I'm rather wounded by the thought," said Horsa as he swung at another branch.

With Horsa's hand raised, Matthew saw his opportunity and he lunged forward, slicing Horsa across his waist, a superficial cut less than a quarter of an inch deep but it was first blood and it belonged to Matthew. If this were a dual, first blood would designate Matthew the winner of the match, but even though this dual would be decided by death, the moral victory belonged to Matthew and Horsa knew it. From that point on, Horsa was in earnest and he roared angrily as he rushed from under the tree toward the only worthy opponent in the world. His speed was incredible for his size and before he could ready himself, Matthew had to fall to the ground to escape the lethal swing of his sword, the air from the blade blowing past his ear. The swing of Horsa's sword continued past the spot were Matthew stood and slammed into a gravestone, breaking it in half. As the battle continued, they both jumped and wove in and out of the crowded graveyard, both with their share of near misses and close calls. With a formidable stone between them, Horsa pulled a dagger from his belt and threw it with inhuman speed and accuracy as if a bullseye were painted on Matthew's face. Without thinking, Matthew felt a harbinger-like instinct takeover his reaction to the approaching blade and as if in slow-motion, he jumped backwards high into the air while the dagger passed under him. Completing a full 360 degrees, he landed on his feet and thrust one of his swords back at Horsa, who was in close pursuit behind his dagger.

The tip of Matthew's sword grazed Horsa's forehead just as Horsa's sword connected with it, breaking it in half. Shocked, Matthew threw the broken sword in Horsa's direction and it surprisingly hit him in the head just above his right eye. Such a blow was an insult between such equally matched opponents and adding to it, Matthew couldn't help from laughing and said, "Take that bitch!"

Horsa was incensed, the insult wounding him more than any blade and he came at Matthew with the fury of a lion, his sword slicing through the air while fire burst from his palm, connecting with tombstones, sending sparks flying and stones crumbling into the fading evening light. The battle continued as if the men were two bulls in a china shop, the china being the stone grave markers that broke and shattered under their missed blows. Both men were so skilled at their murderous craft, that it seemed neither could take the advantage and as the battle progressed around the back of the church, the graveyard in shambles. The shards from the stained-glass window broke under their feet as they slowly turned in a circle several feet apart until Horsa lowered his sword and smiled. He was obviously looking at something behind him but he dared not turn his back on Horsa for a moment, but he then worried that soldiers were approaching and he spun around quickly to see several hundred harbingers running up the hill.

This was something he had not thought of and even if he had, there was nothing he could do. He knew more than anyone the ferocity of a pack of harbingers and without even weighing the odds, he knew he was a dead man unless he ran, which meant leaving Jess behind. For what seemed like several painful minutes, that were really only fractions of a second, he mourned the abandonment of his friend and brother just as he heard Horsa advancing behind him, taking advantage of the harbinger distraction. A warrior is never more vulnerable and unprotected than when attacking. His arm is extended when making the blow while his whole body is exposed and unable to defend a counter attack, which is why a swordsman waits for the perfect moment—a moment Horsa thought he had found. But Matthew heard him take two quick steps, which he guessed placed him within striking range but since he could not see him, he would have to wait for his blade to touch his skin before moving. The touch of Horsa's blade would reveal his exact position, allowing Matthew to react on instinct and not wait for his eyes to interpret the situation. It was risky in the extreme but as the fractions of seconds ticked by, he soon felt Horsa's sword graze his bare shoulder. Knowing Horsa was right handed, he knew he had to be standing at least two feet behind him and one foot to the right since he had observed that Horsa always positioned himself counter to his target by a few degrees when attacking.

As he felt the cold steel enter his shoulder, he spun around, causing Horsa's blade to slice down his arm, flaying several layers of skin almost to his elbow. Out of the corner of his eye, he saw that his assessment of Horsa's position was deadly accurate and as he came out of his spin, he leaped into the air and came down with a crushing blow that connected with Horsa's wrist, severing his hand just above the joint. Horsa yelled out mostly with rage than in agony over the amputation and his sword fell to the ground, his hand still clinging firmly to it. Matthew knew a wound even as serious as a lost hand would not stop Horsa and he quickly picked up Horsa's sword and pointed it toward him as Horsa stuck his stub into his shirt. Behind Horsa he could see the harbingers quickly approaching and going back inside for Jess meant certain death for both of them. If he fled to safety, he could come back with help and there was the hope that Horsa would also bleed-out right there.

With a heavy heart and with Horsa's sword in his hand, he ran toward the coast with his incredibly nimble and fast harbinger-toned legs. As he ran, he remembered his last conversation with Jess and how it was as if he knew that he would be left behind. "Choose England," he said out loud, "I don't have to choose one Jess, I will be back—I can choose both."

By the time he reached the cliffs, night had completely fallen and he watched the movement on the docks below for several minutes before coming up with a plan. There was a single, two-mast ship tied to the end of the dock and about a dozen men loading or perhaps unloading it. Oddly enough, there didn't appear to be any soldiers or guards around the perimeter or anywhere on the beach but as he stood up, he felt a sword in his back.

"Oops, my mistake," he said, as he reached behind him and grabbed the guard's wrist and threw him over his head and off the cliff.

The guard landed with a loud thud on the rocks below, causing everyone on the dock to stop and look around.

"Did you hear that?" asked one of the men.

"No, and neither did you," replied another man who seemed to be in charge. "Get back to work! Lord Horsa will be here any minute and he expects his ship to be ready to sail."

"His Lord is sailing tonight?" the underling replied, "Alone?"

The man in charge smote the underling on the head, abuse of subordinates being a common theme in Toprak ranks, and cursed, "Don't be daft, his captain is already on board and he's comin' with his crew."

"So the captain is on board without a crew," Matthew said quietly. "A perfect storm if there ever was one."

Matthew climbed down the cliffs to the rocky beach and found the soldier he had thrown off and removed his shirt. Clothing was something harbingers rarely had and with only a tattered pair of pants, he was more fortunate than most. The shirt was too small to button so he just wrapped it around, tucked it in his trousers He waited until most of the men were off the ship in their back-and-forth work before he stepped onto the dock from the darkness.

"Evening fellas, I don't think his Lordship will be making it. I hear he's a little shorthanded tonight," Matthew laughed as the dock came to life with swords being drawn.

With little effort, Matthew either cut down or threw off the dock, every man who approached him and within a few minutes, he stepped on board, ordering all hands to make sail just as he felt a knife in his back.

"I'm the only one who makes orders on this ship," came a familiar voice behind him.

Matthew turned around quickly with his leg extended backwards, knocking his assailant to the deck and then pointed his sword where death would be swift. In the faint light of the deck lamps, he squinted for several seconds and then said, "Well, well, Nicole! I should have known. There's always maggots on a rotting corpse."

Nicole looked up at Matthew but didn't speak. She then recognized whose sword he held in his hand and her expression changed from defiance to surprise. Regardless of whether Horsa was dead or alive, the fact remained that Matthew had defeated him, which meant it might be time for an alliance change and employing her newly honed skills of manipulation she began to whimper, "I'm so glad you're here! You won't believe what hell I have been through since I was captured at the Battle of the Thames."

Matthew slowly lowered his sword with cautious surprise and asked, "Captured?"

"Yes, did you think I joined the enemy?" replied Nicole. "I suppose I could be offended that no one came looking for me but you're here now and that's all that matters."

Matthew took a step backwards, extended his hand and pulled Nicole to her feet. "Well, you're the sailor. How soon can we get off this rock?" he asked.

"Soon," replied Nicole. "Horsa was on his way here so all we need do is hoist sail and cut our lines."

In under five minutes, the *Bizyok* was responding to the stiff breeze that was blowing off the sea toward the island and with Nicole at the helm, she jibed into the breeze and pointed a course toward England just as a large pack of harbingers on the cliff began howling their hateful cry of defeat.

"You sure make a grand exit, as always," said Nicole with a smile.

Matthew observed the set of the sails with the direction of the wind and assumed that with little maneuvering, they should be able to sail in a nearly strait course across the channel. Checking his assumption, he turned to Nicole, who was reading her compass, and asked for confirmation.

"Nearly so," she replied as she reached out to touch his bare chest through his open shirt. "It depends on where you want to land. Our present course should put us in near Blackpool, baring a northwestern off the coast. If that's the case we'll be closer to Liverpool, unless we beat into the wind of course."

"That works for me, and that means I no longer require your services," he replied as he pulled her hand off his chest, grabbed her by the nape of the neck and threw her overboard. "You're not that clever babe," yelled Matthew from the taffrail. "You should probably take off that dress, it'll turn into a sea anchor before you reach shore."

Turning around, he saw the concerned faces of the remaining make-shift crew, wondering what would be their fate. Matthew drew his sword and pointed it at the men and then toward the rail, giving them the option to fight or jump while they were still close enough for an evening swim. Due to Matthew's formidable size, the choice was easy and all of them ran to the rail and jumped into the black waters of the Irish Sea.

On a low rising hill overlooking the Ribble Valley, where the feared M6 line lay less than a mile away to the west, the King, Gus and General Clancy sat on their horses in the damp darkness, waiting for Riley to return with news of the harbinger army encampment. Nearly a week ago, they sat atop another hill in the dark, watching the harbinger army advance over the top of Castle Hill into Woodsome, putting the entire English army to flight northwards for thirty miles where they finally found refuge in the Yorkshire Forest. Before the Minimum, the Yorkshire Wood was only a three hundred acre relief surrounded by a sea of manmade development, but it now encompassed the entire expanse of land from coast to coast and rumor held that it extended as far as the old town of Glasgow and perhaps further. The Yorkshire Forest in the modern age marked the beginning of the English frontier and there were no accurate reports or maps of the area, just myths of endless dark woods and cold rivers, inhabited by creatures that hadn't been seen for fifteen hundred years such as redcaps, bugbears wargs and of course nymphs.

Earlier in the day, the English scouts reported that the harbinger army had dispersed and their human commanders had retreated to the west. Since hearing the news, they had followed the Toprak retreat with a hundred men just in case it was a ruse to draw out the entire army, but the last two miles had not turned up any organized attack. The harbingers seemed to be wandering aimlessly but were still aggressive when approached however. It seemed as if every harbinger was now out for itself without a Toprak commander. The General assumed that for whatever reason, Toprak had retreated back to the M6 so quickly that they abandoned the harbingers, leaving them to pasture as it were, knowing that they could gather them again later no doubt but the news coming back from the M6 line would confirm such a hypothesis and they all waited anxiously for Riley's return.

"Your Majesty," said the General handing the King his canteen, a seamless leather bag fastened with a tie string.

The mist from the coast had been hitting them in the face since early evening and a cold drink of water was the last thing he wanted at that moment and he shook his head.

"It will warm you your Majesty," insisted the General as the King reluctantly took the bag and a sip.

"Whoa!" he exclaimed, and then took several more deep swallows. "Wherever did you get that—and what the hell is it?"

The General laughed. "I came upon a still in the forest and I assured the men that I would not destroy it so long as they furnished me with three leather casks. That one is yours, and Gus, I have one for you," he said handing him a bag. "I figured I would wait until their contents would be the most beneficial."

"Never in life has ale been more welcomed," replied the King taking another long drink and then wiping his mouth on his sleeve. "Don't misunderstand me, it's not the most desirable taste but it is incredibly stiff. I am not just a little surprised that it has not corroded the bag."

"Or eaten a hole in my stomach and drained out my leg," replied Gus in surprise after taking his first drink.

As their laughter began to die out, they heard a horseman approaching and they all instinctively drew their swords until the rider came within the light of their torches and they sheathed their weapons. Riley saluted to the General and then bowed as best he could on horseback to the two Kings.

"Your Majesty, Your Majesty, Sir," he began respectfully, "We found ample signs of the Toprak encampment but no personnel. I rode as far as Bilsborrow and I sent a detachment south to Buckshaw. They returned shortly after I did and their report is the same—encampments and equipment galore, but it's a ghost town."

The King turned to the General a gasped, "What the hell is happening?"

"It's as if the power went out and they've all gone home," said Gus.

"Indeed," replied Riley, nodding.

"Gentlemen, it is still much too early to assume a full retreat, especially since they had us on the ropes. Let's continue our march to the sea with the same trepidation. Inform your men that we are most certain to meet up with the Toprak army any moment," commanded the General.

"Do you think?" asked Gus.

The General turned to Gus with a weak smile, shaking his head and said, "It doesn't seem likely now, but we must continue to advance as if we are still at war, lest we march in into a fool's trap."

"Very well, Sir," saluted Riley as he turned and rode into the darkness.

"Shall we gentlemen?" said the King, suggesting that they ride.

"Indeed," replied Gus, taking another drink from his leather flask.

At the bottom of the hill, they made their way over the destroyed M6 that was now covered with thick vines, making it hardly noticeable other than the strange embankment twisting across the countryside like a snake, waiting to be discovered by some future archeologist. Coming down the other side, they began to see signs of the Toprak encampments and just as Riley had reported, it all appeared to have been abandoned in haste. As they rode thorough the empty camp, they continued to look at each other from time to time, shaking their heads in disbelief, wondering what was the meaning of it all. Continuing west, they left the Toprak encampments behind them and proceeded to the coast, trailing behind the main detachment with a dozen personal guards. If Toprak was planning an ambush to capture the King, they had ridden into it with no escape, which made the General very uneasy and as they rode, he continually looked in all directions like a doe in an open meadow, being startled with nearly every twig snap.

Just before first light, Riley had finally found a Toprak soldier taking refuge in one of the many ancient church ruins in the region and by the time the General and the two Kings caught up, he had already interrogated the prisoner and tethered him behind his horse, hands bound and gagged.

Upon seeing the prisoner, the General sighed with relief and exclaimed, "At last maybe we can have some answers. What have you been able to learn captain?"

"Strangely enough, he sounds as confused as we are," replied Riley after saluting. "He was very cooperative however and responded to all my questions without hesitation."

"A soldier who so easily spills his guts is usually a plant intended to deceive," replied the General.

"I thought of that of course, but he is French Sir," Riley said with a knowing look.

"Oh—all right then, what did he say?" asked the General dismounting.

"He claims that the harbinger armies all of a sudden did not respond to the usual commands," said Riley as he walked with the General toward the prisoner, "and that when the soldiers saw they could no longer command them, they fled for their own lives—he doing the same. He also says that several ships docked near Blackpool departed in the night but he was too late to board."

The General placed his torch near the prisoner's face who was sitting on the ground behind Riley's horse to make sure he was not a harbinger. The prisoner looked up with a cheap smile, trying to save his life and saluting with his bound hands.

After the General was satisfied the prisoner was not part

harbinger, he cut the gag from his mouth and asked, "How does a Frenchmen come to work for Toprak?"

The prisoner swallowed hard and explained that he was captured in Algiers before the global destruction and then was offered to join the Toprak army in exchange for food. "But I would gladly exchange my allegiance to England and serve an even greater General," he said with his smile becoming cheaper as it grew.

"Flattery is a dull blade," scoffed the General turning his back and walking away, "kill him Captain."

"Yes Sir," Riley replied, saluting.

"Wait! No, I can be of great service, please," begged the prisoner.

The General paused without turning around and said, "I believe I am a just man so tell me. You join an army in which you do not share in their cause, only for self-preservation and you invade His Majesty's Kingdom leading an army of demons. You are clueless or withholding information about your retreat and you are French. If I have missed something, please tell me but I have heard nothing that compels me."

"You kill me because I am French?" asked the prisoner in horror.

The General slowly turned around and looked at the man intently and said, "No, that you can't help. I condemn you because you wage war on my island for self-preservation with no moral compass." He then turned and walked back to his horse as the prisoner continued to plead for his life.

Just then one of the King's men rode up exclaiming that a

ship was seen on the horizon in the first light, directly approaching the beach. The General stopped and turned on his heel, walking back to the rider.

"We could not make out any other details but the commander on the beach ordered everyone out of site," said the soldier catching his breath.

Riley slowly turned to the General and asked, "What do you make of that?"

The General slowly shook his head as the prisoner stared up at him. "It's—I know that ship. It's the *Bizyok*—Lord Horsa's ship!" said the prisoner sounding as if he had made it up.

The General looked down at the prisoner incredulously. "You know that from only hearing that it is a ship?"

"Oui, oui! His Lord's is the only two masted in the fleet," he lied. "All the others have three."

"And how large is this fleet?" asked the General, hearing the first bit of information he found valuable.

The prisoner stalled since he really did not know but his goal was to stall time for his life and he offered to go down to the beach and positively identify the ship and if it were Horsa, he would intercede and allow his capture. His willingness to desert his army surprised the General until he reminded himself that he only joined Toprak to preserve his life and he was simply doing the same thing now. After thinking through the scenario several times, the General nodded and told Riley to take the Frenchman down to the beach.

"Let him be the only man seen and secure your men as

close to the landing site as possible. We will have to run this one with our gut-sense since we do not know the beach nor who and how many are in the ship. Be prepared for the worst—meaning harbingers," commanded the General before walking back to inform the King.

When they reached the beach, the King, Gus and the General saw the ship just over a mile away, heading straight for them. They did find it curious that it was not heading for the Toprak port near Blackpool but like everything else Toprak, there was certainly a well thought out plan and purpose. Out of site, they continued to watch the ship draw within a hundred yards of the beach and Gus suggested that at any moment they would see the sails dropped and an anchor lowered but to their great surprise, they saw neither. The ship continued its head-on course for the beach with a strong tail wind of at least twenty knots until it ran aground, its hull crashing into the rocky shore and finally coming to a painful stop where the surf relentless pounded against it, eventually rolling it on its side.

Everyone remained out of site, waiting and expecting to see Horsa and an army of harbingers descend out of the ship but they saw nothing and no one. After twenty minutes had passed, the General finally ordered everyone to remain alert and out of sight while he and Riley went to investigate the wreckage but before he climbed over the berm, the King tapped him on the back and pointed. Ducking back down, they watched a figure approach the railing that was almost in the water now and a very large man leap overboard. The water was less than four feet deep and the man that was exactly Horsa's size, waded through the rough surf and walked toward the Frenchman who wasn't sure what was going to happen. It was light enough now to identify faces but this man was certainly not Horsa, however, the Frenchman was convinced he was

Toprak, after all this was a Toprak ship. Trembling and still on his knees, the Frenchman bowed and stuttered, "L-L-Lord Horsa ex-t-tends his hand of fe-fellowship."

Matthew was beyond irritated to hear such a greeting on English soil and with a giant leap, he lunged forward and kicked the Frenchman off his knees, hurling him into the air and landing him on his back unconscious. He then threw Horsa's severed hand on the Frenchman's chest and laughed, "No my friend, he certainly does not!."

CHAPTER 16

CROSSING LINES

Nicole struggled to unbutton her dress while being churned in three foot swells off the Saxonice coast as she watched her ship sail away toward England in the darkness. The wet heavy velvet around her waist was like concrete, making treading water with only one arm impossible—just as unbuttoning with the other was equally futile. Every time she tried, she quickly sank beneath the waves no matter how violently she kicked. At last, she gave up the fight and with a deep breath; she used both hands to unfasten twelve buttons down the back of her dress while she sank deeper and deeper into the cold, black abyss. Nearly out of breath, she ripped out the last two and pulled the dress down over her shoulders and kicked the anchor from her feet as she began pushing upward.

Push, push, push and still no air as she started to grow dizzy from the lack of oxygen in her bloodstream, making her arms and legs lethargic, refusing to obey the command to save her life. In desperation, she opened her eyes in hope of seeing how far she was from the surface, but the forbidding darkness of the Irish Sea offered no hope to its victim and she pushed one last time with all the strength her body could wield as the sea water burned into her eyes. She felt her body ease upwards and then slowly coast to a stop, still not finding the surface and life. Being the accomplished sailor that she was, she had often wondered what it was like to drown and the last thought to pass through her conscious mind was; *now I know.*

It was already as black as a grave under the water but it grew even darker as her consciousness faded and survival gave way to the indisputable supremacy of the sea. She was no longer aware of where she was nor could she feel the stabbing cold of her watery grave and with instinct taking over, she involuntarily opened her mouth and drew one last deep breath. With a mixture of water and oxygen filling her lungs, her reflexes began choking on the waves that were continually dumped over her head as she was thrashed about in the heavy seas at the surface. With air reaching and reactivating her conscious mind, she rolled over and arched her back into a float, keeping her mouth out of the water as she bobbed through the swells, gasping and coming back to life.

When she finally felt as if she could move again, she heard the sound of the surf and was then immediately thrown over the crest of a wave, spitting her naked body onto the rocky beach. When she came to a painful stop, she rolled onto her back, several yards from the Toprak dock. For the next ten minutes, she lay on the sharp rocks, filling her lungs with pure air that wasn't mixed with water and with every breath, she coughed and groaned until her mind finally became clear again just as she heard voices approaching.

"I'm tellin' ya they're real!" she heard a voice say as it grew closer. "And that's no fish, it's a mermaid I tell ya!"

She raised her head off the rocks and saw two Toprak dock hands timidly approaching her, unsure of what had just washed up on the beach; a monster or mermaid.

"Don't get near it. I hear them mermaids can be right deadly to a man—on boat or land," said one of them as the other drew within a few yards.

On any other evening, she might have played along and maybe even scared the unsuspecting mermaid hunter for fun, but tonight, she was barely alive and in no mood to be stared or poke at in the nude. She picked up a palm-sized rock and then pulled her ragged body to her feet as the closest man froze, not believing what his eyes beheld. As Nicole staggered passed him, she made a tight fist around the rock and landed it squarely on his jaw, knocking him unconscious as she shook her head and sighed. Seeing that the walking mermaid was none other than Nicole, the Madame Captain, the second man stood at strict attention and saluted, his eyes painfully staring upwards instead of the pleasant nakedness of the Captain. At her command, he took off his pea coat and gave it to her as she continued up the beach to find Horsa.

To her surprise, when she reach the top of the cliffs at the end of a narrow path, she saw dozens of harbingers running aimlessly through the open countryside. Some of them were still in a chaining, pulling in every direction but strangely, they were not violent to one another as they always were when a Centenary went bad. Scanning the surrounding hills, there was no sign of any Toprak personnel and even the chaining camp in the valley below the church was empty. It was then she remembered Matthew having Horsa's sword and she wondered if he had defeated Horsa since there were few other scenarios where Matthew could have taken his sword. Whatever was going on, she decided that it could wait until morning or at least until she stopped shivering as the night wind continued to chill her wet body to the bone. The only sign of life and the only light on the horizon was coming from the old church and since light in this day and age meant fire, it also meant warmth and she began making her way toward it.

Arriving at the church doors, she was surprised to find them locked from the outside and had she not been so cold, she might have concluded that perhaps there was something inside that should not be let out but as her teeth chattered, setting the rhythm for her body shakes, she lifted the plank that held the door and pulled it open. In the center of the large vacant room was a small fire with a cloaked figure sitting behind it, its head bowed and motionless, even at the sound of the creaking door. Stepping inside, she pulled the door shut and cautiously approached the fire, waiting for the figure to look up but even after she reached the warm flames, the person under the brown cloak didn't move. In a heap next to the fire was a small pile of wood, timbers from the roof cave-in, and she slowly bent down, picked one up for a weapon and cleared her throat. The cloak didn't move at first but then slowly looked up then returned to its slumped and crippled posture.

"Well—Father Jess. I wondered where they had thrown you," said Nicole, chattering and tossing her make-shift club on top of the fire, causing sparks to drift up with the smoke. There might have been more she would have ordinarily said to him but the only thing on her mind right now was to stop shaking and she stepped closer to the fire, neither of them speaking. Once Nicole's lips changed from blue to red, she looked around for something to sit on but found nothing and then tried to sit on the floor, struggling with the short pea coat she was wearing. Modesty was not something she usually worried about, in fact it rarely crossed her mind at all but being in Jess's presence, it was strangely important to her and she struggled to cover herself with the short wool coat.

Finding her behavior odd, Jess finally looked up and realized who was sharing his fire, not having identified her previously. He then noticed her long, bare legs disappearing under her short pea coat and her self-conscious disposition, a trait he had never before witnessed in Nicole. In the cool evening air, her pale legs were covered in goosebumps and he couldn't imagine being so ill-clothed on such a late summer night. Without a word, he stood, removed his riding cloak and handed it to her with a smile. He then sat back down and resumed his slumped position while Nicole removed the coat and pulled the cloak over her head. As she sat across from Jess, she repeatedly thought about her actions in Conwy Castle and she wondered how he could possibly be kind to her after what she had done to him. It also puzzled her why she even cared at all what Jess thought—but she did. While she was trying to understand her tangled feelings of remorse, she heard herself say, "Thank you."

Jess slowly looked up and smiled warmly, nodding once before looking back down at the fire. He then picked up another piece of wood and after stirring the embers; he placed it on top of the fire and said, "You're welcome."

Jess had heard of war stories where enemies became isolated and upon finding each other alone, shared a civil and even warm interchange over a meal before returning to their respective sides. Even though he believed such stories were true, he never anticipated that such a meeting would change things for either party so profoundly as it seemed to be changing for him. Previous to this night, he never had much to do with Nicole, not since arriving in England almost five years ago, but he had heard what she was capable of—her unwavering evil disposition—and he looked up into her steel eyes wondering if she was experiencing the same thing.

Nicole smiled superficially and then looked away, the fire providing a grateful distraction to the awkward situation.

Jess also looked away, after all, what do two enemies say to one another. Jess tried to think of a benign topic they could discuss, the most obvious being why she was here but given the fact that she was almost naked, that too was an awkward topic so he quietly sighed, saying nothing. Just as he concluded that Nicole wasn't sharing any of his fuzzy feelings she asked, "What were those swords you drew from the well?"

Jess looked up slowly and protected, wondering what her interest was in the swords but regardless of her slant or cunning, the truth was, he didn't know anything about them and after a few seconds he shrugged and said, "I don't know."

"They're Viking," she said as if making a piece offering.

"Excuse me?"

"Those swords Ted pulled from the Conwy well, they're Viking steel. You really don't know anything about them," she laughed. "Viking swords were forged out of high carbon steel, which allowed them to be brilliantly polished—something that really freaked-out the Europeans."

Jess nodded, smiling as he realized she was just trying to make conversation not extract information and he returned the favor by telling her that they were following the trail of a medieval myth but before he became too comfortable, Nicole reminded him that they were on opposite sides.

"So you risk your lives traversing England alone, all over a curiosity? Honestly Father, lies are not becoming," she said smiling harmlessly but reaffirming the line separating them was just as real and dangerous as the fire between them.

While the conversation was still awkward, they managed to converse for several hours, steering clear of sensitive subjects and secrets, the dialogue completely failing at times until they spoke only of their lives before the Minimum which was a completely benign topic.

While they shared their tales, Jess continually wondered how she could so easily switch sides and turn her back on her friends until he blurted out, "Why did you leave us—what really happened at the Battle of the Thames?"

Nicole looked as if she were going to be angry but quickly softened, assuming a reflective mood as she sighed in a defeated manner and said, "It's just who I am Father."

Jess's question had a dousing effect on their conversation and for several minutes they both stared into the fire until Nicole voluntarily expanded upon his question in a very sober tone. "When I was seven, I became an award of the State of Mississippi and spent the next ten years in more foster homes than I can remember, all of them only taking me in for the extra three-hundred dollars the State gave them for looking after me, but they never really did—look after me or take very good care of me. I learned at an early age that survival was a means of allying myself with those who had the best chances of winning. When you're faced almost daily with what feels like life and death, right and wrong become rather meaningless. As I saw it, when I was the nice girl and did what I was told, that was when I got hurt. I'm sure you can't understand but when you suffer every kind of abuse imaginable, it changes you in terrible ways. When I was seventeen, I finally stopped waiting for God to answer my prayers and killed my guardian with a table leg and ran to Texas. I suppose you could say I'm still running but the only difference now is, I'm in charge."

"I'm so sorry Nicole," replied Jess, shaking his head.

"Don't be Father, unless you were the one who did it., but to answer your question, I'm just surviving and it's immoral for mė to do otherwise. Life has taught me to always side with those who have the best chances of winning."

"So you don't believe England has a chance?" replied Jess somewhat irritated.

Jess could tell Nicole was trying to be kind but after a short pause she replied, "Well, perhaps—but not after tomorrow."

Still irritated, Jess shot back but with restraint, "Please don't be offended but, how is it you are in control? Surely Hengist and Horsa rule supreme."

"For now," Nicole replied, smiling and raising her hand. On her right palm were two intersecting cuts that appeared very fresh and before Jess could ask what it meant, Nicole placed her hand back in her lap and continued. "Another skilled I developed was strict observation. You can learn anything and everything about someone if you watch them long enough and I've learned where Toprak's true power comes from."

Jess was about to ask her to explain but then remembered the unspoken rule about certain subjects and he nodded, even though he didn't really understand. Then as if she could perceive his unspoken question, she shook her head and said, "It's not what you think."

"No?" replied Jess.

"It's not the devil—at least not directly I guess, though Horsa does give me the creeps at times," Nicole said laughing. "Only you can appreciate and understand what I am about to say; that we mortals are not alone on this earth and all that is happening, has all happened before. Granted, the situation is different and even the people, but the world's history is flowing through our veins like a tape player. The power and the victory will go to them who understand the past. Not just know it, but understand it—intimately."

"And you believe Horsa and his brother have such understanding?" replied Jess ignoring the rules.

Nicole's countenance became very flat as her head first nodded and then shook contradictorily. "You have no idea Father." Nicole's face then turned blank as if she were weighing something very heavy in her mind after which she turned to Jess and smiled mournfully. "I'm sure this will not be a surprise but Horsa plans to kill you tomorrow."

Jess nodded, having already considered the possibility.

"I'm sorry but nothing can be done to change that. However," she paused. "I can't imagine anyone not knowing what I know and even though you can only savor it for a few hours, will you allow me to give you something?"

"Give me something?" replied Jess, confused.

Nicole laughed. "I was going to ask if you trusted me but certainly you do not, so let me rephrase. You *can* trust me in this moment, besides, there is no advantage in killing you right now and Lord Horsa would be really ticked off if I did."

Still confused, Jess slowly shrugged, giving her permission

to continue. Nicole got up and walked over to his side of the fire, the symbolism firmly in Jess's mind that she had just cross lines, at least for the moment. She then reached out and took Jess's hand in hers, slowly unwrapping the bandages from Matthew's blood atonement ceremony but to his surprise, she didn't enquire about his wounds. She held his right hand in hers and carefully pried apart the freshly sealed wound, ensuring that it bled profusely and then told him to lie down.

Jess slowly reclined with apprehension but as his head rested on the floor, he realized that she truly believed Horsa would kill him in the morning and that meant she may very well divulge some deep Toprak secret. If he was rescued before high noon tomorrow, what he was about to learn would be more valuable than gold and he prayed silently that that would be the case.

Nicole got up and walked over to the broken window that Matthew had destroyed and picked up a shard. She then knelt back down and he watched her carefully place the piece of glass on her palm, turning it several times, as if she were taking a measurement, but for what? His question was quickly answered when he saw her place the sharp glass in a precise position on her palm, the one already containing two cuts, and then watched her press down until it cut very deep. Surprisingly, she didn't flinch or wince, not even when she dragged the jagged edge across her entire hand, the cut crossing the two other wounds. Blood drained down her arm as she took his bleeding hand in hers and held it high above his head. Then, just as Horsa had done to her several days ago, she squeezed Jess's hand tightly as a drop of blood fell from their clasped hands and landed on his forehead.

"Damn-it!" she cursed, having missed Jess's eye, but the second drop was true and his entire body immediately went stiff. Jess thought he heard thunder as he violently began spinning in darkness as if he were free-falling in space, but there were no stars or lights of any kind. He then felt a pain in his chest so intense that he looked down to see if he had been stabbed, just as he sped through an endless hall; like when two mirrors are placed together. On each side of the hallway, doors were violently thrust open as brilliant light burst through them and into his consciousness, with it, a flood of memories that were not his own, although strangely familiar. He sped through the endless hall for what seemed like hours if not days, until he flew out and then immediately into another free-fall but this one in slow motion. He spun from end-to-end several times before he saw Nicole holding his hand on the floor of the old church, a church he now knew everything about. When he opened his eyes, he was looking up at Nicole from the floor while she held him tightly, anticipating the next phase of the blood-memory recall, which was the feeling of molten iron being forced through one's veins but the sensation never came and Nicole looked down at him puzzled.

"Don't you feel anything?" she asked, thinking that the dark ordinance had failed.

Jess couldn't speak. Not only were there no words to describe what he both saw and felt but it would take several hundred lifetimes to tell it. The only thing he could do was nod, and he did so repeatedly as amazement spun in his mind. "I was a blind man, but now I can see," he said, slowly sitting up. "This room, this building—so much sorrow here." After getting to his feet and surveying the chapel in minute detail, he smiled, although weakly and placed his hands to his mouth like a prayer replied, "Though not without its tranquil moments."

He then walked to over the altar and ran his hand along

the top of it as if it were speaking to him from the dust. For several minutes, he seemed lost to the present while he recalled memories from the past concerning both the alter and the church, presenting to him sacred memories of both tragedy and triumph. He now understood how divine, eternal timing worked and to his enlightened mind, it was no longer a mystery or even a miracle. Events continually repeated themselves not only because they happened once before in a person's ancestry, but the very buildings and landscape participated in the story of mankind and the same locations played out the same scenes over and over, something that the ancients understood which is why they erected monuments and memorials.

"I feel as though I could fly," he finally said laughing with joy.

"Indeed Father," replied Nicole with a knowing smile as she walked back to her side of the fire. "Now you can understand where Hengist and Horsa derive their power; they've both done this war before."

Try as he might, Jess could not recollect any memories about Hengist's or Horsa's past no matter how far back he turned the pages of history in his mind and he finally looked back at Nicole with wonder.

"You won't be able to find them," she said, perceiving his question. "Yours and their ancestry never crossed in history, something I can determine as the blood-memory arbiter."

"So I'm guessing Hengist and Horsa are able to do what you just did?"

"No, only Horsa," she replied shaking her head while

anticipating his next question. "And yes, Horsa can see into a person's past, except he is able to do it just looking into their eyes without the ordinance."

Jess slowly nodded as major pieces of the Toprak puzzle fell into place. "Horsa stared at me in Conwy Castle as if he were looking into my soul. I can guess now that he was reading my history," he said as he realized how powerful such a skill would be. "Whose history does Horsa know?"

"Everyone's," replied Nicole without further explanation as Jess realized that this was the reason Toprak had a hit-list, complete with dates and times for the person's removal; everything calculated with precision. With his new knowledge seemingly about to split his parietal lobe wide open, he realized that no matter the risk, he had to escape and get back to England. What he now knew could finally give the King the upper hand against Toprak once and for all but he was still weak from his extreme blood loss, making a run for it out of the question. However, he still clung to the hope that Matthew would return just as he had promised.

Historical events were still passing through his consciousness as he fixated on a particular thought or object, connecting all similar memories together. In amazement he laughed, "How long does it last?"

Nicole smiled. "The unbroken flow of memory every time you look at something or even think a thought? A few days and usually all night," she replied. "Then after a few days it slows down somewhat—mostly because the mind runs out of questions."

Jess continued to laugh with amazement as memory after memory effortlessly flooded his mind. He then froze in thought and motion as he recalled an ancestor standing at the side of a grave. It was late evening; the last rays of an orange sun, illuminating the western wall of a church—a church he knew. Whomever was being buried, the feeling was not one of mourning and loss but of fear. The burial was very rushed as several deacons kept watch while the body was lowered into the grave with ropes.

"What is it?" asked Nicole, sensing that Jess was in the midst of a very interesting blood-memory.

Realizing that he could return to the memory at will, he quickly changed his thoughts and asked, "About those swords. How did you know they were Viking steel?"

"Horsa has one. For an antique it is in remarkable condition. When I mentioned that to him, he told me about Viking blades and how enduring they are. He also claims they have magical powers," she said laughing.

Jess laughed with her, trying to underscore the absurdity of the notion even though he knew there must be some truth to the story. "So are they all the same?" he asked, wondering how she identified some rusty old swords so confidently.

Nicole had resumed her casual disposition as she placed several more pieces of wood on the dying fire. "I don't know if all Viking blades are the same but Horsa's and the ones we kicked back into the well are an identical match—that's the only way I identified them. I'm no medieval weapons expert."

Jess nodded casually, trying desperately to hide his zest for answers as his thoughts flew at near light speed. The first thing he had to do before anything else was determine just how much Horsa knew but to go there directly, Nicole would certainly become suspicious, so he plotted a series of questions that would be seen as benign but that would lead to the answers he needed.

"How much of my history could you see during the procedure—all of it?"

Nicole looked at him suspiciously, wondering where he was going with such a question but then quickly determined it was harmless. "Only bits here and there. It all depends on what you're looking for."

"And what were you looking for?" asked Jess, being a little more direct.

"I needed to know if your past would reveal anything about Hengist and Horsa," she replied with a smile. "We *are* enemies you know, you and me."

"And what would you have done if I had shared any history with them?"

"Nothing," she said reticently. "I was trying to rob you Father. There is much I still need to learn about Hengist and Horsa."

Jess nodded, wondering about the moral implications of stealing a memory. It was a sin he had never considered since previous to a blood-memory recall, one's memories had to be shared and no one could simply take one from you. With the sun now beginning to rise, he knew he had to act fast since Nicole would be leaving soon but he wasn't sure his question would be innocently received like he had planned. With precious time escaping, he swallowed hard and asked as casually as he could, "How much can Horsa see at a glance?"

Nicole's disposition seemed to change with the pale

morning sky and as she pulled his robe up over her head, she replied under the muffle of the heavy fabric, "Only what he is looking for."

Being completely unprepared for her abrupt and shocking disrobing, Jess nervously looked into the smoldering ashes away from her naked body as she put on the short pea coat again. She then walked over to the rain puddle that doubled for Jess's drinking water and threw several handfuls on her hair. Hearing the sound of splashing, Jess looked up, wondering what she was doing.

"I have to make it look like I just came from the sea, I can't have Horsa wondering where I've been all night," she said with a smile. "He is very insecure and violently jealous."

Jess smiled weakly as he watched her walk toward the door but before she pulled it open, she stopped and turned around. For several seconds she stared at him and then finally said, "I still wish I would have voted for you Senator. You are a very good man—perhaps too good for this evil world." She then walked over and knelt down next to him, placing her had on his cheek while she continued to look into his eyes. In alarm, Jess realized what she was doing. Somehow, she too was now able to see someone's history by looking into their eyes and he closed them tightly. Nicole laughed slightly and then to his surprise, she kissed him on the lips before getting up.

"It's a right shame that the truth about The Seven will never reach England," she said as if pushing a dagger through his heart.

Jess shook his head in despair as he considered what had just happened. He was sure his brief vision of the burial had something to do with The Seven and now that vision was in Nicole's mind, probably in its entirety even though he had not witnessed it all. Never had he known a woman so cunning and completely deceptive as Nicole. All night she had not only made him feel at ease but had convinced him that she was a lamb—misguided and perhaps even sick—but harmless. Only now did he realize she was the wolf and having feasted all night among the flock she was now walking away with blood on her lips, along with his stolen memories. Above that, she had even made him believe that she was giving him a gift but all along, her intensions for giving him a blood memory were only so that she could steal them from him.

His rescue was now even more desperate than before and he walked to the large shattered window and looked toward the sea, hoping to see Matthew. He knew he had escaped last night since he heard Horsa groan in pain but by the time he had the strength to look out the window, both he and Matthew were gone. Seeing that the ship which brought him to Saxonice was gone, he correctly assumed that Matthew had commandeered it from Nicole—which also explained why she was wet—however the reason she was naked was still a mystery.

Not seeing a ship on the horizon, he leaned on the altar and sighed. It then occurred to him that he could not hear any guards surrounding the church and he walked from window to window looking for any sign of a Toprak army but found none. As he reviewed the last twelve hours in his mind, there were so many strange events; he concluded it could only mean something sinister that had forced Toprak to focus their efforts elsewhere. Looking around once more, he pulled himself up on the sill of the large broken window and rolled through it, falling onto the dew-soaked grass. Looking up at the clouds blowing inland from the sea, he waited, anticipating at any moment for soldiers to look down at him with pointed swords but none arrived.

The air was very humid and silent, only the sound of the wind blowing up the cliffs and across the barren highlands, ghostly in their tone and empty. Without even looking around, he could sense that he was alone and for several minutes, he lay motionless, listening to the howling wind. He then rolled onto his stomach and then to his knees, surveying the countryside. As he already knew, the only movement was the grasses, bending to the wind and whispering out a hymn that is only heard by the lonely and lost. As he struggled to his feet, he saw workers in the fields gathering wheat into large stalks. The men were cutting with large sickles while the women gathered and children bound them with cords. It was a scene that could have happened more than a thousand years ago and as he studied the countryside in greater detail, he realized it *was* a scene from over a thousand years ago.

His blood-memories were so strong and vivid now, it was difficult to discern them from reality. The only evidence that the gatherers were not mortal was that their bodies were slightly transparent and would suddenly disappear and then reappear when they walked behind a tree or building that was no longer part of the present landscape. He also found it odd that the memories would randomly shift. One second he would see the wheat gatherers, the next, winter snow drifting across the fields. After several minutes, he realized that *he* was changing the scene by his uncontrolled thoughts and for the first time in his life, he understood how distracted the human mind is and how difficult pure concentration truly is. Every random thought was manifesting itself in his visual world, linking his mind to every blood memory in his genealogy.

With winter snows blowing past him, he laughed in utter amusement as he focused on the present time of year—

late summer/early fall—and resumed his observation of the gatherers. It was a peaceful scene and he lamented the loss of such a time and place where the noises of the world consisted of only nature and man conversing with his kinsmen. He then saw a rider pass through the fields that was markedly different than the workers and he realized it was Nicole, making her way to the opposite end of the island and he was thrust back into the cold present.

He needed to get out of sight since he knew the absence of Toprak personnel would not last and he turned and quickly made his way toward the cliffs, as fast as his weakened condition would allow him. Ducking over the edge and onto the narrow path that lead to the docks, he paused to catch his breath, amazed that he was still so weak. In the small bay below, he stared at the mesmerizing waves beating against the shore as they had done for countless centuries. He then saw something move to his right, down by the sea but his alarm quickly turned to amusement. He saw an elderly gentleman casting a fishing rod over his head and then sitting down on the rocks, getting comfortable for a long day. As he watched, it occurred to him that he was observing more blood memories—his ancestors, which also meant that the gatherers in the fields were also his ancestors, at least some or one of them. More than just seeing the past, whatever his ancestors remembered, he could also remember since their blood flowed through his veins. It wasn't just their memories, but their very thoughts and the more he watched the old man, the more he intimately came to know him. It was the middle of the ninth century and Dane invasions had stripped England of her will and the whole land was sinking deeper and deeper into despair.

For many years, the Vikings had landed wherever they desired and took all that they saw whether it be gold, weapons, food or women.

King Ethelred had done all that he could but drawing from the old man's memories, he knew that the King's army had been defeated and the King himself was captured and killed only days ago. Alfred, the King's younger brother was to be crowned any day in Winchester but the Kingdom was not encouraged. Alfred was young and impulsive, not a seasoned war King like his brother that had stood up to the Danes at every advance, despite being repeatedly beaten. England desperately needed a hero at this dark hour since everyone knew the Danes would return in the spring as they always did, except this time they feared there would be no one to oppose them.

The old man's thoughts then turned to his daughter who had been stolen away by the last Dane invasion and Jess also learned that he fished at this same place nearly every day, not so much for the want of food but so that he could watch for her hopeful return. His sorrow was immense and it intensified the longer Jesse watched. The old man had also lost his only son in a Viking raid and since his wife had past many years previous, he was alone.

The man's story was pitiful enough but knowing that he was his forbearer, a tear rolled down Jess's cheek and he closed his eyes, groaned and forced his thoughts to focus elsewhere.

CHAPTER 17

THE WAY OF MARTYRS

Jess slowly opened his eyes with trepidation. All he could see was darkness and a pale mist, ghosting passed him as if it were animated and moving on its own power, swirling, leading him onwards. Unable to alter what was before him in his blood memory, he followed until he came to a medieval churchyard as a heavy rain began to fall on a small group of men standing around a gravestone. Knowing that he could not be seen, he quickly walked over so that he might learn more about the memory. They were all speaking an obscure dialect of Latin he was not familiar with but after a few minutes, he realized it was an infusion of Old English and Latin, an oddity the history books failed to record, among at least a million other things he had noticed in his blood memories.

Stepping nearer, he first noted their coarse dress and complexions that spoke of a lifetime of severe hardship in a brutal world. However, the world in this blood-memory was not unlike his own since the Minimum, but these men had lived their entire lives in such a world and it showed. The man nearest to him wore a medium-length beard that had the appearance of being trimmed with a sword, coarse and jagged. He wore his hair down to his shoulders that was similarly unkempt. He had always assumed the modern world had romanticized the medieval period but just how much surprised him. All the men around the grave wore a very simple cloak, woven from thick wool threads which made them appear like gunnysacks but much heavier. From the smell, he could tell the rude fabric had been soaked in pine tar in an effort to make them waterproof and from what he could see, it worked surprisingly well.

As he studied his medieval companions, he suddenly felt the eyes of someone behind him and turning in the direction of the stare, was a woman standing with a lantern looking right through him. From under her hood, he could see that her hair was long and braided. The light of the lamp danced in her blue eyes that radiated brutal integrity and trust, a disposition that reminded him of Veronica. Without knowing anything more about her, he knew she was trusted and very powerful. As in his previous memories, he then tried to identify which one was his ancestor and he finally decided it was the humble abbot who, like the woman, was watching the men working around the grave.

He had assumed that the scene he was witnessing was a burial but it quickly became apparent that the men were exhuming a body not burying one and when they reached the prize, they fastened ropes to it and pulled it from the wet ground. Jess was surprised to see the body was in an actual coffin and not wrapped in cloth as most medieval corpses were. The men then pried open the lid and began taking out longswords and handing them to the abbot and the woman. They carried them to a waiting wagon beyond the graveyard that contained a very large object underneath a tarp and the woman, who was certainly senior in authority to everyone present, commanded the driver to proceed to the castle as she climbed upon her own horse and carefully followed behind.

Jess determined that whatever this secret event in English history was, it was of great importance and he desperately wanted to follow the wagon but his blood memory was tied to the abbot and as the wagon and riders disappeared into the darkness, he found himself following the abbot inside the church and it was then he recognized where he was—Saint Mary's church inside the walled village of Conwy. Retracing the last few minutes, he accurately concluded that the exhumed grave was most certainly the grave of The Seven.

He watched the abbot cross himself as he entered the dimly lit chapel and slip out of his rain cloak that was taken by a young deacon who appeared to be no more than twelve years old. Jess remembered that medieval deacons were a type of internship to the Cloth and were usually a child from a prominent family or a gifted orphan.

"Father, what were you at in the yard and why was the Queen so far away here in Conwy?" said the young deacon, who shook the water from the bishop's cloak and hung it on a rack near the door.

The abbot said nothing as he, slowly walked to the last pew and sat down with a tired grunt. He stared at the crucifix at the front of the chapel for several minutes and then crossed himself again. Finally after several more minutes and a deep sigh, he motioned for the deacon to sit next to him.

"The Queen is old my son and we must now face the inevitable end of the house of Tudor. The Stewarts will soon rein over England, so there are a great many preparations that must be attended to before that dark day is upon us."

Jess was now finally able to place the memory in chronological history but the preparations the abbot spoke about were still lost on him, at least until the abbot reached inside his robe and handed the deacon a Seven of Swords tarot card.

"In a day not far distant, you my son, will be abbot of Saint Mary's. The archbishop has declared it. You shall be the keeper of a very grand secret that you must not ever reveal—never, to no one. Especially not Queen Mary or any other king or queen."

The deacon's eyes grew larger and he sat up on the edge of the pew and asked, "What is the secret?"

The abbot smiled and placed his hand on the boy's shoulder and said, "If you knew it, you would most certainly tell it for there will be those who will torture and kill to know it. All you must do my son it keep this card safe. Never let another person's eyes set upon it.

The boy nodded with disappointment as he took the card and began studying it.

"Perhaps not commit it to memory my son, lest someone extract it from you," said the abbot as he placed his hand over the card.

"And what of the Locker, Father?"

The abbot considered the deacon's question as he slowly got to his feet and leaned against the pew. "It is also best if you not know where it has gone but it will also be hidden from the Stewarts—such power in such unfit hands," he replied, shaking his head with disgust.

Jess's memories were now scrolling without his control and though he desperately wanted to stay and learn more about the secret of The Seven and the Rain Locker, he felt the memory fading, as he slowly drifted backwards through the dark churchyard and then upwards. Before the memory completely faded from view, he saw the destination of the wagon and the Queen—who he now understood was none other than Queen Elizabeth, enter Conwy Castle. The last thing he saw was the Queen's lamp, like a single star in the night sky.

As he watched the star, it eventually began to bob, rising and falling to a rhythm like a ship on the sea. Drawing closer again, he saw that it was a ship, the light coming from a lantern on the quarterdeck. The night was dark with no moon and heavy clouds as the ship quietly coasted to a stop and silently dropped anchor in three fathoms. The lantern was then doused and all was quiet. The night was terribly cold and even though Jess was only observing the scene, he was chilled to the bone. When the sun began to rise, he saw that the sea had frozen solid around the silent ship with icicles hanging from the yardarms.

The ship was anchored off an unknown shoreline near a small village. Just to the south of the ship, he saw fishermen cutting holes in the ice to catch the day's fish but his attention quickly turned back as the cargo hold was violently thrown open and untold numbers of dog-like creatures poured out of it and onto the ice toward the unsuspecting fishermen.

As the creatures closed the distance between the ship and the shore, he wondered which one of these fishermen were his relative, but try as he might; he couldn't feel a connection with any of them. The creatures quickly advanced and fell upon the men, killing them all where they stood before they continued on to the village. From his high vantage point, he couldn't make out any details and just as he desired to be closer, he was suddenly standing on the cobblestones of a narrow street, looking out to sea. The creatures were advancing quickly and the closer they got, he began to realize what they were hellhounds!

He finally saw his relative run out of a house with something in his arms towards the forest and as he drew closer, it suddenly occurred to him why he knew this memory. In his relative's arms was his daughter and the man was none other than Colton. This particular memory was only a few years ago, just before Colton ended up in Margate, sullen and alone.

Jess shook the vision from his mind and for the first time in what seemed like many hours, he returned to the present. The last thing he remembered was crouching below the bluff above the Toprak docks but he had now somehow made his way to the beach and was walking northwards, the docks a quarter of a mile behind him. It was then he noticed his legs and shins were aching and bleeding from stumbling over the rocks along the rocky shoreline in his trans-like state. He sat down in a small cleft near a tide pool and washed the blood from his chins, while cringing from the sting of the seawater. He wondered at what he now knew about his past and how profound it was that he and Colten were related and for the first time, he felt a strange connectedness with the whole human race. In addition to his strong visions, there were also a million other things he just knew—things he couldn't explain how he knew other than that were now just very distant memories as if from a single, very long lifetime.

As he caught his breath, sitting in the cleft, it reminded him of the narrow grave in the St. Martin churchyard when he discovered the buried books and he paused for a moment wondering if it was a memory or an event from his life. So complete were his blood memories that he had great difficulty distinguishing the two but when he finally concluded that the experience was real, meaning that it was something he had actually done, he began to remember other details about the event he had forgotten—or did he?

Once again, the present world grew dark around him and he could hear hushed voices discussing the content of the grave, its ensured protection and the urgent need for the two men standing above the fresh grave, to meet in Conwy in a fortnight's time. However, this memory was different from all the rest. This time it seemed as if he were not merely observing the scene, but was part of it, seeing the events from the eyes of one of the participants.

"God bless you John," Jess hear the other man say as the two men embraced.

Just then, the dark peace of the graveyard was interrupted by the sound of soldiers, approaching with torches and mastiffs. The two men ran to their waiting horses and fled northwards toward St. Albans or was it Holmhurst Hill. Jess found his modern mind conflicting with his ancient one as memories of the past and present fought for supremacy. Shortly after his arrival in Holmhurst, the Roman soldiers burst through his door, demanding the Christian he had been hiding over the past few years. He heard himself deny that he was harboring the fugitive but then stop and boldly declared that he had taken pity on the helpless Christian and that he would never divulge his location. He remembered that he and the Christian had not only become friends but that the Christian had also taught him how to read and write. The Christian was the very best man he ever knew and his very best friend in the whole world.

The soldiers dragged him out of his house, into the garden and rudely commanded him to comply with the proclamation of Caesar; to turn over all Christians to

Rome. John said nothing and humbly stared down at the ground. After a few minutes when the soldiers determined that he defied their authority, he heard one of them say, "John Alban, you are sentenced to death by the decree of Caesar!" He then felt himself rising above the scene but before the memory completely faded, he saw a soldier step forward and slice off his head.

The rising evening tide was now approaching the cleft where he sat and as he made his way to higher ground, he remembered all the martyrs he had learned about in seminary and determined that he had just witnessed the martyrdom of St. Alban. Jess found it odd that he not only saw it, but experienced it as if it had happened to himself.

In the early evening light, he scanned the horizon for a ship and the rescue Matthew had promised but the sea was empty. With hope still in his heart, he continued to make his way northward, getting as far away as he could from Toprak as his mind continued to rehearse the stories of the Christian martyrs. Suddenly he found himself in a small cart being pulled by a single horse, led by a small hooded figure. The sun was setting into a red horizon that bled into dark clouds and a black sea. With each successive blood-memory, he was becoming more and more of a participant rather than a mere observer. In this one, not only could he feel the sea air blow through his hair but he could taste it on his lips. He could also feel the tight hemp rope cut into his bound wrists as he tried to keep his balance in the cart that bounced on the dirt path. The only thing he didn't feel was kinship. With all the other memories, he was able to identify his relation and just as he was about to conclude that the reason he didn't feel kinship was because he was alone, he saw an aged man appear beside him.

The man smiled with sadness in his eyes as one might who

understood every detail of another's darkest moment. He was dressed in a black tunic with a white undergarment, the unmistakable dress of a medieval bishop in England. He had a long grey beard that was darker and parted at the ends with matching hair that hung to his shoulders. His eyes were kind with bushy brows that looked down a slightly oversized, plump nose that was also reminiscent of the dark ages. They traveled together for several minutes before he reached out his withered hand and placed it on Jess's back. His touch was comforting but he wondered why he was trying to comfort him. Surely, he should be comforting his ancestor and just as he was about to protest, the cart lodged into a rut, causing them both to grab the rail. With the old man's hand next to his, he noticed it wasn't withered with age but scared by fire. Jess slowly looked up as he considered who the man might be and as if perceiving his thoughts, the man nodded.

Jess began shaking his head in solemn pity as he recalled the man's fate, considering that he was about to witness first-hand, one of the most immortalized martyrs in history. The man standing next to him was none other than Thomas Cranmer, the Archbishop of Canterbury during the reins of Henry VIII, Edward VI and Mary I. Cranmer was instrumental in formulating the doctrines and structure of the early Church of England, including an addition to the small book Jess took from Conwy, but after Mary came to the throne, he was denounced as a heretic and imprisoned for years. Rather than just kill him as Mary did to three-hundred and fifty others during her brief reign of terror, she tried to get him to recant his heresies and thereby use him as a tool of winning back Protestants to Catholicism. Faced with certain death, Cranmer agreed to Mary's demands and officially reconciled himself with Rome. He signed many public recantations that were used in Mary's propaganda campaign but on the day he was to give his official address to the Kingdom, he could no longer sin against his conscience.

During a service at the University Church at Oxford, he departed from his approved speech and renounced the recantations that he had written with his own hand. Knowing that he would certainly perish in the flames, he raised his right hand and declared that his hand would be the first to perish for the sin of recanting truth. Before being pulled from the pulpit, he concluded his speech with his famous words, "As for the Pope, I refuse him as Christ's enemy, an antichrist with all his false doctrine!"

He was immediately dragged out to the churchyard and tied to a stake. Before the flames grew around him, he stretched out his hand as he had promised, causing it to burn first, yelling, "This unworthy hand!" His last dying words were, "Lord Jesus, receive my spirit."

"Bishop Cranmer, Your Holy Grace, you are a pillar for the earth," said Jess. "I am honored more than I can speak that I have risen from your legacy."

The Bishop looked confused and then finally began to shake his head with great pity as he realized Jess's error. Just before the cart stopped, the Bishop placed his arm around Jess and said, "My brother—this is not my memory."

Jess looked back confused as the Bishop sighed deeply and said, "It is yours."

The Bishop disappeared just as Jess was pulled from the cart and dragged up to the top of Maughold Head on Saxonice, high above the sea where a stake had been prepared for him. As he was chained, he saw Horsa whose arm was in a sling and Hengist arrive on horseback along with a score of their general officers, including Nicole. The late summer brush was very dry and when it was lit, it exploded into flames around him, rapidly approaching the stake and his robes. His eyes however, were fixed on Nicole and he waited for her to look up from under her cloak but she never did. He also noticed that Horsa did not look up, only Hengist and he smiled with pure delight. With the flames growing ever closer, he saw a multitude of people appearing before him, both male and female of seemingly every age, including children. Then like his blood-memories, he understood and immediately knew each of their stories. They were all of England's martyrs and they counted in the hundreds. Their presence was powerful as they stood to welcome one of their own into the eternal world. Jess looked for John Alban but he strangely could not find him. The last to appear was Thomas Cranmer and he stood only a few feet from Jess in the flames with his pitiful but also hopeful look, the look of someone who knew in every depth of the soul what he was experiencing.

Following the Bishop's example, Jess stretched his bound hands over the flames and called out to the darkening sky, "Oh that I had more hands so that I might purge all of my sins before worshiping at your feet O' Lord! Burn these wretched hands that have sinned in life, whilst my intended heart has always been pure!"

As the flames caught his robes, he began singing *Gladsome Light* with all his heart and was joined by the chorus of martyrs. Jess's unbroken spirit infuriated Hengist and not being able to stand the hymn for a moment longer, he ordered arrows to be shot until there was scarcely place for more in his riveted body as the flames ascended up into the night sky.

Far below in the dark Irish Sea, the *Bizyok* was making its way back toward Saxonice under a faint moon, carrying with her a hundred men, led by the King and Matthew, who was fulfilling his promise. For the past hour, they had been navigating by the firelight on Maughold Head, a beacon Matthew insisted was Jess, signaling for their return but as the flames died away, the wind also receded into a great calm and the *Bizyok* slowed to just three knots. The calm frustrated everyone on board but none more than Matthew as he worried greatly over Jess's safety but there was nothing that could be done except wait. In the stillness of the night, a comet flew through the heavens which many of the hands on board took as a sign of something important, though they knew not what.

In the smallest hours of the morning, they finally drew within heralding distance of the Toprak docks but they were deserted. While the crew tethered the ship, Matthew went in search for Jess, assuming that he was secluded on the beach somewhere near the place where they saw the bon fire, but since its dousing, it was difficult to ascertain its exact location. Not finding Jess near the shore, the armed party proceeded up the cliffs to the flats of Maughold where they were met by the lonely wind that mourned across the desolate landscape. The lifeless scene left Matthew at a loss of what to do. He had expected a waiting guard at every turn with harbingers howling for human flesh but as they walked through the tall grass, even it felt devoid of life. Not knowing where else to search, Matthew led them towards the old church thinking that perhaps Jess had given up hope for the night and sought shelter but entering the church, they also found it empty. The only evidence of Jess they found was his cloak, lying in a heap in the middle of the floor where Nicole had dropped it.

Matthew's optimism was fading and as he picked up the cloak, he sighed heavily, remembering how Jess nearly gave his life for him. He looked over at the blood-stained altar as he began to shake with both fear and anger. Other than the remnant of the small fire, the room was just as it was when he left it, but the ashes were no longer warm, indicating that it was at least a day old. Everyone in the rescue party stood silently while Matthew weighed the very scant clues in his mind. If Jess had escaped, why did he leave his cloak on such a cool night and if the signal fire was not Jess, then whom? Turning from the altar, the small book fell from the pocket of Jess's cloak and knowing it was of great value to him, Matthew picked it up and placed it in his own pocket and walked out to the churchyard. By the light of the moon, he scanned the horizon in the direction of the sea, hoping to discover the exact location of the signal fire. Based upon their approach, he guessed the signal might have been north of the church and as he proceeded in that direction, the King, Gus, Shay, Ted, the General and his men followed.

As they drew nearer to Maughold Head, Matthew thought he heard a familiar sound, the sound of harbingers scavenging. Calling for a torch, he drew his newly acquired sword and approached the highest outcropping along the cliffs. In the faint light, he could see a tall post in the moonlight and then the smell of an extinguished fire riding on the wind blowing off the sea. Hurrying his pace, he rushed ahead with his pulse racing in anticipation of what he might find but before he reached the place of the fire, he was met by several harbingers. They were not in pentacode and appeared to be quite harmless, staying to the shadows beyond the light of the torches. Matthew sheathed his sword, ignoring them as he approached the place of the signal fire. From the large burn circle he determined that the fire must have been enormous, which made sense since they could see it so far out to sea but as he walked through the ashes to the center of the burn, his heart and breath stopped.

Raising his torch, he came face to face with a black skeleton, still hanging from the charred post where it had been chained, its skull bowed in benediction to the devouring flames. Though he needed no further evidence, he saw a silver chain around the skeleton's neck bearing a cross, the symbol of Jess's devout faith and perhaps Toprak's vindication for his death. Matthew's sorrow was complete and he groaned as he fell to his knees in the ashes but before he could sob, the previously timid harbingers rushed in upon him. It then occurred to him that the harbingers had been picking the bones and in indignant rage, he roared as he drew his sword and slaughtered them all before any of his small army could assist. As the last harbinger groaned its final breath, Matthew dropped his sword and once again fell to his knees and sobbed.

The small army knelt on the stony ground behind him, bowing their heads as the requiem wind placed a hollow benediction on a life so perfectly lived. For the better part of an hour, no one broke the sacred silence until Matthew slowly got to his feet and cut the chains that held the skeleton with his sword. He carefully placed Jess's bones in his cloak then made his way back to the ship after wrapping them tightly in his arms.

What the medieval world would look like now after Jess's passing, no one dared guess but everyone knew the loss to England was devastatingly immense. While Matthew and the army proceeded to the ship with the reverence of a funeral procession, Gus and Ted went back to the old church and tolled its bell forty-two times, long and slow for every year of Jess's reverenced life. The ancient, mournful tones of the bells could still be heard as the

Bizyok drifted away from the dock and disappeared into the early morning mist of Saxonice.

ABOUT THE AUTHOR

Greg T Meyers (1964) was born and raised in the U.S. Rocky Mountains but unlike most six year olds in the 1970's who played Cowboys and Indians, long before the days of video games and cable, if you came to the Author's backyard, you would have seen a skinny, blond-haired kid wearing a suit of armor made of cardboard with an old Clorox bottle for a helmet. One of his most-cherished gifts from his parents was plastic sword, encrusted with plastic jewels in the hilt—much more beloved than even his bicycle. Where his love for chivalry and the medieval age originated is anyone guess but the Author concludes he was most certainly born with it. To make matters better or worse, during the nineteen-eighties he lived in London, England while Margaret Thatcher was Prime Minister and his intrigue and utter fascination for the medieval age was solidified.

Over the past 30 years, the Author studied the medieval period and though he often romances it, he is not disillusioned by the history. He makes no mistake in his writings that it was a terribly difficult and brutal time to live and yet, in many ways, he reminds us that it was much more kind and honorable time than our own. One of the reasons Greg loves the medieval age is because he longs for men and women (himself included) to live so honorably, bravely and without guile. In his inspiring works, Greg often reminds us that there is greatness in all and it swells and rises up when physical and emotional needs are starved, which is why we find such tales of human greatness during the darkest of all ages of the world.

Instead of following his love for history, Greg fell into corporate America as a marketer and copywriter for most of his professional career. He often laments that while we all take the wrong bus from time to time throughout our lives and wake-up on the wrong side of town, there is always another bus and another train if we can just muster the courage to get on board.

Greg sees his writing career as being raised from the ashes, mostly because of the love of a woman, his very own Veronica Paige. Parts of his life's tale is woven into this series, enriched and greatly fabricated with color, wild fantasy and blood—all good story elements. Having lived without it, he loves to write about hope. Hope against impossible odds, where miracles happen and truth prevails, a world where Greg always wants to live. Man can live without a lot of things, says the Author, but hope isn't one of them.

Greg currently resides in a little town up in Rocky Mountains where his imagination runs free and sometimes finds its way into his books.

Connect with Greg exclusively at: